VIRTUOUS SINS

A 12TH CENTURY THRILLER

DEREK ROY

Derek Roy Stories

ISBN: 979-8-9856219-0-7

ISBN: 979-8-9856219-1-4 (ebook)

AUTHOR'S NOTE

Dear reader,

Thank you. Thank you for discovering this book and giving it a chance. Historical fiction is a notoriously complex genre to write. That is why I wish to begin this book by establishing my thought process. I'll try to keep this succinct, as I'm much more interested in introducing you to Edith, Fraunce, Godfrey, and the other unique characters awaiting you in this book.

Virtuous Sins is a novel that can be enjoyed by all.

You don't need a prior understanding of twelfth century European politics to appreciate the story found within these covers (or on this tablet/phone, for you wonderful eBook readers out there!). I'm a storyteller, first and foremost, and this book is a thriller that centers around the complex relationships of the characters. You can think of the cast of characters found within Warin's Inn as a microcosm of European feudalism. And while there'll be historical characters and references within this novel, the story focuses much more heavily on these characters and how they react to each other.

My goal with this narrative (and this saga) is to make you experience life as it was during the third medieval renaissance. Like most people today, these characters simply want to survive and live their best lives. And just as it is in real life, where we experience every type of genre possible, so do the characters in this novel. This is a mature book for mature audiences. You'll find vulgar language and themes that branch into love, violence, horror, forgiveness, guilt, sex, abuse, friendship/companionship, drugs, mental health, faith, and much more; so please, take this as a trigger warning for those sensitive to such content.

All of this is to say, *Virtuous Sins* is an **entertaining** and **emotional** story first, while it is an intriguing exploration into medieval society second. I did my best to appease history buffs and casual readers alike. I hope I did both justice.

If you're one of those people who are in search of a thrilling, engaging story, you can now skip the rest of this and dive in. The dramatic and extraordinary lives of these eclectic characters await you . . .

This next section, however, is for those die-hard historians, especially those who have done extensive research on this fascinating and influential time period. You'll no doubt catch some liberties I took.

Firstly, I would like to touch on my portrayal of linguistics. After the Norman conquest of 1066, England went through a significant and prolonged transformation of the English language. There was a clash between a mixture of five languages: Old English, Old Saxon, the assimilation of French by the Norman aristocracy, the nascent formation of "middle English," and of course, the remnants of Latin that still lingered within the clergy. It was important to me that the peasantry spoke differently form the educated members of society; however, it was equally vital that I didn't give in to common "Hollywood" tropes of peasantry—tropes that depicted them as filthy beggars without any intellectual thoughts. For this novel, I chose a stylish version of classic "Shakespearean" language, one that nullifies the "thee's" and "thou's" of the language for "ye's" and other simplified, streamlined words. I wanted the semantics to be absorbing and modern while still giving the impression that you are hearing archaic syntax and discourse.

Next, I'd like to touch on the main thrust of the story: the wedding of Duke Rowan's son with Duke Richard's daughter. As I'm sure you know, these dukes did not exist. From the extensive research I did, there are limited historical sources that investigated the lives of lesser barons and dukes. That being said, I did find plenty of evidence that suggested the barons and dukes of neighboring fiefdoms did, indeed, quarrel and have skirmishes. The domains of Duke Rowan and Duke Richard expand into what is modern day Wiltshire, Gloucestershire, and Somerset. During the 1130s, this section of southwest England had vague borders between William I de Moyon (first baron of Dunster), Robert FitzRoy (Earl of Gloucester and bastard to King Henry), and Harvey of Leon (future, albeit short-lived, Earl of Wiltshire); thusly, there were many lower nobilities who fought for territorial control. They believed picking a side in the upcoming succession would give them legitimacy in their region. I created two fictional barons, who fancied themselves dukes, to help portray this formation prior to the Anarchy. I hope you can forgive these fictitious elements.

Finally, I would like to touch upon the depiction of religion. Spirituality and the Church played major roles in the lives of everyone during this time, and I wanted to emphasize that without diving too deeply into the structure of the clergy. As this subject has been thoroughly explored and dissected in other novels set in this time period, I was mostly interested on delving into the impact religion had on the individual, especially in the light of a radically mutating society. Consequently, my focus is on the impact God and the divine had on the individual rather than the Church's effects as a whole. It was important to acknowledge that religion was paramount to everyone and everything, while also acknowledging the complex hypocrisies that individuals felt due to this fact.

I hope with the aforesaid you can understand why I wrote the story I did, with the characters I did, and with the emphasis I did. My goal was to write an engaging and passionate story above all else. My hopes are that the historical setting helps people realize that, while foreign, the lives and dilemmas of humans almost a milllennia ago weren't that different from ours today.

I hope while reading this novel, you truly feel like you have had a chance to live in the twelfth century; I also hope you feel like you've experienced something riveting and spectacular.

—Derek Roy (January 2022)

PROLOGUE

HERE, HERE:
BY DECREE OF DUKE ROWAN 'THE JUST,' ALL MEMBERS OF HIS FIEFDOM ARE HEREBY CORDIALLY INVITED TO THE EXTRAVAGANT AFFAIR OF ROYAL MATRIMONY BETWEEN DUKE ROWAN'S SON, LORD MEREK, WITH THAT OF DUKE RICHARD'S DAUGHTER, LADY LORENA.

WITH THE BLESSING AND BENEVOLENCE OF KING HENRY BEAUCLERC—SON OF WILLIAM THE CONQUEROR, DESCENDANTS OF ROLLO, COUNT OF ROUEN, FIRST RULER OF NORMANDY—ALL PEASANTRY, NOBILITY, AND PATRONS OF *HIS* HOLY LAND ARE TO BE INVITED TO TAKE PART IN THE CEREMONY OF BELOVED LORD MEREK AND LADY LORENA.

THE CEREMONY WILL BE ORDAINED BY GOD ABOVE ON THE 21ST OF APRIL ON THE 1132ND YEAR OF *OUR LORD*, WITHIN AND OUTSIDE THE WALLS OF DUKE ROWAN'S MAGNIFICENT, ROYAL KEEP.

PART ONE

A NIGHT OF TERRORS

PASSIONATE INDIFFERENCE

*T*HE HORRIFIC BEAUTY OF *the Lord's wrath is insignificant compared to a mother's desire to glance upon her precious child.*

This is Edith's main thought as she stares out the window into the abyss before her. A furious storm descended upon the English countryside earlier in the day, and it refuses to release its hold. During the brief bursts of lightning, Edith spots the grass fields that surround Warin's Inn. The silvery, wanton blades dance in synchronous turbulence until they reach the edge of the tree line. Usually that forest is alive with the chorus of fowls, but those pleasant sounds have been replaced with the creaking and rustling of its ancient boughs. Looking out through the curtain of rain, all Edith can think about is her daughter.

Emma.

It feels like a lifetime since Edith last saw her daughter. Edith imagines Emma's lovely features, desperate to have any source of comfort within the thundering storm around her.

Emma. Her hair is as black as her mother's, and her mane already reaches the bottom of her spine. Her eyes, however, green as springtime grass, are a constant reminder of her father.

Her father.

Edith shakes out that formless void. She needs something real.

Emma has already survived five summers. She's recently developed a new habit where she puffs up her cheeks and taps on them when she thinks. It's a silly habit, but Edith can't think of anything else she'd rather see at this moment.

Thunder jolts Edith out of her head, evaporating all thoughts of Emma. Edith looks away from the window, back to the compact kitchen that is her workspace. The intermingling of both cool and hot air causes her to perspire uncomfortably. The storm outside Warin's Inn has been unrelenting for the past three hours, and only God knows how much longer it'll last. The magnificent storms which haunt the English countryside during early spring are beasts to be avoided and abhorred. To be caught in one is certain death.

Emma.

Edith shakes her head. She can't think of her daughter, not now. She has to get through her shift, and more importantly, she needs to save that woman who just stumbled in—the poor soul who got ensnared outside in that tempest.

What was her name? Verona. Verona and Paris.

The couple appeared to have gone through Hell and back. Edith needs to help them. But to do that, she is going to need rosemary and sage. What had the alchemist said? *Mix rosemary and sage with a canteen skin of fresh water. Let it settle. Make sure they fully drink it.* Edith nods.

A large central fire occupies most of the kitchen where a cauldron hangs upon a metal post above the flames. The pottage should be fully cooked by now. Edith wipes sweat from her eyes. The humid storm and simmering hotbox of the kitchen cause her to sway. She steadies herself. Herbs and preserved meat hang on the walls around the kitchen. The floor is uneven dirt. The wooden walls and ceiling bounce candlelight into sharp, unflattering shadows.

Lightning flares outside the window. Edith glances back out it. The weather really is getting worse. Emma must be terrified; she always did hate storms.

"Edith, what are you—stop looking out the fuckin' window!"

Edith spins. Warin the innkeeper bursts into the kitchen. His bloated belly shakes with the room as he thunders to the cauldron. He breathes in a series of constrained wheezes. Edith pushes herself against the wall as he passes. The smell coming off him is unbearable, or at least, Edith hopes it's from him.

"Sorry, Warin. Won't happen again," says Edith.

"We have two knights who just walked in," he says sluggishly. "I need you to take care of them."

Warin doesn't bother to look at Edith while he orders her around. He moves erratically with quick, sudden changes of direction, as if his body struggles to catch up with his mind. Warin knocks a wooden pot off the wall, which ricochets across a table into an open candle. The wax and flame tumble off the precipice, catching the wooden wall alight.

"Blast it! Whole place is gonna burn down one of these days," says Warin as he stomps out the growing flames. Once he is content that the fire is fully smothered, Warin grabs a pewter dish and scoops up pottage with it. He hands it to Edith. "Here, take this food with ye. Give it to the farmers."

"'Course, sir."

Edith spots a few dead insects in the corner of the room. She shudders at the thought of what ingredients Warin puts into his cooking, especially during the famine seasons of late winter and early spring.

Better off avoiding any customers asking about it, she notes.

Edith glances up at the wall of herbs. Her eyes linger on the rosemary and sage. She must help that couple.

But no one can survive after being caught in those storms.

The thought circles in Edith's mind.

Maybe if I give it to her soon enough . . .

Her fingers wrap around the sage. She didn't even know she was reaching for them, yet here she is with her fingers already around the herb. Edith glances behind her. Warin stares into his cauldron of better-left-unsaid pottage.

Edith tears the herb off the wall. She stuffs it into a small pouch tied onto her belt. No turning back now. Edith steps over to the rosemary. The herb glistens in the warm candlelight. Footsteps cause Edith to glance over her shoulder.

Warin hobbles to the far wall, grabs firewood, and feeds it under the cauldron. The innkeeper studies his concoction. Edith turns her attention to the rosemary. She *needs* to help them. Edith reaches for—

Warin yanks Edith's arm. She drops the pewter dish. It tumbles to the ground and flings out a torrent of flying pottage. Warin brings his mouth inches from Edith. Spit and other foulness spew from Warin's tongue and wet her face.

"What'd I say 'bout stealin' food? Huh?" hammers Warin.

"I'm sorry, I—"

"Belt it, you daft wench. You're done after t'night. You hark?!"

Edith wrings her neck, shielding her face from his beratement. Warin pinches his swollen fingers around her cheek. He forces her to face him.

"I should have you beaten, taken before the duke," he threatens.

"Oi! We need our damn food!" rings a voice from outside the kitchen door. Warin turns his rage away from Edith. She whispers a small prayer.

"You'll get it in a moment," Warin yells in response.

He cranks his neck back toward Edith and stares her down. Edith sticks up her chin in an act of defiance. It won't do much, but it makes her feel stronger. That's something.

"If we didn't have so many patrons, I'd throw you into the storm." Warin spits. "You steal any more food, I'll have the duke hang ye. You and your daughter."

Warin throws Edith backward into the wall. Herbs flicker to the ground around her like the leaves of a shedding tree during the cool autumn season. Edith braces herself before she collapses.

"Get movin'," says Warin. "Don't forget the bread."

With his last order given, Warin thunders out of the kitchen. Edith is left catching her breath. Thunder rumbles the walls of the inn. Edith stifles a cry. She breathes in. The air flows through her, powering her, as the crisp chill of it mellows out her burning blood.

Emma. Do it for her. Black hair, green eyes, puffy cheeks. Emma.

Edith straightens her rumpled tunic. Her hands come away with a slimy grime. She wipes it away on the window. Her sleeveless tunic is covered with sweat, food, mud, and other unknown substances. She's never fully appreciated how much it betrayed her work as a bar maiden. Edith flattens her frizzy hair. The humidity is awful this time of year.

Emma's hair will be perfect, though. It's always perfect.

Edith picks up the pewter dish from the floor, noting that there's still enough pottage to serve. She then snatches the burned bread from the side table and takes a deep breath. She can't allow herself to slip up.

Why do I always need to help? Someday it'll get me killed.

Edith takes another breath. She can't allow herself to get killed. Warin is capable of it. He's not a man who makes idle threats. She only needs to look at his son for proof, the poor lad. It can't happen to her. Not with her daughter a whole town away; not when she's by herself during a storming night.

Edith holds the rosemary in her hand.

Shit, when'd I grab this?

Edith glances up at the wall. There's a blank space where the rosemary just hung. Edith stuffs the herb in her tunic. She shakes her head.

Why am I always like this?

The common room of Warin's Inn is a large square with not much in the way of decor. At the northern side of the room, next to the kitchen entrance, a fifteen-foot bar counter stretches across the space. A few scattered tables and chairs placed around the room, seemingly at random, allow for patrons to eat and relax. The "tables" are nothing more than a barrel with a wooden plank balanced above them, making them a distant relative of the well-crafted carpentry of those found within castles and palaces.

A huge stone hearth fills most of the western wall. The fire that blazes within it shines out, warming the air and lighting the inn with the same economic fashion of a miniature sun. A staircase adjacent to the hearth leads up to rentable chambers on the second floor. The dirt floor is covered with a thin layer of hay that insulates the common room. Even with the torrential rain and bellowing wind,

Warin's Inn manages to stay cozy and warm; in fact, the storm has even caused the inn to smell *better* than it usually does. If the owner wasn't threatening to have her and her daughter hanged, Edith may have even enjoyed working on this night.

Edith stands under the doorframe to the kitchen. The two knights that Warin told her to check on sit at the bar. Edith recognizes one of them. *Sir Algor.* His tan-colored gambeson is torn and scratched. The hauberk he wears under it has various links broken and molested. Edith notices he has a bloodied bandage around his forearms, while his left eye is black and swollen. Edith stores her physical queries of Sir Algor in the back of her mind. She has more pertinent matters, considering that this particular knight is visiting on this particular night. He has stayed at this inn numerous times before, and he usually does so for Edith. She imagines this evening isn't any different.

The boy to Sir Algor's side looks even worse. His padded armor is similarly devastated, but his hair is thick with mud and rain, while Sir Algor's head appears relatively clean. There are more scratches and nascently-formed scars on his face than Sir Algor's. The boy has a distinct bruise around his neck. *Actually*, Edith now notices, *Sir Algor has a similar bruise as well.*

And . . . and are those tears in the young knight's eyes?

The boy rubs them away. Edith watches Sir Algor scratch his young companion's back. Interesting. She stores all of her observations away for later. As a bar maiden, she never knows when she may be expected to ask a patron about their woes.

Edith's eyes flicker to a hunched figure that sits and rocks before the hearth. His shirt clings to his back. His black shoulder-length hair sticks to his neck and forehead. He twitches back and forth. The figure glances at Edith, his blue eyes gripping her into a stare down. *Paris.* She has to help his lover, Verona.

No. First she has to attend to her work duties. She can't have Warin hunting her down in the meantime. Edith approaches the two knights. Sir Algor straightens up as she crosses to them. He fixes his armor and brushes back his hair. The young knight seems to laugh. Edith takes a deep breath. *Best get this over quick.*

Edith puts the pewter dish on the counter. She sets her hand on the young knight's arm hospitably, squeezing it lightly. "I'll be with you sirs in a moment," greets Edith.

"I'm looking forward to it, madam," says Sir Algor, grinning a stupid grin. Edith avoids eye contact and gives a considerate smile in response. *Move on, move on, move on.*

Edith picks up the dish and trudges onward. At the southern wall of the inn, next to the main doors, rests the largest table in the establishment. It's pushed against the wall with one of the few windows right above it. Five farmers sit around the table. Edith hasn't bothered to learn their names, as these peasant types are more usual, and with the royal wedding tomorrow, it is likely all the inns and taverns in the surrounding land will be filled with more patrons than typical. Despite the deadly storms and roaming banditry, people will never miss an opportunity to masquerade their misfortune for a night. *Perhaps,* Edith ponders, *even in spite of them.*

"'Bout damn, fuckin' time," the filthiest looking farmer complains. Edith sets their pottage in the center of the table.

"Sorry, we wasn't expectin' so many people t'night," says Edith.

She catches the oldest looking farmer glaring at the filthy one. He smiles up at her. "No worries. Thank ye," apologizes the oldest one.

Edith spreads out the stale bread to all of them. The filthy one scoops pottage with his hand and slops it on the bread. He scoffs it down. The only female farmer does the same.

"Let me or Warin know if you need anythin' else," says Edith, turning away from the table. She catches Paris storm up the stairs. Edith feels the stolen herbs in her pocket.

Sir Algor peeks at her from the bar. Edith sighs. She has to do her job first, then she can venture off and help the helpless. Paramount to all other objectives, she needs to guarantee she'll see her daughter in the morning. If that means dealing with horny knights, so be it.

Edith stands outside the door to Chamber 1. The second floor of the inn is one long hallway that connects to four guest chambers. At one end of the hall are the stairs that descend to the main room; at the other end is a large window that usually shines light into the hallway. On this turbulent God-forsaken night, however, only the occasional flash of lightning gives any glimpse at the tenebrous hall.

Edith opens the door. The contrast of the bedchamber to the common room is immediately apparent. There is no light or warmth here, no comfort that one can become lost within. The foul, acidic smells of puke and deteriorating flesh burn Edith's nostrils and cause the hairs on her arms to stick up. Diffused moonlight shimmers through the closed window shutters.

Paris kneels at the side of the bed. His lover lies on it. *Verona.* Her jet-black hair, damp with rain and oil, soaks into her forehead and into the sheepskin sheets. Her brown eyes stare at the ceiling, focusing on nothing in particular. She coughs. Saliva seeps onto her lips. Paris wipes it off and continues his prayer. Edith watches their quiet moment together.

"How she doin'?" asks Edith.

"Worse," says Paris without looking up. He brushes Verona's hair back with trembling hands.

"Let me see."

Edith takes out a full canteen of water. She stuffs the rosemary and sage into it. Paris wanders to the shuttered window as Edith replaces him next to Verona. She shakes the canteen, dissolving the stolen herbs within. Paris paces back and forth.

"'Tis my fault. We knew a storm was comin'. We were warned, but I made us leave."

"Matters not. It be in the past," consoles Edith. She feels Verona's forehead with the back of her hand. Verona squeaks. The smell coming off the woman is gut-wrenching. A pitiful smile curves the corner of Edith's lip. Verona stirs under the blankets as she tries to lift a hand. Edith stops her. She tucks the sheepskin around Verona tighter. "Stay still."

"The storm brought her death," croaks Paris. He wrings his hands restlessly. His voice grows thin, and his breaths become shallow as he stares out the window. Shafts of moonlight glisten through the shutters, sparking particles of stagnant dust that twinkle like a clear night full of stars. "She would have lived longer if we stayed. We believed this was the only passage."

"Paris, you must stay calm."

"Stay calm. Yes. Stay calm."

Edith looks into the canteen; satisfied, she shows it to Paris. "Give this to her. It shall remedy some pain."

Paris snatches it from her. Edith jolts back at the sudden move. Paris doesn't bother to apologize as he moves his full attention immediately to his lover.

"Verona, it's me," whispers Paris sweetly. "Ye hark? You must drink." Paris puts the canteen to Verona's chapped lips. When she opens her mouth, the crackle of splitting skin soars into the electric air. She drinks.

"That's it," says Paris, relieved and smiling. Verona guzzles the medicinal tea like she hasn't drunk anything in days.

"Make sure she drinks often," says Edith, standing over the two lovers. Paris nods.

"I will. Thank you, ma'am. Thank you." Paris lays his head on Verona's stomach. He kisses her chin. Edith smiles. She backs out of the chamber.

"Let me know if you need anything else." Edith bows.

She considers the pair for a final moment before she exits and closes the door behind her. Edith sighs. Lightning flashes through the far hallway window, followed immediately by earth-shaking thunder.

"What are you doing there?"

The masculine voice makes Edith's skin crawl. Goosebumps climb up the back of her neck as she spins to face the voice.

Sir Algor stands between Edith and the staircase. The knight blocks her path, anchored into the floorboards as a bulwark of muscle and steel. The darkness of the hallway coerces Edith to see only a monochromatic outline of the man. His eyes, however, reflect a single, brilliant white light that pierces the humid air and stares straight into Edith's being.

"Helpin' a patron," says Edith faintly.

Sir Algor takes a step to her. His padded armor chaffs against each other as he steps. The chainmail shudders. The sword and scabbard tied to his waist clanks against him.

"You've always been so tender, so nurturing," compliments the knight.

Thunder booms. The walls shake. The inn bellows. Moonlight spills into the hallway, making Edith and Sir Algor fully visible. His eyes are trained on her. The moonlight disperses, and they drench back into shadow.

"I've missed you, Edith, so much. Are you working tonight?"

I knew it. Edith closes her eyes and curses under her breath.

"Not t'day," strains Edith.

"Why not?"

"I'm sorry, sir," is all Edith can muster before she attempts to scurry past him. Algor swings his arms around. He catches Edith between him and the wall, clasping his two trunk-like arms around her body. The knight steps to her, pinning Edith back. The hilt of his sword pinches into her groin. Edith instinctively yelps.

"You always do," whispers Sir Algor.

Every sensation in Edith's body becomes enhanced to the extreme. Every patter of every raindrop on the roof, every warm breath from Sir Algor, every footstep and distant voice from the floor below them. Everything is loathsomely thrown into the precarious present with Edith.

"Not t'night. Please," begs Edith.

"You've never refused me before."

"T'day I am. Now, Sir Algor, if you'd please."

Sir Algor studies her for a long moment. Edith shakes her head at him. She can't have this tonight. He has to know that, right? He has to be able to tell. The knight lifts Edith's chin up and gazes into her eyes. Lightning flashes across his face. Sir Algor steps back, releasing his arms. Edith slides past him and rushes toward the staircase.

Get downstairs, tend to the guests, survive the night. Emma. Don't forget her. You're here for her.

"It's the innkeeper, isn't it?" echoes Sir Algor.

Edith freezes in her tracks. Thunder vibrates the very air around her.

Keep going downstairs, keep going downstairs . . .

"He dismissed me, starting in the morn," says Edith scornfully.

She faces Sir Algor. Seething blood courses through her veins, injecting an anger into her that Edith hadn't known was possible until now. Judging by the look on Sir Algor's face, the vehemence must have surprised him as well.

"That corpulent dolt," spits Sir Algor. "Do you need him taken care of?"

Sir Algor grips the hilt of his sword. He stares at her. Edith knows the threat isn't idle, but she finds herself unable to immediately answer. She should say no, shouldn't she? She can't possibly be considering—

If he's dead . . .

Then what? How would she be in any better position?

"No. No," answers Edith.

"I've always known he was cruel. How could one abandon a woman so beautiful?" wonders the knight incredulously. He steps closer.

"Sir Algor—"

"Edith, a woman as comely as yourself should be thoroughly indulged, not strewn aside to the gutter," whispers the knight as he comes upon her. He combs back Edith's hair, which appears to have become frizzy again. Edith reaches to deny his touch. "And what of your daughter?"

Edith stops herself. She glares at him.

"A daughter without a father?" wonders the knight. "It's unnatural. What's her name?"

"Emma." Edith can barely squeak out the word, her name. Her daughter feels even more distant when talked about aloud.

"Emma. Poor, poor Emma. How can a single mother raise a begotten child with no means?"

"I . . ."

"But you have means, don't you, Edith? You have me." He scans her from head to toe. "You've professed I'm your favorite. Am I not? Privilege me with alleviating your sorrows."

Sir Algor places his fingers on Edith's bare shoulder, slowly drifting his touch down the side of her arm. He moves to her hips and pulls. Edith snatches his hand away. Her chest thumps. She clears her throat.

"Edith," begins Sir Algor, dropping his voice to its lowest octave. The breathy rumble of it is faintly audible over the molesting storm. "Let me take care of you. My heart never fails to yearn for your touch. I'll pay double."

Double.

The money jingles inside Edith's head. She doesn't have a job any longer. That money can make the difference between her daughter eating or starving. Prostitution itself isn't the problem. Edith has used her body to earn money numerous times, and Sir Algor is a regular patron of hers. Warin knows about Edith's side gig, but he's never stopped her. It means more revenue for him. The clients have to rent a bedchamber somewhere.

But tonight? Tonight, when Warin's Inn has had more guests than ever before? Tonight, when the looming extravagance of Lord Merek's wedding has been overshadowed by the threat of Edith's broken neck drooping from a noose? Tonight, when a storm has hit the countryside that'll be remembered for ages to come?

Edith can't do it; at least, not for double.

"Triple," demands Edith.

"Triple, then."

Blast it! Should have asked for more.

Sir Algor grins at her. Edith sighs. Within her mind, she tries to navigate all the ways this can go wrong. There's too many to comprehend.

"Madam, don't abandon a knight in the cold. Don't leave me yearning any longer," says Sir Algor, holding Edith's arms with both hands. She stares at him, contemplating, deciding.

Chamber 2 is identical to Chamber 1, with the only difference being that the window shutters were left open. A small pool of rainwater seeps into the floorboards below it. Edith releases Sir Algor's hand, crosses to the shutters, and closes them. She then turns to the nightstand next to the bed, where she takes out a match and lights the beeswax candle above it. The light dances in the turbulent air while shadows blacker than death leap around the bedchamber. Sir Algor closes the door. He unclasps his scabbard and leans it against the wall next to the entrance.

"Sit," commands Edith, pointing to the bed.

Sir Algor sits on it. The rain beats off the window shutters, and occasional gusts slam it harder. The pitter-pat creates a soothing lullaby as Sir Algor undresses himself. He undoes his armor first, placing it very carefully on the floor. He unstraps his belt, sliding his trousers to his ankles. He uses his legs to toss his trousers to the opposite side of the space.

"Money first," says Edith.

"In my trousers."

"Why'd you just kick them then?"

"My bad." Sir Algor grins in a playful way that moderately vexes Edith. She sighs and walks over to the pants. Edith catches the knight staring at her backside as she walks away from him. He groans. Edith ignores it. She reaches into one of the pouches on his belt and takes out three handfuls of silver shillings.

"Happy?"

"Lean back," she dictates.

Sir Algor does so. Edith drops the currency into her belt pouch before she slides the filthy tunic off her. Sir Algor props his upper body up. He now only dons an oversized shirt. Edith shakes away the desire to stare at how his muscles fill it up. This is business only. She strips down to her night gown and lies next to the knight. He slips off his under garments.

"What are you doin'?" questions Edith egregiously.

"What?"

"Do you think I'm magically ready?"

"Oh, right," chuckles Sir Algor.

"At least warm me up first, ye fool."

Sir Algor pulls Edith into a kiss. Their bodies intermingle as she folds over him. Edith clears her mind, letting the sensations of her body overtake the turmoil in her heart. She escorts Algor's hand under her night gown, begging to quicken the process of erasing her mind. The knight bites her neck. She slaps him.

"I'm in charge here," says Edith definitively.

"Yes, madam," moans Sir Algor.

Bloody hell, he enjoys being told what to do.

Edith further guides his hands around her curves. Their breaths hasten. Thunder rumbles. Rain drips on them from the ceiling, adding to their increasing perspiration. The knight grasps her body. A piercing rush of heat spikes through her. For a brief moment of sensual pleasure, Edith forgets the threatening maelstrom. She straddles him. Edith allows Algor's hands to wander freely, and they do. She pushes down on his chest, feeling him, slowly losing herself in the passion.

Emma.

Fuck, not now.

Edith wraps her arms around the knight's chest. She twirls her body, flipping Sir Algor on top of her. She curls her fingers around his face, combing his short brown hair. She needs to get this along and leave her daughter entombed in the back of her consciousness.

"So, get to work," says Edith shallowly. She hopes he can decide what that means. Sir Algor smiles. He lowers his head between her thighs. Edith stiffens.

That'll do the trick.

She closes her eyes. Their moans echo into the howling wind. Three loud bangs bellow throughout the bedchamber. The rain pounds on the walls. The roof continues to leak. The muggy, condensed odors of dust, humidity, and human fluids tinge the air.

Three more audible booms thunder through the atmosphere. *Odd,* Edith momentarily thinks, *that sounds like it's coming from the door.* Sir Algor quivers between her legs. Edith squirms, all inquiries on the audible qualities of the chamber gone. They are both gasping. The titillation of lust and chaotic cacophony of the storm disguise all other sounds.

The window shutters blast open. Rain and wind shower into the chamber. The one candlelight distinguishes into a fume of wispy smoke, leaving Sir Algor and Edith steaming together in the dark. Sir Algor rips his shirt off. Edith feels him up. She pulls his neck to her, and they embrace into a kiss.

I may as well enjoy this.

"Edith, we need your help!"

Edith opens her eyes. Sir Algor kisses down her neck to her collarbones. She flickers her eyes around the space. There's no one else here. No voice reverberates within the storm. She shakes her head; clearly, she imagined the voice.

Emma.

Edith pulls Sir Algor over her. The financially incentivized lovers ignore all else around them. The storm climaxes with them. All sounds crescendo into indistinguishable, utter chaos: panting, howling, splatting, banging, whining, thundering, yelling. Even if someone were screaming for Edith, there's no way she'd be able to hear them over—

The door bursts open. Lightning and thunder flare through the open window as Paris stumbles into the bedchamber. He's drenched in sweat. Edith yelps. She pushes the knight off her.

"Edith, she needs help!" begs Paris, tears streaking down his cheek. He is hyperventilating. Sir Algor spins around on the bed. He spots Paris's silhouetted figure.

"Aye! Get the fuck out!" clamors Sir Algor.

Paris curls his hands into fists as he stares down the knight. The peasant spins his head. He rushes to the door and unsheathes Sir Algor's sword. The knight springs out of the bed, his completely nude body glimmering in the occasional moonlight.

"Whoreson, give me my sword," commands Sir Algor.

"She's gonna die," pleads Paris.

"Paris, I'll be there soon," says Edith frantically. "Put down the weapon."

"She's gonna die!"

Sir Algor jolts forward. Before Paris has time to lift the weapon, Sir Algor tackles him into the wall. The door bellows closed as the two men bounce off the boards. Lightning flares them into blazing white angels. The knight slams the peasant to the ground. Paris barely manages to hold on to the weapon. Blood seeps from his nose. Thunder rumbles as Sir Algor reaches down for him.

Paris slices.

Blood splatters across the chamber. Sir Algor collapses to the ground, his stomach cleaved in two. A waterfall of blood splurges from his wound and drenches the floor in a maroon puddle. The floorboards soak it in.

Paris stands over the knight, the traitor sword still in his grasp. Edith covers her mouth, unable to process the carnage of the naked man she had just known. She watches the body of the knight convulse.

I'm dead. This is it. There's no escape from this. Not for her, not for Paris, not for Verona. He's doomed them all. She'll never get to see her daughter again. *He* took that from her.

It all vanishes: the color of her daughter's hair, the vibrancy of her daughter's eyes, the habits of her daughter's thought processes. Edith can't recall any of it.

She can't even remember her daughter's name.

UNABASHED SHAME

PARIS HAD NEVER KILLED a person before, so he was surprised to discover that when he vomited out his dinner, it was not because he murdered the knight but because he was proud of it. His puke settles above the expanding blood, forming an opaque, protective layer over the gore beneath. Paris would have certainly been disgusted from the stench if only his nose wasn't broken. He clears his mind. Before he does anything else, he has something important to do.

Paris spits on the cadaver of Sir Algor.

That bastard got what he deserved. *Their* lot did this to them. Paris glances up at the bar maiden. She has yet to move from her spot on the bed. She stares at him with dread in her eyes. Whether that dread is directed at Paris or the situation itself, he isn't certain.

What if she won't help him now? What if she won't tend to Verona?

Edith glares at his hands. He follows her gaze. He still holds the knight's sword. The blood-soaked steel reflects the bedchamber in a mirrored, red glaze. Paris drops it. It rattles as it hits the floor. His hands shake violently. He didn't notice them doing that before.

"Verona. She needs help," mutters Paris.

"Y-yes," stumbles Edith.

"She is dyin'."

"Yes."

"I didn't mean to."

Paris himself isn't sure if that's a lie or not. He's not a beast. The knight lunged at him first. He was justified . . . he was . . .

"Yes," confirms Edith. Or is she just repeating herself?

She slips her feet off the bed. Paris notes her shallow breaths. Her face is blanched white, although that could be from the storm. It probably isn't from him. The knight had it coming.

Edith teeters forward, covering her mouth and nose as she carefully slinks around the cadaver and its leaking fluids. The bar maiden throws her tunic over her night gown. She has yet to take her eyes off the body.

"I didn't mean to," implores Paris.

I didn't mean to. The averment solidifies within Paris's dilapidated psyche. Edith shushes him. She reaches into the pouch of her belt, and the sound of clanking metal rings out. She grabs Paris by the hand, calming his shaking muscles instantly. She pulls him out of Chamber 2. They abandon the hemorrhaging knight in the dark.

"Stop cryin'," says Edith as they close the door behind them. Paris wipes away his tears. He's weeping. Curious, that.

It all felt surreal as soon as Edith shut the door behind him. The hallway is no different from when Paris stood within its walls mere minutes ago. The wood appears no different. The ceiling still leaks occasionally, and brief flashes of lightning continue to flare at the far window. Even the quiet sounds of people eating and talking keep seeping up from the floor below them. Everything is as it was. There were no guards waiting for them, ready to execute Paris before his ill wife. The world is indifferent to the abominable sufferings that transpired within Chamber 2, and it is equally devoid of any adjudication for the crime of butchering a man. If Paris is lucky, the verdict of his transgression will be determined in the court of his inner soul, where his faith shall be pitted against the discrimination of his sins. That he can live with.

"What are we goin' to do?" worries Paris.

"I need to think."

"Don't leave us." The words slip from Paris's mouth before he even realizes his fear.

He *needs* her with him. He reaches for the bar maiden. Edith slumps away from his touch, backing into the wall behind her. Her pupils widen. Paris flinches back. She fears him. Paris has been a small man all his life; no one has ever feared him. He bows his head, ashamed. What would Verona think of him? The thought singes a hole into his heart.

She must never know what he did here. Never.

"Whatever you decide," says Paris, "help her first. Please."

He closes his eyes, waiting to hear her objection. If she could just save Verona, he wouldn't care if Edith hated him. He would trade every good grace he has ever earned, from any person, if it means saving his wife. The entire world can be set against him, but if Verona's warmth is pressed against him every night, it'd be all right.

"Stand guard," answers Edith. Paris looks up at her, unable to keep the shock out of his face.

"I'll come with—"

"Stand. Guard."

Edith's declaration melts Paris's feet to the floor. He nods his head. Edith slinks around him, keeping a good arm's length away from him at all times. As long as Edith fixes Verona, the bar maiden can detest him all she likes. She can wish the foulest of plagues upon him and condemn his soul to an eternity in Hell. He would take it, too. He would accept any fate of reviled mockery that the world can throw at him.

It's my fault. Dear Lord, please deign her life worth saving. I've killed for her. I've killed.

E DITH TALLIES UP THE facts of the night so far: Warin threatened to have her and her daughter killed, she stole from the kitchen (which validates Warin's threat), Verona becomes closer to death at every moment, Paris became a murderer, and a knight in service to Duke Rowan was slaughtered on the eve of the biggest event this land has seen in ages—not to mention his squire is currently awaiting him downstairs.

When Edith was calculating all the ways that sleeping with Sir Algor could go wrong, his imminent death was honestly not one of them. Isn't it funny how life always finds a way to be surprising? Edith opens the door to Chamber 1, longing to abandon the threats of the night behind her. And the murderer.

Paris, what have ye done?

Verona lies still in the bed. She squeaks a breath out of her mouth, followed by a forceful pull as she sucks air back in. Edith closes the door behind her, entrapping a cerebral calmness in the bedchamber that Edith hadn't realized was possible, especially when next to someone who is on death's doorstep. All the various sounds and smells of the inn vanish in an instant. The quiet drum of heavy rain and the shallow breaths of two women at the ends of their ropes are the only hints of this room being real and alive. Everything else could be a dream. *Well,* thinks Edith, *a nightmare is more like it.*

"Paris . . ." murmurs Verona as the door closes.

Edith walks to the bedside. The pillow behind Verona's head is soaked in an oval of sweat. Verona's black hair, which must have once been lush and vibrant, now splits and grays at all its ends. Verona struggles to open her eyes, but Edith can spot the pooling of popped blood vessels in the whites of them.

"No, 'tis ye . . . our angel," says Verona, smiling. Edith grabs the herbal drink. She shakes it.

"I ain't an angel, only a woman. Open your mouth," says Edith.

She slowly pours the rest of the drink down Verona's throat. Edith places her hand on the sick woman's brow. She's burning up. Edith picks up a rag that was on the ground, carries it to the window, opens the shutters, and wets the fabric. The rain splatters off the side of the inn and showers the upper half of Edith's body. It cools her down, now feeling refreshingly sharp. Edith takes a deep breath, closes her eyes, and lets the rain splash off her face.

Edith still hasn't come to a decision on what to do next. She feels a twinge of guilt crawl through her as she realizes she didn't care much about Sir Algor's fate. She saw him die; surely that should upset her more. He may have been a bit rash and crude, perhaps more than a little bit manipulative, but did that merit death? And even more hauntingly, did those facts deservedly subjugate him to an apathetic death?

The repulsive conclusion comes upon Edith like a star plummeting into the earth. It isn't the blunt reality of Sir Algor's demise, a man she had known both intimately and superficially for many years, that bothers her; it is simply the gruesome nature of how it was done. She isn't shocked that Sir Algor lies dead upon the floor of the opposite chamber. She is merely surprised to witness that a human has so much blood, and that they can lose it so quickly. It is the sudden confrontation with mortality, the blunt reminder that life enjoys throwing back at a human: *you're just a bunch of meat and bones, no different from the cattle that are slaughtered every day for the nobility to feast on.*

Edith opens her eyes to the pouring rain. Her guilt for the knight's death magnifies tenfold. She crosses back to Verona and places the moist rag on the woman's head. Verona clasps Edith's forearm. Edith smiles down at her.

"My husband is frightened," says Verona.

"'Course he is. He loves you."

"Yes," whispers Verona. "But there's more. More you should know."

Edith tilts her head. When she found Paris and Verona crumbled on the ground of Warin's stable, she took them in at face value: a couple of pitiful peasants destined for the great wedding tomorrow evening who were caught in the storm. What else could they be? Why else would they be traveling through that thunderstorm? They are just a couple of peasants like her . . . or so she thought.

"Who are you two?" questions Edith, the words slipping off her tongue like the warm glaze of honey. The sweet yearning of information is too powerful for her to refuse. There *was* something in Paris's eyes when he killed the knight. Edith was unsure of what to make of it at first. A sadistic kind of glee it seemed to her. He didn't appear like that type of man, but perhaps Paris *has* killed before. Does Verona, his lover, know what he's capable of?

Before Edith knows it, her heart is pounding out of her chest and her ears ring with the quietness of all the world. Nothing matters but for the secrets hiding between the thin gap of Verona's lips.

That's why, when Verona releases Edith's hand and stares up at her in true earnestness, Edith lowers her head so she can listen with every ounce of her body.

PARIS STANDS GUARD IN the God-forsaken hallway. Thunder shakes the inn around him. He startles and falls back into the wall. The wooden walls are rough and sharp, not finely shaved like the nobility have. Splinters shove their way into his fingertips. Paris retracts his hands and pulls at the burrowed wood.

Good, I'm jumpy. I am still human. See?

Paris looks around the hallway as if expecting an answer to come from reality. He braces himself against the wall. He feels more comfortable with at least one side of him secured. Lightning flashes the hallway into white flames.

Sir Algor. He appears in the light. His face . . . it's twisted, mangled. His gut splits open. It speaks to Paris. Sir Algor's cleaved stomach yells for help. Paris falls onto his backside. The lightning disappears in an instant, along with the knight. Paris is left alone in the hallway. He stands, sweat dripping down his temple.

Thunder rumbles.

Paris orients himself. More lightning glares at the far window. Sir Algor stands within the brilliant light once again. He disappears back into the darkness. Paris huffs. He moves toward the window, drawn to it like a moth to a flame.

Lightning. Sir Algor. Thunder.

The closer Paris gets to the window, the more defined this pattern becomes. Lightning. Sir Algor. Thunder. As the knight appears more and more within the heavenly fire, his form slowly perverts to greater extremes. His eyes blacken. His skin seeps into bones. His cleaved stomach forms into a severed torso. His mouth gurgles blood.

Thunder rumbles.

The hallway remains pitch black behind Paris as he reaches the far window. The inn has reached a lull in the storm. The low grumble of distant thunder can hardly be felt in the ground any longer. Paris watches lightning bolts electrify the faraway sky. Thick, burly clouds cover parts of it. The purple glow of the bolts simmer the condensed clouds, leaving wisps of it trailing to the ground. The brief flashes of light reveal a glimpse of the distant rolling hills and allows a small comfort to crawl to Paris. The torrential rain that drenches this land is only temporary.

"Paris?"

He pivots on his heels. Darkness shrouds the hallway into an abyssal tube that vanishes before him.

"What are you doin' over yonder?"

Paris forgets to breathe. The air freezes around him. All becomes still. "Who are ye? What do you want?" Paris yells back.

A footstep answers his call. Then, a figure. The figure's black form slowly distinguishes itself from the shadows around it. It floats forward, like a wraith gliding through the sky.

Sir Algor. The spectre of the knight towers before Paris. His nude body is caked in blood. The slash across his abdomen is dried and swollen, looking no more than a grisly scratch. Blood drips from his hair and hits the floorboards like a person who just stepped out of maroon-colored rain.

He stares Paris down. His scratched stomach opens up to form a severed mouth. His intestines spill out of it like a perverted tongue.

"I'm sorry. I'm sorry. . . ." Paris catches a lump in his throat. The knight steps toward him.

"What? 'Tis me," says the knight's stomach.

Sir Algor gingerly steps forward. His face is hit with the soft glow of passing moonlight. Except, it's not his face. Edith's face now appears—her face on Sir Algor's body. The bar maiden's black hair droops down to her slashed stomach.

"Paris, what's wrong?" the Edith–Sir Algor fusion demands of him.

Paris stares at the abomination in horror. He can't breathe. His mind screams at him to speak, but the words become trapped in his throat.

Lightning flashes. Thunder rumbles.

Edith appears. Just Edith. She stands before Paris in the exact spot that abysmal beast just stood. Paris sighs. Relief floods over him as reality sinks back in. Paris runs up to her.

"Verona? Will she—"

Edith cups Paris's head between her hands. He holds fast. Her warmth radiates from her hands to his cheeks. A pleasant sensation flows up his back. It feels good to be held, but it feels even better to be anchored to reality.

"You have my help," says Edith.

A bottled tension releases from Paris. He had no idea his shoulders were even tense until they finally drooped down. "Thank you," sighs Paris.

"But if we're gonna get out of this, you have to do what I say, when I say. Ye hark?"

"Whatever ye say, I'll do."

"Good. Follow me," commands Edith. Paris trails behind her toward Chamber 2.

"How is she?" Paris asks, failing to keep the worry out of his voice.

"She will live, for now. I can craft her another drink, but you'll have to give me some time. It's up to her to fight it in the meanwhile," says Edith.

They enter Chamber 2 and bolt the door behind them. Sir Algor's mangled body spreads across the floor. His blood continues to slowly expand away from his body while congealed portions of it soak into the crevices of the floorboards. For a long moment, Paris and Edith neither move nor speak. They simply stare at the cadaver, transfixed on its hollowness.

"Get the head," begins Edith, breaking the silence.

Paris steps through the blood. It sloshes underfoot, pulling at the bottom of his feet as he steps up. Edith slides through the gore, carefully balancing herself. She grabs both of his legs. Paris steps around the head and bends down to grab it. His hands slip around the knight's bloody face. He reorients. Paris finds a handhold under the knight's armpits. They lift.

The stench immediately finds Paris's nostrils. He instinctually throws his arm over his nose. The body drops. The knight's head slams into the floor. The ground rumbles. Paris steps back, but his foot slips. He kicks blood up as he windmills his arms, desperate to stabilize himself, but unsuccessful in the slightest as he crashes backward straight into the carnage.

Multiple knocks rap from the door. They echo through the bedchamber.

"Oi! Who in there?!" a voice yells through the door.

"Help me open it," orders a second, more feminine voice.

Paris, now covered in gore, stumbles to his feet. His whole backside is soaked. He feels a sticky substance gluing his hair at the back of his head. Wind bellows at the open window. Edith glares at it.

"Quick. Out the window," commands Edith.

"Wha—"

"Quickly."

Paris and Edith heave the body up. Paris readjusts his grip, unable to get any good hold on it. Edith awkwardly pushes forward, making Paris stumble back. They don't make any ground by the time the door is knocked on again. Then again. Dust flies off the door as a loud crunching noise erupts from it.

"Kick it open!" The female voice again.

Panic swells within the lower portion of Paris's body, like the storm outside has buried its way into his abdomen. Paris and the bar maiden continue to stumble over the slick ground.

The door shudders and splits in the center. A hinge breaks off the wall. It flings across the crimson floor. The door goes askew, letting in the slightest bit of light.

They get the body to the window. Rain showers their face, and wind blows them back. Their hair becomes a tangled knot of furious vengeance, blinding their eyes as they try to lift the knight.

The door shudders again. The middle hinge comes loose. The sound reverberates through the chamber before it's overtaken completely by thunder.

"Open it!"

Edith and Paris lift the body. It tilts off center, throwing them back into the bedchamber. They quickly shift their weight to center the knight's mass between them. Paris pushes with all his strength. He manages to rest Sir Algor's upper body on the windowsill.

A final kick shatters the edge of the door. The last hinge bounces off the far wall.

Paris helps Edith push. They fold the knight's body over the precipice. Sir Algor tumbles out the second story window as two figures stumble in. Paris and Edith twist around. Paris catches the glint of steel. With a surge of dread, Paris realizes they each hold a knife. He bumps backward into the wall. Edith immediately holds her hands up.

The figures scream as they surge forward, knives held into the air. Confusion and terror overtakes Paris all at once. His mind races with possibilities. Did they hear him murder the knight? Where'd they come from? Will they strike Paris and Edith down without needing any semblance of proof?

The figures freeze a few steps into the bedchamber. They glance down at their feet. One of them bends down and sweeps a finger through the blood. They lift it up to their eyes. The two figures look at each other. They lower their knives together as they amble up to them.

Paris recognizes them as they step within the light of the window. They're members of that group of farmers at the long table, specifically the female one and the one that looked like he had bathed in mud. Paris follows Edith's lead and sticks his arms up. She'll know what to do.

"You part of the coup?" asks the female farmer.

Paris lets the question wash over him. Then he lets it wash over him again. Then again. By the fourth time Paris reiterates the question in his mind, he decides he has no idea what the hell she's talking about. Paris glances at Edith. She peeks at him, too.

Great. She has no idea what to do.

"Ed, give him your shirt," the woman commands.

The dirty one, Ed, takes off his shirt. Paris's blood-soaked body begins to itch. He becomes overwhelmingly conscious of the gore and stench that must be permeating from him. Paris reaches for Ed's outer shirt; however, Ed yanks it back at the last moment. Paris is left swatting at air.

"Can we count on you both . . . if the squire . . . y'know?" says Ed, looking them dead in the eyes. Paris catches a fire smoldering behind them. The transparency in Ed's tone made even Paris understand the threat behind them. Paris peeks over at Edith for help.

". . . Yes. You both can," nods Edith.

"Good to know there are more of us out there than we thought," the female farmer nods. Ed hands Paris his shirt.

"Me too," says Edith. She nudges Paris.

"Yes," fumbles Paris.

He fondles the farmer's shirt nervously in his hands. The female farmer takes off her shoes. She hands them to Edith.

"Ye need clean shoes. I can get away with being shoeless. A workin' bar maiden can't," advises the female farmer.

"Thank you."

"You both can ride with us t'morrow then. We leave at first light. My name's Vivian. This 'ere is Edmond."

"Nice to meet you."

"What'd you do with the whoreson, anyway?" inquires Edmond. Paris hears the genuine curiosity in his voice. Paris glances back at the open window.

"Ye threw him out the window? Nicely done. He'll be covered in mud and foulness by morn," compliments Edmond. "How'd you do him in?"

Edith nods to the sword on the ground.

"With his own damn sword as well? Couldn't have done it any better myself," says Edmond.

"We head for the keep t'morrow. I'll let the others know what you've done. All we have to do now is survive the night," says Vivian, sighing.

The others? Paris's eyes widen. What has he gotten himself into? He holds on to Edith's tunic. He has to ground himself with something. Anything.

"We look forward to it," croaks Edith, clearing her throat.

"Ed." Vivian nods to the bedchamber door. The two farmers head for the exit.

"Fuck. We didn't even need to kill the bastard," whispers Edmond.

"Don't tell Fraunce," says Vivian.

"'Course."

With those final words spoken, the two of them vanish from the chamber. Paris and Edith glance at one another: Paris holding Ed's shirt and Edith holding Vivian's shoes.

A coup? Heading to the keep?

No words are spoken between Paris and Edith. They share a glance. It says everything.

What is happening at this inn?

NOBLE PEASANTS

"**O**F ALL THE DAMN, bloody nights to have a storm," groans Edmond. "This is a bad omen if I've ever seen one. A fuckin' omen, let me tell ye."

"You clearly are," says Oswyn.

"Belt it," Edmond snaps back. He returns to tapping his fingers nervously on the table.

Fraunce gazes around the table at his companions and conspirators. They're his friends and his fellow martyrs. That's the inevitable conclusion of this uprising. Fraunce accepted his fate to martyrdom long ago on that fateful night he saved Vincent and himself from certain doom. If only he had been faster, he'd have been able to save their parents and his wife from damnation. Now here he is, years later, leading a revolt of hundreds of peasants. They are destined toward a fate that will become greater than their individual selves, but it'll cost them their lives.

We might get lucky.

Fraunce glances across the table at his brother. Vincent is the youngest of them all, nearing his seventeenth year on this terrible earth. Vincent stares out the window at the storm. Sitting there, watching his younger brother's gloom transparently plastered on his face, Fraunce can't help but liken it to seeing a younger version of himself. Vincent is the exact copy of Fraunce. He has the same shade of light brown hair as Fraunce, and his skin is the same pale shade. His hazel eyes even have a similar green ring circling the outer part of his iris. Vincent is starting to grow muscles, shedding the layers of fat that have filled his skin since he was a babe. Fraunce knows those muscles will continue to refine until Vince becomes a fit, strong man like himself. He'll likely become even stronger than Fraunce. In a heartbreaking punch to his gut, Fraunce realizes that the only thing separating Vincent from his younger self is that his brother has the scars and wounds of a traumatic childhood weighing him down.

Unlike Fraunce, his brother never had a chance for normalcies. It was stolen from him, and in due course, it had wreaked havoc on what should have been a handsome young man; instead, dark bags hang under his eyes, and his hair is already starting to thin. He always slouches his shoulders forward and never holds his chin up. His brother never deserved this life, and now Fraunce is shepherding him into an uprising that will surely get them slaughtered.

"Vincent," says Fraunce. His brother flinches around. Fraunce has recently noticed his brother often daydreams when he isn't being directly talked to. "You must follow along. 'Twill all be over soon."

Fraunce smiles. He reaches across the table and shakes Vincent's hair playfully. Whether they live or die, his brother won't have this burden weighing him down much longer.

"'Twon't if we can't finalize a plan," harps Vivian. "Fraunce, he isn't ready."

Fraunce looks around the table at the other farmers: Oswyn, Vivian, and Edmond. Together, them plus Fraunce and Vincent, they make up the leaders of their underground coup.

"He's just a kid," defends Fraunce.

"Kid or not, he needs to be full in," says Edmond.

"He is," says Fraunce. He makes sure to put extra emphasis on his declaration. There could be problems, even before tomorrow night, if they start to doubt him and Vince now.

"Quit it. Your ruckus makes me nervous," Oswyn snaps.

Fraunce appraises them. Edmond taps the table furiously. Ever since the storm hit, Edmond's mental state has been expressing itself more and more clearly; Vivian has stayed stone-cold as ever. There has been few times when Fraunce has ever seen her express her true emotions. The death of her husband a few years back at the hands of some knights had been one of the few exceptions. Oswyn . . . well, he is just Oswyn, except now he sweats a little more than usual.

Fraunce takes a deep breath. He needs to make sure they all stay under control.

"Everyone needs to stay calm. Our plan will work," says Fraunce.

"What fuckin' plan?" croaks Vivian.

Edmond throws his shoulders up, visually agreeing with her. Fraunce sighs. Here they go again. Fraunce opens his mouth, about to object, but is cut off when a small boy wanders up to their table. The young boy looks no older than ten with his hair trimmed almost to the skull and baggy clothes that appear to be weighing him down.

"How is *you* doin'?" asks the boy.

"Awe. Look at you. Ain't you precious." Vivian smiles.

"Thanks," grins the boy. The boy's infectious smile causes Fraunce to grin. Fraunce hasn't smiled in a few days. This is nice. "Are *you* here for the lord's weddin'?" wonders the boy.

"We are," answers Fraunce. "We came all the way from Pressington to see Duke Rowan's son marry. Are ye excited for it?"

"Yeah! Me have never been to a weddin' before."

"Ye Warin's boy?" Edmond interjects.

"Yes, sir. The name's Leif," says the boy. He bows to them, failing miserably at doing it properly. It was still cute.

"Good. Scamper off and tell 'em to get our fuckin' food. I'm starvin'," says Edmond. Vivian and Fraunce glare at him. Leif stumbles back from the table, his smile disappearing and turning to a serious line. He nods.

"Yes, sir."

"Go. Off with ye!"

The boy runs off. Fraunce feels a flush of heat rush to his cheeks. He suppresses his anger the best he can.

"What was that?" growls Fraunce.

"'*What was that?*' Let me tell you what that was. First, you tell him where we're from. Then, you tell him where we head. Do you want the whole kingdom to find us after? I know your family is dead, but mine is still alive, and I'd like to keep it that way."

"You kind of fucked up there," says Oswyn.

"That's no excuse to pick on the boy though," says Vivian sternly.

"Exactly," agrees Fraunce. Edmond rolls his eyes.

"But, Fraunce, he's right. You need to be more careful," snaps Vivian.

Fraunce leans back in his chair. He moans. He catches his brother carefully watching them argue.

"This isn't a joke," harps Vivian vexingly. "We're killin' a *duke* t'morrow. Not some village fool. The duke of the whole Goddamn fiefdom."

"Do you not think I know who we're fuckin' killin' t'morrow fuckin' night?" Fraunce couldn't help but let some of his anxiety crawl into his anger. Together they form a sharper and more crude tongue than Fraunce means to use, but he needs to gain their trust back. He can't be having a mutiny on the eve of their assault. "I despise Duke Rowan and his knights as much as any of ye. You know what they did to my wife," Fraunce points to Vincent and himself, "to our parents. Me and Vince want His Lordship dead like all of you. Lest ye forget, I was the one who set this up."

"Then what's the plan, Fraunce?" sighs Vivian.

"We stab him," says Fraunce. The bluntness of the reply gives him the reaction he desired. Edmond scoffs over it. *I have their attention now.*

"'Tis that simple, is it?" chuckles Oswyn. "We just sneak past all his knights and nobility and stab 'im?"

"Hark. This ain't no peasant weddin'," says Fraunce. He looks all of his companions in the eyes, playing up the scene. He has to make this sacrifice worth it to them. They have to know it's not for nothing. "Duke Rowan promised a mystic affair. There will be thousands at the castle. Nobility, peasantry, merchants, and the like. All we must do is wait till after the ceremony. By nightfall, Duke Rowan will be too soused to piss straight. Same with his knights."

"Attack when their guard is down," nods Vivian.

Fraunce grins. *Even better, if they start forming the outcome themselves, they'll feel even more so that the plan is their own. That means they'll be less likely to betray him.*

"Less deaths that way," reasons Fraunce.

"God, I am so fuckin' hungry," says Edmond.

"How 'bout the others?" asks Oswyn.

Fraunce considers this. When he started recruiting the members of their coup, it had started as a small subsection of their village. Over time, however, as the miscarriages of justice from Duke Rowan's knights became more prevalent throughout the land, it became easier and easier to find members willing to sacrifice their lives for the cause. Soon it became a life of its own. Their movement was a hushed legend, quietly but enthusiastically gossiped about in the smallest villages and farm towns throughout the land. Fraunce has even heard that the rumors of their uprising have begun to crawl its way into the taverns and inns of bigger cities. When the notices of the wedding were posted around the fiefdom, Fraunce knew this was their chance. It was difficult to get a number on how many, exactly, were a part of their efforts and how many were only privy to their existence. A few—fortunately untampered—letters gave Fraunce, at the very least, a baseline.

"They be meetin' at other inns and taverns t'night. Should be a few hundred of us come t'morrow," Fraunce answers.

"Won't King Henry come after us? After, me means," says Vincent.

Fraunce spins his head. The whole table turns their attention at once to his younger brother. Vincent shies away from their sharp glares. Fraunce sighs. Even through all the pain in his life, his brother is still soft at heart. *Lord, help him maintain his innocence.*

Fraunce reaches out, grips Vincent's forearm, and squeezes it. "Don't worry 'bout that," consoles Fraunce. "No one will miss him, 'specially the king."

"But he's a duke."

"The Duke of Cocksuckery," laughs Edmond.

Fraunce rubs his brother's arm. "Point is, we just have to remain calm till morning. If we do, nothin' can stop us," says

Fraunce, smiling comfortingly.

The front door flies open next to their table. A chill rudely seeps itself into their muscles. The crackle of thunder bellows throughout the room, louder than ever, shutting up the table of farmers for good. Wind and rain shower into the common room as two knights saunter into Warin's Inn from the storming darkness outside. Fraunce feels the whole table tense up.

"Fuck me," curses Edmond under his breath.

The younger knight closes the door behind them, entrapping the conspirators inside with the knights. The racket of the storm diminishes instantly, altering to the quiet, unnerving sound of straining wood like the haunting moan of a ship's hull as it's berated from monstrous waves. And similar to the uninitiated seamen who embark on their first voyage asea, Fraunce feels the very ground beneath him sway while the walls slant toward him. Fraunce keeps his eyes locked on the newcomers.

The glow of the hearth glistens off the knights' rain-soaked bodies. Fraunce notices their wounds. The armor on both of them is badly damaged. The older one places his hand on the hilt of his sword, but the ginger nature in which he moves his arm betrays his pain. Upon closer inspection, Fraunce notices a wrapped bandage around his forearm that is stained red. The younger one's face is cut and bruised all over. These knights may be in no condition to fight.

The knights walk past them and halt in the center of the room. Rain continues to drip off them as they stomp their boots, flinging mud onto the hay-covered ground. The older knight points to an insignia sown onto the shoulder of his armor, the wing-stretched form of a raven—the insignia of Duke Rowan.

"We are members of the knighthood, in service to Duke Rowan the Just," begins the eldest knight. "Long may he reign sovereign over our great land! I am Sir Algor. This here is Kendrick, my squire. We do not wish to instigate any hardships. We simply seek refuge from the brewing storm until we head for the wedding of Lord Merek and Lady Lorena tomorrow. That aforesaid, if we must, we will honor our sworn duties to protect the glory of the duke, his land, and his people."

The table of farmers glance at one another. A silence creeps over the room, causing the knight and squire to scan the inn again.

"And you shall be welcomed."

The room turns to face the southeastern corner of the inn, where a man sits upon a chair with a pipe in his mouth. The man takes a drag. The bowl flares red, a satisfying popping sound bursts into the groaning air. The embers of the pipe reveal a purple shiner under the man's left eye.

Fraunce lifts his eyebrows. This is the first time he's heard the man speak; in fact, he completely forgot that man has even been here the whole night. The man has an odd sense of style. He wears black stockings that climb up his legs under a pair of tightly fitted brown hose. An undertunic sloppily sticks out from under a dirty doublet, which must have once been a centerpiece for his outfit. Golden silk trimmings around the doublet still sparkle out from areas; however, the majority of it seems to have been dulled from mud, rain, and other happenstances of life. Perhaps even more odd, notes Fraunce, is that Leif hides behind the man. What is the innkeeper's son doing with him?

"Thank you, sir. Who might you be?" asks the knight, Sir Algor.

"I am but a traveling bard," says the man, "no one of note. Merely one who wishes to experience the extravagance of royal matrimony."

"You bless us with your eloquent speech."

"Speech is only a mannerism of education, hardly a factor for appraising one's character," says the bard, a devilish grin spreading across his cheeks.

"What is your name, good sir?" asks the squire, Kendrick. His voice betrays that he must not be much older than Vincent. Fraunce glances at his brother. Sure enough, Vincent has his eyes trained on the squire.

"I really am no one of importance. But if you must have a name—"

"We must."

"Well, if you insist, you may call me Godfrey. Godfrey the bard. Or simply Mr. Bard, as this young fellow likes to fancy," finishes Godfrey the bard as he points to Leif behind him. The knight and squire smile at him as all three bow to one another.

"Ah! Sir Algor!" bumbles Warin. The room turns their attention away from the bard. Warin the innkeeper raises his big arms into the air at the bar, emitting the warm glow of hospitality which many decades of work has trained him for. "Good to see you again. Please, sit 'ere!"

Sir Algor and Kendrick the squire pace to the bar. The table of farmers turn back to face one another. The fear in their eyes catch Fraunce off guard. He hoped, perchance, that sharing such an intense emotion would calm them all down, similar to how grief can be staved off with fellow communion. It turns out fear doesn't follow such petty contrivances. Whence fear is shared, it flourishes. Like a sickness that grips the countryside, it simply expands in scope and strength the more contact it has. Fraunce catches a glint of firelight off an object in Edmond's hand. A knife. Its sharp blade peeks up from partial concealment under his tunic.

Where there is fear, there are limited options. Where there are limited options, there is always an opportunity for violence. This could be dangerous.

"Put it away," strains Fraunce. Edmond cocks his head at him.

"We can—"

"No."

Fraunce makes certain to be definitive and final. He adds a hint of threat behind his words. *Me hopes this doesn't backfire.*

Edmond slides the knife back into his trousers. Vivian and Edmond eye each other up. Fraunce sighs. He has to keep them distracted. They have to stay out of trouble until morning. Fraunce thinks of something fast.

"Ed, check on the food," says Fraunce.

Edmond glares at him. Fraunce tightens his jaw. He keeps his chin up, maintaining eye contact, not backing down. Their eyes pierce one another and lock them up, like daggers pressed against each other's throats. Edmond laughs. The tension shatters.

"I *am* fuckin' starving," he bellows, slinking to the kitchen. Fraunce studies him the whole way.

"What do we do 'bout the knights?" whispers Vincent once Edmond is out of ear shot.

Fraunce regards his brother. The fear and pain glistening off Vincent's eyes melts Fraunce's soul and shoots a fire up his spine. His one job is to protect this boy, this last remnant of family he has left. Now he has forced his brother into a coup, and on the eve of battle, he has brought his brother into another dangerous situation. Even worse, he has exposed his brother to even more fear. Hasn't this boy seen enough of that?

For the first time since the formation of the revolution at Fraunce's hands, he begins to doubt the very vengeance he has set out to achieve. Is it worth the cost of his brother's innocence?

They've already taken his innocence, bites Fraunce. They killed their parents. What could be more damning to a young boy than that?

Your brother dragging you into a path of vengeance, perhaps?

"Don't worry about 'em," mumbles Fraunce. He feels tears swelling up inside him. Fraunce stifles them with a grunt. He can't be seen crying.

"I don't want to kill anyone," squeaks Vincent. Fraunce brushes his brother's hair to the side.

"Me knows. That's why I need ye," admits Fraunce. The truth slips out of him so easily that Fraunce half-expected every other earnest, bottled-up expression of his soul to seep out as well. Fraunce spots his brother's confusion even before he opens his mouth.

"What do you mean?" asks Vincent.

"Oi! We still need our damn food," yells Edmond into the kitchen.

"You will have it in a moment," Warin's voice yells back.

Fraunce uses Edmond's interruption to choose his next words carefully. He needs to make his brother understand why they're doing this. Vincent has to know why their sacrifice matters. If Vincent ever finds it in his heart to forgive his older brother—or even simply accept an understanding of why Fraunce is doing this—the seeds of that germination will be sowed here, on this night and this night alone.

"'Tis for the good of everyone. Remember what he did to us. Those knights pillage and rape. It must end," says Fraunce. A sourness drips onto his tongue that Fraunce grimaces at.

"Can't they be good?"

All else in the world evaporates around Fraunce. It's only him and his brother. Fraunce relaxes more than he has in months. It has always been just the two of them.

"Once one is spoiled, the whole patch must be disposed," says Fraunce. His brother nods his head, not saying anything further. Vincent looks back out at the storm.

In that precious moment, looking into the replica of himself, the younger version of him that could have been, should have been—if it weren't robbed from him in his youth—Fraunce realizes he can't have his brother with him tomorrow, no matter how desperately he wants Vince next to him during his final moments. He can't tow his brother into the castle, within the walls of the keep, where only death awaits them. Perhaps they will kill Duke Rowan and get their vengeance, but many of them will certainly perish.

Fraunce discovers in that moment that he isn't dragging his brother with him because he needs Vincent to help them; he is bringing his brother because he doesn't want to die alone, without him. It's a perverted selfishness that is causing Fraunce to lug Vincent into mortal danger, a cowardly narcissism he didn't know he was capable of, especially with family.

What would his parents have thought?

What would his wife have thought?

They would be ashamed, and that shame cascades over Fraunce like a wave pulling him under into the currents below. And similar to how those currents tumble and carry a man treacherously out to sea, the remorse hauls Fraunce to a sickening darkness within himself that any man would desperately shy away from. But not tonight. Tomorrow Fraunce will die, avenging the death of his family and redeeming the lost hope of every peasant throughout the land, but at least he'll be given the good grace of seeing his wife again.

Dawn.

How the name of his wife shudders him so. Fraunce spent a long time forgetting her, banishing her image and likeness to the pit of despair he dwelled in for so long. Now he'll get to see her. His wife. His Dawn.

Vincent, however, has the potential to live a normal life if they succeed in their plan. Another realization shakes Fraunce like the force of thunder. Vincent was *never* Fraunce's younger replica; he was his better. A vehemence overtook Fraunce on the night his family died that never corrupted Vincent. His brother *did* maintain his innocence. It was only Fraunce that changed. Vincent carries the same trauma. He has all the same reasons to despise life and the duke himself, but he doesn't. Vincent is everything Fraunce wishes he could be—everything their parents and Dawn would have wanted after their deaths.

Fraunce leans back in his chair, a self-pleasing smile plastered across his face that has been absent for years. There's a happiness within himself that he believed would be dormant forever. He pleases himself with that understanding which now rests easily upon his conscience.

"He says it is comin'," says Edmond as he sits back down at the table. The rest of the world comes back into reality around Fraunce.

"Ye get a good look at the knights?" asks Vivian.

"Don't see nothin' but them swords. They look roughed up as well. Methinks we can take 'em," says Edmond eagerly.

"Take 'em?" Fraunce frowns.

"We kill 'em now, two less knights t'morrow," says Oswyn.

"Who will stop us?" Vivian nods aggressively. "There be a storm. No one else is comin' t'night. Anyone caught in that rain is good as dead."

Fraunce shakes his head. Vincent will never live a life beyond Fraunce if he dies here tonight. Fraunce will kill Vivian, Edmond, and Oswyn before he lets that happen. Even if they are his friends, his confidants, they aren't family. Fraunce opens his mouth to interject, but the bar maiden approaches the table with their food.

"'Bout damn, fuckin' time," complains Edmond.

"Sorry, we wasn't expectin' so many people t'night," responds the bar maiden. Fraunce glares at Edmond. *Why does that fool always have to be so rude?*

"No worries. Thank ye," apologizes Fraunce. He gives her the best smile he can muster. The bar maiden spreads out the stale bread to all of them.

"Let me or Warin know if you need anythin' else." The bar maiden bows as she turns away from the table. Fraunce watches her as she turns back to the knights at the bar.

"So, what ye say?" mumbles Edmond as he inhales the pottage.

Fraunce leans back into his chair. He rubs his eyes in a futile attempt to ward off exhaustion. For a brief moment, Fraunce loses himself in the calming thump of rain and wind. The sweet smell of salt water lingers around the open window, transporting Fraunce to a place called a beach. Fraunce has only heard of the ocean in the stories that traveling merchants, priests, and vagabonds tell—of waves that calmly brush over the pebbled sand and wet your toes. He could imagine the sun rising behind the endless expanse of water, the sky turning hue and welcoming the warmth of life. He had hoped to stand on a beach with Vincent one day. Maybe his brother will reach the shore of their land without him. That thought makes Fraunce smile again. All of these false memories because of a simple little smell.

Thunder booms outside, but rather than discombobulating him, it stabilizes Fraunce's state of mind. He is powerless, trivial, in the face of the power of nature . . . the power of God.

God. The Lord.

Fraunce had a major disturbance of faith after the butchering of his family. He did his best to keep Vincent and himself from all aspects of the Church. He temporarily fell into a pact with heretics a few months after they fled the destruction of their hometown. The pagans spoused tidings of sin and evil—both of which ironic, since their very reasoning against the Church was drenched in religious rhetoric—about how the Church was in bed with the nobility, and how King Henry was little more than a puppet for, at the time, Pope Honorius II and his cardinal subordinates. They're tidings gained even greater handholds in Fraunce's mind when the pope died two years back. The world became still as the Church fought internally over his successor. When the papal election became a double election and the cardinals split between Innocent II and Anacletus II, even the peasantry became hostile toward one another. It was as if the tension within the Church became the tension between man and his neighbor. "The end is nigh" was a common whisper amongst tavern-goers during this time.

Fraunce began to understand the very brittle foundation that society stands upon when they are beckoned by the whims of faith. *Faith is a solid core for an individual,* as Fraunce later came to terms with, *but not for a kingdom.*

When Pope Innocent II was officially elected, the world slowly started moving again. Life went back to how it was: both the Church and the Norman aristocrats tax and regulate the peasantry, all the while leaving little pittance in the way of alms for compensation. Of course, it was all ruined again when Anacletus II was declared antipope. As it turns out, humans need to feud to gain eternal salvation.

Either way, Fraunce decides now will be as good a time as any to be a good Catholic and follow His commandments. *When death is at your doorstep, you don't have any time to play chicken with God,* Fraunce humors.

"You not really thinkin' 'bout it, are you?"

Vincent's question tears Fraunce right out of his religious indulgence. *How long was I thinking for?*

Fraunce realizes the whole table turned their attention to Vincent. They have pitifully hidden scowls of disgust at his brother's question, mainly from Edmond and Oswyn. Vivian's eyes flicker between Vincent and Fraunce. Fraunce knows Vivian will be more compassionate for Vincent's naivety. She almost had a child of her own once, the last memory of her husband, before she miscarried. Fraunce knows that, for her, this answer isn't about where Vincent stands but about Fraunce's own dedication and allegiance.

Killing a few knights here and now *would* give them an advantage. Duke Rowan is one of the lesser royalties. He probably has one of the smallest knighthoods in all the kingdom. He has Commander Rayner, whose ruthlessness made up for what they lacked in quantity. But if they were to make that quantity even smaller . . .

"Fraunce, no," pleads Vincent.

Bloody hell, grins Fraunce, raising an eyebrow, *that boy knows how to read me.* That gives Fraunce a warm, fuzzy feeling—a feeling of comfort that not even that giant hearth could give him. That is his brother's gift to the world. Comfort. Loyalty. Compassion.

"Vince, why don't you grab some food and tend to the horses," demands Fraunce, layering the patronizing tone thick.

Fraunce has to make his younger brother believe he is a monster. He knows the pain it'll cause him to consciously make Vince think of him as such, but the reaction on Vincent's face when he saw what Fraunce was going to do still dug a sickness so deep into Fraunce's stomach that not even throwing up could evade it. His brother might learn to hate him, but that will, in turn, lead him to hate violence. If his hostility sets Vincent on a path toward becoming the man Fraunce only wishes he could be, that will be worth his soul and more.

"Do as you're told," says Fraunce sternly.

Vincent glares away from him. He petulantly slops pottage onto some burnt bread. He takes it and storms across the common room. He vanishes into a small door on the eastern wall leading to the stables.

Fraunce releases a deep sigh. A lingering anger to his conspirators claws to the surface of Fraunce's being. They forced him to make this decision now. Fraunce takes another breath.

No. No, it's not their fault. He started this, *him*. It is too late to turn back the wheels of time. The assassination will be carried out with or without him. It *will* lead to a better future, not only for his brother but for all peasants. No more harsh taxes, no more capturing of peasant women for their own sick pleasures, no more rules thundered down from God-ordained nepotism.

"One of the knights is movin'," says Oswyn. The table turns to face the raven-crested knight and squire.

The knight shakes the squire's shoulders, almost in a playful and loving way. They laugh. The knight straightens his padded armor before he walks up the stairs.

"They both alone now," licks Vivian.

That they were. It would be easy now, like cornering two chickens at separate ends of the coop. Fraunce feels the heat of hatred boiling up inside him, energizing his muscles to perform a task that is merely animalistic in nature but noble in thought. For the greater good.

"So, what it be?" questions Edmond.

The three farmers . . . no, conspirators . . . nay, revolutionists, stare at Fraunce: their leader, their martyr, their redeemer.

Do it for a better world, justifies Fraunce. *Do it for justice and love, as well as for the innocent, the naive, and the helpless. Do it for religion to prosper in the hearts of men and not in the decrees of nobility. But most importantly, do it for Vincent.*

STOIC INDULGENCE

R AIN ASSAULTS GODFREY FROM all sides. The wind swirls around him, causing the bard to imagine he's caught in the middle of a maelstrom. Water even manages to pierce his face from below. What a bugger this whole mess is.

Godfrey made a point—internally, of course—to not cuss anymore; however, the present storm of colorful adjectives knocking on the strings of his vocal cords are making it particularly strenuous. It's quite a shame, really. He would have been able to create a whole ballad of exotic expletives if he were caught in this storm a few weeks back. Knowing how much the peasantry love their profanity, it would have been a hit as well.

Godfrey shakes his head.

What am I thinking? Obscenity-laden or not, none of my poems will gain any popularity. You're a right fool, Godfrey. An expletively desolate fool at that. You're better off worrying if your drenched breeches are causing any hostile rashes near your pecker.

Godfrey readjusts the garters keeping up his hose, stealing a look down at his breeches as he does so. *They most certainly are, aren't they?*

Godfrey continues to push through the storm. It's been about an hour since the stormfront crashed into him with all the force of a horse-drawn wagon. A wagon might have been preferable—at least that wouldn't kill him so slowly. The headache from being pummeled earlier in the day starts to latch onto Godfrey's brain. Even worse, it thumps right behind his eyes.

Fantastic, scoffs the bard, *now I'm being blinded from both sides. Someone might as well come behind me and—*

Godfrey shakes his head. No language. No swearing. *They might as well, though. I need all my holes corked shut.*

Every inch of Godfrey is drenched. Water leaks in and out of pores that he didn't even know he had. The thick density of the fog and wind make it impossible to see the lightning flare right above him. Luckily, Godfrey had made it out into the open grass plains before the storm hit. Some people might prefer the cover a forest would provide during a storm like this, but Godfrey knows he's an idiot, so . . . at least he's being true to form?

He feels the inside pocket of his belt. The sack is still there. Godfrey sends a brief blessing up to the heavens. *Hopefully, it makes it past all these clouds.* If the Church is correct about its teachings, and if Godfrey's extensive education doesn't betray him, Jesus and the Lord Himself should be right around him anyway. They'll get the message. *Please help this dim-witted, doltish, irresponsible, daft, obtuse, no-good, waste of space—*

Are those lights?

Godfrey strains his eyes. Sure enough, flickering in and out of existence between gusts of rain and wisps of mist, is a sharp amber light. It's still a fair bit off, and it's impossible to hear if any civilization is close over the clamorous gale. The light *is* promising, though. If nothing else, it gives Godfrey a warm glow to head to, even if that glow is death. *That's a curious juxtaposition*, thinks Godfrey, *death being a glowing light of warmth and comfort.* Godfrey stores that visual in his head for later use in another poem that'll surely be forgotten.

Blast it. Toward the light we go. Maybe it'll be that inn I was told about.

It is, in fact, that inn Godfrey was told about.

Hah! Let those deft cowards hiding in the forest be lost forever. My genius knows no bounds. Only one trudging through the open in the middle of a typhoon can get so devilishly fortunate.

Godfrey smiles. The inn stands as the sole source of light in countless miles of storming darkness—a beacon, a haven, for anyone who is unfortunate enough to be caught in the storm like Godfrey. It's a good thing he just sent the Lord a blessing; now he doesn't need to send a follow-up thanks.

Godfrey pushes the double doors inward that lead inside the inn. He stumbles into the common room. His hair plasters to his forehead. Large, heavy drops of rain slink down the strands of his hair and fall to the floor. The warmth of the ginormous hearth immediately salvages the ache in his bones. The strong smell of ale, salted meat, and horse dung simmers in the air. Godfrey takes a deep breath. The surprisingly human amalgamation of it all is an unexpectedly pleasant scent compared to the hours of painfully fresh air the storm threw at him. Wrapped up in the satisfying comfort of human hospitality, Godfrey reaches down and loosens the drawstring around his breeches, releasing an uncomfortable buildup of water and grime between two particular, spherical objects.

"Hello, sir!" reverberates a high-pitch, little voice.

Godfrey quickly removes his hands from the vicinity of his bollocks. It would be unfortunate if someone caught him with his hands down his breeches next to, what sounds like, a small child. Godfrey turns and finds, sure enough, a little boy running up to him. The boy stops, sliding on the hay that covers the ground and almost falling on his backside. The boy has black hair that is cut close to his head, looking like dark, tiny needles sticking up in all directions. His baggy clothes appear more like sacks with holes cut in them than any type of actual fabric. The boy also has some slight discoloration around his arms and neck. Godfrey watches the boy look him up and down. A grin that shows every tooth he has cleaves across his face. "Are ye a minstrel?!"

"You're very observant." Godfrey smiles back.

"Thank ye—or, me means, thank *you*, sir," corrects the boy. He performs a terrible attempt at a wink, which makes Godfrey chuckle some more.

"There *you* go."

"Me pa be cookin' up supper. We expects a busy night on accounts of the duke's son's weddin' t'morrow."

"I see."

"Ye—me means...*I* means, *you* can sit there till he comes out," says the boy. He points to a chair in the southeast corner of the room with a tiny table next to it.

Godfrey sits at it. The boy stands uncomfortably close to him. Godfrey gives him a polite nod. The boy just stands there and smiles. Godfrey catches the boy tapping his own legs. He's contemplating something. The boy rolls his tongue under his cheek.

"My name is Leif," the boy blurts out.

Really? After all that mulling over, that's all the boy wanted to say? Godfrey laughs again.

"My name's Godfrey." After the boy continues to stare at him for a few seconds without saying anything, Godfrey adds, "It's nice to meet you, Leif."

"Do ye know any songs?" Leif's eyes widen as he asks the question, probably imagining a wonderful world full of songs and dances and exciting stories. It's a world Godfrey had once believed in. He'll have to burn that image down.

"'Do *you* know any songs.' Unfortunately, no, singing isn't my forte, my specialty, if you will. I recite the music of verse: poetry."

"So...you talk funny?"

"I guess you can say that." Godfrey chuckles.

"Are any from tomes or scrolls? Me likes 'em."

"You can read?"

"No," Leif admits flatly. "But sometimes lords and ladies leave 'em tomes. Then I looks inside them and pictures in me head what it might say."

"It would certainly help your grammar," comments Godfrey. Leif cocks his head at this. The bard waves the confusion off the boy's face. "Most folks believe reading is useless, that scrolls and tomes should be used only for kindling and the like."

Leif shrugs. "They feel like magic in me hands. I wish me could read 'em." Leif frowns.

Godfrey studies the sad boy. He feels the instinctual need to reach out for him, to comfort the child. He really can't be touching random boys, though. For obvious reasons, that'd look quite bad. Godfrey thinks of the next best thing.

"I'll have to recite one for you at some point."

"Really?!"

"Really."

They both smile at one another. Leif's brown eyes glisten with excitement.

"Boy! Get back to work," orders a large man from behind the bar. "Mister, ye can come speak to me."

"*You*," mutters Leif under his breath. He hurries off to do menial tasks somewhere else in the inn.

What a clever boy, humors Godfrey. *It's a shame he is rotting away here.*

Godfrey stands up and wipes crusty dirt off his doublet. He sets a mental reminder to get it cleaned and fixed at a tailor. The bard steps over to the bar. The man behind it stares him up and down. His whiskers poke out at various spots. His hair is cut down to the skull, much like Leif. A foul stench flows from him as well. Godfrey tries his best to not cover his nose.

"Are you the owner?" asks Godfrey.

"This be my inn. You stayin' the night?"

"If you'd allow it."

"What happened to your face?"

A sudden pang shoots from a bump under Godfrey's left eye. Trudging through the chaos outside, he completely forgot his fight earlier. Fortunately, the headache had dispersed quickly after it formed in the thunderstorm. The bard has actually had a unique string of fortune recently. How long could that last?

"What are you getting at? I was born like this," says Godfrey innocently.

"Ah. Funny guy," spits Warin. "Now ye hark. This here is my inn. That means it's my law."

"Understood."

"No ruckus t'night."

"No, sir. I would never fantasize of being such an encumbrance."

Warin growls. Godfrey lets a grin slip. When in doubt, he can always use his education to dance around the peasantry. Words never did any harm, other than maybe make a few of them feel a little foolish. Godfrey has already decided he is fine with making the innkeeper feel that way.

"A guest chamber is five pence. Ye can pay that?" Warin eyeballs him.

"Pence of the silver kind?"

"I'd take the gold kind, if ye have 'em."

Godfrey reaches into his pocket and pulls out five silver pence. He flicks the coins onto the bar. He looks back up at Warin. The men meet eye-to-eye.

"Anything else?" asks Warin wolfishly.

Godfrey squints at the innkeeper.

Warin cocks his head and gives a self-satisfied smile. "Me can see it in your eyes," he rumbles. "You'd be surprised how much you can learn about a man from his eyes. Ye educated folk always be lookin' down at us, so we have lots of practice at it."

The hot surge of *want* creeps its way into Godfrey's being. Spit swells in the inside of his mouth. He's forced to swallow it down, only for his mouth to refill with saliva a few seconds later. A high-pitched scratching noise rises from his nails clawing at his breeches; it's the loudest sound in the world, only to be counteracted in audible strength by the thumping of his heart within his head.

"You have some?" Godfrey licks his lips. They were suddenly chapped, the crevasses of dried skin forming maze-like canyons. He tastes blood. He tastes *it*.

"Ten shillings apiece." Warin grins. He knows he has him. All Godfrey has to do is refuse. *Just walk away, you daft idiot.*

The small sack in Godfrey's pocket suddenly feels incredibly light. It will never last. And . . . he survived the storm. Blast it! Godfrey overcame all odds and persevered through Hell and back to get to this very inn. If that didn't grant him the right to enjoy a few well-earned smokes, then what did?

He will be indulged.

Godfrey lights his pipe. The aroma hits the bard first, even before the smoke passes into his lungs. A pine scent, full of depth and an earthy sting, pierces his nostrils. The scent swells within his nose, almost burning, like he wafted too much cinnamon. Then, the relief; a hint of sweet citrus folds itself around the pine, forming a package that together pushes a satisfying aroma deep within Godfrey's mind. Godfrey isn't sure what turns him on more, the smell or the sensations that follow.

By the time that eclectic, aromatic package is delivered to his brain, the burning fire of smoke begins to scold the muscles within his throat. His body's visceral reaction comes next. A shudder of intense contractions zap at his throat, almost forcing the bard to cough out the invading smoke. He refuses. Godfrey is a man, and he isn't about to let something as pitiful as deadly debris escape from within him. Godfrey often makes a game with himself to see how long he can contain an inhalation of smoke. He has found himself getting exponentially better in recent months. During some more high-stake bets in various taverns, Godfrey has managed to keep smoke swirling in his lungs for up to a minute. It has won him a good amount of money in recent outings. He feels like taking it easy today, though. He releases the cloud of white fumes and relaxes into his seat.

Godfrey knows the mixture he is smoking quite well. It's the modern favorite amongst smoke lovers in the southern parts of the kingdom: light amounts of henbane and mandrake, which are then coated in frankincense oil. There is a fad coming on that includes adding trace amounts of a plant called hemp. Godfrey is less knowledgeable on hemp, since it is still a fairly rare herb that was just introduced to their region. Apparently, travelers from some of the places down south and far to the east, even farther than the republics of Venice and Florence, carry sacks full of the plant. Godfrey isn't sure if the plant is even really called hemp, or if that is simply some slur used by foreigners. Either way, it seems like a big tradition for travelers to smoke the hemp. It didn't take long for the substance to slink in with the more traditional smoking mixtures they loved so much.

Godfrey doesn't want to admit that he'd try it, but he certainly would if the opportunity presented itself.

He can't help it. He has yet to hear of anyone who has died from smoking. Some people have been poisoned here and there, but that is of little consequence to Godfrey. It won't happen to him, and that's the important distinction. The worst thing Godfrey has ever experienced was a coughing fit that went on for an hour or so. Other than that, smoking seems to do little else to be concerned about. The calmness it subdues on the bard's hyperactive mind—and the lovely images it occasionally inspires after—are well worth the risk.

The bard closes his eyes and drifts off, finally releasing his mind from any internal monologues. Now is a time for the present. The chair crackles lightly under his weight. Godfrey smiles and listens to the soothing sound of popping wood at the hearth, the distant rumble of thunder over far countries, the soft murmur of—

"You want food?"

Godfrey startles, rudely jolted out of his substance-induced relaxation. The pipe topples out of his mouth and lands on his hand. A fierce pinching sensation buries under his skin. Godfrey yelps, just managing to hold back a string of obscenities. Godfrey wrings his stung hand, which tossed his pipe to the ground. A small circle of red sizzles his skin, while a ring of dark-colored hair singes around it. Godfrey glares up.

Leif stands before him. The boy looks every bit as startled as him.

"Where'd you come from, boy?"

"Well," begins Leif, "first me had to go help 'em farmers over yonder. Then me had to go tell Edith—oh, Edith is our bar maiden. But sometimes Edith cooks our meals and attends to the guests in their chambers, as me pa likes to say." Godfrey reaches for his pipe on the ground as Leif rambles.

"I got it," declares Leif, lurching for the pipe.

"No!"

Before Godfrey can contain himself, his arms slam against the boy. Leif flings back and crashes onto the floor. He thumps his head hard, an audible boom reverberating off the dirt. The bard flinches back, already feeling the flustered heat of embarrassment and shame on his cheeks. Godfrey glances up. Warin glares at him from the bar. Godfrey readies himself for a fight, for Leif's father to rush over and teach him some manners.

To his surprise, however, nothing of the sort happens. Warin merely scowls and dips back into the kitchen. Godfrey wonders at this for the briefest of seconds, before the sobs of the boy drag him back to what's important.

"I'm sorry," says Godfrey softly, "I didn't mean to push so hard." *Already making excuses. Good job apologizing, you child beater.*

"'Tis fine, sir." Leif sniffles.

"No, it isn't. Are you hurt?"

"No. Me ain't cryin'," snorts Leif as he wipes away a liquid from his eyes that surely can't be tears. Godfrey sticks his hand out and helps the boy up. He grips Leif around both his shoulders and directs him to stand before Godfrey. He holds the boy still. For the first time, Godfrey truly studies Leif.

He's so small.

It's strange what that simple awareness does for grounding the bard. Godfrey has spent so many tumultuous years learning and diversifying his vocabulary as a scholar and scribe. Time and time again, Godfrey has embellished his snarky comments and wit with unreasonably complicated syntax. He does it all in the vain hope of creating a veneer of worth and prestige. And of all the complex adjectives in his arsenal, only one very simple word feels right to describe Leif: small.

Within that unadorned and unpretentious description of the boy, Godfrey discovers a homely comfort. It's the kind of serenity that usually only washes over the bard when he's smoking. But here is this boy standing timidly before him, so small yet so human, so plain yet so honest, that he gifts Godfrey with a warmth he could only pay for prior to this night.

Godfrey combs his fingers over Leif's prickly hair, brushing out all the straw that stuck to his head after the fall. With the gentleness that Godfrey presumes a father should have, he continues to pick off stray strands of hay from Leif's oversized outfit. Godfrey's eyes briefly flicker to the discolored parts of the boy's skin. A ring of dark green and blue wrap around the upper bicep of Leif's left arm. A similar ring of purple and red constrict Leif's right wrist. Then the scar above Leif's left eye buys Godfrey's attention. The scar stretches about two finger lengths across the boy's temple to his eyebrow. It must have been very pronounced at first, but time has weathered it down to match—both in color and bulginess—with the rest of his head.

Godfrey glares at the kitchen door Warin has recently entered.

"There. Now you look like a proper lad again," says Godfrey as he pats Leif on the head.

"Thank you, sir," mutters the boy.

"No need to call me sir. Call me Godfrey or . . . Mr. Bard."

"Me likes Mr. Bard," smiles the boy finally.

"It appears I certainly owe you a story now."

"Yeah, you do," says Leif. A mischievous smile spreads across his face. Godfrey laughs. If he didn't know any better, he'd imagine Leif set this whole thing up just to get him to tell a story.

"You cheeky bastard," huffs Godfrey.

"The cheekiest!"

Godfrey rubs more dirt off the boy. They watch each other for a short moment. Godfrey feels the conversation coming to an end. A strong urge infuses the bard, pushing him to continue their talk, to make this moment with Leif last.

"Well," begins the bard, "I have a novel idea. Why don't we create our own story together?"

"Really?" Leif's eyes burst wide with amusement.

"It can be our own little story, only between the two of us. You can become a storyteller yourself and tell it to all your friends."

"Me don't have many friends. Well, except Emma. Emma is Edith's girl. She comes over and visits some, but pa makes me stay here most times. Even when he goes to the village to collect wares and such, he leaves me to tend to the inn."

"Your father doesn't let you out?"

"Well, he does sometimes. Not often though." Leif nods. Godfrey pulls his lips tight. He flicks his eyes to the kitchen again.

"This can be a story to keep you company then," says the bard. "Who should the hero be?"

"Hmmmmm."

Five seconds pass. Leif continues to think. Godfrey watches him intently. Five more seconds pass. Another string of hums spill aloud from the boy's lips. Godfrey nods to him, egging him to speak. About ten more seconds pass. Leif continues to think. Godfrey rolls his head, moving with the rhythm of the boy's continuous, audible hums. Another five seconds. Godfrey sighs. Leif looks nowhere closer to landing on an answer. The boy glances around the room, as if searching for the answer in the plainness of the inn. Leif begins to tap his foot. After another ten seconds of Leif internally deliberating to no avail, sending more minorly annoying hums into the world, Godfrey opens his mou—

"How 'bout a giant rock monster who hides in the forest and makes friends with all the animals and such. But he wants to be friends with humans, but can't 'cause he is made of rocks and the like, so he always has to stay in the forest," Leif says matter-of-factly, like the solution to finding the hero of their story is so obviously a rocky fiend.

Godfrey shuts his mouth. He was going to suggest making the hero a small ten-year-old boy with short hair and baggy clothes. Godfrey had a whole arc planned out where the boy meets a traveling jester, and they soon become best friends.

Perhaps the analogy was too blatant. A rock monster *is* much more interesting. At least they both want to go with the friend theme.

"A rock monster who hides in the forest it is," says Godfrey.

"What happens now?"

The door from the kitchen explodes open. Leif jumps. The boy spins on his heels and looks back to see his father enter. Warin thunders behind the bar counter. Godfrey catches Leif twitch his fingers nervously.

"Leif?" entreats the bard, waiting for the boy to glance at him. "Are you happy here?"

For a long second, the query hangs in the air like a botched joke. Leif twists his head at him. An odd expression crosses his face.

"What?" questions Leif cautiously.

The front door to the inn flies open. Godfrey and Leif crank their necks to glance over. The crackle of thunder bellows throughout the inn, louder than ever. Wind and rain shower in as two knights—no, a knight and his squire—enter the room.

Godfrey grabs Leif instinctually. He tucks the boy between himself and the wall, blocking Leif from the newcomers. Godfrey has seen drunkenly emboldened knights terrorize taverns across the fiefdom.

He won't let anything happen to Leif.

Godfrey has to get on the knight's good side, and he's better off doing that right quick. Godfrey picks up his pipe from the ground and places it back into his mouth. He uses a candle on the table next to him to light it up. He inhales and exhales smoke as the knight finishes his speech at the center of the room.

". . . honor our sworn duties to protect the glory of the duke, his land, and his people," concludes Sir Algor.

Time to sound sophisticated again.

"And you shall be welcomed," greets Godfrey, making sure Leif's small body is secured safely behind him.

". . . you may call me Godfrey, Godfrey the bard. Or simply Mr. Bard, as this young fellow likes to fancy," smiles Godfrey. He points to Leif behind him. Godfrey feels a flutter in his chest for a tense moment as the knight and squire glance at Leif. Sir Algor and Kendrick smile back at him. Godfrey bows, reaching into the depth of his education to remember the proper way to do so. Godfrey glances up. It must have worked since they both bow back.

Nicely done, Godfrey. You didn't ruin everything for once.

"Ah! Sir Algor!" Warin yells from the bar. "Good to see you again. Please, sit 'ere!"

Sir Algor and Kendrick wander to him and take seats on two barstools. Godfrey sighs. The muscles in his back relax, which allows him to finally slink fully into his chair.

It worked! It actually bloody worked. I'm on their good side, which means Leif is too. Godfrey releases a smile, relief rushing over him. Leif steps out from behind him but keeps his eyes on the knight and squire.

"Don't worry. They won't harm us, not now," comforts Godfrey.

"Me ain't worryin'. Sir Algor visits us 'bout a few times a year," says Leif simply.

"Oh." *Well, it was a noble attempt.*

Godfrey places his pipe in his lap. Leif still faces away from him, staring at his father and the knight at the bar.

Godfrey clears his throat.

"So, Leif, I was thinking we could start the story by having our rock monster—"

"Sorry, Mr. Bard. Me needs to do some work, or else me pa will get mad," says Leif as he turns back to Godfrey. The bard peeks at Warin, who glares at him and Leif before he exits to the kitchen.

"I understand." Godfrey frowns.

He stares down at his lap. He finds his fingers turning the pipe over and over again. A tightness grips the bard's throat. Godfrey scrunches his brows, unable to tilt his head up from his lap. Why is it suddenly so hard to look at this boy? Unable to glance up, Godfrey speaks with his head bowed. His voice breaks ever so slightly as he continues. "If you, um, want to continue the story or talk . . . I'll be in this here corner all night."

"Bye, Mr. Bard."

Godfrey listens to Leif's small feet run off. The patter of his footsteps echo in the inn, more thunderous in the bard's ears than the storm. He twirls the pipe in his hand, spinning it, caressing it, crushing it. Godfrey sucks in a sharp breath and forces himself to sit up. He clears his throat again.

How could I have ever thought . . .

Godfrey laughs at himself. A sluggishness overtakes him as a higher level of exhaustion strains his muscles. Godfrey shakes his head. He must look like a crazy old fool to whomever is watching him.

No one is watching me. I'm a wasted life with an idiotic mind. There's no popularity for me or my verses; not with anyone and not with anywhere.

Godfrey puts his pipe up to his mouth and drags. The warm smoke and citrus scent overloads his senses. Godfrey closes his eyes. *Odd,* reflects the bard, *I never thought about smoking when I was with Leif.*

Godfrey takes that as a challenge. He thinks back to a situation when he had ever gone a substantial amount of time without being distracted by the need to smoke. None comes to mind. That boy grants to Godfrey what a lifetime of searching has never divulged: unadulterated contentment, even if only for a few minutes.

"Get in there, boy!" Warin's scolding yell shakes Godfrey out of his reflection.

Warin tosses Leif forcefully through the door to the stables. The yelp that escapes from Leif as he flies through the doorway causes Godfrey to stand. Warin bull-rushes through the door after his son. The thunderstorm around the inn comes into focus as Godfrey moves to the thin walls.

The bard looks around the room. Sir Algor, Kendrick the squire, and three of the five farmers have all disappeared from the room.

How long was I smoking for?

"Sorry, pa," squeaks Leif's voice through the closing stable door.

A loud *smack* pierces through the air, followed by a rumble as something falls to the ground hard. "Stay away from that swine," berates Warin's muffled voice, "ye hark?!"

Godfrey moves quicker. The voice dies down as the door shuts completely. The bard strains his ears, unable to hear much more than the dull murmur of a different voice.

"Hey!"

The muffled yell squeezes through the walls. A colossal *boom* vibrates the wood. Godfrey sprints for the door. The walls shake again. Multiple voices scream at once, the grunts of a fight. Godfrey bursts through the door into the stables.

He finds Warin wedged into the wall. The corpulent innkeeper tries to squirm out, but his body is stuck between two wooden panels. Kendrick the squire stands over him, panting, his hands curled into fists. Godfrey spots rain behind Warin. The squire must have managed to push the innkeeper straight through the walls of the stable. The bard christens an immutable reminder to not pick a fight with the young man. That squire is strong.

Godfrey spots Leif laying on the ground. The right side of the boy's face glistens red. Godfrey helps him up. Tears stream down Leif's cheeks. The bard wipes them away.

"What happened?" asks Godfrey.

"This fat bastard slapped him," growls Kendrick.

Godfrey keeps his attention on Leif. The red glow on his face begins to disappear. Godfrey had his speculation, with the cuts and bruises and marks all over Leif's body, but now he has proof. He holds back a snarl.

"Go inside and find the bar maiden," Godfrey tells Leif softly. "What's her name?"

"Edith," sniffles Leif.

"Good boy. Go find Edith. I'll find you after."

"Son?" rumbles Warin. He writhes his body in the wall, trying to squeeze himself out. Leif runs for the door. "Son?! Don't ye listen to him! I'm your father! Not him!"

Leif rushes out of the room. Godfrey stands as the door closes behind the boy. Godfrey and Kendrick confront Warin, who thrusts about like a hare caught in a trap.

"You fuckin' cunts! I will have ye both hung. This is my inn. Mine!" Warin spits at them. Godfrey keeps his glare on the innkeeper.

"I got this," says Godfrey sternly. The squire nods at him. Godfrey seizes his hands around Warin and pries the innkeeper from the wall. The shattered wood splinters around him.

"Don't touch me, ye whoreson!"

Godfrey twists both of Warin's arms behind his back. This isn't the bard's first confrontation with a man bigger than himself, and this is far from his first violent encounter. Godfrey commands Warin with ease, forcing the innkeeper to the back door of the stables.

"Knight, ain't you gonna help me? Huh?! You're a fuckin' knight," cries Warin.

Kendrick simply smiles. Godfrey nods his head at the squire, thanking him for all his help. He saved Leif, which makes Kendrick good company in Godfrey's books. The bard pushes Warin forward.

"Out the back," directs Godfrey as he kicks open the back door. A gust of rain immediately slams into them. Lightning flares in the distance, granting a glimpse at a densely packed wood on the horizon. The incredible darkness that follows is haunting.

"Let go of me, ye bastard," grunts Warin.

Godfrey bunkers behind the bigger man to avoid the assault of rain. The back stable door shuts behind them. A waterfall douses them, rainwater spilling off the roof two floors above. He twists Warin to walk across the northern side of the inn. He kicks the back of the innkeeper's leg. Warin wobbles. They trudge uphill, their feet seeping into the earth beneath them. Every time their feet sink into the mud, a dreadful stench reminiscent of fecal matter bursts up to greet them. Warin wrestles with the bard's grasp, but Godfrey is too strong. He yanks Warin's shoulder down and the innkeeper cries out in pain.

Finally, after they made their way uphill about halfway across the northern face of the inn, Godfrey twirls Warin around and pins him against the wall. A blast of wind and rain screeches between them, as if there is a cyclone of water separating them. Godfrey lets his long hair hang down in a damp net across his face. He feels more threatening this way.

"You touch that boy?" demands Godfrey, holding Warin by the front of his tunic.

"Piss off."

Godfrey punches the innkeeper in the liver. The fat of Warin's stomach disperses much of the blow, but enough of it vibrates through the innkeeper to collapse him to his knees. Godfrey yanks him back to his feet and shoves his face through the cyclone. Water sprays him from the side.

"Did you touch your boy?!"

"Why do you care?! He's *my* son!"

"He's a boy! You don't hit a child."

"Don't preach nobility to me, you drug-laden pissant! Me've seen your type, time and time again. All ye do is destroy in your self-pity. Aye? Ye know I be right."

Godfrey yells. He slams another fist into Warin's liver. Lightning flares and thunder crackles as Warin crumbles again. Godfrey flings Warin away from the inn. The innkeeper lands face first into the mud about three feet behind Godfrey. Warin climbs to his knees and glares up at Godfrey. Mud drips off the innkeeper's face as he squints through the rain.

Godfrey kicks. It careens against Warin's temple. The innkeeper slumps to the wet earth again, this time with rain, mud, and blood dripping from his face. Warin wheezes. He crawls back to his knees before feigning a poor attempt at groveling.

"You touch that boy again, I'll kill you myself!" says Godfrey. "I'll tear this whole inn down, to Christ above, and I'll take your boy from you. He doesn't deserve your abuse!"

"Why do you care about Leif, huh?" Warin spits on the ground. "You're a vagrant! You know no codes of hospitality! Like a leech, you take and take and give nothing back to the world. Ye think you're so kind and noble?"

"No," admits Godfrey, "I don't. Love was never an honor I gifted myself."

"Then ye can't give it to him. At least I can give him a roof. And food. That's more than most people can say, ain't it? More than you can. What would ye know of raising a child?"

Godfrey stares at the innkeeper. The bard's lips tremble. He's right. Godfrey has no knowledge of child rearing, and he has no land of his own. All he has is his failed poetry and his unlovable personality. Who would want to be with him?

The bard sighs. Whatever the outcome of the night is, if Godfrey can keep that boy from being beaten any longer, then perhaps his life wouldn't be that much of a waste after all.

Warin sits back onto his knees. The rain washes away all the mud and blood. Godfrey can now see Warin's eyes clearly. The bard points at him.

"If I see you touch him again—"

"I hark, bloody cunt," says Warin, grimacing. The innkeeper tries to stand. Godfrey extends a hand.

A body!

Warin splats into a pile of broken bones under a pale, naked figure. Godfrey yelps. He slips on the mud and sprawls back into the inn.

Godfrey manages to abate any foul language, but his body lurches for any other avenue to release fear. He hyperventilates. Air becomes stuck in the bard's throat, blocking off his windpipes like a chunk of rogue food. Godfrey claws at his throat, but his fingers shake too ferociously to be delicate. He slaps his throat instead. The air bubble bursts out of his mouth like a cannon. The world spins as rain beleaguers him from every direction. Godfrey shoves his thick hair out of his view.

Two limp bodies lie crumpled before him. They ooze into the mud.

Godfrey, unable to flee from such a surprise, crawls to the devastation. There has always been an inquisitiveness to the bard; he is never able to look away from death or destruction. This morbid curiosity of Godfrey's had deeply troubled his monks and teachers.

Godfrey reaches the cadavers. He rolls the top figure over. The nude person—the nude *man*, Godfrey now realizes—has a disemboweled stomach. A lump of hot coals climb up the bard's throat. Godfrey pushes down the urge to puke. He wipes mud from the nude man's face.

"Jesus," mutters Godfrey as he recognizes the human. "Jesus Christ."

It isn't actually Jesus, but rather the knight, Sir Algor. Someone murdered the knight! Why couldn't it just have been Jesus Christ? There'd be less repercussions that way.

Godfrey glares up at the inn. Lightning flashes. Godfrey glimpses a tenebrous shape moving at a window on the second floor. *They're trying to hide the body*. The bard shoves the knight off Warin. *Dear Lord* . . .

A bone tries to bulge its way out of the innkeeper's neck. Warin's eyes protrude from their sockets. Blood flows out of his nose and mouth. The knight landed right on top of Warin's head.

No, no, no!

Godfrey shakes the pile of bones and fat. It doesn't reanimate. The two cadavers rot away into the mud, sinking deeper and deeper into the filth. Godfrey closes his eyes and tries desperately to compose himself. The instinct to move overwhelms him. It doesn't matter where he moves to. He just needs to walk, run, slam something, punch someone, drink, yell—something, anything! He has to do it now!

No. No, Godfrey won't let animalistic instincts take over. He's been a slave to his desires all his life. The bard starts to tap on his leg.

Great, now I need to smoke. Those monks really taught you something about self-control, didn't they, Godfrey? How could you be so foolish? What is Leif going to think?

Godfrey laughs. It is a horrible, empty cackle that can only be enjoyed by the phantoms that haunt all men—the spectres that haunt *him*. The mystery of who killed the knight and tossed him out the window matters less to Godfrey than Leif's reaction to this whole tragedy. Warin is dead. Sir Algor is dead. And even worse, they both appear to have died next to each other. The squire watched Godfrey come outside with Warin. He will know. It'll be obvious when Godfrey comes back without the innkeeper.

I knew my lucky streak had to end, laughs Godfrey. *I'm a dead man walking. What an idiot and fool I am to ever have believed a soul like Leif could care for me. I'm not deserving.*

Godfrey watches the bodies for one last moment, devising a prudent plan for surviving the rest of the night—a plan that'll navigate him out of this predicament and will help Leif come to terms with this nightmarish accident.

The first step involves getting very high.

VILE BLISS

FRAUNCE CAN STILL HEAR the screams of his dead wife.

Her terrible wails haunt him every second of every day. He wishes they came only at night. He so desperately wishes they didn't intrude on his life during the day, when the sun is still shining and life is supposed to grow anew. His days could then be relegated for the living, to be in the present with Vincent and all his other friends who survived. But they don't. Those terrible screams don't only keep him awake at night; they also force him to slumber during the day. At all times, his grief cries out to him. Fraunce hears his wife in the howling winds of storms. He hears her screams in the quiet whispers of villagers. He even hears her in the songs of birds and the strains of trees. Not even nature is sacred to the horrific wails of the dead. Grief is all consuming.

The hate came next.

Dawn, please forgive me.

Fraunce detested his wife. He hated her with all the strength he could muster from months and months of sleepless nights. Why is she haunting him? Why is her spirit refusing to detach from him? Why *him*?

He hated her so much that any time Vincent dared speak her name, Fraunce would release his anger onto his brother. Fraunce cursed the day he ever met Dawn—her putrid musk that never leaves his nose, her horrid face that always lurks in the shadows. Curse it. Curse it all! Where is the Lord to take her spirit? Where is the Heaven that is supposed to accept her soul? Why is she still here with him? Why couldn't she just fucking leave?!

Why is she still weeping?

The screams. Those terrible screams. And the more Fraunce loathed his wife, the more he despised himself. The months went on to years, and the years stretched on to last innumerable lifetimes. The hate festered within him, so pungent and visceral, that Fraunce was tempted to end it all. All it takes is the flick of a dagger, but that'd be too quick for him. He wanted Dawn to be banished from his mind. She was the single worst thing to ever happen to him.

Her voice. Her damn, fucking voice.

Death by dagger is too quick for Fraunce. He deserves so much worse than that. Fraunce deigned that starvation was his destiny. Slow and arduous . . . a perfect fate for the likes of him. So, he stopped eating. Fraunce gifted all his spare food to Vincent. Surviving off the nourishment of his bereavement, Fraunce struggled on. For a week, he watched his brother eat his food begrudgingly. He swore Vincent hated *him* more from it. Imagine your older brother forcing you to strip him from life, and not only that, but doing it slowly, deliberately.

At the time, Fraunce wondered if he hated Vincent, too. It was easier for Fraunce to disregard his commandeering of Vincent's sanctity toward him as ignorant negligence, proliferated by an abundance of desolation. Reality is never easy though, and the truth is that a cold resentment had been forged within the smoldering ashes of Fraunce's heart, hammered and annealed ceaselessly, and grinded to a scolding bitterness. How could his kid brother move on so swiftly from the butchering of their parents? Why is it only Fraunce who goes on, day after day, grieving for the life they had lost? And so Fraunce figured his voluntary suicide, which he compelled Vincent to involuntarily abide by, was both an act of nescience and indignation.

Imagine being forced to participate in all of that but refusing to abandon attempts at descrying the humanity in your older brother. The fragility of relationships is none weaker than when lamented by the wraith of grief. The chasms it cleaves between partners and friends, families and confidants, can be insurmountable by the bridges of empathy. Fraunce and Vincent found themselves at separate cliffs of the void, an abyss wrought by senseless murder but exasperated by self-pity. The canyon between them was too great for any bridge to be built, and the foundation of sympathy too weak. The torment of sorrow remained overwhelming. Vincent was the one who suggested they leap into the crevasse together. Rather than remain aloof and alone, they should dive into the terror and face it head on; and so they did. Leaving the dust of the past behind them forever, they plunged, hand in hand, into that abyssal gorge. Fraunce was surprised to learn that at the bottom was life rather than death, and with it, the possibility for him and his brother to build a new world together.

It was Vince who saved Fraunce's life.

From that point on, Fraunce made certain to find purpose in life, and if not for himself, then for his brother. Vincent deserves that much.

The screams continue, of course. The truth is Fraunce will hear them for the rest of his life, during dawn and dusk.

They never got quieter either. They simply began to fade in with the other noises of life. Oswyn suggested for Fraunce to sleep with another woman once. Fraunce refused. He knew he would see Dawn's figure at the corner of the bed and that he would hear her deathly screams rather than any pleasureful ones. He is forever going to live with the phantom of his wife.

It took an even longer time after he decided to keep living, but Fraunce eventually forgave his wife, too. That was the hardest part, forgiving Dawn for a crime she never committed. But Vincent, his mind well beyond his years, had told Fraunce that he needed to forgive Dawn before he could forgive himself. He was right. That's when Fraunce actually accepted death. That's when he decided he could give his life for the cause, to get revenge on Duke Rowan.

There's only one issue now. Fraunce has already forced his brother to watch him die before, and now he is making Vincent do it again.

Vincent saved Fraunce's life; it is time for Fraunce to repay the favor.

Vince isn't a murderer. He isn't enslaved to the dead like so many. He's a sigil of the living. Fraunce needs to believe that life will keep going after his death. And thus, pondering so at the table after sending Edmond and Vivian to kill the knight, Fraunce concludes that he needs Vincent to flee from here. Vincent must get out of this coup. He needs to fly far, far away. Fraunce desperately wants to believe that his brother will live a long life, and if not a prosperous one, then a life surrounded by people who truly care for him. A wife maybe, perhaps a few children. Fraunce smiles. He wipes away tears.

Vincent doesn't need to die surrounded by so much vitriol and hate. He doesn't need to *watch* people die with so much vitriol and hate. He deserves love, and Fraunce is going to make sure his little baby brother is granted that.

Fraunce notices commotion at the door to the stables. The bard who was sitting in the corner of the room moves toward it. He disappears through the doorway. Fraunce stands. Only a little while earlier, he had sent Vincent to the stables. The squire entered the stables a little after that. It made Fraunce a bit nervous, but he didn't want to make a scene.

The innkeeper's son bursts through the door. The boy stands, panting, with his back to the stables. Fraunce crosses the room. His brother is in trouble. He knows it. Leif peeks through the stable door as Fraunce approaches. The boy stares intently at something inside. What happened to Vincent? Fraunce hears yells leap from the doorway. What are they doing to his baby brother?! Fraunce shoves Leif aside and crashes through the door.

The first thing Fraunce focuses on is an enormous dent in the wall. The wood is split back like someone threw a boulder at it. Fraunce pivots. The stable is a small, damp room. Rain leaks from everywhere. Chopped firewood is stacked four feet high against every wall in the room. There must be, at least, two months' worth of fuel for the hearth in here. Four horses strain at a picket line they're tied to that spreads from the eastern wall to the western one. They neigh and ruffle their manes, clearly perturbed by a recent disturbance. Fraunce spots Vincent next to the horse they had borrowed for their travel. The squire stands next to Vincent.

Too closely next to him, worries Fraunce.

And . . . wait, they appear to be—

They're talking to each other?! This is bad. This is very bad. A dreadful beast overtakes Fraunce. The nightmare from his past slinks into his head. He hears Dawn scream somewhere outside. The squire will harm Vincent. He's going to hurt his brother! Fraunce runs to them.

"Fraunce?" stammers Vincent as he spots him. Kendrick the squire turns to face him.

"We got to go," says Fraunce harshly.

"I wasn't—"

"Never mind that. Let's go." Fraunce grabs Vincent's tunic and drags him away from the squire.

"It was a pleasure to make your acquaintance," the squire says to Vincent. Fraunce turns to face Kendrick.

"We want nothin' to do with you."

"Fraunce—" whines Vincent.

"We want no trouble."

"Neither do I, sir," says Kendrick softly.

"Good. Then ye should know why to leave us be."

The squire nods at this, understanding. Fraunce stares Kendrick in the eyes. He swears he spots earnestness in the squire. That can't be right. Fraunce drags Vincent after him.

"He was just bein' nice," Vincent says half under his breath.

"It matters not. 'Tis dangerous to be around them. What if the others saw ye?" Fraunce suppresses a knot in his gut. Members of the knighthood are dangerous, but tonight, their conspirators might be a bigger issue if they see Vince with the squire.

"What do you mean?" whispers Vincent as they enter back into the main room. Fraunce places his hands on both of Vincent's shoulders. He leans down to get inches from his brother's face.

"I love you," says Fraunce, trembling.

"Me knows." Vincent looks at Fraunce curiously. His brother can always read Fraunce like a book. *He feels my fear.*

"I will get you out of this, I promise. But ye need to listen to me very carefully, ye hark?"

"What's wrong?"

"Nothin' ye can't fix," says Fraunce. Vincent frowns. Fraunce rubs his brother's head. "Please, just stay at the table for a while, ye hark?"

Vincent nods. He takes a few steps toward the table before he turns and faces Fraunce again.

"He really is nice," states Vincent.

Fraunce watches his brother meander back to their table. Footsteps rumble from the stairs. Edmond and Vivian hurry down them, whispering amongst themselves. Did they do it then? Fraunce quickly paces to them.

". . . a man with nothin' is a dangerous man indeed," finishes Vivian right before Fraunce stops them at the bottom few steps. Edmond and Vivian glare at him. Fraunce waits a few moments. They say nothing.

"Well? Did ye do it?" blurts Fraunce.

"Aye. 'Tis done," whispers Vivian. Another few seconds pass without either of them adding anything else. Fraunce taps on his leg nervously.

"Should I be worried?"

"Me should be askin' you the same," says Edmond. Fraunce frowns; Edmond points. Fraunce, Edmond, and Vivian watch as Vincent ambles up to the squire—who appears to have sat back down at the bar—and shakes his hand. Fraunce closes his eyes. He curses under his breath. *I just told that boy—*

"What is your brother doin' with that bastard?" growls Edmond.

Fraunce yanks Ed toward him faster than lightning. He bunches Edmond's undershirt in his hands. Fraunce snarls at him. Edmond, infuriatingly, smiles back.

"Ye implyin' somethin'?" spits Fraunce.

"Me did."

Fraunce holds Edmond in a death grip. They glare into each other's eyes, and Fraunce feels a sharp pinch at his side. He looks down. Edmond presses a dagger straight at Fraunce's ribs. Fraunce puffs hot air at him. The damn bastard continues to smile.

"Ye want to play this game?" grins Edmond.

"Go anywhere near me brother—"

"Try it," scowls Edmond. The grin disappears into a serious threat.

"Boys, come on," sighs Vivian. "Ye both be makin' a scene."

Fraunce and Edmond continue their stare down.

"Fraunce," says Vivian softly. Fraunce snaps his eyes over to her. "Let him go, please."

Ed flicks his eyebrows up in a quick motion, then lowers them. He knows how to burrow under Fraunce's skin. Vivian is right though, and so Fraunce releases. Edmond brushes off his undertunic. Why was he only wearing an undertunic anyway?

"Thanks, bud," says Edmond.

"Come on, Ed," Vivian huffs as she pushes Edmond past Fraunce.

"I'll be watchin' him," threatens Ed as he slips by. Fraunce glares at Edmond and Vivian as they reach their table at the same time as his brother.

Vincent, I asked ye to stay at the table.

Fraunce sighs. He buries his head into his hands. He feels thunder shake the earth deep below him. This night will never end.

THE NIGHT AIR BUZZES with electricity around Godfrey. He scrambles to his feet. There's an energy to the night that's terrifying, as if any atrocious possibility is able to bear fruit. A dreadful feeling overtakes Godfrey that this is only the beginning.

The bard slips his way back down the small hill along the northside of Warin's Inn—or, previously Warin's Inn, that is.

We're all in a heap of trouble.

Godfrey scurries to the back door of the stable. The howling wind and rain continue to barrage his back. Godfrey humors that he can be permanently pinned to the inn if he lets the storm take full control of him. But he refuses, opting rather to tumble through the wooden door.

Godfrey stumbles straight into Kendrick the squire.

Godfrey gasps. The ghastly perverted figure of Sir Algor flickers over Kendrick's face. The squire cocks his head. The bard wipes rain off his face, buying himself precious time. He can't tell Kendrick about the knight. He'll surely kill him on the spot. Godfrey trembles.

"What happened?" asks Kendrick.

"What?"

"How do you fare?"

"Everything is swell," says the bard, forcing a smile. *Did that work?*

"Where's the innkeeper?"

Nope, not at all. Quick, Godfrey, think.

"Who?" stammers the bard.

And . . . we blew it.

"Warin, the innkeeper?" pushes the squire.

"It's cold out there, y'know?" says Godfrey stupidly. *I am the worst wordsmith in history. Apollo, strike me down.*

The squire stares at him for a long moment. Godfrey gulps.

"Perhaps," begins Kendrick, "you should warm up by the fire."

"Excellent idea, sir." Godfrey nods. The bard sends a silent prayer of thanks to the angels above. He also fires a prayer to Mount Olympus as well, just to be safe. "Pardon me."

Godfrey quickly slips past the squire and enters the common room. The bard glances around for Leif, but the boy is nowhere to be seen. Kendrick strides past the bard and sits at the bar. The youngest peasant walks up to the squire. Godfrey shakes his brain; a headache is closing down on him. There are too many things happening at once.

The bard stumbles back to his corner seat. He reaches for his pipe, picks up a candle, and tries to light it. Nothing happens. The bard glares at his pipe. The bowl is empty. Godfrey brings it closer to his eye as if willing for more henbane and mandrake to grow. His temples sweat.

"No, no . . ." He feels his pockets. Nothing. He used it all. *This is bad.*

His fingers scrape at his breeches again. Godfrey burns up. He gouges at his skin as itchiness molests him in patches all around his body. *This is very, very bad.*

EDITH TAKES A MOMENT to reflect on her initiation into a coup. Paris trembles next to her, clearly as dumbfounded as she is. Whatever pleasures Edith had allowed herself when in bed with Sir Algor is but a blurry, distant memory. Now all she knows is survival. She needs to be willing to fight to whichever lengths necessary to be reunited with her daughter.

Emma. Don't you forget her name again.

Edith rests her hand on Paris's shoulder. The gore of Chamber 2 surrounds them. The pool of blood seems to have ceased its spread across the wooden floor; however, it continues to grow darker in spots.

It's soaking into the wood, realizes Edith. She thinks about what area of the inn Chamber 2 is above. Horror slaps Edith across the face for the second time that night.

"Tend to Verona," orders Edith. "Stay hidden."

"Will you—"

"Yes, I will get ye more of the drink." Edith leaps across the chamber, being careful not to soil her new shoes in the guts across the floor. Edith wraps around the damaged door and ducks into the long hallway. She heads for the stairs.

Edith has to escape. It's the only option left. She listens to the rain bounce off the roof above her. Her mind flashes to Verona. What good would Edith be to her daughter if she were slowly dying from an illness? She can't stay here until the storm clears up, though. A dreadful feeling sinks its teeth into Edith, a horrifying instinct that the inn will become a tomb for many more of its inhabitants before sunrise. Edith can take her chances outside. It's only an hour-long trek to her village.

In perfect conditions, Edith argues with herself.

How long will it take with little-to-no visibility? Two hours, maybe three. How much energy will it take to stomp through mud the whole way? What if she becomes lost in the storm?

There's a chance Edith could get lucky. Some people possess the ability to stave off the sickness like nothing happened. That funny fellow in the corner seems to be that way. He was soaked from head to breeches but didn't appear ill even by happenstance. Edith can steal a horse, but doing so is a crime liable for execution—although, everything is punishable by death nowadays, and dying later is preferrable to dying now.

But what of Verona? She will die without Edith's aid.

Emma is more important. She's more valuable than Verona. A warm trickle flows down Edith's palms and congeals between her fingers. Edith looks down. Her palms bleed. She appraises the culprit to be her nails as dark blood soaks her skin underneath them.

With all these thoughts and more flooding her mind, Edith steps down the stairs. She spots one of the farmers—or revolutionists?—at the bottom of the staircase. It's the man who was kind to her earlier. He buries his head in his hands. Edith clears her throat. Until she decides how she'll make her escape, Edith needs to stay in character: the loyal bar maiden.

"Can I help ye?"

The man stares up at her. He scans her body. "Nice shoes," he says flatly. Edith glances down at Vivian's shoes on her feet. She meets the man's gaze. He knows.

"Bar maiden, over here," calls the squire from the bar.

"Excuse me," says Edith to the man, trying her best to keep the tone of relief out of her voice.

Edith scurries past him and slides behind the bar. She gambles a brief glance up at the ceiling; there are no traces of the devastation directly above them. That's good, at least. Edith pushes down a lump in her throat as she looks at the squire. The phantom image of Sir Algor sits next to him. She shakes her head. The guilt wreaks havoc in her lower stomach. A gaseous build up swells inside her. Edith tries to ignore it and feigns the perkiest face she can.

"Yes, hun?" smiles Edith, managing to be semi-convincing. Edith watches the younger man start to blush. What did Sir Algor say his name is? Kendrick?

"Is my partner . . . you know," stumbles Kendrick. His face transforms to a peachy-red color. "Is he *done* yet?"

Ah, this is about the prostitution.

Edith releases an authentic, gentle smile. The young man is actually kind of cute. He hasn't fully grown into his manhood yet. Baby fat still clings above his concealed muscles, and a patchy stubble of beard splotches across his face. If Sir Algor is the hardened sensuality of prime manhood, then Kendrick is the beguiling potential of youth. *He's going to be quite the bachelor when he learns to be not so coy about sex,* muses Edith.

"He's asleep now," she answers.

"That sounds like Algor. You must have really worked him," chuckles Kendrick. Edith raises an eyebrow at the squire. She wasn't expecting such a sly remark. Her eyebrow raise works its wonders though, as Kendrick's chuckle swiftly evaporates into a blushing embarrassment.

"That was, uh . . . I apologize. That was a terrible jest."

"Methought it was funny," says Edith.

Kendrick scratches his small patch of beard, probably in an attempt to stave off awkwardness. Edith decides to let him speak first. An amusing comfort soaks into her as she lets the young man embarrass himself a little. There is a tenderness in the graceless nature of human beings, and Edith eagerly needs some solace.

"Is our food done yet?" asks Kendrick.

"Should be. I'll check."

"Thank you." Kendrick beams at her. He has a great smile, the kind of grin that glistens no matter what the situation. It triggers a natural response for Edith to smile.

"No problem, hun," says Edith. She turns her back to the squire, still reluctantly beaming from Kendrick's smile. Edith steps to the kitchen doorway—

Splat.

Edith freezes. She holds her arm up before her, eyes straining through frizzled hair. A red dot. The drop of blood soaks into her forearm. Her smile vaporizes. Edith rushes to the kitchen door. She glances at Kendrick, but fortunately the squire didn't notice. Edith scans the room to be certain no one is watching her before she slowly looks up at the wood ceiling.

The usually light-colored timber warps with a red liquid. Drops of blood congeal directly above the squire. It swiftly grows in diameter.

The world folds in upon Edith. A lump of spit blockades her throat as she squeaks in a breath. She stumbles back into the kitchen, tripping over her own feet and slamming into the wall. A few herbs tumble onto her hair and shoulders. She covers her mouth. Her chest pumps. Air, air, she needs air. Edith gasps for life. Her eyes flicker. The heat of the kitchen grips her as it squishes her to the ground. Edith fights for the strength to keep standing. The world wins however; the world always wins. Edith collapses to the ground, bouncing her butt off the floor.

"Edith, you all right?" asks a fragile voice.

Edith gazes toward the voice. Her watery eyes have turned the world into a glossy streak of uncontained colors and lines, like a painter's pigments have all washed together in some terrible accident. She spots Leif through her water-colored vision.

"Are you cryin'?" asks Leif innocently.

Her lips tremble at the boy's pure concern. He reminds her so much of Emma. Warin didn't deserve such a son.

"Ye sayin' *you.* You a lord now, huh?" Edith smiles through the pain. "Come here, little guy."

Leif embraces Edith. He has to bend over slightly to hug her properly. They hold their embrace. Edith lets his little warmth power her. She sniffles away the tears.

"Thank ye," whispers Edith.

"You better now?"

"Much. You're the best."

They release their hug. Edith maneuvers onto her knees. She straightens her back, allowing her to become eye level with Leif. She takes his hand in hers, and as she does so, an idea forms in her mind. *She* might not be able to take Warin's horse, but . . .

"Leif," says Edith, "me needs you to hark my words. Keep your eyes and ears open. No fantasies t'night. Ye hark? If any trouble happens, ye take your father's horse and ride to my place. There you'll be safe with me daughter. Me needs you to keep her safe. Promise me, Leif. Promise me you will protect Emma."

"Promise," whispers Leif sternly. He understands, and Edith can't be more appreciative. She kisses the top of his head.

Lord, protect this boy.

F RAUNCE SITS NEXT TO Oswyn. He ignores the glare from Edmond, opting rather to spend his precious time to observe his brother. Vincent stares out the window again. What does his brother see out there in that storm-ravaged countryside? By some internal voice or gut feeling, Vincent turns to look back at Fraunce. Fraunce spots the fear in his brother's eyes. It is the same fear that had terrorized him for so many years, until Vince pulled him out of it. Fraunce gives him a reassuring smile.

They'll survive this night. He's not going to let their last night together be drenched in pain and sorrow.

"Shit."

The surprise in Edmond's voice makes Fraunce's heart stutter. Apparently, it had the same effect for the rest of the table as everyone snaps their attention to Edmond. They follow their conspirator's gaze toward the squire at the bar, then up, up to the ceiling, and then at—

Is that blood?!

An expanse of crimson pools directly above the squire. Fraunce glares at Edmond and Vivian. Did they chop the Goddamn knight into pieces? There's so much blood.

"What did ye do to him?" asks Fraunce, aghast and astonished.

He meant to keep some restraint in his voice, but the horror takes over. They give him no answer. Fraunce peeks at his brother. Vincent's eyes grow wide as he understands the direness of their situation. So much for living their last night together without fear, pain, or sorrow.

GODFREY FIDGETS HIS FINGERS. His face twitches. The bard fights for control. He gains it momentarily, but the corner of his lip decides to hop again. Godfrey takes out his pipe, reaches into his pouch, and feels around . . . still nothing. The bard molests it. His search is in vain. He bites his lip.

Godfrey peers up. Leif and Edith enter from the kitchen. The bar maiden pats Leif's back. The boy walks off from behind the bar and glances at Godfrey. The bard stiffens. Leif can't see him like this. Godfrey presses the back of his head against the wall behind him. He shoves it there, as if it can make him disappear from Leif's sight. He knows the boy will peek right through his veneer. He'll know the exactness of Godfrey's failures as a man and poet. Leif will see that he is nothing but a plague in human form.

Godfrey rocks back and forth.

EDITH TAKES A DEEP breath. She waits for Leif to move from the danger zone before she glances at the ceiling. She thinks fast. Edith places a bowl of pottage on the bar one seat next to Kendrick.

"Would ye mind movin' to this stool, sir?" says Edith sternly.

"Something wrong with this one?"

"That there stool needs a fixin'," lies Edith. "It might break. Wouldn't want ye to be sittin' on it when that happens." Edith holds her breath. The urge to vomit prods at her throat again. Kendrick rocks the barstool.

"It feels solid to me."

"Take your chances, if ye wish." Edith forces a chuckle, trying to keep it lighthearted. She hopes it appears more earnest than it feels.

"I'll take your word for it."

The squire moves over to the adjacent barstool. Edith watches a drop of blood fall onto the now-empty stool. Within the act and noise of switching seats, Kendrick doesn't notice the falling blood. Edith slides him the bowl.

"Perfect. I was famished," says Kendrick. He leans his scabbard against the bar. Edith notices he no longer has his chainmail on either. He must have taken it off when she was upstairs in the—

I can't think of that chamber. Not now. I'll go crazy.

The squire strips a knife from his belt and uses it to take a bite. He smiles. He slices another clump into his mouth. "Mmm. This is a fine good meal, madam," says Kendrick, grinning. "Succulent as any food I've ever had."

"Glad ye like it, sir."

Two more red droplets splatter onto the bar. Edith quickly sweeps them away. The liquid smear remains on the wood, but its red hue desaturates into the grain. Edith wipes her hand on her tunic, which is luckily dirty enough to disguise the blood. Edith peeks up at the squire. He's enamored with his food. Somehow, mercifully, he didn't notice. Edith steps back from him.

"If ye need anythin' else, let me or Warin know," says Edith. A voice inside her head yells at her. *Get out of here. Flee!*

"Thank you, madam." Kendrick smiles at her warmly.

Splat.

Kendrick flinches, his hand instinctively bracing in front of his face. The squire, slowly, timidly, lowers his hand, revealing to Edith the horror she dreads. Edith tries to run. Too late. Her legs are already frozen in place. Her body loses all its warmth.

A streak of blood slinks down the squire's cheek.

Somewhere in the firmament above them, thunder forebodes their misery. The room goes silent. The barstool groans under Kendrick as his weight shifts. Edith watches, helpless in her dismay, while the squire wipes the back of his hand across his cheek. The blood smears, leaving behind three maroon streaks like the claw marks of some ferocious beast. Kendrick lowers his hand and watches the blood seep into it. The squire tilts his head. Confusion overtakes Edith briefly. The squire doesn't react. He just watches his hand.

The maroon bead soaks into a brown coat on his skin. He still does nothing.

A second drip splashes onto him.

The squire jolts back. The barstool fires out from beneath him. It ricochets off the ground, bouncing and screaming as it contorts under his force. Edith's legs release her from their stillness. She stumbles into the wall behind the bar. Kendrick glares up at the crimson-soaked ceiling where the lumber sheds tears of gore and rain.

Kendrick glares at Edith. His lips quiver with hers. He unsheathes his sword.

FRAUNCE GRIPS HIS KNIFE. Edmond and Vivian have already taken theirs out. Oswyn follows. Knives are one of the few things that every person owns, no matter how rich or how poor—man or woman, priest or criminal, everyone carries a knife. They are used for eating, crafting, farming, and, of course, self-defense. Fraunce begins to wonder if they don't cause more trouble than they're worth.

The squire's sword rings out as he unsheathes it. Its razor edge sings for death. Lightning flashes the room into white as the squire charges up the stairs.

Wind howls through the window next to Fraunce and his brother. They're out of time.

"Vincent, get up," orders Fraunce. He wraps around the table and drags his brother from his seat.

"Sit down, 'fore ye get yourself killed," says Vivian. Edmond turns in his chair. Fraunce points his knife at them.

"Lest ye forget, Fraunce, 'twas your plan," says Vivian.

"What's happenin'?" asks Oswyn, looking as confused as ever.

"They killed him. The knight," answers Fraunce.

"'Tis'nt a good thing?" questions Oswyn, hardly less bewildered.

"Would be if they didn't do such a shoddy job," says Fraunce bitterly, failing to leave any anger out of his voice. Edmond flourishes his dagger at Fraunce and Vincent. Somewhere, Fraunce hears the wails of his wife . . . perhaps in the wind at the window.

"Fraunce," Edmond speaks carefully, "if ye ain't with us, you's against us."

"We want freedom," says Fraunce. He embraces the preachiness of his stance. "I want the freedom ordained to us by God. Not gruesome deaths to be abhorred."

"Christ only gives freedom of the soul," contests Vivian. "Here, we must claim our own, by any means."

"We ambush him. As soon as he comes down the stairs," says Edmond.

"No," says Vincent, stepping up to them. "Kendrick's nice. He wants to help people like us."

All attention turns to Vincent. Fraunce pushes his brother behind him, abating him from the wrath of their conspirators.

"Ye know his name?" asks Fraunce in surprise.

"He's a vicious whoreson," argues Edmond. "Don't let him fool ye, Vincent."

"Think of your parents he killed," adds Oswyn.

"Or me love," says Vivian reluctantly. Her voice breaks. She wipes tears that form in her eyes. "Me love that they took, me everything."

"He wasn't there though," reasons Vincent. Fraunce feels Vince try to push past him, but he keeps his brother back. He won't lose him. Not tonight.

"They be all the same," says Edmond. "Believe me."

"No."

"Vince, 'tis for the good of everyone," comforts Vivian. The manipulation in her voice is transparent for all to hear. Fraunce grips his knife tighter.

"Abdicatin' the duke is," contends Fraunce. "We don't want to kill more than we must."

"We must destroy them all, lest they come back stronger. 'Tis the whole system at fault," growls Vivian. Fraunce can spot the ferocity on her face now.

"Don't spit your venom at us!" Fraunce thunders.

A loud step reverberates from the stairwell. It quiets the room. Another step echoes out. Then another, another. All of them thunder heavy, foreboding. Kendrick the squire reaches the final step at the bottom. His body and padded armor are drenched, both in gore and rain. His leather greaves are stained a dark red, and his vambraces don a matching pigment. The squire's hair latches to his brow. The room remains utterly silent as Kendrick, so intimidating in his armor despite his age, steps off the stairs. He leaves a bloody trail of footprints behind him.

Kendrick erects himself before the hearth. Its blazing fire silhouettes him from all angles. His bloodied, meter-long sword gleams the hearth-fire off its iron blade. The blood groove along both sides of the blade proclaims its lust for human skin. Sparks of fire and ash blow around him, shrouding everything into shadow but for the intensity of the squire. The entire room appears dark in comparison.

"You." Kendrick growls to the bar maiden, glaring over his shoulder. "You were with him last."

The bar maiden shakes her head. The squire slithers to her. Even with his body no longer blocking the hearth, the room seems to remain in darkness. *This is Vincent's opportunity,* Fraunce realizes.

"Get up the stairs," whispers Fraunce to his brother.

"I want to stay with ye," says Vincent.

"Please go," cries Fraunce. "Me can't lose you too."

Vincent hesitantly nods. Fraunce kisses his brother on the cheek. Vincent's eyes, the reflection of his own, pierces a hole into Fraunce's soul. They'll get out of this. They will. Vincent slowly moves toward the stairs, keeping close to the walls, similar to how they escaped from the sacking of their home.

EDITH BITES HER TONGUE. The squire is on her within seconds. The young man's kind eyes glare at her with a ferocity that she had only seen once before. That same viciousness was within Paris's soul when he killed Sir Algor. Tears boil in Kendrick's bloodshot eyes. He trembles all over. It shakes Edith to her core.

"He loved you," says Kendrick faintly.

"He thought he did," quivers Edith.

"He did."

"I'm so sorry," says Edith quietly.

Kendrick leans within whispering range of her without forfeiting eye contact. He remains silent. It locks Edith up. She feels her hair stick up all over.

"I know it wasn't you," he says at last.

His eyes change. The intensity swells into a soft sadness. Edith comes to a pitiful realization: he's simply a heartbroken, young man. A boy who has lost his mentor and friend. The evil seething underneath remains ever present though. "Edith, don't let me hurt the wrong person. Just look at who it was."

Someone punches Edith in the gut. Her brain rattles within her head, like some giant dog is thrashing her about endlessly. As far as Edith knows, Paris is upstairs with

Verona. The squire wants her to reveal who it was, in other words, to be responsible for the death that follows. Her heart aches for her daughter. She only wants to hold Emma, for pity's sake.

"Please," begs Kendrick. Edith catches the regret in the squire's voice. He must feel that he has to do this, that he *needs* to get revenge. She can try to use that.

"You can let it go," beseeches Edith. "You don't have to hurt anyone."

"Edith, just look," says the squire. She spots the humanity fighting within him. It's caged behind rage and grief, but it's there. If only he lets it free.

"Don't make me do this," whispers Edith. She senses warm tears streak down her face. Her jaw quivers. *Don't make me kill anyone. Please. I just want me daughter.*

"Look."

Kendrick stares into her eyes. She glares back at him, fearful to accidentally glance at anyone else. Tears form under his eyelids as well.

Find your humanity, Kendrick.

"Look," he begs again.

Edith shakes her head and sticks out her chin. Strong. Defiant.

"LOOK!"

Edith's eyes flicker on their own accord. They flinch toward an object in her peripherals, the only thing with movement in the frozen room: Vincent.

T HE SCREAMS OF EVERYONE Fraunce has ever lost shout at him at once. He watches the squire snap his head from his brother, to the bar maiden, and back to Vincent. Fraunce imagines a world where he must listen to the screams of his brother every waking moment. His parents, his wife, and now Vince—all dead and all haunting him.

"V-Vincent?" stammers Kendrick.

Fraunce loses control over his body. His knife drops to the ground with a dull thud. He stares in uncontrollable horror as the squire steps toward his younger brother. Kendrick points the tip of his sword at Vincent.

"How could you?" gapes Kendrick incredulously. "Did you do it before or after our talk?"

Fraunce watches as Kendrick's body shifts. He spots the squire's resentment, wrath, and anguish evaporate all semblances of compassion. Fraunce himself had lost that same touch with humanity. He knows what loss does to a man. That's how Fraunce knows what cruelty will follow.

"You did this to me? Why?"

Vincent remains frozen in place. He puts his hands up, surrendering himself to the whims of Kendrick. Vincent shakes his head.

"Why did you kill him?!" Kendrick raises his sword.

"Not him."

Fraunce steps forward, past his conspirators and their knives, within five paces from Kendrick and Vincent. The squire moves his blade toward Fraunce.

"What do you know of this?" questions Kendrick.

The screams go silent. For the first time since that fateful night, Fraunce no longer hears the wails of Dawn, the yells of his father, nor the cries of his mother. They are watching him now, he knows. They are with him. They will protect them. Vincent *will* get his life.

Fraunce and his brother make eye contact as worry overtakes Vincent's face. Fraunce smiles at him. Vincent shakes his head, pleading for Fraunce to not say it.

His brother can always read him so well.

"'Twas me who killed the knight," says Fraunce. He keeps his eyes trained on his brother. No more pain tonight. No more fear.

Vince never deserved this life that Fraunce coerced him into. He will get out of it. Fraunce is certain of it now, looking at the honest distress displayed on his brother's face. Vincent will never have to kill anyone. He'll never have to become the monster Fraunce became. Vincent is the world that Fraunce wanted, the forbidden fruit that doesn't sprout for the likes of him; but because of some divine benevolence that he'll never understand, he is honored with it anyway. He'll never stop thanking God for the privilege of knowing his brother, for having Vincent when no one else would have Fraunce.

Fraunce lets all fear shed away so he can only show Vincent his love. His brother will get out of this horror. That's all that matters, and so Fraunce smiles.

"It was me," repeats Fraunce. "Don't hurt him. Vincent is pure. He's the kindest soul I've ever known. He would never —"

Fraunce loses control of his voice. He tries to speak again but fails. A fuzzy, tingling sensation lingers at his stomach. Fraunce prods with his hands. They touch something cool and hot. Fraunce glances down.

A blade sticks through his belly. Odd, that.

Fraunce feels a hard object, like a rock, behind his back. Bones? Even odder. A gushing warmth of liquid streams from his mouth. Fraunce glances at the ground. The straw-covered floor is lathered in offal. How'd that happen?

Fraunce falls onto the gore. Why are his legs not working?

He convulses over himself, but no pain hits him. He just convulses, again and again. Fraunce tips his head up in time to see his baby brother open his mouth. No sounds come out, though.

His brother has always been a quiet one.

Fraunce closes his eyes. For some reason, he's unable to keep them open. He no longer feels the coolness of the ground, nor the heat of the hearth. He no longer smells the sweetness of the rain, nor the spice of the earth. He no longer tastes the iron of the liquid, nor the tang of the dirt. All he knows is darkness.

But he can still hear.

He listens as Dawn shrieks in his ears. Her beautiful voice fills his head. She isn't screaming at him, though. She isn't crying for help nor wailing from pain. No, she's shouting in joy to see him.

What a wonderful sound, the screams of his wife. How could he ever hate her voice?

PART TWO

A PAST OF REGRETS

IMPOTENT RESOLVE

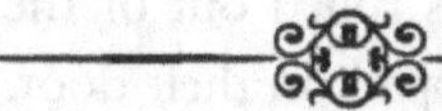

PARIS AWAKENED TO THE sound of frantic knocks at his door. He grumbled and rolled over onto his stomach, wrapping a single arm over Verona. Her hair smelled entirely like her—a musk impossible for Paris to describe but inconceivable for him to forget. She had washed at the public baths yesterday, and so her hair had a soft residue left over that made Paris feel at home. Verona stirred in his arm. A second sting of knocks rapped on their cottage door.

"Paris?!"

Paris grunted. Verona shifted her weight and pushed him to the side. He opened his eyes. Their bedchamber remained dipped in darkness, giving him all the environmental clues he needed to deduce that it was still way too damn early for visitors. A third series of knocks erupted.

"Verona?! Paris?! Open up!"

"For the love of God," mumbled Paris.

"Paris, dear, methinks there is someone at the door," said Verona, smiling slightly. Paris moaned. The environmental clues also warned Paris that it was way too damn early for jests.

"Ye think so?" Paris whined.

Verona stood up next to their straw bed. Paris reached out with his arm, but all he captured was the emptiness of the bed. He sighed but consoled himself with the lingering heat of Verona's body. She yawned and stretched her arms. Her beautifully imperfect figure, even first thing in the morning, managed to stun Paris. She threw a long, blue-trimmed tunic over her night gown. Paris rolled out of the bed as well. A fourth series of knocks rapped on their door. The thumping continued on and on, building in intensity and severity.

"Bloody hell. Hold a damn minute!" said Paris at the rude awakener.

Paris threw on his tunic. The thundering at the door continuously invaded his privacy. Paris stuck his hand out, trying to navigate around his tiny cottage in the dark. Verona found the door first and swung it open.

"Good mornin', Verona," greeted a masculine voice.

Paris stumbled about in search of his belt, scouring under scattered silks, dresses, and straw laden throughout the bedchamber. Paris finally found it and wobbled to the brighter light of the door.

"Who is it?"

"Johnathan," said Verona.

"Johnathan? What is John doin' here so early?"

Paris wrapped his hand around Verona's waist. Sure enough, it was Johnathan. The bastard. Well, John wasn't really a bastard. He's their closest friend, or at least, he *was* their closest friend, until he decided to wake them up so Goddamn early.

Johnathan leaned over, resting his hands on his knees, and panted furiously. His clothes stuck to his body. The village of Salisbury silhouetted him from behind. The morning air was silent, as if the whole world was holding its breath. The blackness of the sky was already being eviscerated by a deep blue, which meant the weather would be immaculate. It would be a lovely day.

"My God, Verona," stammered Johnathan, gulping down air. "How do ye manage to look so good right out of bed?"

"Oh, me knows," said Paris. "'Tis witchcraft, I tells ya. Witchcraft."

"Stop it, boys," blushed Verona. Paris chuckled. His wife's skin glowed in the light of dawn. Her black hair hung around her in thick, vivid ropes.

"Ye goin' to have to teach my wife that spell," laughed Johnathan half-heartedly. "She looks like a real witch comin' out of bed."

"Shush. Elizabeth is stunnin'."

"I wish ye could tell her yourself," said Johnathan, his tone slamming them in the face like a gust of muggy air. Verona and Paris glanced at one another.

"Everythin' all right, John?"

"We need to talk. I came as quick as me could."

"Clearly," Paris remarked sarcastically, waving his friend in.

Paris and Verona sat at their dining table. Rather than the barrel–plank combo of most peasantry dining boards, their table was a finely crafted work of art that could rival those found with the higher nobility. It was a wedding gift to Paris and Verona by a carpenter they helped house a few years back. The table was expertly hewed and sawed off, with its rich brown oak frame glistening in the early morning light. A Latin inscription was etched into the frame of its decorative apron. Paris and Verona don't know how to read, but their carpenter friend assured them it was a lovely poem about eternal love. The poet's name was Virgil, or something comparably silly. Paris had a vague idea of who he was, as some aspects of that archaic Roman culture was still being forlornly preserved within educated circles. Paris never understood the allure. What use were these dead Romans to him and other peasants? They just want to live.

Johnathan circled them. He scratched at his mop of hair. It strung around him in thinning strands. He was in his late twenties, and thus only a few years Paris's elder, but his wrinkled skin from decades working in the fields around Salisbury have made him appear much older. Johnathan finally scrounged up the courage to speak, but only in a harsh whisper, as if the angels of God were spying on them.

"He wants Verona."

Paris forgot to breathe. Verona frowned. She picked at her fingernails, a nervous tick that Paris usually found quite charming. But on this terrible morning, it made him even more anxious.

"He can't," said Paris stubbornly.

"Duke Rowan proclaimed it before his inner court the day before yester. A few servants were in the room. One of them got word out. I caught wind of it at that tavern a partial league from town. I came as soon as me could, but those damn guards refused to open the gate until sunrise."

Verona grabbed Paris's hand. A silence crept into the room as a gentle breeze invaded their home. Johnathan plopped onto a chair, his disgruntled appearance betraying his lack of sleep.

So, he tells the truth.

Paris turned his attention to the window. The sky was turning blue at the horizon. "How long do we have?" Paris finally asked.

"Sundown, at the latest."

"How do they know?"

"Must've been some villager tryin' to get on their good side." Johnathan sighed.

The pity and sorrow on his face could have slaughtered Paris right there in his home. It was well known that the duke—in his sick perversion of lust and gluttony—loved the recently bewedded, to take them upon his bed and defile them. It was a fictional horror story promulgated by the peasantry, or so Paris thought. It was also illegal and strictly forbidden under the monarchy of King Henry; however, it seemed dukedom had its virtues.

Paris slammed his fist upon their hospitable dowry. The table shuddered under his might, and Verona jumped in surprise. Paris thundered to the window and stared out it despondently.

"How can Duke Rowan do this?" croaked Verona.

"He's the bloody duke," stated Johnathan bluntly. "He can do whatever he wants, even claim it is ordained by God."

"The Good Lord would never ordain this."

"That no longer matters. Four knights have already left the keep. Paris, Commander Rayner is with 'em."

Paris turned pale. A chilling rush of despair pierced his blood. *Commander Rayner.* That bastard was known far and wide within Duke Rowan's fiefdom. He was a ghoul, a bogeyman who preyed on the feeble peasantry and smote them down before his liege lord. Commander Rayner was spoke about in hushed terms within taverns and churches, often becoming the fiend of many horrific rumors that traveled from the mouths of the inebriated and liberated alike. He had become the nightmare that parents alerted their children to beware if they didn't do what they were told. The grotesque mystique of Commander Rayner had put him at the center of every reprehensible act Duke Rowan's knighthood had performed.

"The commander?"

"He's ruthless," said Johnathan. "Satan's own begotten child, through-n-through."

"The other wives say he is three meters tall. That he carries a blade longer than him," shuddered Vivian.

"Me can't decipher truth from hearsay, but me knows that ye must leave. Now."

Paris nodded. If Johnathan was right, and Commander Rayner was leading the pack of knights who had ventured out to capture Verona, they wouldn't stand a chance at all.

They moved quickly. They tossed their clothes into a burlap sack: breeches, tunics, hats, silks, belts. Above all their clothes, they placed Verona's wedding gown. It was a beautiful heirloom, passed down amongst the female lineage of Verona's line. It was a single dress, sewed together with delicate care, which flowered at the bottom with large turquoise ruffles. When in motion, it gave the illusion of bubbling waves, like an ocean that continually rose and folded upon itself. Paris had never seen anything so beautiful in all his life. Their marriage was coronated by their town bishop, and a small festivity was held in the back lot behind a few of their homes. It was a wonderful ceremony held in secrecy, lest the duke caught wind of the affair. They weren't careful enough.

"Head east," advised Johnathan.

"East brings us closer to the keep," said Vivian hesitantly.

"Me knows. But it's the quickest way out of this land. Do ye have any family elsewhere?"

"Me does," nodded Paris, "up in Glucester. Kin from my mother's line."

"Good. Head north as soon as you cross into Duke Richard's fiefdom," said Johnathan.

Paris and Verona packed the last of their items. They placed it on the English oak table. Paris knew the table would hurt the most to leave behind. It wasn't as valuable as Verona, though. Nothing would ever be as precious as her. Johnathan approached Paris. He took Paris's hand into his own and plopped something cool and heavy into his palm. Paris gaped down at the handful of pence within his hand now.

"'Tis not much," said Johnathan regretfully.

Paris stared up at his lifelong friend. Johnathan was the first person Paris ever connected with. They went through all stages of life together. They learned the trade of being farmhands together. They pulled pranks upon the unsuspecting townsfolk together. Whenever they drank, it often leads to them being locked up for the night, much to the dismay of their wives. And whether at church, a ceremony, or some major life event, the townsfolk could always guarantee they'd find John and Paris next to one another—probably snickering amongst themselves about some silly joke. Johnathan was the type of friend who only came around once in a lifetime and often too early on to be fully appreciated. He'd never again have a friend like John.

"Thank ye," said Paris. He pulled Johnathan into a hug. Paris wasn't going to argue about the money. He knew refusing Johnathan's offer would only offend him.

"I wish me could see ye both grow old together," said Johnathan as they stepped back from their hug. "See you start a family of your own. Me can't imagine the trouble of tiny Paris spawns runnin' about."

"We love ye," mumbled Verona. They embraced.

"I love you too. No cryin'. Stop that. You're too lovely to cry."

They severed their embrace, permanently cutting ties to a past they'd have to forget. Johnathan stepped back from them. He looked between Paris and Verona. The grin—the fake, empty grin—Johnathan plastered across his face would forever be seared into Paris's mind. Paris would go back to it time and time again whenever he needed some light to look to. Paris and Verona have people that love them. They have people who are thinking of them. Paris could think back to this day, when on this morning, his childhood best friend standing aloof from them in the waxing light of dawn, Johnathan benevolently gifted to them that expression that conveyed everlasting companionship.

"Tell Elizabeth me loves her too," beseeched Verona.

"'Course."

Verona blew him a final kiss before she exited the cabin forever. Paris and Johnathan remained intimately close but catastrophically apart in the room. Johnathan knocked on the oak table.

"You mind if I take this? Elizabeth would be happy," implored Johnathan.

"Go ahead."

"Ye protect her," said Johnathan, nodding his head to the doorway left open by Verona.

"Me will."

"Watch for storms. They can kill ye out in the open."

"Me knows. You stay safe as well. Them knights find out you helped us—"

"They won't," Johnathan said confidently. "Besides, I won't tell 'em shite."

Johnathan and Paris laughed. Paris knew Johnathan would never betray them, not to Commander Rayner nor the Devil himself. They would die for each other. They both knew it but neither had to say it. It was a given fact of life, no different from stating the sun will rise again; it simply does.

"Now fly," said Johnathan. "Me don't want ye caught."

"You have me thanks, John. Always."

Paris hefted up his sack and ambled to the front door. He stopped under the doorway. A temptation too powerful to override forced him to look back one last time. Johnathan stood over their ornate table, and his fingers traced the grain of the wood. Paris suppressed the urge to say one last thing; it would only sour the moment. Paris sighed and turned away, leaving his best friend behind in the tomb of their old life.

Paris and Verona were well outside the city walls of Salisbury by the time the sun hoisted itself from its slumber and shined, like a coin of silver molten, upon the far green country. The lovers steered clear of the well-trodden roads. The chances of stumbling across the pack of knights hunting them would be less likely if they roamed across the uncultivated, hilly provinces of Duke Rowan's domain. There was, admittedly, an edge of risk in their assessment: crossing the countryside so far from the main roads would make them stand out like a nobleman in a peasant's brothel. Why would two people need to avoid the refined, traversable comforts of civilization if not for nefarious purposes? Paris hoped that "to avoid the torrent of human hostility," wouldn't be the answer that jumped into anyone's mind. The lovers took their chances.

They ventured through much of the morning without trouble. It took an hour of laborious trudging to get through the farmlands that surrounded Salisbury. The two burlap sacks of clothes and spare food hung heavy on their backs, and Paris's shoulders began to ache even though he was used to ploughing fields for hours on end. He could only imagine how it must strain at the limbs of his wife, but Verona kept trekking on, like a draught horse whose majestic power relentlessly surprised the weak muscles of man; and so, she blessed Paris with the inner strength to keep moving on, one foot in front of the other. Paris was merely a mule laboring in the awe-inspiring wake of his wife.

His love for her grew with every step.

When they were around an hour outside of the Salisbury farmlands, Paris and Verona had to hide behind a lonely oak for half an hour. They spotted two figures upon horseback about a furlong west of them. The horse riders were cresting a hill when Paris discerned them against the brightening sky. He swore he saw a glint of light flash off them, giving him the uneasy feeling that they were more than mere travelers. The sudden realization came over Paris: *If I can see them, they can see us.* Paris and Verona promptly hunkered down behind a slender oak that sat isolated on the brink of the massive green sea. After a comfortable amount of time had passed since the lovers saw the figures upon horseback, they set out again for freedom.

Two more hours passed with little commotion. It was becoming one of those rare spring days where the sun could amble, unabated, through a cloudless sky, and where the warm, vibrant colors of the wilderness were beseeched to radiate out in all their bewitching glory. Their kingdom was so often covered in a gloom of rain and humdrum bleakness that a brilliant sunny day, such as this, was a divine privilege. It should be a sin for Paris and Verona to labor on such a day.

They traveled through the sea of grass. Its knee-high blades undulated in the cool breeze, pushing and pulling at their legs like the flow of an ocean tide. Paris and Verona became well entrenched within the lush, hilly landscape by midday. The sun beamed down on them, and the humidity forced their bodies to weep. The lovers bitterly fought against the burlap sacks they carried. They switched shoulders occasionally, granting much needed relief to their screaming muscles. After a while, Verona began to tow the sack behind her; it left a trail of crushed grass that slunk its way conspicuously through the grasslands. Paris shortly followed suit, and by the time the sun dipped to the western horizon, there was an irregular, parallel wake of ruptured grass that cuts over a league into the rolling plains.

Paris and Verona talked very little. They opted, rather, to share the companionable silence of drudgery. The grueling journey wreaked havoc on Paris's body, and he knew it must have been wearying the same on Verona's. There was a comfort in their mutual affair with anguish. This could only make them stronger in the end, so there was no need for words.

The clouds appeared two hours later. They begot from under the western horizon and spread across the azure sky like smoke from a monstrous inferno, reaching up its terrible black tendrils to encompass the sun, as if the night was too impatient to await the natural extinguishing of sunshine. Before the lovers had a chance to search for shelter, the dense clouds of ink sprung upon them. The yellow sun, which, mere moments ago, was simmering Paris and Verona alive, became smothered by the storm clouds. The calm breeze perverted itself into a frightening gust. Dirt and leaves slammed into the lovers before the rain did. The sea of grass contorted into a darkness of gray hairs that tumultuously splayed about in the wind.

Verona tapped Paris on the shoulder as he shielded his eyes. She pointed to an object in the distance. A few kilometers away sat a two-story building. Paris nodded. Salvation rarely materializes to the helpless at the onset of despair. It was their only chance. Between them and the building lay a few furloughs of descending grassland, and then another quarter of a league or so of dense woodlands. Once they exit the wood, they would practically be at their safe haven.

"Worth tryin'!" screamed Paris over the onslaught of wind.

Verona grabbed his hand. She pulled Paris into her. Their lips connected, and a jolt of rejuvenation shot through him. Paris released his sack and pulled her closer to him. They embraced and kissed and made obvious their love as the first few drops of rain slopped onto them. The lovers heaved up their burlap sacks and raced down the slick slope to the woodlands.

The forest was a terrible decision.

They were lost; hopelessly and terribly lost. The woodlands were even denser than they had appeared. Paris and Verona squeezed sideways between the massive trunks, pinching their overburdened sacks through the narrow gap between trees. The wind swirled unimaginably loud around them. Paris's ears felt as if they would burst if the pressure continued to increase. The canopy did little to block any of the storm, as rainwater doused them from above in chilly torrents. The wind took on the form of a gale within the maze of thickets, contorting and combusting into itself until only a frightening tempest remained. This self-perpetuating windstorm within a storm pushed back at the lovers. Verona's long black hair flew violently into Paris's face and impeded most of his vision—not that it would have mattered; the denseness of the wood shrouded all sight anyway. Only the occasional flicker of lightning allowed any vision through the boughs and shrubbery, and all it revealed was even darker shadows and an even more profound sense of terror.

Prickly plants and thorny branches bit at their legs. Paris's feet sunk into the ground. A stream of water and mud washed around his ankles like a river swarming around a tree trunk.

Verona lurched Paris forward. She stumbled over some root, dragging Paris on top of her. Paris's body jolted back, though, as the burlap sack in his opposite hand caught on a thorny thicket. His arms stretch out in opposite directions. A loud crack erupted from one of his shoulders. A sharp pain pierced his armpit and fired down his back. Paris yelped. He collapsed to the ground between Verona and his supply sack.

"Sorry, I fell," said Verona sheepishly.

Paris ignored the temptation to berate her as she pulled herself out of the mud. Her legs, like Paris's, were now caked with slimy dirt. She had a series of red lines across her skin from cuts the forest had subjected her to.

"'Tis'nt your fault." Paris groaned. He swirled his shoulders into a circular stretch. The ache remained, but it subsided substantially. *Good,* thought Paris, *me didn't destroy anything.*

Verona stood in the swirling wind. She gripped her burlap sack and readied to drag it again. Paris tramped back to his sack. He pulled it to him. The fabric stretched a little, but the sack didn't budge. Paris tried again. He heard the slight sound of ripping linen as it bulged in the center.

"Oh no."

Paris felt around the bulbous sack stuck to the thicket. A few thorns had pierced through the sack. Paris pulled it again. A scar sliced across the bottom, and a pair of undergarments slinked out and soiled themselves on the ground. Paris gingerly pinched the sack and tried to lift it out of the thickets but to no avail. Paris screamed a mighty, powerful roar that lost all impact as a gust of wind swallowed it up. He yanked and thrust and twisted the sack this way and that. The bushes swayed but refused to release their hold. The linen ripped more as the ground became littered with torn clothes.

"Darling, we need to go!" yelled Verona behind him.

"Damnit!"

"Paris, please." Verona laid her hand on his shoulder. She sneezed. Paris leaned his head against hers. They mourned over the lost contents of the sack before continuing on.

I can never have kids.

Paris had no idea why this sprouted into his mind as they continued their descent into the wood, but it was true. It was an awful truth. Other men mentioned their nights with their wives on occasion, but Paris could never relate. Verona and he had tried on their wedding night, but alas, it still didn't rise. It was embarrassing, and Verona had taken it personally at first. When Paris explained his predicament to her, Verona suggested visiting a local herbalist to consult about it, and if that didn't work, they could always find a witch. The witches in the wood were said to have incredible potions that caused all sorts of miracles. Paris wasn't too sure he wanted to take a chance with that one, it being such a sensitive region.

Paris had met with his local cleric on numerous occasions to discuss it. The priest believed it was a punishment set upon Paris by God, that the Lord ensnared him with this illness to curse him for some sin Paris hadn't atoned for. Paris, for the life of him, didn't know what sin he had committed, but it must have been something particularly atrocious for such retribution. All Paris knew was he could never fully satisfy his wife. It was a terrible guilt he carried within him. The worst part was that it loomed around him every time they were in bed together. It was a demon that never ceased to rear its ugly head. In a depraved way, that was what made Paris's blood boil about the duke's decree. Duke Rowan could give Verona something that Paris couldn't. It was disgusting to think of an assault on Verona's virtue that way. Paris knew it, but he couldn't help it. All he had to remember was that she chose to be with him regardless of his deficiency. For a long time, Paris believed no one would want to be with him because of it. The Church preached that it took purpose out of life, for a man and a woman to not bear children. Verona had saved herself for marriage as well, whether it was because of the fines women have to pay for copulating before marriage, or if it was for her own saintly virtue, Paris wasn't entirely sure. Either way, he owed her much more than life.

Paris led Verona now. He shook his head. They needed to survive. *Stop thinking about the past and your own damn woes.*

"Hang on!" Paris screamed as a blast of wind knocked them back. Verona held onto Paris's sleeve for dear life. Rain splattered against them like miniature arrows.

"Paris!"

Too late. A branch twirled from the darkness and sundered apart as it collided with Paris's face. He collapsed to the forest floor. He reached up to his nose and clogged the stream of blood. Verona hoisted him up by the back of his shirt. She sneezed again. An irritating, ringing noise reverberated throughout Paris's head. He grimaced. The foul taste of iron flooded over his tastebuds. Paris spat it out. The roof of his mouth declared to him that he bit his tongue. Wonderful.

They trudged on. They had no other options. Paris promptly decided they would have been better off facing the storm in the open countryside. The cover of trees seemed like such a great idea—how wrong they had been. Verona's grip on his sleeve started to shake. She sneezed again and followed that with a soft whimper.

The building

Paris espied it momentarily in the flash of Heaven's light. He lost it in the following gloom. Paris turned his body to where, he thought, he saw it.

"It's this way!" Paris yelled over the storm. Verona didn't respond. She merely held on as Paris dragged them through the blackness.

Paris was correct; the building sat just beyond the tree line. They crossed the small grass plain to the two-story shack. They navigated to its front side, and Paris discovered that it was an inn. Paris smiled. A fortuitous turn of luck at last.

A smaller shack lay to the side of the inn where a set of barn doors closed it off to the world. Paris tried that first. It opened. A warm, orange light greeted them as they stumbled into the stables. Only two horses were stashed on a picket line that crossed the space. A rampart of firewood lined the walls of the room, and a mound of hay was crammed into the corner. Verona collapsed into the pile of straw.

Paris kneeled next to his wife. He rubbed snot off her top lip. Another drip of slime slinked from her nose. Paris wiped that away, too. She shivered.

"Verona, ye fine?"

Verona nodded her head, but it did little to calm his nerves. Paris rubbed her arms. Their one remaining burlap sack was soaked next to them. A sharp clap swung Paris's attention up to a door in the western wall. A little boy stared at them. He held a bucket of water.

"She fine?" asked the boy.

"No," said Paris. "Can ye help us?"

The boy didn't bother to respond. He sat down the bucket and rushed back through the door. Paris combed Verona's hair back. She sneezed into him.

"Sorry," she apologized softly.

"'Tis fine. We'll get out of here soon." Paris forced a smile.

The door opened. Paris glanced up. The boy stood at the doorway with a woman about their age. Her tunic was littered with filth, and her wanton hair was clumped into ragged knots. Paris recognized she was a hardworking woman. He liked her already. The woman stared at him and Verona for a moment, presumably appraising them.

"Please," begged Paris.

The woman bent down to the boy. "Don't tell your father she is sick. Ye hark?" she said. The boy nodded. "Good. Back to your chores."

The boy took the bucket of water to the horses. The woman crossed to them.

"Can she stand?" the woman asked.

"Me can," Verona grunted. She forced herself up. Paris flung Verona's arm over his shoulder. She coughed. It was a wet snarl of a cough that hinted at a battle of phlegm within her throat.

"Take her inside," said the woman. "Cross the common, up the stairs, first guest chamber on the left. This key will let you in. Me knows a remedy that might help, heard it from an alchemist. It needs a few specific herbs, which me can get from the kitchen."

"Thank ye," said Paris.

"Make sure the other patrons don't see her. They might panic if they think a sickness will spread out."

"'Course."

"What's your name?" Verona asked limply.

"Ye can call me Edith," said the woman. "I be the bar maiden here."

Verona grazed Edith's arm with her hand. His wife smiled at her, and Edith returned the friendliness. Paris put more of Verona's weight onto himself. They hobbled to the stable door.

"Leif, get that sack there when ye finish," ordered Edith.

"Yes, madam."

Verona coughed again. She spat out phlegm this time. Paris inspected her cautiously. Her face turned deathly white. Drops of sweat beaded from her temples. Paris suppressed an anger within him, one that raged to be released.

This was Duke Rowan's fault. Duke Rowan and all his accursed knights. Those cowards. They kidnap women to be violated by their ruler. They all deserved eternal damnation. Why did they have to go after Verona? Why did they choose them? Duke Rowan and his knights were despicable to the highest degree, a plague cursed upon the peasantry.

Damn them all to Hell.

CALLOUS REMORSE

AN EARLY MORNING HAZE rolled over the boundless green hills. Sheep roamed across the plain. Dozens of eclectic and ecstatic birds sang aloud, praising the dark passage of night and the fresh aurora of a new day. A rosy-fingered dawn stretched from the east. It couldn't be any more beautiful of a day.

Kendrick cantered his horse, Fortune, up the shadowed slope of a hill. They crested the mound and sauntered into the nascent sunlight. Sir Algor ambled up next to his squire upon Brandy, a caramel-colored horse with black streaks throughout his mane. Brandy had a distinct scar that ran up the side of his neck and face. Sir Algor had told Kendrick that it came from a collision with a tree, but he left the particular set of circumstances that would have led to such an accident a mystery. Unlike Brandy, Fortune was a mare with a deep black coat cleaved in two by splotchy white spots.

Kendrick always loved horses. They were majestic and magnificent beasts, with the power and speed to make any man jealous. Fortune's warmth radiated from her body and comforted Kendrick. He never felt alone when with her. The barrel of her body bloated and contracted with her every breath, pushing gently on Kendrick's legs and letting him know definitively that she was alive. She was a sentient creature, with all the beauty and flaws that God put into every being. It was a privilege for Kendrick to ride upon her. He knew he would give his life for Fortune, as she would for him.

Kendrick and Fortune watched as the dozens upon dozens of sheep flocked in the distance. They grazed silently as they moved. He smiled as he took a deep breath; the swirling scent of morning dew filled his nostrils.

"It never gets old," said Kendrick, moaning pleasurably.

"What?" Sir Algor frowned.

"The smell of morning's first light." Kendrick closed his eyes and relaxed. His mentor sniffed the air.

"Smells like sheep shit to me."

"How can you not be romantic about a new day?"

"Do you have any idea how many *new days* I've had in my life?"

"With that attitude, it's clearly been too many," said Kendrick.

"Aye. When you reach my age, you realize each day is just like the prior. Once you've seen one sunrise, you've seen them all."

"That's because you're no fun. Lo, and hark, the sun warms and life giveth. You can't possibly suggest that the sunset has more beauty?" contended Kendrick, raising his eyebrows at Sir Algor.

"When you reach your forties like I have, you'll speak a different timbre. The sunset is the promise of tranquility. It's a spiritually ordained peace on Earth, an interlude between the violence of man," proposed Sir Algor.

"But dusk begets darkness and dread. Can you say the same about dawn?"

"Are you calling me pessimistic?"

"All I'm arguing is that the sunrise harbors the promise of a new life. It evaporates the horror and chill of the night, while bringing forth the possibility and warmth of the day. I believe one to be clearly preferrable." Kendrick smirked.

Sir Algor rolled his eyes. "Don't get a hard-on, lad. It's just a bloody sunrise."

"Clearly you don't read."

"Reading is for the young. Life is my greatest teacher." Sir Algor nodded.

"'Life is my greatest teacher,'" mocked Kendrick playfully. He laughed. Sir Algor glared at him. "Oh, lighten up," cheered Kendrick, pointing his head to the rising sun. His pun fell flat. Kendrick sighed.

"It was a good jest," said Kendrick defiantly.

"I'm going to smack that insolence off you one day."

"Don't lie, you found it hilarious."

"I do find your guilelessness to be particularly humorous."

"Oh, look at you, throwing out the big words today." Kendrick grinned.

"Jesus, help me," groaned Sir Algor. "I've had more enlightened conversations with the higher nobility, and their ignorance knows no bounds."

"You know, you can enjoy life every once in a while," said Kendrick, taking another deep breath of the morning air. "Look at us, we're free. We get to roam the countryside, two pals—"

"You're my squire, don't be presumptuous now."

"Fine. We're *practically* two pals who get to experience the world and bring peace to those around us." Kendrick sighed.

Sir Algor looked at him with a strange expression. Kendrick tried to read it. There was an odd sadness to it, but it was intermixed with a degree of loving admiration.

Kendrick had seen that same expression before, on his father, when he told him he was joining the knighthood.

Kendrick's father was the top blacksmith west of London and worked exclusively at Duke Rowan's keep. Kendrick was his father's top apprentice, and his father had been quickly grooming him to take over the mantle. It was tough to let the old man down. Kendrick had avoided the confrontation for months while giving reluctant glances at his father as they forged their final weaponry together. When Kendrick had finally gathered up the courage to tell him, his father didn't say a word. They sat for a few minutes, on their midday break to avoid the deadly heat of both the sun and furnace, while Kendrick waited in the unbearable silence as his father stared off into the distance. Eventually his father had looked back at Kendrick, giving him that same enigmatic expression that Sir Algor was giving him now.

"Son," Kendrick's father had finally said, "after your mother gave birth, and I held you in my arms for the first time, do you know what me thought? Ye were so little and so light, I thought certainly this being couldn't grow up to be a strong man. I was wrong. Ye have. But a deep sadness also came over me when I held you that day. You were so pure and innocent, and me wanted nothing more than to protect you, but I knew me couldn't. I knew this small babe would have to face the world and, in turn, be thrashed and scarred from it.

"Do ye hark me, son? No one gets through this world unscathed. I knew when that moment came, I'd have to let you go. That be the great sorrow of parenthood. We give life to our children, but we know that also guarantees them pain. No parent can protect their child from it. I reckon this is when I have to let go."

Kendrick entered Duke Rowan's circle of knights the next day.

"Don't give me that look," Kendrick whined to Sir Algor. The knight chuckled and shook his head. He pat the side of Brandy's neck. The horse nodded his head in loving response.

"Let's keep going," said Sir Algor. "We have seven leagues still. Duke Rowan wants all knights at his keep by midday tomorrow."

Kendrick whistled. He rubbed Fortune's neck and pat the side of her thigh. "Looks like you're getting worked today, girl," whispered Kendrick into Fortune's ear. She neighed. It made him smile.

"I know an inn we can rest at for the night," said Sir Algor. Kendrick raised an eyebrow at him. "I visit a wench there from time to time," he clarified.

"A wench?"

"The bar maiden."

"Ahhh." Kendrick grinned salaciously. "And what be her name?"

Sir Algor shook his head.

"What? Surely you don't call her wench."

"Edith."

Before Kendrick had a chance to ask another question, the knight clicked his heels, and Brandy cantered down the hill. Kendrick grinned. *This'll be fun!* He nudged Fortune after them.

"Oh, you really do fancy her," teased Kendrick.

"Jesus Christ," complained Sir Algor, still trying to keep ahead of his squire. "In the knighthood for three months, and you're already an ass."

"Isn't that a prerequisite?"

"No, usually it takes a year or two. You're quite advanced in that respect."

Kendrick laughed as they rode away from the rising sun. They headed west for most of the morning. Kendrick tried multiple times to get Sir Algor to open up about his bar maiden muse, all to no success. That didn't stop him, though. Armed with the ambitious stupor of youth, Kendrick was determined to uncover all the secrets of the world. Everything in God's green country was set there for him: its mysteries were to be solved, its conflicts were to be resolved, its women were to be courted, and its riches were to be won.

The world was a fantastic, wonderous arena for Kendrick to uncover. It was up to him to make it a better place, and he was damned if it wasn't going to be that way.

The sun was a particularly devilish mistress, and the cloudless sky did naught to relieve its intensity. The hottest part of the day descended on them quickly, so Sir Algor and Kendrick both decided it was best to find some shade to rest out the heat. Their padded armor did little to keep them cool, and the sun appeared to be perfectly content with baking them.

As the sun reached its zenith, they found themselves reaching a tree line that divided the grassy plains from a sizable wood. Sir Algor and Kendrick tied off their horses onto two trees. Brandy and Fortune grazed on the surrounding land. The knight and squire rested under a birch tree, its long and slender white trunk weaving up into a tall canopy. Kendrick helped Sir Algor strip off his hauberk. He threw it to the ground beside him.

"Ah, much better." Sir Algor sighed pleasurably.

Kendrick followed suit. He always forgot how much the chainmail weighed, and the pressure it released off him made Kendrick believe he could fly, as if his body could float off the earth with the slightest push. The cool breeze from the west chilled his sweat, stilling the salty perspiration on the spot. Sir Algor and Kendrick sat in hospitable silence, basking in the daylight with only their undershirts and leg armor on. Deep within the forest, a choir of birds sang their wonderfully abstract songs. Kendrick imagined what they must mean. One high-pitch chirp must be a mating call, vibrating an alluring plea to all females around him. Another lower-pitch, repetitive squawk must be a territorial warning, keeping at bay all those vile fowls who dared enter their territory. At all times, there was a world of conflict and resolution at play. Kendrick heard various twigs snap and crunch, hinting at the multitude of mammals that lurked in the forest as well. It was alive, and therefore, it was beautiful.

"Tomorrow will be a farce," said Sir Algor.

"How so?" Kendrick queried.

"The last tally I heard from Commander Rayner is that we're expecting short of five thousand people to be present, and we're supposed to protect *all* of them. I can't possibly imagine how that can go wrong."

"Shouldn't Duke Richard's knights be there?"

Sir Algor raised a questioning brow at him.

Kendrick wiped sweat off his temples. The sun beamed down on him like he was standing outside a furnace. The heat made it hard to think. "What?" questioned Kendrick.

"Duke Richard won't send his knights. You really think he cares about the safety of Duke Rowan's castle?"

"But it's his own daughter getting married."

"I don't keep an open ear to court politics. I'd much rather spend my evenings at my estate. But I do know this much: Duke Richard wants nothing to do with this arrangement. Lord Merek's marriage to Lady Lorena is supported from up top."

"Up top?" Kendrick thought back to his recent lessons on contemporary world politics. "What, you mean from the Earl of Warenne?"

"No. William de Warenne has no reason to interfere with the squabbles of lesser nobility. He has strong ties to the king. He fought alongside King Henry in the Battle of Bremule, and he married his granddaughter, for Christ's sake. No, not the Earl of Warenne. I've taught you enough about current events; who would have something to gain from marrying off Duke Rowan's son to Duke Richard's daughter?"

Kendrick pondered on it for a moment. His mind traversed over the various barons, dukes, and earls who'd wanted to contend with their region of England. "Maybe some of the more traditional Normans?" Kendrick thought aloud.

"Think more specific than the Normans. Who needs support right now?"

"King Henry?"

"Precisely."

"Why would Duke Rowan let himself be maneuvered so? He's smart enough to realize what King Henry is up to," said Kendrick, truly baffled.

Sir Algor glanced around them, as if paranoid someone could hear them. Hundreds of birds continued to interact with their various vocal pitches behind them. Sir Algor leaned closer to Kendrick, nonetheless, and dropped his voice to a whisper.

"I swore an oath to protect Duke Rowan, and I will fulfill it to the end of my days, but he isn't a righteous man. He has a lust for power, and his greed often gets the best of him. Just look at the ceremony he's throwing tomorrow. To call Rowan a duke is a modern embroidery, and to tell you the truth, it'd be a stretch to call him a baron. The same with *Duke* Richard. Both Rowan and Richard are small-time barons with big-time ambitions. Them having the title of duke is more of a courtesy that others oblige in. Someone who already has power doesn't need to flaunt their wealth like our lord is tomorrow. Duke Rowan and Duke Richard both want each other's land, and sooner or later, one of them is going to make a move."

"Who would win out?"

"Whoever correctly bets on the next ruler."

"Ah, so that's why King Henry wants to help our duke."

"Exactly," said Sir Algor. "I've heard rumors: the king doesn't have much time left. After his son drowned, King Henry has been trying desperately to convince the higher nobles to install his daughter as successor."

"Empress Matilda? A woman?"

"William Adelin was King Henry's only legitimate son. His daughter is the Queen of the Germans, the Holy Roman Empress, Queen of the bloody Romans. If there's anyone with a good name to back up their right to rule, it'd be her. The only issue—"

"She's a woman," nodded Kendrick.

"Which brings us to the king's nephew, Stephen of Blois. Word is, he's contending for the throne. King Henry wants nothing to do with him, which means everyone who disagrees with the king will back him."

"Let me guess, Duke Richard wants Stephen on the throne then."

"And who do you think Duke Rowan will back, especially now that King Henry has personally blessed his son's marriage?" Sir Algor dropped his voice to an even more gentle whisper. "Don't speak of this to anyone, but our liege lord doesn't want to be a baron masquerading as a duke forever. He wants to be an earl, which means he needs Duke Richard's land."

"But to do that, there's going to have to be—"

"A war. Yes. There's already tremors of a split between many of the barons, dukes, and earls throughout the province. Each day, more and more Normans are arriving on our shore from the south, and more and more Saxons are gathering in the north. Even the clerics are picking favorites. Imagine if the king dies before he can instate his daughter as queen."

Kendrick nodded. He understood.

"Hence the extra taxes Duke Rowan is taking from the peasantry. He's not building revenue for his own ornate gatherings. Well, not entirely anyway."

"What does this mean for us?" asked Kendrick, a sudden realization coming upon him.

"You've vowed to protect and serve Duke Rowan for life, under the eyes of God no less. That includes during wartime." Sir Algor sighed as a soft, warm breeze glided across the serene grassland. "Our country is falling apart. We'll all have to choose a side, eventually. Peasants, nobility, the Church. Everyone has a part to play. This peace won't last forever. In fact, I believe it'll end very soon, and you and I will have to decide what we want with our lives."

"Don't we have to do what our lord commands?"

"We do." Sir Algor grimaced. "But I didn't become knighted to protect the court from itself. I wanted to travel, explore the edges of our land, kill bandits."

"There's that romanticism," grinned Kendrick, glad to have finally changed the subject. He hated court intrigue. "I assumed you did it for the women." *Women* are *much more interesting.*

"Well, that's a lovely perk." Sir Algor smiled.

"So, this bar maiden—"

"You never give up, do you?"

"Let me guess, she's young?"

"Older than you, actually. She has a kid."

"She's already courted?" asked Kendrick, surprised but smiling slyly.

"Kid's father isn't around."

"Why's that?"

"I never bothered to ask," admitted Sir Algor. "How about you, lad? Spellbound by any maiden?"

Sir Algor drank out of a wine skin. He handed it to Kendrick, and he took a sip. The wine, surprisingly, was still cool from the night before and had the flavorful explosion of cherry; the light hints of earthy spices settled between his tastebuds. The chilly aroma of the drink sent a frigid wave of relief through Kendrick's roasting face. He contemplated whether he should tell . . . wait, who's he kidding? He couldn't help but divulge.

"There is one," said Kendrick timidly. "She visits the keep every fortnight or so."

"Oh shit. Don't tell me—"

"Yeah, she's, um . . . Duke Rowan's niece. Lucia. You know her?"

"A blacksmith courting a royal maiden. I don't expect Duke Rowan would have been too happy . . ."

He trailed off. Kendrick watched as Sir Algor connected the dots. He snapped his head to face Kendrick. "Don't tell me she's the reason—"

Kendrick gulped down the wine. While its cool, bitter taste refreshed his starched mouth, it failed to chill his embarrassment.

"Jesus, kid. You joined the knighthood for her, didn't you? You fucking dolt," said Sir Algor.

"She wasn't the *only* pretext," said Kendrick.

This was partially true. Kendrick joining the royal knighthood of Duke Rowan *did* allow him to court higher nobility. He met Lucia during one of her routine visits from northern England. They ran into each other following a party Lord Merek was throwing. Kendrick hadn't been invited to the affair, of course, but his father had needed Kendrick to deliver a ceremonial dagger to one of the attendants. He accidentally bumped into Lucia while navigating through the swarm of nobility. Her beauty was beyond words, and Kendrick found himself unfit to even apologize. He was spellbound, and she knew it. She gave Kendrick a sly grin. From that moment on, Kendrick was unable to forget her.

Her stay at Duke Rowan's castle only lasted a few days. It didn't matter. On her final night, Kendrick—or rather, Lucia—had successfully courted them. It was the greatest night of Kendrick's life. For Lucia, he imagined, the whole affair was founded purely on the allure of the forbidden fruit. For Kendrick, however, it was the allure of Heaven. Kendrick's eternal happiness lay dormant within Lucia, and the sweetness of her lips blossomed with the zest of desire. But alas, as the sun does set at the gloom of day to spread its warmth elsewhere, Lucia must leave him behind and travel back to her life of comfort and stability in the north.

That is, unless Kendrick can formally court her.

"Let me guess," said Sir Algor, slapping Kendrick out of his Lucia fever dream. "You also joined the knighthood for honor and virtue? To whet your fantasy on—"

"Hold on, someone's coming," interrupted Kendrick.

A small figure hobbled over a hill about a furlough to their west. An animal strode behind it. The figure slinked across the main road that ran parallel to the tree line.

"What do you see?" asked Sir Algor. "You have better eyes than I."

Kendrick squinted. The sun was dipping to the west now, and in doing so, cast a glare right above the slow-moving figures. Kendrick shaded his eyes.

"It looks like an elderly man, a peasant. He has a donkey with him," said Kendrick. The elderly peasant ambled within twenty paces of them. Sir Algor rapidly threw on his cuirass and tightened his vambraces.

"Get your armor on but leave the hauberk. We don't have time to fasten it all," commanded Sir Algor. Kendrick looked at him sideways. "Heed my words, lad."

Kendrick threw on his cuirass. He tightened all of Sir Algor's armor first. Sir Algor then did Kendrick's. Kendrick strapped on his vambraces as the elderly peasant reached them. They could make out all his features for the first time. He had shriveled and leathery skin, which must have once been white but had slowly browned over a lifetime of work under the sun. His face had wrinkles upon wrinkles, and it was especially difficult to see his eyes under the droop of his fuzzy unibrow. His hair was a wanton mess of gray strands, and his trousers and tunic were shredded like they had been mangled by some beast. He towed a donkey behind him by a length of rope.

"Unsheathe your sword," hissed Sir Algor under his breath. Kendrick did so, although he knew not why. The elderly peasant had a lame leg that he ambled gingerly on, and he appeared to Kendrick to be no more a threat than a rabbit ensnared in a trap. Weren't knights like them supposed to help the helpless? That was one of the virtuous deeds Kendrick had to rehash during his coronation.

"Greetin's, fair knights." The elderly peasant waved. He had a rough voice, and his words gurgled together like a jumble of tiresome breaths. Sir Algor raised his hand and stopped the peasant in his tracks.

"What do you require?" Sir Algor asked.

"Can ye point meself yonder to Sherborne?"

"What do you seek there?"

"A man, calls 'imself Rhys. He traveled to me village a few nights back. Saw me and me ass there," said the elderly peasant, pointing back to the donkey as if it weren't obvious what he meant. "Said he'd pay extra if me delivered the ass to 'im, he did. Said he lived in Sherborne. Trouble is, me has never been to no Sherborne. Me 'ave only heard of it once or twice."

"Sherborne is northwest of here," answered Kendrick. *Strange, he had just come from the west.*

"Would ye know how much farther?"

"I'd reckon around two leagues," replied Sir Algor.

"Ah. Methanks ye kindly."

Kendrick noticed Sir Algor tightened his grip around the sword's hilt. The elderly peasant looked back and forth between them. The soft breeze died around them. Total stillness crawled over the countryside, as if the Lord himself wanted to listen to this one moment. The nagging pestilence of intuition itched at Kendrick. *Why does something feel off?*

"Ye headin' to the lord's weddin'—"

"Why do you still linger, old man?" Sir Algor said.

Kendrick noticed that the birds had stopped singing. The choir had been muted, as if the forest had been abandoned of all life. They stood with their backs to the vacant tree line.

"Do ye have any water ye could spare?" asked the elderly peasant.

"No. So why don't you go on your—"

"We have wine," said Kendrick, burying his annoying intuition. Intuition was dangerous; it could be perverted by prejudice. It was their job to maintain peace and order, to strive for prosperity among the people of their province. There was no reason to refuse this old man—who was traveling across the fiefdom under the blazing heat of day—a simple drink for his wares. He was participating in commerce, after all. That must be a good thing.

Sir Algor glared at him. Kendrick ignored the look and threw the wine skin to the old man. The elderly peasant bobbled it briefly. He straightened his back, which made him seem much taller now, and bowed his head to Kendrick.

"Thank ye kindly, young knight. Thank ye kindly. It be a hot one t'day," the elderly peasant said, smiling at them, which revealed a maw only half filled with teeth. They watched the old man gulp a monstrous mouthful of red wine. A few drips overflowed off the side of his lips and poured down his chin like rivulets of—

An arm constricted around Kendrick's throat like a snake coiled around its prey. Kendrick felt his heartbeat pulse in his neck. He tried to scream, but only a string of spit flew out.

Kendrick's mind raced. He flailed at the arm around his neck. He peeked at Sir Algor. A bandit held the knight in a similar death grip.

Sir Algor pushed back against the attacker who strangled him from behind. He slapped at the bandit's face. Kendrick, unable to think for himself, tried the same attack. His hand slapped haphazardly against skin. The man grunted behind him, and Kendrick's body twisted, his chest violently thrusting out to face the tree line. Kendrick fought for control over his air. He sipped in breaths. He twitched his neck to find Sir Algor.

He saw nothing, though. He could only hear the struggles of men.

The forest moved. The bushes, the shrubbery . . . they swayed. Kendrick couldn't believe it. The leaves vibrated.

His breath. *Air.* Kendrick gulped. *Breathe, brain. Work.*

Kendrick pulled. The arm clamped around his neck. *Breathe. Air. Suck in.* Kendrick did. He tugged down the arm. An odorous smell filled the sky. His head felt light.

Sir Algor, was he. . . . Air. Kendrick breathed. Wait, he was breathing. He had plenty of air. Why was he still dying?

Kendrick slapped skin. Wet. Oily.

A knife. It stabbed at Kendrick's face. *How was the knife floating?*

It wasn't. His brain caught on. The bandit choking Kendrick held it. The knife pierced for his neck, but Kendrick blocked the bandit's arm. He stopped the knife. The snake pulled tighter around his throat.

The bushes moved again. A spear. The bush held a spear. How? Kendrick marveled. His legs thrusted apart. Kendrick grappled with the bandit's knife.

Air. Lucia. Breathe.

Kendrick fought. Kendrick lost. His mind. It was jumbled. The bush with the spear—no, a man—ran from the forest. *He* held the spear. The iron blade glimmered in the light.

It was beautiful.

It aimed for Kendrick. The bandit tightened his hold on him. The man with the spear charged. Kendrick. Unable. To. Move.

Air. Life. Sir Algor. Help. Spear. It thrusted.

A collision.

Kendrick bounced out of the bandit's grip as they tumbled to the earth. Kendrick gasped for life, and he devoured it down greedily. His hands reached instinctually for his throat as he rolled on the ground.

Sir Algor mounted a bandit right next to Kendrick. *That's the one who was choking me*, Kendrick realized.

Sir Algor beat the bandit's face in. Kendrick scrambled to his feet, quickly appraising his surroundings. Three bandits remained up; two of them held spears. Sir Algor must have broken away from the bandit who was strangling him and then tackled Kendrick and his foe to the ground before one of the spearmen impaled Kendrick.

Kendrick swiveled. His sword lay exposed on the ground. Kendrick fumbled for it right as the two spearmen charged after him. Kendrick lifted the sword up, swung it to face his foes, and readied himself for death. The bandits yelled out as they charged. One of them hurtled their spear.

Kendrick froze. The spear screamed after him as the air seemed to cleave in two between them.

Sir Algor shoved Kendrick to the side. The spear ripped Sir Algor's bicep open above the vambrace. If they had their chainmail on, that wound would have been avoided. Sir Algor's scream hurtled across the kingdom. It made Kendrick shudder.

The knight ripped Kendrick's sword from his grasp. Kendrick remained on the ground, out of breath and stunned from battle. Kendrick swiveled his head and found the bandit who was choking him. The bandit was on the ground and his face was unrecognizable, beaten to a pulp so badly it was impossible to tell he was once a man. The gore was vicious, animalistic, but it made Kendrick glad.

What a wicked feeling.

He glanced up in time to spot Sir Algor with Kendrick's sword held before him as he squared up against the three remaining bandits. Kendrick pried the thrown spear from the ground and turned it against them.

Two versus three.

Kendrick had never been in a fight before. His training was limited, and it mainly centered around swordsmanship. He turned the spear around, finding the balance between the weight of the head and the length of the shaft. It couldn't be too difficult to use a spear, just stab them with the blade. The bandits readied to charge. Sir Algor held up his sword in a hanging guard position. Kendrick thrust the spear.

A rumble erupted within the earth.

Kendrick lost his balance for a brief moment. The frightening image of the world splitting apart beneath them vanished from Kendrick's mind as soon as it had appeared.

A pack of knights upon horseback crested over the vast hills next to them. The knights charged after them. Kendrick was so caught up in the spectacle of charging knights that he didn't notice Sir Algor rip the spear from his hands until it was already gone.

Apparently, the bandits thought the knights were as spectacular looking as Kendrick did, since they hadn't moved from their positions. Sir Algor heaved the spear. It penetrated the second spearman's belly. The spearman collapsed to the ground in a spasm of gore.

The other two bandits fled for the safety of the forest. The knights on horseback stormed past Sir Algor and Kendrick and reached the bandits. The knight at the front of the pack sliced his sword at the slowest one. The bandit's back cleaved in half at the whim of the blade. The faster bandit managed to dive into the dense tree line before they reached him. The lead knight halted his force, and Kendrick finally recognized who it was.

Commander Rayner.

The commander, clad completely in steel plating, sat upright upon his horse. His silver armor shimmered in the sunlight, almost blinding anyone who dared look upon it. It was truly a spectacular sight to see someone in full steel. Kendrick, as the son of a renowned blacksmith, knew the immense resources, toilsome labor, and prodigious expertise it took to craft such armor. A blacksmith needed to harness the power of rushing water to create enough force to hammer sheets of steel, and beyond that, they needed to layer, temper, and form fit the armor so no weaponry of man could penetrate or avoid it. The artisans who forged Commander Rayner's armor must have been the best in the world. Kendrick couldn't spot a single gap between all the pieces, which gave the illusion of the commander being made of metal.

"Spear," demanded Commander Rayner joyfully.

The second knight, who Kendrick now recognized as Sir David, rode up to the commander and handed him a spear. The bandit with the sliced back groaned on the ground. Commander Rayner punctured the bandit in the neck with his new toy. With a twist of the commander's wrist, the bandit's head separated from its neck.

"Fucking bandits," spat Commander Rayner. "Sir Tobias. Sir Ivan." The last two knights rode up to him. They each held an axe in their hands. "Track down that bastard who got away. I want his tongue."

"Yes, Sir Commander," said Sir Tobias.

The two knights dismounted their horses and raced into the wood with their axes. Commander Rayner directed his steed to Kendrick and Sir Algor. He navigated the horse around two of the corpses. He loomed large above Kendrick.

"Sir Algor. Kendrick," greeted the commander. "I'm delighted to see you are both safe from harm."

"As am I, Sir Commander." Sir Algor bowed.

"Kendrick, how was your first scuffle? You fare well?"

"I suppose," said Kendrick hollowly. He wasn't too sure how he felt. The battle ended as abruptly as it had started, and Kendrick was certain he didn't do much more than roll around on the ground and survive. His father would probably tell Kendrick that surviving was enough. Even if that was true, it still didn't feel right.

"You didn't kill anyone, though?" questioned Commander Rayner, a hint of disappointment in his tone.

Kendrick shook his head.

"What a shame," said Commander Rayner, frowning. "Well don't fret, there'll be cause for celebration yet."

Sir David shoved the elderly peasant over to them. Kendrick lost sight of the old man during the fight. He honestly forgot about him. Sir David was a broad-shouldered, slender man with a tall frame. He wore the simple padded armor that Sir Algor and Kendrick donned. He still managed to intimidate the elderly peasant, nonetheless.

"Sir Commander," hollered Sir David.

"Stop pushin'," moaned the old man. "Me did nothin' wrong."

"Who is this peasant?" inquired the commander.

"He greeted us right before the attack," said Sir Algor.

"Awfully convenient."

"Is not," disagreed the old man.

"I wouldn't advise such a temper for a man convicted of treason," said Commander Rayner.

"Treason?" The elderly peasant gasped, his eyes wide with surprise and horror.

"Yes. We believe an insurrection is in the works."

"Insurrection?" questioned Sir Algor, who appeared to be every bit as baffled as Kendrick and the old man.

"I've been meaning to inform you, Sir Algor," said Commander Rayner. "Our spies have informed us that the *respectable* peasants of our domain are planning a coup. We suspect they will attack at Lord Merek's wedding tomorrow. It's quite a boring plot, all things considered."

Kendrick and Sir Algor shared a glance. They had heard nothing of the sort. Who would dare threaten the duke in his own stronghold?

"Hark," begged the elderly peasant. "Me just tryin' to sell this here ass to a man in Stoford." For the first time, suspicion of the old man docked inside Kendrick's mind.

"Stoford? I thought you were selling it to a man in Sherborne," said Kendrick.

"Yes, Sherborne."

"Humph. Sir David," said Commander Rayner.

Sir David kicked the elderly peasant to the ground. The old man gasped as dirt puffed up around him in a brown cloud. He tried to crawl away, but Sir David flung him back by the holes in his tunic. The elderly peasant flailed about until he lost all vigor within him. Tears streamed from his eyes, and he fell to the ground in a pitiful act of submission.

"Please, sir! Me'ves done no wrong."

"You betrayed your duke and lord." Commander Rayner smiled.

"No, sir. Me adores Duke Rowan."

"Then why are you convicted of conspiring to murder him?"

Commander Rayner's question silenced the elderly peasant. He gaped. He tried to speak, but his words stumbled from his mouth. He was absolutely baffled. He crawled and wrapped his arms around Kendrick's knees. The elderly peasant kissed Kendrick's hand.

"Young knight!" he cried. "Ye knows me am innocent. Ye were kind. Give me your grace once more. Please."

Commander Rayner snorted. He dismounted his horse. The dirt exploded into debris under his weight, and as he walked, the sun glimmered off his steel plates in flashes of blinding light. The trail of dust left in his wake trickled into Kendrick's nose and made him want to sneeze. Commander Rayner peeled off his helm, and his most notorious feature, his vivid green eyes, pierced the air like daggers. Only a fool would dare remain under their gaze for too long.

"You even grovel pathetically." Commander Rayner smirked.

A rustle from the forest diverted their attention away from the old man. Sir Ivan and Sir Tobias emerged through the tree line dragging the bandit between them. The bandit's face was brutalized, and his legs tripped over themselves relentlessly as the knights hauled him to doom. He gurgled blood out of a deformed mouth.

"Ask 'im! Ask the bandit! He don't know me. Me prays it," said the elderly peasant.

"Bring him here," ordered the commander.

Sir Ivan and Sir Tobias discarded the broken man in front of Commander Rayner. The bandit fell to his knees. His hands shook uncontrollably. Kendrick never knew it was possible for a person to shake so ferociously.

"Do you know this man?" questioned Commander Rayner.

The bandit lifted his head. His eyes flickered over the elderly peasant. A soft squeal seeped from his lips.

"Speak up."

The bandit's lower jaw quivered. He opened his mouth again, but only a rasp of air filtered into the daylight.

"This is your final chance," warned Commander Rayner. "Do you know this man? Speak up and we will grant you a quick death."

The bandit looked the elderly peasant up and down. His hands shook even worse.

"Please, son . . ." whispered the old man.

The bandit's glossy eyes bounced between Commander Rayner and the elderly peasant. He wept. The bandit leaned his forehead to the ground. A surge of pity eroded at Kendrick. This was a man who just tried to kill Sir Algor and him. Kendrick knew if he would have died, this bastard would have been a ball of joy. Now here he was, soaked in the piss and foulness of his own defeat, yet Kendrick couldn't help but feel sorry for him.

"Speak!"

Commander Rayner kicked the bandit in the ribs. Blood squirted from his mouth. The bandit keeled over onto his side. He squealed. His mouth opened wide, but all Kendrick could see was a stream of bright red. Behind them all, Sir Tobias cleared his throat.

"Sir," said Sir Tobias hesitantly. "We cut out his tongue, like you dictated."

The group faced the two knights. Sir Ivan held up a severed tongue.

The bandit rolled on the ground. His formless cries stung the peaceful air. The liquid of death poured from his mouth, and Kendrick noted that, indeed, he couldn't see any tongue in the poor bastard's mouth. Commander Rayner glared up to the heavens in transparent disbelief. He bit his lip and suppressed a growl. Kendrick took a step away from him.

"It's a figure of speech. You wait until after I question him," he scolded.

Sit Ivan and Sir Tobias glanced at one another. Sir Ivan slowly lowered the tongue. Commander Rayner sighed, more out of general annoyance than incompetence, Kendrick imagined. The bandit continued to writhe on the earth in a howling fit of pain.

"One of you cretins 'kill him and end his wretched weeping," said Commander Rayner as he massaged his temples. Sir Ivan ran up to the bandit and slit his throat. The bandit's grotesque gurgles ended after a few long moments.

"Your prayers failed," said Commander Rayner to the elderly peasant.

The insouciant disregard his commander displayed to death revealed to Kendrick that Commander Rayner had killed many people before.

How many people must you kill before death becomes frivolous? One? Five? A hundred? Kendrick shivered at the thought.

Commander Rayner's beautiful green eyes became something much more sinister. Kendrick now understood the fear the peasants had of him, why he was the nightmare that fueled compliance. He was the ferocious canine Duke Rowan would sic on the peasantry, even though he had already fatally wounded them in his hunt for acclaim.

"Young knight, save me. Me begs ye," sobbed the old man onto Kendrick's leg.

Commander Rayner kicked the old man. The elderly peasant crumbled to the dirt. Kendrick wasn't sure if it was the suffering of the bandit, the elderly peasant, or both that built the foundation of guilt he suddenly found within his gut. Either way, it was there nonetheless. The guilt hung in his stomach like he ingested a boulder. The weight of it pinched down on his intestines and caused his discomfort to grow to a degree at which Kendrick felt no heed for his own safety. He only understood that he needed to relieve this unbearable weight.

"Sir Commander, there's no evidence of guilt," said Kendrick smoothly. He determined it was best to start with reason. Reason would be the most efficient way to stop the commander without Kendrick being tried for treason himself.

"You believe him innocent?" asked Commander Rayner.

"I do."

"Sir Algor?"

Kendrick glanced at Sir Algor, his mentor and friend. Sir Algor had to have the same feeling in his gut, right? This was wrong. There was no rhyme or reason to it. Kendrick knew he didn't have any more proof of the old man's innocence than Commander Rayner did of his guilt. This whole situation was a nasty scar on what should have been a wonderful day. Kendrick felt even worse now.

"It's too much of a coincidence," said Sir Algor finally.

"No," cried the old man.

Kendrick's heart dropped into his gut as well, leaving all he cared about within his bowels.

"So be it." Commander Rayner sniffed. "Your name, peasant?"

"Please, m'lord," he begged. The elderly peasant hobbled to Commander Rayner and wrapped his hands around the commander's legs.

"Your name, lest you be forgotten for all eternity," said the commander. The elderly peasant bawled at Commander Rayner's feet. Snot ran from his nose.

Kendrick shook his head. He faced away and found that his eyes lingered on the man's donkey. The animal stood at the edge of the road and slanted its head at them. No emotion came across the donkey's face. It only watched.

"Eliot. Me name is Eliot," sobbed the old man.

"Eliot, you've been found guilty of treason, treachery, and conspiracy to assassinate the crown—"

"No—" wept Eliot.

"For these crimes, I, Sir Rayner, first of his name, sentence you to death."

"Please—"

"Bring him to his knees," Commander Rayner ordered.

Sir David yanked the old man up. Kendrick noticed that the lower thread that connected the frontal greave of Commander Rayner's armor to the back one had come slightly loose. Eliot must have accidently untied them while groveling at his feet. The old man now writhed in Sir David's arms, but he failed to shake off the knight's grip.

"Quit squirming unless you want multiple cuts," said Sir David.

Eliot cried silently to himself now. Kendrick stared at Sir Algor who gave him an empty look in return. Was this what Sir Algor had become a knight for? Murder?

Commander Rayner unsheathed his sword. His eyes met Kendrick's. "Do us the honor." He smiled maliciously.

"What?" mumbled Kendrick. That was the daftest thing he could have possibly said, but it was the only thing that felt remotely right. Commander Rayner handed Kendrick his ornate sword.

"To be a knight you must learn to serve justice, for that is our purpose," he said.

"This is justice?" questioned Kendrick. The sourness in his voice betrayed how much he detested everything about this.

He couldn't do it. Kendrick didn't have this kind of wicked piety in him. This wasn't what he wanted.

The truth was Kendrick joined the knighthood for a woman.

The truth was Kendrick joined the knighthood because he was a spoiled kid who grew up at the hands of a master in his craft. He joined because he knew he could never live up to his father's great name, and for that reason he never wanted to speak of him. Kendrick wanted to see the world, to become his own man. What greater way to do that than becoming a knight? The books he read made it seem so virtuous, a lifelong dedication to selfless ideals and protecting those who couldn't protect themselves. Was it all a lie?

No. It couldn't be. Sir Algor was better than this. *He* was better than this. Kendrick has met other knights, those from other provinces, who had made Kendrick believe in the Codes of honor. Those knights reinforced that virtue was still alive in the hearts of men.

"We all here agree that he is a dangerous criminal," reasoned Commander Rayner. "Even your knight, Sir Algor, admits so. Eliot here put your life in danger. He distracted you so they could ambush you from behind."

Kendrick thought back to the attack. The bandits had come from the forest. Eliot mixed up Sherborne and Stoford, even though both towns are on opposite sides of the fiefdom. Kendrick found himself staring at his commander's sword. Was Eliot really trying to kill them? As if to answer his question, Sir Algor stepped up to Kendrick.

"I'm sorry, lad. But the world isn't kind to us. People want us killed," said Sir Algor softly. He rubbed Kendrick's back.

"Not me. Not me," repeated Eliot.

Kendrick's hands shook, and now he was even more horrified to find out that he possessed the capability to spasm like that dying bandit. Sir Algor leaned close to Kendrick's ear.

"You're just torturing the poor man now," he whispered.

The unsentimental attitude in which the knights spoke of murder, of the unadorned bequeathing of life, shook the very faith Kendrick has spent the last three months acquiring. When Kendrick first joined the knighthood as squire to Sir Algor, he had given Kendrick an epic poem titled the "Song of Roland." It was a contemporary piece of literature that quickly garnered traction within both the higher and middle-class Norman aristocracy. Sir Algor gifted it to Kendrick on the basis that he should take to heart the exploits of Count Roland and King Charlemagne's Twelve Peers. The Norman knights had extrapolated a steadfast list of standards from the poem called the Codes of Chivalry. A few of those Codes popped into Kendrick's mind now as he stood above poor Eliot as his executioner: "to protect the weak and defenseless, to live by honor and glory, to fight for the welfare of all, to eschew unfairness, meanness, and deceit, and to, at all times, speak the truth."

These were the Codes by which Kendrick had given over his life. There was no abandoning the knighthood except by retirement or release from the liege lord, Duke Rowan. The "Song of Roland" made this clear by Ganelon's betrayal and the drawing and quartering of his body. Kendrick would demonstrate an offensive punishable by death if he denied the dictation of his commander. Commander Rayner knew this.

Is this all a sick game to him? He's asking me to kill a man!

Kendrick's hand gripped tighter around the hilt of the commander's sword. Kendrick knew, in the way all people instinctually know before they performed the act that would change their life, that he would never be the same person again. His father warned Kendrick that there were turning points in life, moments that gave meaning to the abstractness of time, at which all events in their legacy would be declared as merely *prior* and *subsequent*. No person should have to cross their Rubicon knowing it would be their destiny. That moment should be one studied in postmortem, when the winter stages of life had already withered away the consequences of such a moment.

Kendrick was furious. His fury stemmed from not only Sir Algor, Duke Rowan, and Commander Rayner, but also from Eliot. Why did Eliot have to make this so difficult? Why did he have to distract them, whether intentionally or not?

As the stares from his fellow knights began to push Kendrick to action, he found himself turning to religion. He was a Christian. Kendrick was raised in his church by His Church. To kill was a sin—that was always plain as day—but the enigmatic morals of man seemed to tamper with those sins. *It's all hypocrisy*, Kendrick decided, *all of it.*

The Codes of Chivalry ordained that one should fear God and, therefore, maintain His Church; but in the same breath, it also commanded a knight to never refuse a challenge from an equal and to never turn thy back upon a foe. How could he fear the wrath of God if he must also embrace his sins with virtuous vigor? The Codes asked him to refrain from the wanton giving of offense, but it also forced knights to obey those placed in authority, no matter their whims. Above all else, the Codes of Chivalry dictated that knights should guard the honor of fellow knights. The events that symbolized this rule were circled in the poem Sir Algor gave him. This was the unspoken rule of brotherhood that all knights shared: judgment could not be placed on them from the outside world. Their deeds and sins were their own to adjudicate, and only internally could their pleas and faults be evaluated. The Lord was the only one granted permission from the outside.

The "Song of Roland" was a joke, and the Codes of Chivalry were merely a series of loopholes for the codes that came before it. Kendrick was on his own. There was no salvation in the Codes, there was no salvation in scripture, and there was certainly no salvation in his brothers in arms, whom he had to defend adamantly, no matter the plight, because they would do the same for him.

There was only Kendrick, Eliot, and this decision.

Kendrick's tears dribbled from the precipice of his eyelids. They collided on his feverishly shaking hands. He balanced the sword above the peasant's neck.

"Keep it straight. Eliot doesn't want us to have a messy blade," said Commander Rayner.

Kendrick took multiple uneasy breaths. He twisted the sword slightly, so the entirety of its cutting force lied upon the center of his mass. If Kendrick's arms bent even marginally, then the blade would not cut down straight, and it would become stuck within the flesh of this pitiful old man. It would make the horrifying ordeal even more nauseating.

Eliot pleaded into Kendrick's eyes. He searched into him. Eliot nudged his soul next to Kendrick's heart. His soul screamed at him, *I am alive! Don't do this!*

Kendrick closed his eyes and shut out the pleas of Eliot's spirit. He raised the sword. His heart pumped numbness through his muscles. Every inch of him tingled. Kendrick's heart couldn't possibly beat any faster; it was certainly going to burst. He opened his eyes.

"Please, young knigh—"

Kendrick sliced.

The donkey brayed behind him. Kendrick heard it race off into the countryside, no longer watching him make his decisive moment.

The commander takes good care of his sword.

The blade cut through Eliot's neck with ease. The difference between skin, muscle, and bone was so minute that Kendrick wasn't sure he cut through Eliot at all. It was the blood that gave it away. The once green grass of a beautiful day perverted itself into a horrifying black sludge beneath the headless corpse.

The blood kept gushing. That was all Kendrick could think. It kept gushing.

"You made it quick," soothed Sir Algor, placing his hand on Kendrick's shoulder.

Kendrick wiped the blood off his face as Commander Rayner seized his sword back. The commander took out a rag and wiped the gore off his blade. More blood splattered on the molested ground. The grass was so green. The day was so beautiful. What happened to it all?

The blood kept gushing.

"Where do you head?" asked Sir Algor as the knights mounted their steeds. Commander Rayner placed his sword back into its scabbard.

"Salisbury," he answered. "Some peasants just got married. You know how Duke Rowan is with engaged women. Apparently, this couple went ahead and had their nuptial affair already. Duke Rowan isn't too pleased. He hears she's very fair."

"We're capturing brides now? I thought that was a peasant myth," said Sir Algor.

Kendrick shook his head. *Thou shall respect the honor of women.* Yet another Code of Chivalry beaten down at the mercy of obeying those in authority.

"I don't agree with it either. A man's wife is his own possession, but a lord's command is a lord's command."

"Why didn't you bring your squires?"

"We don't need them for such a simple operation," stated Sir David, Commander Rayner's second in command. He hovered around them.

"It's but a single day transport. They were starting to get on our nerves anyway," continued Commander Rayner. "I'm quite enjoying my break from mine." All the other knights nodded in agreement. Commander Rayner mounted his horse and maneuvered to Kendrick. He shook Kendrick's hair.

"I'm proud of you, Kendrick," said the commander. "This is a world of life or death. When we have an advantage over death, we must take it. Always."

"Yes, Sir Commander," mumbled Kendrick hollowly.

"Keep your eyes out, gentlemen. From our reports, it's more than a few peasants who are plotting to assassinate our lord. And worse yet, I believe Duke Richard may have a part in all of this."

"You think this has to do with the throne?" asked Sir Algor.

"I never trusted the bastard nor his insufferable knights. Either way, stay alert, of peasants and nobles alike. We have a full-scale coup on our hands. Death is near."

With his last words of dread given, Commander Rayner and his pack of knights raced off as quickly as they came. They stranded Sir Algor and Kendrick behind upon the battlefield of lost innocence, with neither a thought nor a consideration for the irrevocable mutation it forged in the lives of those involved. Sir Algor massaged the nape of Kendrick's neck as if it could thaw the icy barrier Kendrick would forever carry within him. Not even the sunlight, which just that morning had been the ultimate warmth of life, could melt this moment away. The decision was made. Kendrick had killed. It was in the past. But the events of the past could solidify in one's mind much like the carcasses of the damned could be preserved in a frosty glacier, held there for all eternity until it was either found or forgotten at the world's end.

As if understanding this turmoil swelling within Kendrick like a tempest, Sir Algor pulled him into an embrace, one so tight and so warm that it shattered a thin layer from that hardened ice. It melted out of Kendrick's soul in the shape of tears, and those tears of past's remembrance slid down Kendrick's face with a biting frost. It was ironic. When he was a child, his tears had always seemed hot and impassioned, but now that he has experienced true pain, they were cold and forlorn, and the inside of his being was bitter and empty. He was a frigid shell of his prior self, and all Kendrick could do was weep away the remorse one glacial layer at a time.

It would take an eternity for him to shed it all away.

The donkey stared at him in the distance. It judged him. Kendrick watched dark thunder clouds rapidly approach behind the animal, like the shambles of his own psyche were manifested by the heavens. His tears disappeared. His eyes dried up. Kendrick was lifeless.

SERENE MELANCHOLY

"**F**UCKIN' CUNT!" Godfrey hurtled through the air. The frozen mud jumped for him. They collided. Something that probably shouldn't crack cracked under Godfrey's weight. He grimaced. The hard sludge warped around his body, sticking him to the earth like a trap. The mud smelled terrible, an unbearable amalgamation of dead matter and the little creatures that decomposed them. It was a retched, foul stench.

Actually, this seems perfect for me. I might as well stay here.

"Get the fuck outta here!"

. . . so much for that idea.

Godfrey wormed his body to face the peasant charging after him. The tavern Godfrey was just so rudely thrown out of towered behind the approaching man. *What was his name? Jack?* Jack stood above Godfrey. His head irritatingly only blocked half the sun, which left Godfrey's eyes to constantly readjust to different light levels.

"Would you mind maneuvering a bit to your right?" asked Godfrey innocently.

"What ye sayin' to me?"

Godfrey sighed. "Nothing. I think I'm just going to stay here for a while if you don't mind."

"Me does."

"That's a little discourteous, don't you reckon? I've been nothing but cordial to you. I believe our little skirmish in there—"

Jack kicked into Godfrey's stomach. A burning sensation flowed up the bard's throat, but he constricted it back at the last second. A repulsive aftertaste lingered in his mouth. Godfrey coughed out the leftover fumes of vomit.

"Your fancy talk won't save ye!" yelled Jack.

"Was I being fancy? That's marvelous! I wasn't even aware I was ejaculating such an aura," wheezed Godfrey. A small gathering of townsfolk circled around them. They watched with fascination. This was the most entertainment they'd get all week.

At least my pain is enthralling.

Jack stormed up to Godfrey. He threw back his foot for another kick—

"Wait, wait, wait! Jack!" said Godfrey, raising his voice like a scolding mother. Jack hesitated. Godfrey grinned; he had an entrance. "Your name is Jack, right? I can make you famous. I'm a poet, you see."

"Me have never heard of ye."

"Someone here has heard of me, right? Anyone?" Godfrey looked around desperately at the other villagers. No one responded. Godfrey frowned. "No one here has heard of Godfrey the bard? I wrote the "Ballad of A Thousand Swans" . . . "The Epic of Hermes" . . . nothing?"

A few villagers scratched their heads. An older man opened his mouth, as if to exclaim something, but then clammed up and looked around confused. Jack glared down at him.

"I'm going to internalize this revelation as a good thing," said Godfrey. "Who really likes pretentious storytellers anyway? It's best for everyone that I'm not well known."

"Ye ain't known at all."

"That's a very bold statement, my friend. Someone is bound to have heard of me somewhere. I would be quite concerned if truly no one knew of my existence. That would be doubly true for you, since if I didn't exist, what would that make a person such as yourself. Yourself being a man, are you not? But if you weren't, and I weren't alive, what would that mean for a good Christian such as yourself if you're seeing phantoms in the middle of the day?"

Jack stammered for a moment. Godfrey smiled while watching Jack's brain try to catch up with his frenetic reasoning. The reasoning wasn't even correct or witty in the slightest, but they'll believe that it was, and that was good enough for him. Godfrey spotted the exact moment where Jack gave up.

"Then get ye goin' there," spat Jack, not sure if he responded correctly to anything Godfrey said. He tossed a small leather sack onto Godfrey. "Never come 'round here again."

Jack stormed back into the tavern. Godfrey hugged the leather sack close to him. He collapsed back into the frigid mud. The cool earth relaxed his aching muscles. The villagers dispersed around him, many of them sidestepping to keep an arm's reach away from Godfrey. He must have looked horrible. A sharp pang struck under his left eye. He felt where a swollen lump of skin has formed under it. When did he get punched?

I really did lose that fight quite spectacularly.

"Get up," commanded a firm voice behind him. Before Godfrey had time to face the voice, he was hoisted off the mud. A stab of pain locked up Godfrey's back. "Ye came here just to cause a ruckus?"

Godfrey swiveled to the voice. He recognized the bailiff instantly. Godfrey had heard of the stern steward who guarded this small town. Bailiff Rosenstein was an older man —he must have been in his midfifties—with a surprisingly muscular frame. It was the old type of muscular, with sagging skin that appeared to melt off his muscles. *The bailiff is clearly one of the more prosperous people in town,* deduced Godfrey based off his finely woven clothes. Bailiff Rosenstein's receding hairline contrasted sharply with his full beard. The most important feature of the bailiff, however, was the cudgel he spun in one hand.

Why is it always a blessed cudgel? And wait—why does this one have spikes?!

The bailiff's cudgel did, in fact, have wooden protrusions sticking out of its heavy face. This wasn't Godfrey's first encounter with a bailiff. He had been arrested multiple times, by multiple bailiffs, in multiple cities, during his multiple travels. Although, if he was being quite honest, he wasn't planning to be arrested today. He would never get the opportunity to drink himself, or preferably, smoke himself to death at the royal wedding tomorrow if he spent the night in a cell.

"Why are ye starting fights in my town?" Bailiff Rosenstein scowled.

"I'm not starting any confrontations, my good sir."

"That so? Then what was that?" He pointed to the tavern.

"More of a pissing contest, if I do say so myself," then, after a dramatic pause, "which I do."

"You're disturbing the good folk of this town."

"Really? They looked quite entertained to me."

"We don't want no entertainment," dismissed the bailiff. "We be a hard-workin' bunch here. The duke confiscated the last of our winter harvest for his damn weddin'. We have men, women, and children workin' extra to make sure we don't starve. Meanwhile, ye vagrants—"

"Aye now," said Godfrey, more than slightly offended. "I ain't no vagrant."

"Ye vagrants," continued the bailiff, ignoring him completely, "are comin' into town and eatin' all our food and drinkin' all our water."

"Hark, I'm paying for everything. I was giving that tavern good business until that big fellow decided to throw me out."

"That's not what I heard. I heard ye were getting possessed, taken over by the Devil with those herbs you smokin'. Is the Devil inside of ye, son?" the bailiff asked suspiciously, squinting his eyes at Godfrey.

"Yes. I'm most certainly possessed by the spirits of evil. Can you see it in my eyes, you mortal fool? Can you see the fires of Hell?!" Godfrey snarled his teeth. He barely kept back his laughter.

The quick smack of the cudgel knocked the sarcasm out of him.

The bard collapsed into the mud again, the hot iron of pain in his arm completely mitigating the tightness in his back. The black mud mingled with Godfrey's shoulder-length hair. The putrid stench of the earth would now follow him the rest of the day. Great.

"Ye are under arrest," said the bailiff.

"You could have arrested me then, rather than break my arm," groaned Godfrey. The bailiff pulled him up. "I have to remark, you're phenomenal at throwing me around. Would you mind carrying me all the way to the cell?"

The bailiff pushed him forward instead. Godfrey sighed. He should have known he was asking too much. What a pity. It felt nice to be carried . . . probably.

"Bailiff Rosenstein, where are you taking this poor man?" asked a soft-voiced woman.

Godfrey and the bailiff both turned to find a comely middle-aged woman facing them. She had auburn-colored hair tied up atop her head and covered with a piece of green cloth, contrasting beautifully with her sparkling pale-blue eyes. A few red strands of her hair hung down and wrapped themselves around the sweat-soaked nape of her neck. A simple gray wool tunic modestly covered her, as it drooped loosely around her figure. The bottom half of the tunic was pinched up by her leather belt, which kept the hemline flowing right below her knees rather than at her ankles. She wore no hose. Her bare legs, slightly stretched and wrinkled from the woes of a longer life, were strangely alluring to Godfrey. When everyone was dressed from head to toe, reluctant to expose even a modicum of the Lord's grace beneath, it could be quite a shock to remember that everyone hid beauty with them. Godfrey stared down at his hose, which were now stained brown from lying in the mud, and chuckled to himself about the absurdity of him exposing his own legs. It would not be as pleasing as this woman.

"I'm locking him up, Miss Regina. He be disturbing the peace of our town. Startin' fights, driftin' about. I have half a mind to—"

"Why don't ye let him go?"

The bailiff stumbled, taken aback by her preposterous—

Hey, preposterous, thought Godfrey, *that's a good word. I have to use that in one of my poems. Anyway . . .*

Bailiff Rosenstein was taken aback by her preposterous proposition. "Miss, why would I do such a thing? He would simply wander around and cause more trouble!"

"Would he?!" Regina gasped, putting a suspicious amount of dramatic flair onto it. Godfrey became amused as he cued into what this lovely Regina was doing. "But why ever would he do such a thing?"

"Why? 'Cause he is a vagrant! He has no place to go, no work to perform."

"Actually, I'm a bard," interrupted Godfrey.

"Precisely!" The bailiff smiled as if Godfrey proved his point. "He has nothin' to give to our town."

"But why does he need to be locked up for that?" questioned Regina.

"Trust me. It be best to keep these sorts holed up until we can push 'em out of town."

"What if he stays with me?"

Godfrey furrowed his brows. Regina looked him in the eyes for the first time. By outward appearance, she appeared ten years younger than Godfrey, but as he stared into the gateway of her soul, he encountered the many decades of toil and heartache that were laden within her spirit. It gave her a maturity and grasp on life that Godfrey could only ever dream of expressing in his art. She must only be five to ten years his elder, but she carried with her the wisdom of someone who had walked the earth for many generations, even though she was only a peasant. The peasantry never failed to surprise him.

"Miss Regina," said the bailiff. The words caught in his throat, and he was forced to push them down and restart. "Miss Regina, ye can't possibly be considering keepin' someone such as this so close to yourself and your daughter?"

"Bailiff, it be our duty as good Christians to be hospitable to the less fortunate, is it not?" She smiled softly. Godfrey jutted his mouth to the side and rocked his head. He was surely not *that much* less fortunate than peasants. Was he?

"Miss, I highly suggest—"

"Me appreciates the gesture, Bailiff Rosenstein. But I assure you, me can make my own decisions on the matter," said Regina with the perfect amount of harshness. She winked at Godfrey. The bailiff growled at him. Godfrey pointed his head at Regina and gave the bailiff his warmest "got you" smirk. The bailiff huffed.

"Don't ye try anythin' with her or her daughter," he quietly threatened into Godfrey's ear. He pushed the bard to Regina. "Ye know where to find me if anythin' happens."

"Me does, indeed." She nodded.

Bailiff Rosenstein reluctantly stomped away. Godfrey wiped the remaining clumps of gunk and dust off his outfit. His once sparkling, golden-trimmed doublet now resembled the ragged leftovers of a noble's discarded corpse.

"Me thinks your clothes are ruined," said Regina.

"I am inclined to agree," said Godfrey. "Thank you, madam."

"Huh? Me ain't no madam. Does me appear to wear fancy clothes and whatnot?"

"Madam or woman or not, I appreciate the help," said Godfrey. Regina gave him a confused grin at his bow. Godfrey stood awkwardly under her gaze for a few quiet moments. He cleared his throat. "Well, I don't wish to occupy too much of your time. You happen to know where I can find another tavern? One with less . . . quarrelling?"

"Me knows an inn, but I meant it when me said ye can stay at my place."

"You don't want me staying at your home."

"How do you know what me wants?"

Godfrey smiled. "I just don't think you'd like me around."

"Humph," Regina snorted.

"What?"

"Ye literate types, ye always sayin' your big words and struttin' in your fancy clothes, but ye never seem to have faith in yourselves."

"Maybe I'm intimidated."

Regina stared at him for a long moment. Godfrey shunned his eyes from her. "It ain't that," she said finally.

Godfrey glanced at her. A soft smile spread across her lips, an elegant display of her pity for him, wrapped in all the warmth and comfort of a mother's love—a feeling Godfrey had never felt before.

I don't deserve it.

That was the truth. Godfrey didn't deserve the radiance of humanity that Regina extended to him. The bailiff was right about him.

"At least stay for a while to have some food," she said.

"I can't take your food."

"Hark, I saved ye from a night in a cold cell. The least ye can do is repay me by humorin' my offer."

Godfrey released an exaggerated sigh, and Regina retaliated by releasing one of her own, except hers managed to be five times louder. It took another few seconds before they both smiled.

Godfrey's fingers began to feel tingly as he got to Regina's house. They always did that when he went too long without smoking. Godfrey grasped at the leather sack he tied to his belt. Feeling the contents staved off the shadow of his looming need to smoke.

He followed Regina to a wooden home crammed between two houses which were further crammed between other houses. Godfrey knew they called these types of homes "townhouses" in the big cities. London was full of such living spaces, where houses were built vertically to accommodate as many people with as little space as possible. Apparently, Sherborne was being given the same royal treatment. Regina's home was only a single story though, as if the town were afraid to fully commit to its big-city aspirations. Two large, blocky posts sunk directly into the ground and made up the corners of the house, while long planks were attached vertically from the ground to the roof. The whole façade of the home and all the surrounding townhouses were whitewashed to give the illusion that cheap wood wasn't used in their creation. The roof was made of wooden shingles that hid under a thin layer of thatch. He imagined it wasn't the most effective protection against the spring monsoons. There were only two front-facing windows that looked out upon the town, but even calling them windows was a stretch; they were merely two vertical slits through the planks, with neither a pane of glass nor any type of wax covering it.

Regina's home was truly the definition of a typical peasant's abode.

Regina welcomed Godfrey inside. The first thing he noticed, admittedly, was the very attractive younger woman who kneeled on the ground. Godfrey discerned with some surprise that she was weaving on a horizontal loom. The art of weaving was predominately a trade of men, as it worked naturally for weavers to toil near tanners, another almost entirely male trade, on the outskirts of towns and cities.

Godfrey flinched his eyes away from the young woman, who must have still been in her teens, as to not stare at her too long; he was a guest after all.

The interior of the home was undoubtedly small, but it retained a cozy quality. It was quite a bit longer than it was wide, giving the home an elongated rectangle shape rather than a square cabin. The ground was solidly packed earth, exposed to the barest extent with neither straw nor clay covering it. There were two rooms divided by a thin layer of timber frames at the back of the home. A firepit, buried half a yard or so into the ground, sat in the middle of the space and breathed out a smoldering wisp of smoke, which traveled up, twisting and biting into itself past a loft up in the rafters that stretched the length of the house, until it jettisoned out of the room through a small ridge in the roof designed solely to let out smoke. There were a few cheaply made chairs and an equally well-designed table in the home, but outside that, there really wasn't much to enjoy. A ladder led up to the loft, but Godfrey couldn't see anything up there that looked interesting enough to climb for. All things considered, it was still a home they shared. And that was something.

"Welcome to our abode," Regina smiled. "This be me daughter, Juliana. Say hi."

"Hi. Nice to meet ye," said Juliana.

"You as well," agreed Godfrey.

"Juliana, ye can put that down for now. Why don't ye help me attend to our guest?" asked Regina in a tone that implied a statement more than a question.

"Fine with me." Juliana yawned, stretching her arms before she stood. She must have been weaving for quite some time, as her joints popped and exploded as she swiveled them.

"Do you both know how to weave?" asked Godfrey curiously.

"Yes, me husband taught us. He runs our clothing store down in the town square," said Regina. Juliana crossed into one of the back rooms, leaving Godfrey and Regina together.

"And where's your husband now?"

"Let's say, he's out," said Regina with a degree of finality. Godfrey got the message: don't mention the husband.

He stood around awkwardly for a few seconds, staring off into the corners of the house. Regina kindled the fire in the center of the room, not possessing any of the same discomfort as Godfrey. He shook his head. His whole life he has had a problem connecting with other people. It was one of the reasons he traveled so often and so far; there was a comfort in his own mind that he had trouble embracing in the arms of others, a deep-seated distrust of the love of others. Godfrey confronted this social demon when he was in the midst of his poetry, when he had to delve into the soul of humanity, into his own spirit . . . where that demon lurked. Everyone else appeared to get along well in social settings, but not him. There had always been a part of Godfrey that resented people for their natural inclination to welcoming the cradle of civilization, the reassurance of human contact.

Juliana carried a block of cheese as she entered back into the room. Godfrey recognized it as gorgonzola, a white marble cheese with vivid blue-green veins that branched throughout the curdled milk like the plentiful strikes of a lightning storm. Gorgonzola cheese started off as a luxurious delicacy only enjoyed by the very rich, as it had to be transported from its origins in the Holy Roman Empire. Over the course of a few hundred years, however, a more streamlined process of transporting the cheese—along with a new salting technique—had significantly lowered the cost of gorgonzola, making it affordable to the peasantry and nobility alike. There had even been some local cheese makers who were trying to reproduce the cheese, although it had been to underwhelming results. The real surprise, then, was the butter that Regina grabbed for them to go along with the bread. Butter was an even rarer food item for the poor, and Godfrey was actually quite excited to taste the creamy saltiness of it. He has only had the privilege to taste butter on a few occasions, and most of those were back when he worked as a scribe under his former master.

"Scrape off the wax," Regina told Juliana. "Me will get the plates."

Juliana took a knife and gingerly peeled back the protective coating over the gorgonzola. Godfrey readied himself for the typical rancid stench that most cheeses possess, but he became pleasantly surprised by the nutty aroma that bloomed outward from the severed wax. Juliana cut the cheese into slices, placed it with the bread and butter on the plates, and handed it over to Godfrey. He accepted with a timid nod and took out his own personal knife. He sliced through the gorgonzola, which was firmer than he expected, and the marbled cheese crumbled around the divide. He took a bite. The punch was instant: a salty creaminess that melted richly around his tongue, then zapped away by a spicy zest that transformed further into a pungent, bitter finish. It was amazing how many eclectic flavors could be compacted into a single food. The salt coating of the gorgonzola reestablished his tastebuds back to their default blandness, already readying up for their next round.

"That's fantastic," moaned Godfrey. Juliana chuckled.

"'Tis a personal favorite of ours. We buy it whenever the merchant comes through with it," explained Regina.

"I'm honored you would share it with me."

Godfrey moved on to the butter. He taste-tested it with the tip of his knife. As expected, the salt covering was overwhelming. Most cooks suggested wiping off the majority of the salt, as it wasn't implemented for taste but rather for preservation. Butter spoiled rapidly, so milk churners and butter crafters found that the only way to preserve them throughout the length of their travels to market was to layer them with a thick coat of salt. It was a tradeoff that most people were happy to make, as it was one of the only ways that anyone got dairy. Milk spoiled instantly, and it was known to be occasionally dangerous when drank raw; thus, it was rarely relied upon for a normal diet. Even nobility didn't drink milk often. Butter and cheese, on the other hand, could be enjoyed by all. And so Godfrey did.

Godfrey spread the butter across the half-stale bread. It crumbled with a crisp snap in his maw. The butter coated the roof of his mouth with a rich combination of both saltiness and sweetness. Godfrey let it stick there for a while as he continuously licked at it with his tongue. As the butter melded with the bread and slinked down his throat, Godfrey lost himself to a distant memory.

Yes, the last time he tasted butter was when he was a scribe's assistant. He could see that child now, a young boy who knew not what the future held for him. A boy who struggled to read and managed to spell every word wrong when tested by his master. He had been a terrible scribe in every sense of the occupation, but Master Ode was an affable old man who was too kind for his own good, and so he had continued to train Godfrey, nonetheless. Master Ode was more than Godfrey could have ever hoped for as an orphan.

Godfrey the bard continued to reflect on his past life as he chewed on the food, sparking memory after memory. Regina and Juliana shared the congenial silence while they ate the cheese, bread, and butter. The three of them stayed silent for a long time, listening to the flight of birds overhead and the passing voices of villagers as they crossed by. A brief argument erupted in the townhouse adjacent to Regina's, and the three of them listened in with curious glee as they tried to make out the fury of words that mumbled through the wall. Gossip was the main source of entertainment for common peasants, and thusly, this was a gold mine for Regina's and Juliana's social lives. Godfrey listened because he loved conflict. It was always good fun.

After they finished their meal and the insult-laden turmoil of the neighboring house settled down, Regina took their empty plates and exited the house to clean them at the family trough. Juliana smiled at Godfrey, which caused him to blush. He nodded, unsure of what to do with himself. She chuckled.

"Have ye ever played Merels?" she asked him.

"I've seen it played a few times but never myself."

"Would ye like to play?"

"Sure," said Godfrey, glad to be doing something other than sitting around awkwardly.

Juliana climbed the ladder to the loft and grabbed a square, wooden board from it. She carried it back down and placed it on the ground next to the sizzling firepit. Godfrey recognized the straightforward layout of Merels instantly, which was painted directly onto the wooden square. Merels, or sometimes called Nine Man Morris, was a simple strategy board game that gained massive popularity throughout the region in the later years of the last century. Its success could be attributed to its unadorned set up but complex intellectual depth. It could be played by child and adult alike, and it was one of the few games not subjugated to one class of society over the other. The board layout was simplistic: a massive, painted square made up the outer limits of the board, a second smaller square was drawn within that one, and then an even smaller square was drawn within the second. From the midpoint of every side of the smallest square, a line expanded from that midpoint, through the second square, and continued until it reached the midpoint of the largest square. By the end of the process, four perpendicular lines were drawn out from the smallest square to the biggest one. Once those steps were complete, the board was ready to be played upon.

"We have these wooden shavings as player pieces," said Juliana. She dumped nine dark-colored chips and nine light-colored chips onto the board. Godfrey chose the dark ones.

"You're going to have to excuse my ignorance," he bumbled. "I'm not a well-versed player of this game. I'm sure you'll beat me easily."

"Ye talk like that but don't know how to play this?"

"Intelligence comes in many forms."

"Me father says wisdom and intelligence are two different things."

"He must be a smart man."

"I don't think he is." Juliana frowned. "Me thinks intelligent people just forget to be wise. Surely all intelligent people must be wise, but not all wise people may be intelligent."

"That's an intriguing perspective." Godfrey smiled. He noticed himself starting to warm up to the situation. Thank goodness. It was exhausting to try to act comfortable.

"Do ye want to go first?" Juliana asked.

"Why don't you go, that way I can watch a bit," said Godfrey, staring down at the board. Juliana took one of her pieces and placed it on the intersecting point between the top line of the middle square and the line extending from the smallest square.

"Now I can put my piece on any of the intersections?" asked Godfrey.

"Or any of the points." She nodded.

"You mean the vertices?"

"I don't know anythin' 'bout *vertices,* but ye can put them on the corners." Juliana pointed to the vertex of one square as an example. Godfrey nodded.

He placed his piece on the lower-right vertex of the middle square. They alternated placing their nine pieces on the different intersections and vertices of the board. The objective of the game was to get three of their player pieces in a row, which was called a mill, that way one player could take one of the other player's pieces. There were three parts to the game: the setup, the maneuvering, and the flying.

Juliana was a fast and aggressive player, Godfrey observed. On two separate occasions during the setup, she tried to get three in a row and captured one of his pieces. It was an effective strategy, as Godfrey had to spend more time defending than properly setting up his own future moves. Juliana effectively outmaneuvered him, placing Godfrey in a vulnerable position by the time they reached the next stage. Regina entered back into the home and watched over them, smiling.

"Let's see what ye got." Juliana grinned devilishly. Godfrey chuckled and shook his head. He was about to be beaten by a teenage girl.

All those years of education are really paying off.

They moved on to the maneuvering phase. There were six open spaces still on the board. The goal now was to reposition the "men" so they lined up as three in a row. The pieces could only move along their line, and only to an open vertex/intersection. Godfrey and Juliana alternated moves. She quickly lined up three of her pieces and captured one of Godfrey's men. A few turns later, she captured another one. A dozen turns passed, with Juliana becoming more and more confident in her boasting, until they reached the final phase. Juliana had five men left while Godfrey only had three.

Regina clicked her tongue behind them. "Not lookin' good for the famous bard, now is it?" jested the mother. Godfrey couldn't help but laugh.

"You both are so vicious with your insults!"

"Father often says we are too smart for our own good." Juliana smiled. She and her mother rubbed their hands, standing in solidarity in their inevitable victory over this educated man. *Fair enough.*

"Let's get this going then," chuckled Godfrey.

The last round of the game was a wild card. Since Godfrey only had three pieces left, he could move his pieces to any point on the board regardless of where it was. His one objective was to block Juliana from getting her last mill. He lasted about four turns.

"Yes!" Juliana shouted in jubilee. She stuck her tongue out playfully at Godfrey. Regina rubbed his shoulders.

"Don't ye worry. She beats me all the time," said Regina.

"You were too fast for me," admitted Godfrey.

Once Juliana got ahead in the set-up phase, making assertive attempts to control the board early on, it was difficult for Godfrey to ever catch up. He was on his heels the entire time, and Juliana, in her intuitive warmongering, smelling blood in the water, stampeded on his defensive front with all the adrenaline-fueled vigor of Achilles, Hector, and all the great generals the tales of yore bespoke of. It was smart, *is* smart. Once Godfrey found himself suppressed by the dealt oppression of her forces, it was near impossible for him to overcome it, almost to a humiliating and despondent degree. There was an apt lesson of life somewhere in there, and Godfrey would have pondered on it . . . if not for his pressing need to smoke.

"Do you mind if I step out?"

"Ye that sore from losing?" bit Juliana.

"Yes. I must smoke myself into a coma for such a devastating defeat," he quipped back.

"Me knew it."

"That be no problem at all," said Regina, rolling her eyes at her daughter.

Godfrey bowed before he stepped out the front door into the main road. Somewhere over the course of their meal and their game, the sun made its decision to heed the inevitability of night. It hung somewhere between midday and dusk, and a series of black shadows stretched slowly away from their sources. A barrage of storm clouds had apparently manifested from the horizon, and they raced up to greet the golden sun. A chill wind blew down the street, stinging the hairs on Godfrey's body to prick up. The town of Sherborne quieted down. The town market, from what Godfrey could see, has largely been abandoned, and the last person on his street vanished behind a house. It was as if the city itself was hunkering down for the long night.

Godfrey took out his pipe, grabbed the henbane and mandrake from the leather sack, and packed them into the bowl. He crossed to a lit brazier, which was spread sporadically throughout the town, and lit the pipe. He took a drag and let the relaxing concoction do its work. The cool wind blew by every so often, giving a fresh bite to his skin that complemented the heat in his lungs quite nicely.

What am I doing here?

Godfrey peeked back across the street at Regina's house. Her tiny home, so vulnerable and bland amongst the multitude of other townhouses on the street, managed to radiate a comfort that Godfrey longed for. He had only been here for an hour or so, but he was amazed to discover it already held a nostalgic place in his heart. A continuous stream of smoke slinked from Regina's miniscule firepit into the graying sky above. The wind jostled with it playfully, swirling the exhaust into the vapors of the other homes until all that was left was a single barrel of smoke, the communitive fumes of individual lives smoldered together. This last breath of individual comfort, contorted into a final exhaust of human hospitality, was blown away by the respiration of the world, forgotten forever by the winds of time.

This stuff makes me imagine some dour things. Godfrey chuckled to himself as he puffed on his pipe some more. *Oh well. I am a lonely man, after all.*

That was the crux of the problem. It always was. Godfrey wasn't meant to belong anywhere. He hated mellowing in self-pity; self-pity was boring. But he had found, time and time again, that his brain had an ingenious way of constantly discovering new ways to doubt the obvious and believe the preposterous. Actually, Godfrey saw it as a personality trait.

Better than having no personality at all, right?

Probably not.

No matter, his mind would do this to him again, so he might as well accept it. Godfrey took another drag, letting the burning smoke contrast with the cooling air. He allowed himself to stop thinking for a moment.

"Ye goin' to stay out here all day?" asked Regina sweetly as she crossed the street to him. The last glimmers of golden sunlight sparkled in her blue eyes. The wind flapped her hair around her shoulders, exposing the gentle skin of her neck. The man who was married to her was a lucky man indeed. "Me didn't realize you took the loss so hard," she teased.

Godfrey smiled. He took a final puff of the pipe. "You have a smart daughter. A little arrogant but certainly intelligent."

"She gets it from her father."

"I don't think so," said Godfrey. He dumped out the burnt plants into the brazier, avoiding Regina's reaction to his implication.

"Looks like a storm is brewin'," she said aimlessly.

"Yeah."

"You often smoke by yourself?"

"Most of the time."

Regina nodded at this. Godfrey stuffed the pipe back into the leather sack. Another blast of freezing wind enveloped them; nothing else could be heard but its whine.

"Ye can spend the night, if you'd like," said Regina. Godfrey nodded his head, but then shook it.

"I don't think I can."

"We have a loft. Ye can sleep up there. Nice and cozy."

"That's the problem." He sighed, glimpsing into her eyes. She read him in that moment, and Godfrey relaxed as he knew she would understand.

"Ye don't have to be so cruel to yourself," she said, smiling warmly.

"Where's your husband, Regina?" retorted Godfrey, realizing instantly he stated it more like a condemnation than he meant. A surge of self-bitterness collapsed in on him; and as Regina licked her lips, Godfrey waited inevitably for her rebuke. But thankfully, her benevolence spread far beyond the insecurities of a lost man, and she simply inhaled a deep breath.

"He left for Lord Merek's weddin'," she admitted. The venomous pain of resentment filled her voice. "Me told him not to go. That weddin' isn't meant for the likes of us. Why not stay here and be with your family? Then he left in the morn." Regina glanced behind her, presumably to make sure her daughter wasn't in earshot. "For all me knows, he could be in some brothel or God-knows-where."

"I'm sorry," said Godfrey. He was amazed by her resilience. Not a single tear appeared in her eyes, and her body didn't convey a hint of her inner turmoil.

"'Tis what it is. He's been out a lot lately, to taverns and distant friends and the like. Me heard him one evenin' in bed, whisperin' in his sleep . . . somethin' about killin' the duke. He has had silly things goin' through his head. How could he possibly kill Duke Rowan? He's one man." Regina scoffed.

"I'm sure he only wants to see the spectacle," said Godfrey.

"Yeah. He could never kill anyone."

They stood silently. In the west, the clouds finally overtook the sun. The wispy outskirts of the storm turned the sun into a silver halo. Their long shadows evaporated, and the world turned gray. The crisp wind, which initially felt nice, now chilled him to his bones.

"Ye sure?" asked Regina again. "Ye sure you don't want to spend the night?"

Godfrey glanced at her home. The orange glow of firelight flickered through the narrow windows and gleamed with the illusion of love. It was a veneer: the warmth, the comfort, the nostalgia, the sense of belonging—it was all a cruel temptress. This wasn't his family. This wasn't his life. Regina's hospitality went beyond gratefulness, to something more perverted and darker on the other side. Godfrey couldn't allow himself to believe that his life could be this good.

"I can't accept," he said.

"Why not?" she whispered.

"I was an orphan. I never knew my parents, and I was cast away to the hands of a monastery. They wanted little to do with me, so they threw me out as well. What do you do when neither God nor man wants you?"

"That's not true."

"I survived, somehow, off the good grace of a few different peasants who couldn't stand to see another child starve. But their love didn't extend any further. I'm a bastard to the world. Eventually, I found myself under the service of a great man, a scribe like none other. He fed me, nurtured me, educated me, maybe even loved me. I didn't have discourse with very many people since we were always working. I was reading scrolls or tomes while he was transferring or transcribing. Then when he died, he left me nothing—which is fine—I didn't deserve any of the treatment he gave me. . . ." He cleared his throat. "I've been roaming ever since."

"And now you're here," said Regina softly.

"I can't step foot back into that house."

"We all have sad lives—"

"True. There have been thousands of humans with tragic lives before us, and there will be thousands who will have tragic lives after. Please," begged Godfrey, "just let me be one of them."

"What are you searchin' for?"

"I'm hoping I'll know when I find it."

"Not prayin'?"

"Not yet."

Godfrey gave her a sad smile, and she reciprocated with one of her own. They had a common understanding, and that was all Godfrey could hope for in this world.

"I suppose I should get going. I don't want to get caught in that," said Godfrey, alluding to the approaching darkness.

"Aye. That'd be quite bad."

"It would. You happen to know where I can find another tavern? The one in town here seems less than inclined to house me."

"Me knows an inn, 'bout a half league yonder." Regina pointed. "Owned by a fellow named Warin."

"Warin's Inn?"

"I suppose. Be careful. Besides that storm, there be the duke's knights too. Me hears they roamin' 'round these parts lately."

"I'll keep an eye out."

They stood silently one last time. Regina grabbed his hand and cupped her own around his. She looked him in the eyes.

"Ye deserve happiness and a family and a life. Don't let yourself tell ye differently," said Regina. Godfrey shook his head.

"You don't have to lie to me," he responded mournfully. He removed his hand from hers and gazed toward the west, toward the black storm. "You said the inn was that-away?"

Regina nodded, a timid little movement that sent shivers down Godfrey's spine. He turned away from her and never looked back. Godfrey trekked out of Sherborne, all while watching the last silver halo of sunlight disappear beyond thick, thunderous clouds.

AMENDABLE DOGMA

VINCENT AWAKENED TO THE screaming of dying children, followed by the wailing of a grieving mother, ended by the gurgling of her demise.

Fraunce yanked Vincent out of his bed. The fuzziness of sleep refused to leave the confines of Vincent's head, and a great dizziness washed over him that caused Vincent to trip over his own feet. Fraunce caught him before he slammed into the wall. Vincent sneezed. His body was still warm from the fever he had been fighting for the past few days. A rampant sickness had gripped their town, and it finally took Vincent just a few days after his tenth birthday. He was one of the lucky ones. It had killed a few dozen people in town over the past few weeks; thankfully, if capricious luck can be thanked at all, the sickness seemed unable to kill the young.

More horrifying screams echoed into the air, barely audible over a constant crackling buzz that permeated all other noise. Fraunce pulled Vincent into another room before he had time to question it. His older brother wore trousers with a long tunic, which was covered in black smudges that looked like soot from a hearth. The house was too dark for Vincent to spot anything else about Fraunce's appearance. The clamminess of Fraunce's hands and the immense heat of the night told Vincent all he needed to know.

"Quickly! Out the back." Fraunce pushed him.

Vincent stumbled through the back door of their house. The night air, thick with heat and moisture, compressed down on Vincent like an animal-skin blanket. All he was wearing was a single tunic over his undergarments, yet his body perspired from every pore. Fraunce yanked Vincent toward him again. Their bare feet bumped against the rocky terrain as they fled around the back corner of their home.

Vincent saw it.

Their town was in flames. Home after home was engulfed in a never-ending inferno. The dark night was alight with a grisly orange glow, as if the heavens themselves were on fire. Villagers who Vincent had known for the entirety of his life rushed both away and toward the fire. Some people fled for the safety of the countryside; others, men and women alike, rushed toward the flames with buckets of water. They splashed the growing flames, having all the effectiveness of a torch evaporating a lake. The immense heat blew back at the brothers, almost pushing Vincent into the fence surrounding their home. Isabelle, their family cow, mooed into the night. She pressed herself against their back fence. Vincent noticed with horror that their barn had already been captured by the hellfire.

"What's happening?" shrieked Vincent, aghast with terror. It was an idiotic question. It was obvious what was happening. Vincent recoiled, expecting Fraunce to slam him with his typical sarcasm. The sarcasm didn't come, and that frightened Vincent even more.

"We need to leave," said Fraunce. Fraunce took Vincent's arm and pulled him past the engulfed barn. The shrill, helpless shrieks of chickens pierced through the fiery walls.

"Where be Mum and Pa?" asked Vincent.

"Me don't know. Methinks Pa ran to stop the fire."

"And Mum?"

"She's with Dawn."

They hopped their outer fence and entered the town proper. The pure chaos streamed around them on all sides. Hundreds of people rushed this way and that, some screaming and others deathly silent. That incessant buzzing noise transformed into a beastly groan as the fire devoured more and more of the town. It was as if Vincent had his ear pressed up against a hearth—deafening rage. They pushed past swarms of people, weaving and bobbing their way like a fish swimming up a stream.

They passed the collapsing house of Miss Eleanor. Miss Eleanor was their neighbor and the kindest old woman Vincent had ever known. She rested peacefully every night, sitting on a wooden chair outside her home while waving and making conversation with the tired populace as they returned from their laborious days at work. During the day, she prodded quietly with the other elderly women at the community garden. Vincent had never seen her upset, not until tonight. Miss Eleanor kneeled before her burning home and cried out in pain as she watched the home of her father, and her father's father, implode without a trace of remorse. Before Vincent realized it, tears streamed down his face. The heat dried them out before they reached his chin.

An older man slammed into Vincent. Vincent lost Fraunce's grasp and tumbled to the dirt road. He looked up in a daze and noticed it to be William Cogg, one of the town bakers. William whipped his head to see who he ran into, and he was about to apologize when Fraunce shoved the older man backward. William tripped and fell onto his behind.

"Watch were ye are goin'!" scolded Fraunce.

William coughed in response. He spat out dust, ash, and mucus. Whether that cough came from the chaos of the night or the nasty sickness that had been going around the town, Vincent knew not. William ran off. Fraunce pulled Vincent to his feet, and they rushed onwards.

The flames stretched to both sides of the road, funneling everyone down a single path like an incandescent cave. A brown lump lay in the middle of the road a little ways ahead of them. As they serpentined their way forward, the lump began to take shape, sprouting appendages and gaining color. Fraunce tried to cover Vincent's gaze as they passed it, but it was already too late. The lump had taken full form before Vincent's eyes, and the perverse, trampled body of Ellis, one of Vincent's closest friends, had already seared into his memory forever. He must have been stampeded on by the frantic rush of human willpower. The time for grief would come later, though.

Fraunce and Vincent pushed on down the road. They passed the ruins of their old marketplace. They crossed through the ashy remains of Miss Eleanor's favorite garden. They fought through crowds and bounced off bodies and whisked over grieving parents and lost children. What caused this pain? Who started these flames? What really happened on this night?

FRAUNCE WOKE VINCENT UP, although, unlike he had on that fateful night seven years earlier, he did so gently now. The rest of that night remained a blur within Vincent's consciousness. He dreamed about it a few times a week, but only the beginning: Fraunce wakes him up, he spots the flames, and they rush past the embers of their old life. The events that followed, the ones that truly changed Fraunce and Vincent's life, were an inconceivable shadow beneath the brilliant lights of their burning town. They came back to him in shattered fragments, a puzzle Vincent didn't have all the pieces for . . . or perhaps one he didn't have the courage to solve.

Vincent could hear the quiet voices of their friends in the other room. In the small cupboard Vincent slept in, only the waking dreams of his imagination held any reality. But Fraunce was with him now, and that was all that mattered.

"Ye sleep well?" asked his older brother.

"Yes," Vincent lied. He woke up numerous times during the night. The dream of their flight from their home had been especially brutal. He woke up in cold sweats and had to stare at the wall for what seemed like hours before he drifted back into darkness, only to be reborn into the horrific blaze once again.

"Good, we got a big day. We have breakfast ready."

"I'll come."

Fraunce smiled and ruffed up Vincent's hair. His brother had a habit of doing that to him. Maybe it was because he wished he had as much hair as Vincent. Vincent chuckled to himself as Fraunce exited the room.

Oswyn, Vivian, Edmond, and them had another league to travel to get to the inn they were told about. Tomorrow, they would head for the royal wedding to do the unthinkable, and the tumultuous pinching of Vincent's stomach squeezed the dread to the surface. Rather than suppress it, Vincent let it overtake him. He allowed the crushing weight of fear and regret to press down on him. It hurt for a second. The unbearable pressure made him feel like he'd compress into the middle of the Earth . . . but then it went away. The pressure eased up, and the crushing weight dispersed evenly over his body. Eventually, after a few minutes, the dread fell away completely. It would come back; it always did. Vincent imagined it would resurface multiple times over the next two days, but Vincent had found that if he accepted the way he felt as truth and allowed them to make their plea to his soul, then the pain that ran tangent with them often disappeared as quickly as it came. He could move forward, and so he did.

Vincent entered the main room of the house they were staying in. Oswyn, Vivian, Edmond, and Fraunce all sat around the firepit in the center of the floor. The house was owned by another conspirator: a fellow by the name of Arthur Herwyk who was kind enough to hide them while they made their way west to Duke Rowan's keep. Oswyn added a few spices to their food within the clay pot he brought with him. Oswyn was the best cook of any of them. If he had the drive to do so, Oswyn could have ended up being a personal cook for some count or countess. His food had a special zest to it, something that brought it alive in a way most people could not comprehend. Vincent liked to fancy that Oswyn would become a famous chef one day, serving all the lords and ladies who lived in the big cities, maybe even the king himself. For some reason Vincent couldn't understand, Oswyn kept his abilities to himself. He'd rather join a plot to assassinate the duke than use his God-given abilities to live a life of relative luxury. It was a funny world.

Vincent enjoyed Oswyn's meal, a rich broth full of complimentary flavors and a comforting warmth. Oswyn apologized to them multiple times about the fact that it didn't have any vegetables.

"It really would taste much better with vegetables. They hold clean water in 'em, and it balances out that chicken taste. Blast it! Me knew I should have waited 'til there were vegetables." Oswyn sighed.

Everyone assured him it was quite all right. His cooking was a blessing during the famine period of late winter to early spring. The winter frost put a hold on most farms and erected a barrier for merchants traveling from the warmer climates in the south. By early spring, most peasants ran out of their stock of food, which they spent all summer storing up, leading to a devastating time every year where people have to eat the same monotonous food. And since vegetables and fruit spoiled so quickly, they were often the first to be consumed. This winter had been especially cruel. Vincent hadn't eaten any vegetables in months, and the repetitive taste of stew and broth had long since begun to taste like sludge in his mouth. Luckily, it seemed like the world was starting to change its tune, and the days had slowly become warmer and more hospitable. Soon the crops could begin to grow anew, and their meals could take on more delectable and wonderful forms. That would be a good day indeed. But alas, for now, they would have to make do with Oswyn's broth and a handful of almonds.

They finished their meal in silence. The air between them was thick with the unsaid, and that pushed them toward greater silence. It had been a long few years since Fraunce first spilled his plot to Vincent. It started out as a silly desire to have revenge, and Vincent assumed it would fade into nothingness like the desires of most men. But what Vincent didn't realize was that revenge was on the minds of thousands, and when thousands of people held a singular desire, it exploded into action. From the moment Fraunce uttered his wish, they were set down a path with no way out, like the caves of flames in his dreams—

No, in my past.

Edmond broke the silence first. He took out his dagger and sharpened its edge. Vivian helped Oswyn carry the pot outside the house to clean it. Fraunce glanced at Vincent. His older brother gave him a comforting smile. He'd been doing that a lot lately. It had Vincent worried. A sudden urge overtook Vincent, and his body moved to act on it before he even had time to consider its implications. He scooted over to Fraunce.

"Me wants to stop by the church," said Vincent.

"Let me get my things—"

"No, me wants to go by myself."

"Ye sure?"

"Yes." Vincent gulped. A brief expression of distress crossed Fraunce's face, but he eventually nodded his head and forced a grin.

"We will get ye when we head out then."

Vincent thanked his older brother and quickly got dressed. He wore the basic garb of most farmers found in the region: a loose-fitted pair of breeches, a long tunic that draped over his knees like a skirt, a belt that clamped the tunic close to his waist, and soft leather shoes tied to his ankles by a piece of lace. Vincent drank from their water bucket, filled from the local well, before he finally gave Fraunce a warning that he was heading out. Once certain that he had Fraunce's permission again, Vincent ventured into the small town.

The day was already hot, a pleasant departure from the months of cold that preceded it. They were in a small village called Newmanton, which hadn't even been properly recognized by the royal court. The village was in close proximity to the Nadder River, giving the villagers enough clean water and fertile land to upkeep a small community. It was unlikely that Newmanton would grow any larger, however, since the surrounding towns of Salisbury,

Sherborne, Corfe, and Bristol had already became the central hubs for trade and commerce. Fraunce and Vincent traveled all around the southern region of England after they lost their home, and Vincent had noticed that more and more people were migrating to these bigger towns. It was hard for a small group of people to live on their own nowadays, especially with Duke Rowan taxing as much as he did. Newmanton would stay on its feet for a little while though, and that was all because of one institution: the Church.

Newmanton had a proper Christian church, which meant it had holy ground that couldn't be easily stripped away. King Henry attempted to take power away from the Church once, and his embarrassing failure led him to become the brunt of many peasant jokes. He tried to become God, to elect his own bishops and abbots. The Church taught Vincent that the words of God should preside over the lives of men, including the government, and not the other way around. All good lives centered around the Church. That seemed proper to Vincent; he was raised on the values of Christianity, so why shouldn't a blessed life be focused around religion?

The church was the best built building in town. Rather than being made of lumber and timber like most other buildings, the church was built using stone and mortar. The bulk of it was painstakingly transported from some far distant rock quarry, making it a spectacle to behold in the vast, natural countryside. Even the smell surrounding the building was different. It had a stuffy, burning odor that made Vincent want to sneeze. It was a far cry from the sweet scent of the wooden homes. The church wasn't quite as impressive as the grand, arching cathedrals of the bigger cities, but Vincent still ogled at its magnificence. A large oak door, reinforced by streaks of metal, glistened bronze in the morning sun.

Vincent entered the domain of the holy.

THEIR TOWN CONTINUED TO burn behind them. The moon turned red under the smoke and ashes of the scorching embers. The wails of hundreds seeped into the humid black air. Vincent stumbled over his own feet as Fraunce towed him forward. They crested a knoll on the outskirts of town, and Vincent got a brief chance to stare at the grief of dozens. From their vantage point, the town looked like the remains of a massive firepit, with the various homes appearing as a multitude of logs, which, chipped and tormented by the fury of fire, left a mesmerizing glow of immense heat in its wake. It was simultaneously the most beautiful and most terrifying thing Vincent had ever seen. He doubted he would ever see anything else so spectacularly abhorrent in all his life.

Vincent bent over, releasing a series of coughs that stripped his throat bare. That damn sickness wouldn't go away. His brother never caught it, thank God. Vincent didn't know what he'd do without his brother. Go mad, perhaps? All Vincent had ever done was look up to him.

"They should be down in the wood," said Fraunce, pointing to the tree line about a furlough away from them.

Vincent nodded. He wanted to see Mum and Pa dearly. His mother would hold him close, and then he could feel her warmth and know that life would be all right. Everything would get better once he had Mum.

A shrill scream echoed into the night. Vincent and Fraunce faced the yell. Three villagers fled to the south from the hellfire, sprinting at full speed and splitting up. The three villagers branched out, and Vincent noticed that they began to serpentine. Strange. They acted as if the fire was chasing them.

A man upon horseback rounded the far end of the town, his horse ornately dressed in a ceremonial caparison. Vincent was too far away, and the night too dark, for him to espy the golden sigil on the horse's caparison. The horseman took out a small stick from his side and lifted it into the air. He rushed toward the first villager.

"Methinks it's a knight." Vincent squinted.

"Yes," said Fraunce, an odd hint of concern in his voice.

"That be good, right? Baron Rowan sent his knights to help us."

"They couldn't get here so quickly."

The knight, glistening the reflection of fire upon his black steed, galloped to the first villager. Vincent couldn't tell who it was from this distance, but it seemed to be an older woman. The old woman peeked behind her at the knight, and a brief scream seeped into the air before being cut off as quickly as it rang out. Fraunce gripped Vincent's arm and pulled him back right as the stick came down upon the defenseless woman. She tumbled to the rocky ground, her forward momentum flinging her body over itself into a horrifying summersault. Before her body had time to stop, the black horse stomped and pinned her unmoving form into the earth. The knight moved to the next villager.

"What is he doin'?" wondered Vincent aloud.

"We need to go. Come on!" commanded Fraunce.

He sprinted down the back side of the knoll, almost pulling Vincent face first into the ground. Vincent peeked over his shoulder in time to see the knight reach the second villager, a younger looking man who was probably around Fraunce's age. The rider of death, mounted upon his coal-black stallion, flailed his wicked mace down on the pitiful soul, and that poor man, now banished from the realm of the living, collapsed to the ground without a head, vanishing down in that valley of fire. That valley, which was once their home and promised land, now reminded Vincent of those terrifying images of Hell that the Church evoked time and time again, and Vincent imagined himself and Fraunce up upon the precipice of purgatory, staring down at the horrors they barely managed to avoid. The angel of death soared across the fiery field of perdition toward the last remaining soul, a boy younger than Vincent, who sprinted toward the safety of the tree line, and struck him down with a similar zeal as the others. The rider cranked his neck, and Vincent froze in fear as the knight seemed to spy him before they disappeared behind the knoll.

"Come on, Vince! Ye need to run!"

"Me am!"

Fraunce stopped, and Vincent slammed into his back.

The two brothers stumbled. Fraunce covered Vincent's mouth and pulled him to the ground. They crouched in the scattered knee-high grass. A few peasants rushed into the open before them. Hollis and Aislinn Fryelond. Vincent recognized the married couple instantly, as their nuptial ceremony was held last year. Aislinn hacked furiously, a combination of smoke and vomit flying from her mouth. She caught the sickness a few days ago like Vincent. A horse neighed, and the couple turned to face their death.

A knight in leather armor, who sat upon a hazelnut steed, slammed his axe into Hollis's shoulder. The man crumbled to the ground. Aislinn yelped. She spun and gazed up at her husband's murderer. The knight raised the axe again.

"Please—"

The axe fell down on her before she could finish her plea. She slumped to the ground as a final cough creaked from her lips.

Fraunce pulled Vincent down until they were both fully prone in the grass. They looked up through the green strands, its skinny tendrils blocking some of their vision. The knight reared back his horse and appraised the surrounding land. He was only a few yards from Vincent. The night glowed orange behind him.

"Sir Ivan!"

The knight steered his horse as a second knight rode up to him. This second knight was slightly younger but more well-built. He hesitated for a second as he spotted the two dead villagers below Sir Ivan.

"Sir Rayner needs your help on the north side," said the second knight.

"He can't handle it himself?" groaned Sir Ivan.

"There's too many people trying to escape that way. We need to keep them all contained."

"Yeah, yeah. I hark. Damn, blasted asshole. I don't see what Rowan sees in that prick," huffed Sir Ivan.

"He's going to promote him to commander soon. I suggest doing what he says."

"You spot anyone on the way over here?"

"Just a woman, a little that ways," said the second knight. Vincent felt Fraunce tense up next to him. "It's a shame. She was cute. Married too." Fraunce and Vincent glanced at one another. Vincent knew what was going through his mind instantly: Dawn.

"Yeah, well, many of these sick buggers are," Sir Ivan scoffed.

"I think Sir Brede might have got her."

"You said Sir Rayner wants me up north?" asked Sir Ivan. The second knight nodded. Sir Ivan turned his steed and clicked it to canter onward. "Watch yourself, Sir Algor! They're trying to make it to the wood!" yelled Sir Ivan as he rushed off.

Sir Algor tapped his horse with his heels. "Damn this, huh, Brandy," he grimaced. "Let's go, boy."

The knight trotted off around the knoll. Fraunce and Vincent remained prone in the grass. A hot swirl of wind broke the stagnant air and made the strands dance around them.

"Hey," hissed a voice. Fraunce and Vincent jumped. "Hey, over here."

They twisted their bodies and spotted three villagers behind a rock formation waving them over. Fraunce quickly glanced over the field before he slapped Vincent to follow him. They stayed low, keeping as much of them hidden in the sparse grass as possible, and crossed to the conspicuous rock. Vincent recognized Oswyn, Nara, and Luella. They were all friends of Fraunce's and in their early twenties like him.

"Am I glad to see you, Oswyn," said Fraunce, his voice shaking.

"Ye too, buddy." Oswyn smiled. Vincent had never seen so many terrified people before. Sweat dripped down all of them, and he could almost smell the dread.

"What's happenin'?" asked Fraunce.

"We don't know. There be knights everywhere, and they killin' anyone who moves," said Oswyn. Nara began to weep. Oswyn glared back at her. Luella punched Nara.

"Belt it!" hissed Luella. "Do ye want 'em to hear us?"

"I'm sorry," sniveled Nara.

"Then shut the fuck up."

Nara curled into herself. Her body trembled all over. Luella shook her head, still annoyed at her. Oswyn turned back to Kendrick and Vincent.

"This whole thing is fucked," said Oswyn, his voice sour. "Why are the knights killin' us? Less of us means less money for Rowan."

"And how did they know there would be a fire?" added Fraunce.

"This ain't right."

"No shit," said Luella. She tore her blonde hair from her face, taking out clumps of it between her fingers. Fraunce peeked around their relative safety behind the rocks. They were still a hundred meters or so from the forest.

"Me needs to go check somethin'," said Fraunce. "Me heard the knight say he saw a woman."

"Fraunce, we don't know if it's her," reasoned Vincent.

"I have to check," said Fraunce stubbornly. He placed a hand on Vincent's shoulder and pointed to the tree line across the empty plain. "Mum is hiding in there, all right?"

"Don't leave me," begged Vincent. His brother pulled his lips tight. He looked up to Oswyn.

"Keep him safe," said Fraunce. Vincent reached for his brother to pull him closer. His older brother couldn't leave him, not now.

"Fraunce, no!"

Fraunce pushed Vincent back. Hot tears streamed down Vincent's cheek as he crawled for his protector. Too late. Fraunce rolled away from him and didn't even glance back as he searched for his missing wife.

"Fraunce!"

"Belt it, kid," said Luella.

His brother left him. Fraunce. Why? Why would he do this to him? Vincent stared after his older brother, the shock and fear overtook him completely. Oswyn pulled Vincent away as Fraunce disappeared among fire and smoke.

FOR SUCH A MASSIVE building, the church felt particularly hollow on the inside. Awe-inspiring and mysterious, but definitely empty.

Vincent ambled his way through the space. Holy paintings of various biblical importance—the crucifixion of Christ and his rebirth, the Virgin Mary surrounded by numerous angels, a depiction of the apostles—was painted on the whitewashed inner walls. They projected a reverence that humbled Vincent on the spot. The church only had a few windows, all of which were simple holes merely hammered directly through the stone, and the sun did little to light the inside of the building. Large, candle chandeliers hung from the vaulted ceiling and reflected harsh yellow light over the walls. Vincent's shadow stretched far behind him, and it jittered this way and that as the candles swayed softly in the air.

The building was shaped as a cross, forcing followers to pass through the pristine artwork as they walked down the narrow neck of the nave toward the central altar. The altar was a long table with a ceremonial cloth knitted with ostentatious precision that sat upon the edge of a slight raising of the ground. Behind the altar was a giant oak cross with a magnificent painting of the Virgin Mary, Jesus Christ, and his twelve apostles. A priest in a simple black hood kneeled below the altar. Vincent realized he was praying and hesitated for a moment, wondering if this was a bad time.

"Come in, my son," said the priest. "Don't be shy." His voice echoed in the empty church, giving the illusion of his voice being projected from the sky.

Vincent treaded across the nave toward the altar. His footsteps reverberated off the stone ground, and the cool air mutated his skin into goosebumps. Vincent stopped behind the priest. The brilliant glow of the candles on the altar gave him an ethereal halo.

"I'm afraid you are too late for mass," said the priest. He finished his prayer and turned to face Vincent. The priest had a kind, old face. His white eyebrows drooped over his deep, brown eyes where long laugh lines extended from. He had some gray beard hairs sprouting sporadically across his face, which hinted that he was due for a shave since canon law forbid clerics from having any facial hair. His black robe hung loose over his body.

"Oh, sorry," said Vincent, unsure of what else to say. He hadn't thought this through. He just *felt* the need to be here.

"That is, unless, you didn't come for mass," said the priest, raising an eyebrow back into its normal position. Vincent's eyes ambled to the painting behind the altar. "What's on your mind?" The priest smiled warmly.

"I'm scared," said Vincent, surprised by his own truth. The words flew out like honey, and it left a sweet joy in his mouth. Another weight off his shoulders.

"We all harbor fear. Even Jesus Christ was afraid when He was on the cross, so you are not alone, my son. The Holy Spirit flows through man and angel alike. It was a mistake by the clergy of the past to not stress the importance of Jesus Christ as a man."

"Thank ye, Father."

"Now what sin has the Devil planted in your soul?"

Vincent's heart jumped a beat. Was the Devil inside of him? Even worse, was the Devil inside of his brother? There was evil everywhere. The sermons Vincent had attended taught him that well. He knew it was true, too. Fraunce and him had a run-in with heretics for a period of time. They could have been burned at the stake if caught.

"Me has no sin—" began Vincent.

"Do not lie, child," cut off the priest. "We all sin. That is why we are out creating new monasteries and new cathedrals, to cleanse this kingdom from hearsay and save you from damnation."

This gave Vincent pause. *I must have sinned then.* Vincent reflected on his past, searching for any sin he must release now. An anxiety started to climb in him as he felt the stare of the priest and the pressure to say something, anything. *Make something up.*

"I stayed quiet," blurted Vincent.

"You were quiet?" A confused look spread across the priest's wrinkled features. Vincent went silent. Of course. He was always silent.

"I'm afraid I don't understand," said the priest.

I don't either.

Vincent shrugged his shoulder. A different feeling crawled under his skin, something he hadn't felt in many years. Vincent struggled to put a name on it, perhaps there wasn't one, but the feeling was real and it was there. The cool air inside the church became humid. A pungent odor—burning skin—filled his nostrils.

That night seven years ago . . . that was where the feeling came from. Vincent felt his body transform. Blisters formed on his feet, and his shirt stuck to his skin. *Is that a black smudge forming on my arm?*

"My son?"

The priest placed a hand on Vincent's shoulder, and it stabilized the swarm of sensations, memories long abandoned, from his present form. Vincent gaped at the hooded man. "There is no need to be so upset," said the priest. "You are embracing the comfort of the wrath of God and accepting the divinity of Christ. You shall be saved of this."

The priest began to utter a prayer in an ancient form of Latin, and even though Vincent couldn't understand all of it, he knew it was a plea for his salvation and absolution. After the priest finished shriving him, he bowed his head and nudged Vincent to follow suit. They stood silently below the altar of the Holy Trinity, and a light wind whined as it squeezed through the narrow windows of the church. It sounded strangely like a hymn.

"Your sin is absolved, my son." The priest smiled. Vincent didn't have the same desire to grin. The priest clearly noticed this, as he raised his thick eyebrows at him again. "If you are still not feeling absolved from your sins, you can accept your indulgence and donate to the church. Your good deed will lighten your crime in the eyes of God."

"Yes, Father," said Vincent. He reached into a pouch tied to his belt and took out a few pence that Fraunce had given him. Vincent would pay any amount to erase the living memories of that night.

"Not to me, my son," said the priest. He gripped Vincent's arm in his hand and pointed to a box near the entrance. "You can place your alms in there on your way out."

Vincent nodded to him. He withdrew back into silence. Something still wasn't right. Vincent didn't know what it was, but some force beyond him locked his feet before the priest. There must be something else he needed to say that tied him to this moment. The priest twisted his head ever so slightly, moving Vincent to speak. But he couldn't. Why couldn't he find the words to move his life forward? Vincent had had more conversations with himself over the last seven years than with anyone else, Fraunce included. Every time Vincent spoke aloud, he felt like a fool compared to the discussions and arguments he had within. But for the first time in years, he found himself unable to speak externally or internally. The very essence of language was crudely ripped from his capabilities, and he found himself abandoned in the vastness of the hollow church. Maybe it was a daft idea to come here. What had he expected to find in the church? Was it a simple ploy to get away from Fraunce for a bit and avoid the finality of the path they headed down? Vincent knew that Fraunce was avoiding telling him the truth—that this usurpation would get them killed. Vincent suspected that Fraunce thought him dumber than he was—which was fine —he couldn't blame Fraunce for always seeing him as that scared kid in the glade. Vincent had seen death and agony; he had felt fear and betrayal. Yet he still defaulted to the good of man, and the others saw him as weak for it.

Maybe I am weak.

A reality swarmed into Vincent's consciousness like a plague of locusts, devouring every doubt within his mind. Only reality remained.

"Me fears change," said Vincent.

"Change?"

"How do you move on when ye know it is toward somethin' different, somethin' you've never been before?"

"Change can often be for the better."

"But it's not."

"Joseph, son of Jacob, went through drastic change. Once his brothers deceived him, he certainly didn't believe his enslavement would be for the better, yet it ended up fulfilling God's destiny for him. David, Moses, Peter, Solomon, all of them went through great change in their life, and often found themselves lost under the splendor of the

Lord's creation. The only certainty of this life is that change will happen. It's not our duty to question why our lives change but rather to accept the responsibility of maintaining our own goodness through it."

The priest's wise words rang true in the lofted ceiling of the church, and Vincent listened to multiple reverberations of his advice, the voice going through its own transformation as it changed pitch in the sacramental echo. The road ahead to Duke Rowan's keep took on a different perspective in Vincent's mind as a new responsibility toward Fraunce took shape. He must show his brother that there was goodness in all living things, that the spirit of God flowed through all people, good and bad alike.

That would be hard. Fraunce was a pagan. He could show him in a nonreligious way, he realized, by focusing on morality rather than religion. In Vincent's mind, they were one and the same. There was a life for them to live away from their past, away from the revenge Fraunce and his friends harbored so dearly. Vincent couldn't live that life away from Fraunce. They were brothers after all—the last of their line.

There was no life without Fraunce.

VINCENT HAD NEVER BEEN more furious with Fraunce than he was now. His brother abandoned him! Fraunce! Vincent's newfound fear crushed his soul to the deepest levels of despair. The roar of the distant fire and the scream of butchered peasants was nothing compared to the retreating footsteps of his older brother.

Oswyn slapped Vincent across the cheek. Vincent stumbled back into the rock formation that shielded them. Oswyn heaved him back toward the group.

"Vincent, me needs ye to pay attention," scolded Oswyn. Vincent nodded and Oswyn released him. Vincent fell backward next to Nara and Luella. Oswyn pointed to the tree line across the hundred meters of open plains.

"We need to cross," said Oswyn.

"We won't make it," stammered Luella. "They'll see us."

"Would ye rather stay here?" After no objection came, Oswyn peeked back out from the rock formation. "We stay low. If ye see anythin', jump to the ground."

Vincent glared across the opening. The forest had never seemed so far away before. Fraunce said Mum was in there. So close yet so far. At least Vincent was tiny, and so he could stay low easier. The other three were much taller than him.

"Ye all ready?" asked Oswyn.

"No," snorted Luella.

Nara whimpered, activating another eye roll from Luella. Vincent timidly nodded his head. A masculine shout screamed through the air, roughly from the direction Fraunce went. Vincent twirled and looked toward the source. What if that was Fraunce? What if he was dead?

No, don't think that.

"We go on three," said Oswyn, a slight tremor entering his voice.

Vincent glared back at the tree line. He mapped out his path. A small boulder rested alone about halfway to the wood. He could slink to it and get cover if something unexpected happened. If only Fraunce were still here. Why did he leave him?!

"One, two . . . three."

Oswyn rushed out, followed closely by Luella and Vincent. Nara limped behind, slow to rise from the rock formation. Her whimper shifted into a full-on weep, and her wails echoed into the darkness. Oswyn quickly separated himself from Vincent and Luella, being the fastest of any of them. Luella stayed in stride ahead of Vincent.

An immense heat and a brilliant glow smothered his backside. Vincent peeked back, but the village blinded him. Vincent threw up his hands to block the light, and his feet betrayed him by stubbing his toe into the dirt. He toppled onto his stomach. A rock bashed into his head, and his hair clumped over his face in a knotted mess of blood and sweat. Vincent stared down at his hands, watching the blood drizzle onto his skin.

He forced himself back up. His lungs burned with all the intensity of the blazing inferno behind him. He ran as fast as he could. Oswyn reached the tree line in the distance. Vincent's thighs shook, and the muscles felt as if they were pulling him back. He forced himself forward. The small boulder loomed a dozen meters ahead of him.

Then his blood turned cold, whether from the screams of Nara or the thunder of hooves, he knew not. But it instigated a primal urge, the urge to get down.

Vincent dove into the grass. The jagged rocks cut at his bare skin as he scraped across the ground. He stifled a grunt. He crawled forward while listening to the haunting pleas of Nara. A heavy thud rocked the earth, and she became silent.

Vincent crawled, pulling rocks and pebbles back as he swam through grass that glistened the vibrant reflection of fire. Vincent didn't dare stick his head up to look back, so he listened.

The ground shook with the footsteps of the horse. He felt the tiny reverberations all around him. The steed released a sharp sniff that sliced through the thick air like a hot knife. Vincent covered his mouth, but his lungs begged for air, exhausted from exertion and exasperated by fear. He jettisoned out breaths between the crevasses of his fingers.

Vincent watched the strands of grass sway beneath his breath. He clamped down on his mouth tighter, but that only caused his lungs to fight back with more fury.

Vincent crawled toward the boulder, listening as the horsemen rode around him. He couldn't have been more than a few yards away. Vincent closed his eyes and squinted away tears. He just wanted Mum, Pa, and Fraunce.

Fraunce had left him to die.

Vincent froze as the horse stomped next to his head. He peeked over and spotted the horse's hoof, steel horseshoe hammered to its underside, press into the rocky earth. He was inches from being unintentionally trampled on. They remained frozen in time. The knight jostled in his armor right above him. Vincent bowed his head into the ground, feeling the hot burn of his blood scar over his wound. The knight's armor shuffled above him again, and Vincent heard him move something heavy. Vincent prepared for the inevitable—

But the horse cantered away, and Vincent used the brief opportunity to rush toward the boulder. He curled up against the rock. For some reason, in the midst of the chaos, his mind only focused on the fact that the boulder was cool on one side but hot on the other. The simple reality that the rock, too, was affected by the mayhem, that not even nature could avoid being horrifically transformed, tethered Vincent to the world in a way he desperately needed. He was not going through this alone.

"Hey," a hoarse whisper drifted to him.

Vincent squinted through the grass and spotted Luella halfway between him and the wood. She waved for him to run toward her. Vincent peeked around the boulder. The horseman rode over the knoll that Vincent and Fraunce were just on. The fire silhouetted the knight. Ash and smoke appeared to rise from him, casting the hell rider into a long, tenebrous shadow that stretched to the very boulder Vincent hid behind.

"Come on!"

Luella waved for him again. Not waiting for a reply, she crawled after the tree line. Vincent leaned back against the boulder to catch his breath, reflecting on his trembling hands and aching feet. A throb of pain shot up from his heels to his neck. His muscles strained and tensed at the discomfort.

Maybe me should sleep here for a while. Fraunce will come and get me, right?

No. He left you.

No.

Yes, he did. He abandoned you for his wife.

"Get out of me head!"

Vincent knocked his head back on the boulder. His vision blurred and his head recoiled, but the pain from his feet disappeared momentarily. A bulge formed at the back of his head, and it felt as if it wanted to penetrate through his eyes.

"Over there!"

Vincent swung his head. The knight upon the knoll pointed to Vincent's boulder. Vincent spun. Another horseman a few hundred meters away twirled his steed and rode toward him.

Run. You have to run!

Vincent cursed to himself and pushed away from the boulder. He flew through the grass. Pointy rocks dug into the crevasses of his torn feet. The pain was numb, though, as a furious concoction of survival flooded through him. His thighs clamped down on his bones, and his knees popped with excitement. It sent a stab through his body, which the adrenaline of survival stuffed down like the placing of a lid over fire.

"Hurry! Get him!"

Luella sprinted up from her spot. Vincent blushed for a split second, realizing he unintentionally guided the knights straight to her.

"Get the girl!"

They raced toward the wood. The ground rumbled as a pair of horses descended upon them. The tree line appeared to stretch farther and farther away from Vincent, like a nightmarish dream that constantly perverted the exit so it could never be reached. Vincent wheezed. The air sucked in through his teeth but was unable to fully fill his lungs.

Luella tripped.

She crashed to the ground hard but pushed herself back up. Grass, twigs, and pebbles tangled in her hair while her pale-green dress gushed red. The knight rode up to her. Vincent flinched as the horseman twirled his mace and slammed down at her.

But Luella managed to duck behind a tree in time, and the mace slammed into a trunk, breaking off chunks of bark. Luella sprinted through the wood, a noisy trail of snapping bushes and plants left in her desperate wake. The knight jumped off his horse and continued his pursuit on foot.

Vincent gasped for air as his tiny legs stretched for the forest. The ground vibrated with greater intensity. The foul stench of his own odor and the wet residue of pouring sweat caused a nauseous sludge to flow up his throat. He heard the puff of the horse behind him. Vincent's own footsteps got lost in the thunder of hooves. The world went transparent. Vincent's vision blurred. The tree line ahead split into multiple duplicates. The rattle of something metal erupted from behind him.

Aim for the center wood.

Vincent yelled, letting out the last of his exertion. The forest collapsed on top of him. Branches sliced his cheeks as he careened into thick shrubbery. Vincent heard a loud collision, the banging and shattering of multiple objects all at once exploding behind him.

The horse neighed and cried. The knight cursed. Vincent didn't stop running, and it was a good thing too, because he caught the sound of two boots hitting rock and the huffing of a man as he chased after Vincent.

All moonlight disappeared, and the radiant gleam of the fire seeped into blackness. Vincent heard the knight behind him—a terrorizing cacophony of trampled flora. Vincent pushed forward, swiping away branches and leaves from breaking his stride. Fraunce and Vincent used to play in these wood all the time. He had an advantage. Vincent ducked and weaved, using his instincts to lead him around obstacles that were practically invisible. The knight didn't fare as well, as a constant series of curses rang out.

After only a bit farther, the voice of the knight diminished behind Vincent. He smiled. He was going to lose him. Vincent dashed between trunks and leaped over bushes. He was young and nimble and could hide anywhere. Now he only needed to find Mum and Pa, then they could search for Dawn and Fraunce.

Vincent burst through the entrance to a small glade. The fresh night air was more humid here, unlike the dry heat of the fire. He closed his eyes for a brief moment and allowed himself to take a deep breath.

He slammed into a solid object. Vincent yelped as he crashed onto his back. He groaned in pain and writhed on the soft moss-covered earth.

"If it isn't my lucky day," crackled a haggard voice.

Vincent forced his eyes open. Towering above him beneath the firmament of Heaven, dark brown eyes gleaming under a leather helm, stood the mace-wielding knight. Somewhere in the far distance, a bird screamed its high-pitch lament into the air. Then all became still.

VINCENT EXITED THE CHURCH into fierce sunlight. A tight, pinching sensation burrowed into his chest; Vincent massaged it away, keeping back the physical reinstatement of that night. Newmanton now bustled with the early-morning goings of its townsfolks; men and women set off to work in the fields or to open their stores as the children who weren't yet old enough to join them ventured off to play and lose themselves in the imaginations of youth. Did all these simple people, with beautifully simple desires and longings, know how much the world was changing?

All we must do is retain our goodness through it.

Vincent inhaled sharply, breathing in the future ahead of him. Yes, these people knew. It was impossible not to. The children, maybe, in their ignorance avoided the truth. Everyone else knew of the rapid mutation the world was undergoing. Peasants may not have high aspirations for power, but they took on the fury of the world as much as any noble.

And it was all taking damage.

The Church, with its schism between Pope Innocent and Anacletus, was at war with itself. There were also rumors of late that the Church was taking up arms and marching against a bunch of pagans in the east. *Muslims,* Vincent thought he recalled correctly. How much would the world change if the religious became the tyrants? The royal court was on the brink of civil war, disputing over the line of succession after King Henry. The duke of one of the bigger provinces of southern England would be assassinated tomorrow, and there were murmurs of follow-up assassinations if theirs went well. To top it all off, the present famine looked like it was in no hurry to whimper out, and Vincent had heard of a city in the north that was having a similar sickness to the one their town had seven years ago.

And, like always, all these woes would trickle down to the peasantry; maybe not immediately, but every man and woman here knew that they'd have to bear the weight of human sin. They'd do it because they must. This was their crucifixion to show their worth to God.

We must retain our goodness through it.

Most people believed that the nobility—the knights, merchants, barons, dukes, earls, and everything they represented—had severed their benevolence toward them. Some heretics even believed that the clergy had done this. They believed that this was the way of the world now, and that they, too, must become vicious to stay alive. If that was the case, then the country had truly fallen into barbarism. A horrifying image of Sodom and Gomorrah penetrated into Vincent's head. How long until God unfurled his wrath and fury on them? If the kindness of men was as forlorn as everyone believed, why hadn't the Lord smitten them like He did those ancient civilizations? He didn't need to break His promise to Noah to do that.

Because there is still virtue in the world.

Vincent nodded. He needed to believe that. Vincent unconsciously rubbed the scar on his chest again. There was something worth saving, something worth living for. Through all the turmoil and all the pain, there was a future out there that could be bliss on Earth. They only had to seek it.

We must retain our goodness.

Vincent set off toward Fraunce, repeating the mantra over and over again in his head. The world sparkled with the allure of faith. That haunting night years ago, which was Fraunce's proof of all that was wrong with the world, was the backdrop to Vincent's hope. Fraunce wasn't there to see what Vincent saw, to know what Vincent knew. Vincent didn't think of that night often. It was a secret that he kept guarded within his soul because no one would believe him if he told the truth. To everyone else, it was the fault of the knights. It was always the nobility. *Maybe it is most of the time*, Vincent admitted. He had stayed silent on that night for so long, that sometimes he himself forgot what happened, especially when surrounded by the hatred of Fraunce and the others. As it turned out, hatred was as addictive as love.

Vincent couldn't allow himself to lose faith that people could be good—not because it was his duty as a Christian, but because he was scared of what he'd become if he did.

THE KNIGHT HELD HIS mace aloft. Vincent tried to push away, but his feet slipped on the moss. His breath caught in his throat, and for a brief moment, Vincent wished for death to come from that. Instead, a coughing fit erupted, and the knight jumped back away from him.

"Watch where you cough, you fucking imbecile," screamed the knight. He quickly appraised his body, and Vincent realized with fascination that he was making sure Vincent hadn't cough on him. The knight glared at him from beneath his helm.

"Fucking peasants!"

The knight stampeded to Vincent. He swung his mace, and Vincent caught the glint of steel, the brightness of death.

The mace *thudded* to the ground next to his head. Vincent winced. The knight's body twitched above him. He stood, unmoving, wavering in the still air, before he slumped to the earth. Vincent remained on his back, confused and breathless. The knight's dead body convulsed next to him, all centered around a knife in his neck. Where did that come from?

"Fuckin' knights."

Vincent jumped. Luella stood where the knight had, her hand a bloody mess. Vincent put the pieces together quickly. Her breaths came out slow and methodic, and she appeared completely unbothered by the murder.

"Ye made it," she said, prying her dagger from the knight's neck. She let it continue to drip red. A twig snapped, and Luella quickly glared toward the sound. She twisted around the glade. No other sound spilled from the dense wood. Vincent tried to stand up, but Luella pressed him to the ground with her foot.

"Have ye seen Fraunce?" Luella asked.

"No," said Vincent, letting her press him back to the ground. "Me just ran here."

"Anyone followin' ye?"

"A knight. Methinks I lost him."

Luella glanced at the wood behind Vincent. In the glade in the center of the forest, the cries of their former life failed to reach them. They were alone in the silence of the world. Vincent pushed Luella's foot off him and stood—

Luella stabbed her knife through his chest.

"I'm sorry," hissed Luella.

Vincent grunted, both out of pain and surprise, as Luella pinned him to the moss. She hushed him, placing her finger over his mouth. A searing pain spread from his chest, then a freezing pain, and then a hot, vicious pain once again. It alternated, sending various waves of different kinds of agony through him. Luella stared him in the eyes. They glowed with intensity as her hair hung in wanton clumps around her head.

"'Tis fine," she whispered gently. Her voice was so soft, like a wool blanket on a storming night. She said something else, but her voice faded out. Then cut back in, "Me had to do . . . ye led 'em to me . . . think ye killed each other . . ."

She tore the knife from his chest. Vincent gurgled. He felt his mortal wound, and his hands come away warm and wet. Luella leaned her head down next to his.

"Thank ye," she said earnestly. She brushed her lips against his ear and pricked it with a kiss. For the briefest of moments, it overflooded the pain in his chest.

"Hey!" a voice jettisoned from the darkness.

Luella burst away from Vincent and blasted through the shrubbery into the trees, stranding Vincent in the center of the glade. He stared up at the stars above. There were so many of them. *I wonder what God made them for.*

A man appeared above him. Vincent forced himself to focus through his vanishing vision. He recognized the man as the knight he saw on the grass plains, Sir Algor. He looked between Vincent and the dead knight.

"Jesus Christ," he said. "Sir Brede bested by a woman. A savage woman."

Sir Algor sunk to his knees and leaned over Vincent. In a daze of illusions and fading starlight, Vincent felt the knight rip off his tunic. He hardly noticed the knight call for his horse, or the needle go through his wound. The world twirled above him in a swirl of intermixing colors like the whisking of stew within a pot. Sir Algor said a few things to him, but Vincent couldn't make out the meaning behind any of it. Like the trees far above them, the knight's voice fused into an indistinguishable pattern.

The next thing Vincent knew, the world disappeared entirely. He plunged into the depths of an abyss, and a faint breeze ruffling through tree branches sounded in the deep. Vincent wandered in the darkness, unsure of what was ahead and what was behind. Somewhere in that dense air, thick and black as tar, he heard the vibrations of Fraunce's voice. Then he heard his brother's voice everywhere. All parts of the air were Fraunce, and all the emptiness within it was Fraunce.

"Vince! Vince!"

Vincent felt his body levitate through nothingness. He flew upward, downward, in all directions at once, until he careened into the precarious form of his mortal self. He inhaled the sharp tang of life and found himself back above the moss-laden ground of the glade. Fraunce, his arms bruised and scraped, stared at him with a frightened look.

"Oh, thank God! Ye alive," he said.

Vincent felt his chest. His wound had been cleansed and stitched together. Vincent tried to remember what happened, but the eternity spent in that dark place left his memories of before in shambles. Luella was with him, and then there was someone else. Who was it? Vincent gaped in surprise at the dead knight next to him. Did he kill him? Vincent grappled to remember what led up to where he was. He woke up, ran through the fire, escaped to the outskirts of town, Fraunce left him—

Vincent shoved Fraunce and scrambled away from his older brother. The stitching at his chest stretched, which sent a new wave of pain through his system. It didn't matter.

Fraunce had left him. Vincent, with gritted teeth and flared nostrils, glared at his older brother. Fraunce crawled toward him. Vincent scooted farther away.

Fraunce was crying. Vincent had never seen his brother cry before.

"Vince, Mum . . . and Dawn—"

"Ye left me!" Vincent growled at Fraunce. His older brother charged after him.

"Vincent—"

Vincent swung his fists. Fraunce knocked his blows away and pulled him into an embrace. Vincent thundered his arms against Fraunce's chest, but Fraunce constricted his body around him, subduing his fury of limbs. A night of grief flooded from Vincent's eyes all at once, and they intermingled with the sorrow of Fraunce's.

"Ye left!"

"They're gone," wept Fraunce.

"Ye left me!"

"They're gone."

Vincent quieted his punches and used his fists to hold onto Fraunce for dear life. He felt his brother's hands curl around the back of his tunic, and they pulled each other into one hunched form of bereavement. They sobbed into each other's arms, their wails echoing into that warm night.

That night had heard too many woes.

Alone in this world, the two brothers sat in the glade, using each other to make the pain hurt a little less.

OVER THE NEXT FEW years, their burning town turned into a ghostly myth. A rumor began to promulgate through the peasantry that the fire was started by Duke Rowan. People believed that he had his knights light the inferno and made them slaughter everyone who tried to escape, all for his own sick pleasure. There were over a hundred people living in that village, and it was unknown how many survived. Fraunce and Vincent had bumped into a few survivors in their travels since, and Vincent had even heard some names in their conspiracy that could be from their village. Over time he slowly got a picture of what happened after he ran into the wood, but the truth behind Luella, and the knight, still blurred into a haze when he tried to think of specifics.

There was only one truth that mattered to everyone: the knights started the fire and tried to kill anyone who could escape, all under the dictation of Duke Rowan and Commander Rayner.

No one ever discussed the sickness that was running rampant through the village, nor of all the people it was already killing, and no one ever would.

It was the knights who did it, and that was all that mattered. It was time for change.

COMPLEX SIMPLICITY

E DITH WATCHED HER DAUGHTER play outside with the other little girls and boys. Emma ran around them and screamed a loud but joyful shriek, one tinged with the self-indulgence only a five-year-old could manage. It was hard for Edith to make out Emma's face from her current position. She could only discern Emma's two most distinguishing features: her long, raven-black hair and her brilliant green eyes. The most prominent features of her parents became the perfect combination on her.

Edith smiled as Emma jumped and wrapped her little arms around another small girl. It was moments like these that made Edith relax and know that going to work was worth it. All for her, her little Emma. Every time she saw Emma, it was like Edith was born anew with a refreshed vigor for life and its worth. Emma's vibrance shined off everything around her.

Well, most of the time.

Emma also had an uncanny ability to make it all evaporate when she threw a fit, but luckily, she only did that a few times a week. Moments like these, thankfully, were much more common.

Emma jumped into the mud, and Edith let out a sigh. Her daughter got up, covered in brown foulness, and beamed with more radiance than the sun.

Fantastic, thought Edith, *she's goin' through a mud phase, isn't she?*

Sure enough, Emma decided to jump into the mud again, flinging that brown goo all over her yellow dress. Another outfit ruined. Edith shook her head. She squinted up at the sun, which rounded her zenith and started its descent to the west. She had to go to work and deal with Warin again.

Edith looked at Emma one last time. She wished she could hug her daughter and feel her little frame wrap around hers. She wished she could kiss her and make her feel loved, but Emma should already know that. She was a smart girl after all, and she would only get upset if she saw Edith leaving her again. That would make Edith more upset, too. It was a lose-lose situation if she said goodbye. Anastasia would watch over Emma until she went to bed. Edith should be back by then anyway, unless those storm clouds in the distance kept her away all night. Emma hated storms.

Edith took a deep breath. She turned away from her daughter and walked out of the village. She thought about Emma the whole way to Warin's Inn. Emma was Edith's whole life. She was the only reason Edith existed.

It be only one night, Edith convinced herself. *I don't know why this feels so much harder than the other times.*

Emma, my dear, my beloved, my everything. . . I'll be home soon.

PART THREE

A GLIMPSE OF SUNSHINE

HOLY BLASPHEMY

"**A**H! SIR ALGOR!" SAYS Warin the Innkeeper at the bar, raising his big arms into the air and radiating the practiced warmth of hospitality. "Good to see you again. Please, sit 'ere!"

Sir Algor and Kendrick stand in the middle of Warin's Inn. The storm barrages the building and shakes its foundation. The planks rattle around them, almost warping from the force of the wind. Kendrick can't help but liken it to his own dismay.

Eliot's final facial expression before Kendrick beheaded him repeats in his mind. His phantom face has haunted Kendrick ever since they left that fateful conflict, staring at him from all corners of the world. When Kendrick finally built up the courage to peek back at Eliot and his enigmatic expression, the old man slid his head off his neck and cackled at Kendrick like it was some kind of perverse jest.

Even now, Kendrick can glimpse Eliot hiding beneath the stairs, waiting for Kendrick to give him a good look so he can slice off his own head once more.

God, what have I done?

"Come on," Sir Algor says softly to him. He pulls Kendrick to the bar. They discard their swords within their scabbards and place the weapons against the bar counter. Warin lays his beefy hands upon the countertop as they sit.

"Who be your friend?" questions Warin.

"This is Kendrick, my new squire."

"Ah, nice to meet you, lad!" Warin sticks out his hand, and Kendrick takes it reluctantly. He doesn't feel like socializing under the gaze of the dead.

"Get us some ale and food," says Sir Algor. "My squire here needs it."

"'Course. Me son, Leif, will bring it at once." Warin motions for the small boy behind the bard. Leif abides and rushes into the stables.

They had just deposited Fortune and Brandy in the stables, but Kendrick hadn't noticed any casks in there. Warin rumbles into the kitchen behind the bar. Yells immediately erupt from the door. This Warin fellow is certainly loud. What could he possibly be yelling at already?

Kendrick's eyes flinch to the stairs, where Eliot waits for him. He gives him that damn, perverse smile again.

"We were attacked," Sir Algor says.

Kendrick glances at his mentor who stares at him earnestly. Why does his expression match Eliot's? Eliot gave Kendrick that same honest stare, the look of a man who is completely in the present, hanging on every second. Imminent death can do that to a person.

"I've sinned a sin the Lord won't forget," croaks Kendrick, "and one I can never atone."

Sir Algor pulls his lips tight. He doesn't respond. How could he? What could he possibly know? He was so damn certain that Eliot was guilty. He holds no shame. He has never been forced to. . . Kendrick bites his tongue before he loses too much control. That's not true. Kendrick doesn't know what Sir Algor has gone through in his life.

"Here *you* are, sirs," greets Leif as he hands them two tankards of ale.

"Thanks, kid," says Sir Algor.

Leif wanders off. Sir Algor slides one tankard over to Kendrick. The squire watches the dark mixture swirl slightly in the cup. His desire for drink and food is long past.

One of the farmers near the door walks up next to them. He gives them a funny look, and Kendrick notices Sir Algor tense up for half a heartbeat. But then the farmer turns and yells at the kitchen door, "Oi! We still need our damn food!"

"You will have it in a moment," Warin's nasally voice jumps back.

The farmer gives them one last glare before he returns to his table near the door.

Sir Algor peeks behind his shoulder at them. He grunts. "Let's keep an eye on that group. I don't like the way they've been staring at us."

"Sure," says Kendrick quietly.

He feels Sir Algor looking at him. Kendrick lets the world fall on top of him between the two stares of Sir Algor and Eliot.

Warin bursts from the kitchen door. A vein protrudes from his temple, and the whole man has turned the color of a tomato. He wobbles into the stables.

"Hey." Sir Algor nudges him. "Look at me."

Kendrick glares at Sir Algor. The pitiful look in his eyes breaks Kendrick down, and he finds himself staring back at his drink again. Sir Algor nudges him again. Kendrick forces himself to maintain eye contact now, no matter how much it hurts.

"You're right, son. The Lord doesn't forget. But luckily, He forgives. You know what's a worse sin? Not enjoying a drink with your friend."

Sir Algor raises his tankard toward Kendrick. The drink hovers in the air, and like some force of magic beyond Kendrick's comprehension, the stare of the headless old man slowly dissipates. Kendrick releases a half-laugh, half-sob, and all the pent-up energy flows out of his body. He even smiles.

They clank their tankards together. Sir Algor and Kendrick sip on their beverage. It's a strong, thick ale. Globs of wheat still petulantly stick together, forming an almost solid in his mouth. It's certainly potent though, as the dryness of the drink sends immediate tingles through the squire's body.

A woman approaches from the kitchen. Sir Algor straightens up and rearranges his leather armor so it sits properly. *Ah, this must be Edith.*

Kendrick becomes self-conscious for the first time of how they must look. Their armor is ripped and torn, and they must have cuts and scratches all over their skin. Kendrick's neck is still sore from being strangled, and he imagines the purple bruising that's formed around Sir Algor's neck is probably around his own.

Edith places a large pewter dish full of pottage on the bar. Her eyes dart between the two of them. She places her hand on Kendrick's arm. Unlike most noblewomen whose hands Kendrick has felt—which, admittedly, isn't many—Edith's hands are rough and coarse, more likened to a carpenter than a traditional woman.

"Be with ye sirs in a moment," Edith says. Her hair is a mess, and her tunic reeks of the myriad substances that are spread over it. Kendrick chuckles at the thought of Lucia ever looking so ravished. That being said, there is something strikingly human about the way Edith appears. She radiates a genuineness and tenderness that seems lacking in this cold world. Kendrick can see why Sir Algor enjoys her so.

"I'm looking forward to it, madam," says Sir Algor with one of the silliest grins Kendrick has ever seen. Edith gives a half-baked smile in return and sets off toward the farmers' table with the pottage. Sir Algor watches her the whole way. Kendrick shakes his head.

"What?" questions Sir Algor bashfully. "What?!"

"I'm not saying anything." Kendrick snickers while Sir Algor downs the rest of his ale. "You're very considerate."

"Bugger off. At least I have a chance with mine."

"Oh. Oh, we're doing this now?"

"Weren't you just wallowing from eternal damnation five seconds ago?"

"More like ten seconds ago."

"You little shit," huffs Sir Algor. Kendrick laughs, but then withdraws back inside of himself. Sir Algor is right, Kendrick *was* wallowing in self-pity a short time ago. He hadn't even realized he stopped doing so. Emotions are confusing.

"What can me get you, sirs?" asks Edith, swinging around the bar to greet them properly.

"It's swell to see you again, Edith," says Sir Algor rather timidly. "How's your daughter?"

"Alive, so better than most. Who be this?"

"Kendrick, my squire."

"How do ye do, Kendrick?"

"A pleasure to make your acquaintance, madam."

"Seems ye have a tongue of silver," says Edith, smiling. "Perchance ye could teach Sir Algor some manners or two?"

"That's a forsaken cause," says Kendrick.

"Yes, yes. Very humorous," interrupts Sir Algor, giving Kendrick a half-serious glare.

"How'd ye get that scab?" Edith asks Sir Algor. She points to his bicep wound from the spear that cut him earlier.

"Ah, this?" says Sir Algor nonchalantly. "We had an altercation earlier."

"He's being modest," snickers Kendrick. "His arm was sliced protecting me from bandits."

Edith raises her eyebrows in surprise. For the first time tonight, she seems to actually *look* at the knight. Sir Algor blushes and swipes his hand across the air, trying to dismiss the heroism of the act. Kendrick hasn't known Sir Algor long enough to guess if he's feigning modesty, or if he actually dislikes being complimented. Kendrick wants to believe it is the latter.

"It wasn't even worth a ballad, really." Sir Algor grunts. He shifts on his stool, as if uncomfortable. "What's available, ma'am?"

"Pottage, per usual lately."

"We'll split a bowl," says Sir Algor.

"Certainly. I will set your chambers first." Edith quickly scampers away and charges up the stairs. *Strange. Why had she ended the conversation and run off so quickly? And why did she need to set their beds first? Couldn't she do that while they ate?*

Kendrick shrugs and drinks from his tankard. Another set of tinges pricks over his body. The two of them sit in silence for a long moment. They listen to the idle chatter of the inn, to the thunder of the storm, to the muffled neigh of the horses in the other room.

Eliot's face flashes before Kendrick's eyes, and the squire stifles a scream. The spectre evaporates instantly. *Blasted! How long will I have to deal with this? Forever?*

Sir Algor sticks his arm out toward him. Kendrick does the same, grateful to have human contact with someone real. They grip each other's forearm, which locks them together.

"You see him, don't you?"

Sir Algor's question catches Kendrick off guard. Kendrick trips over his own tongue. He struggles to find air to breathe. The squire licks the roof of his mouth and fights for the willpower to speak.

"How do—"

"I've done terrible things before," says Sir Algor. "Things worse than you, son. Things I was commanded to do. Years ago, there was this village. It had a plague. A sickness that was quickly spreading elsewhere, killing a lot of people. The court was fearful that if they allowed it to prosper, then it would soon capture the entire kingdom. They ordered us to burn it; kill anyone who tried to flee. Our job was to stop the sickness from spreading. They told us we were saving the lives of thousands." Sir Algor trails off for a moment, and Kendrick can see the man reliving that night. He sighs. "I've done a lot of things to try to make amends for that night. I repented before the altar of God. I accepted my indulgence. And I believed what my commanders told me, that it was for the greater good.

"Everyone believes that they are in the right: the peasantry and nobility and holy alike. We believe our atrocities are the righteous ones, and that we're the martyrs of our own world. Do you believe that, Kendrick? Do you believe in virtuous sins?"

Kendrick doesn't answer. What can he say to that?

Sir Algor sighs and drops his self-reflection. He moves himself back into the present with Kendrick and grips his forearm tighter. Kendrick feels his humanity through his touch.

"We don't live in a perfect world," says Sir Algor. "But you stick with me, we'll improve it together. We won't have that prick commander forever."

"I hope not." Kendrick snorts. For the first time since that morning, Kendrick releases a full smile. It feels good. *Really good.* Sir Algor glistens back.

"You know," admits Sir Algor honestly, "if you smile like that to your noblewoman, you may win her over yet."

Kendrick quickly shrugs off a tear before it can leave his eyes. "Thank you."

"Grant me luck," says Sir Algor, huffing, pumping himself up.

They release from their grasp, but Kendrick imagines a piece of Sir Algor's soul lingers with him. Sir Algor stands and dusts off his armor. He ties his scabbard back around his waist. He winks at Kendrick, turns, and stomps away. Kendrick watches his mentor—

No. My friend.

Kendrick watches his friend exit up the stairs.

The squire glances down into the tankard of ale and swishes the brown liquid around. He tries to picture Lucia on the night he ran into her, if anything to just ignore Eliot who slinks around in his peripherals.

Lucia, the fairest maiden I have ever seen . . .

Kendrick was crossing a majestic courtyard, packed to the brim with the bodies of the inebriated and the sweat of the jolly. The stone courtyard was painted a myriad of vibrant colors beneath his feet, making him feel like he was walking on a rainbow. The exotic outfits of Duke Rowan's guests matched the courtyard's flair for the flamboyant. Many of the noblemen wore hoses that wrapped tightly around their legs, exposing their muscles bare underneath, with a girdle that tied it up to their breeches. Unlike the lower-class populace, a new style was emerging with the wealthy fops that emphasized form-fitted outfits. Most of the men were embracing this style, wearing tunics of the softest silks with impressive wool patterns sewn into them. Their tunics were strapped close to their bodies with leather belts, and the arms of their tunics were trimmed to close perfectly around their wrists. They wore pointy, polished shoes that Kendrick humored could poke a hole in someone if they weren't careful. The noblewomen were just as ornately dressed. They had lustrous dresses of varied cuts and lengths—many reached down to the stone floor and spread away from their feminine source like a melting candle, while others were trimmed to a close right above their ankles—and their hair was covered with veils, barbettes, and wimples based on their preferences. Kendrick noticed that many of the older women wore traditional veils that covered the top, back, and sides of their hair, while younger maidens trended toward the more stylish barbettes and wimples, which had more freedom in design. Many women also had makeup on, whitening their skin to appear purer and more beautiful. That was a shame to Kendrick, since he has always had a thing for darker skinned women. He was certainly in the minority on that front, though. To tie their outfits all together, almost every woman carried flamboyant bags and purses to carry their various expensive items, and the richest among them wore jewelry, mainly necklaces and rings, which shined and gleamed with silver and golden rays under the fading daylight.

As Kendrick made his way through this swarm of slithering bodies, careful to avoid accidentally stepping on some maiden's dress or spilling some count's drink, while listening to the band play somewhere in the distance and watching the nobles dance terribly, he felt a tinge of sadness as the night evaporated the daylight. The sunrise is so much better.

Distracted thusly about the decline of the day, Kendrick rammed into the back of some woman a good bit shorter than himself. Kendrick quickly apologized and steadied her before she fell to the ground. He babbled as fast as he could about how it was an accident and how he would never mean to slam into such a fair, sophisticated woman and all the other rubbish he could think of before she deigned him whipped and beaten for the offense.

Then Lucia turned around.

Her sharp, hungry eyes and gentle, narrow lips shrunk Kendrick before her as if she were the one towering over him. Her hair wasn't covered, a sign of loose morals that generally equated to a bachelorette or prostitute. Kendrick guessed the first. While she wore the whitening makeup that many of the women did, he could tell she had a darker complexion under it. But most of all, there was something in the way she held herself. She was just stampeded from the back, blindsided by a much bigger man, yet she stood firm in front of him, unshaken and, frankly, a little intimidating.

Oh, I'm in trouble.

Of course, Lucia ended up being much more benevolent than most would have been. Kendrick likes to believe that it was because she was instantly attracted to him, but the more likely cause is that she's honestly that forgiving. She did give him a lot of grief for it later though, in the privacy of her own bedchamber.

Kendrick shakes his head and comes back to the present. He smells the clean air of the storm and allows his posture to decline momentarily as he bends over the bar. He downs the rest of his ale. Eliot still lurks for him under the stairs. Kendrick decides to take care of his horse as a distraction.

Fortune has been nothing but good for him, and she rubbed her head against his leg numerous times on the ride here from the battle ground. She was trying to cheer him up. Horses are so smart.

I can't wait until the sun rises again. Tomorrow I get to see Lucia. Maybe I can convince her to come with Fortune and I, and we can get far away from this sinful land.

V INCENT STANDS NEXT TO Sugarplum, the horse they borrowed from the stablemaster in Newmanton. He, too, is a fellow conspirator; lately, it seems like more and more people are. Rain drips down between the wooden shingles covering Warin's stables, and Vincent lets the hollow sound of it ring through his turbulent mind.

Fraunce ostracized Vincent from the dining table, forcing him to attend to Sugarplum in the stables like Vincent is some kind of petulant child. That isn't what upsets Vincent the most, though. It's the fact that Fraunce is making the decision to kill that knight. It hadn't even been a whole day, and Vincent has already failed at keeping Fraunce from doing any more harm. It's difficult for Vincent to speak when he's going up against Oswyn, Vivian, Edmond, and Fraunce. The four of them are so set on their thoughts about the nobility and the knights that Vincent finds he even doubts himself. Maybe they really are that bad?

You must maintain your goodness . . .

The mantra reverberates throughout him. His confrontation with the priest, the conversation that had filled him with so much enthusiasm for the future, seems a distant memory now.

Thunder rocks the walls around the stable. Sugarplum neighs and shakes her body in response, stomping her hooves and pulling on the picket line. The two, more majestic, horses next to Sugarplum glare at her like she's a foal. Vincent pets her long neck.

"'Tis fine. The storm scares me too," consoles Vincent.

There *is* something different about this storm. The springtime always accompanies the worst of the weather, but this one is different, unnatural even. It feels divine. Maybe it's the way it simultaneously strikes fear and awe in his heart, or maybe it's how it manages to make Vincent feel stuck in time. The rest of the world seems so distant, like they're stranded on some patch of land way out in the endless sea. There's no escape. There's only the *now* and all the horror that insinuates.

Vincent pets his horse again.

The door to the stables opens. Vincent glances around Sugarplum and spots the squire. Vincent freezes, a sudden gust of panic pushes him against the wall. He backs up against the logs of firewood that surround the room. They rumble as they roll off to the side. The squire jerks his head and catches Vincent stumbling clumsily out of the wood pile. He must be able to discern the panic on Vincent's face because he raises his hands and reveals his palms in a gentle act of submission.

"I won't do anything to you," says the squire as he slowly ambles toward Vincent.

He stops next to the two horses next to Sugarplum. Vincent should have known those were the knights' horses. Their saddles and breeds betray the wealth divide between Vincent and this squire. Now that Vincent is up close to him, he realizes how similar in age and size the two of them are. Vincent maneuvers to the far side of Sugarplum, using the horse to block himself from the squire. He's careful to not accidentally look him in the eyes.

"That your horse?" asks the squire, digging into his saddle bag and bringing out a brush.

Vincent stays silent. His friends are currently murdering this squire's master. Vincent feels the flood of complex emotions rising in him again.

Did that knight deserve being killed?

Vincent didn't see him do anything deserving of it, and something about him seems oddly familiar. But his friends also made good points: the knights had set their village on fire, they killed people who ran away, they forced peasants to pay money, and they stole brides-to-be.

They have done all those things, right?

"She's a good breed," says the squire pointedly, nodding to Sugarplum. She puffs out air at him. The squire lets a smile slip. "It's surprising to see a peasant own such a steed."

"Not ours," whispers Vincent before he can stop himself.

"Pardon?" The squire's voice has renewed enthusiasm, as if he were desperately hoping Vincent would talk back. Vincent curses under his breath. Now he has to speak.

"The horse master lent her to us," says Vincent.

"You heading for the royal wedding tomorrow?"

"I ain't supposed to talk to knights."

"Don't fret then. I'm not a knight yet, just a squire."

"Look the same to me," says Vincent, taking note of his dilapidated armor.

"True enough," he chuckles. "What's your name?"

Vincent glances at the squire's eyes. He asked him for his name . . . surely a being as terrible as a knight wouldn't care for his name? Vincent squints his eyes, trying to read the squire, to figure out what he's up to. He has to be up to something.

Maintain goodness.

Vincent shakes his head. He turns away from the squire and rubs his horse aimlessly. He can't tell him his name; it'll get Vincent in trouble. Oswyn, Vivian, and Edmond will be furious at him, and even worse, Fraunce will be disappointed.

"What do you have against knights?" the squire asks as he brushes his horse. He really does have a beautiful steed.

"Ye are all murderers and thieves, uncaring of us folk," blurts Vincent. It comes off stilted, almost rehearsed. Vincent cringes at his own voice.

"Is that what you believe? Or do you just repeat what others say?" The squire turns to look at him, but Vincent hides behind Sugarplum's stocky body.

"'Tis what me knows."

"How's that?"

The squire steps around Sugarplum, and his scent hits Vincent's nose. A strong, powerful, earthy tone with some tinge of vinegar. Vincent shoots back against the wall; the logs tumble around him once again. His heart races in his ears, and his hand reaches instinctually for the knife pressed to his thighs by his breeches.

Vincent whips the dagger out before he has time to think through the consequences. Sugarplum neighs and kicks back with her hind legs. Her tail slaps the squire, which pushes him toward Vincent's knife. But the squire stomps his feet into the floor, skidding straw into the air, and stops his momentum before he penetrates himself. He throws his hands up again. Vincent has yet to catch his breath. The world rumbles around him.

"Hey! Careful with that," stammers the squire.

"Stay away!" warns Vincent with a voice that is probably more timid than intimidating.

The stable door swings open. Vincent and the squire whirl in time to see Warin hurl Leif into the room by the back of his neck. Leif tumbles across the dirt floor and careens into a stack of firewood. The logs rupture and collapse on top of the poor kid. One log hits him on the head.

"Sorry, pa," cries Leif.

The boy tries to stand, but Warin rumbles to him and backhands him across the face. The hard slap thunders out and is instantly swallowed by the storm. Leif falls onto his back. The husky innkeeper towers over the boy like a boulder, round and opposing.

"Ye stay away from that swine, ye hark?!" Warin says. "Ye stay away from him. That bard will get you killed." Leif grovels at the feet of his father. Warin shoves him with his foot. "Now get up. Stop ye cryin'."

"Hey!"

Vincent watches with utter shock as the squire clocks the innkeeper across the temple. Vincent was so enthralled by Warin's actions that he didn't notice the squire sneaking his way behind the innkeeper. Warin flies backward from the squire's blow. His colossal frame crashes *through* the wall. The planks sunder and break backward, exposing Warin to the ailments of the storm. *God, that squire must be strong!*

"Don't you hurt your boy. *Ye hark?!*" the squire says.

There's goodness in everything . . .

Vincent's jaw drops as he watches from behind Sugarplum. The squire postures over the big man now. Warin groans and tries to move, but he's firmly wedged between two planks.

The bard flies through the stable door. His movements are frantic. His eyes dart around the room until they finally settle on Leif. Vincent can tell he must really care for the boy. Strange. Why would that be?

The bard helps the boy up and tells him to leave the room. Leif rushes out, and the bard asks the squire what happened. To Vincent's surprise, the bard then pries Warin out of the wall. Vincent notices the stable door creak open a crack as the bard shoves the innkeeper out the back door. *It's Leif.*

Leif watches the bard and his father disappear out the back door, before he vanishes back into the main room.

The squire stands alone now in the aftermath of the mayhem. A few burning candles highlight him before the hole in the wall where the storm and wind can be seen swirling out there in the abyss. The squire walks back to his horse.

Vincent and he make eye contact for the briefest of moments, then the squire turns back to combing his steed. He actively avoids glancing at Vincent now. He removes his chainmail and sits it above the horse. He fixes the saddle so it sits properly again. He doesn't glance at Vincent once. Vincent tries to read his expression. But, as it turns out, it's much more difficult to understand a stranger than a loved one, and all Vincent can tell is that the squire is distracted, or maybe lost.

"Vincent," says Vincent.

The squire peeks up at him. It takes a moment for him to catch on. When he does, he smiles. "Vincent. I'm Kendrick. It's a pleasure to meet you."

"Ye too," says Vincent, and he means it.

Kendrick is the proof Vincent was searching for. A knight, well, the squire of a knight, saved someone. It's only one act of kindness—Vincent understands that well enough—and one act of good nature isn't any more a germination of mass kindness than one act of evil is of mass corruption, but he only needed proof both sides exist. Now he knows.

"I'm terribly sorry about whatever we did to you and your kin," says Kendrick. There's a sorrow in his own voice. Vincent has gotten accustomed to experiencing that sound, so he recognizes it instantly. "Some of us want to make a real difference."

Vincent smiles. It is the first time he ever smiled to a squire . . . knight . . . anyone of any nobility actually. It feels good too. And Kendrick smiles back at him. A genuine smile, more human than any Vincent has seen in recent memory. Maybe the most genuine smile since his Mum . . .

"Perhaps we could even be friends one day," says Kendrick.

Yes. We can.

The stable door flings open yet again, only this time Vincent's heart jumps into his chest when he sees who enters.

"Fraunce?" stutters Vincent. Kendrick turns as Fraunce rushes over to them.

"We got to go," orders Fraunce.

"I wasn't—" starts Vincent, desperate for Fraunce to not be disappointed. Maybe he can show him that Kendrick is good. Maybe he can convince his brother to not go to the wedding tomorrow.

"Never mind that. Let's go." Fraunce grabs Vincent's tunic and drags him away from Kendrick. Vincent stomps his feet petulantly and tries to glance back at Kendrick.

"It was a pleasure to make your acquaintance," says Kendrick. His older brother halts in his tracks. He twists Vincent around so he can face Kendrick.

"We want nothin' to do with you," says his brother. Fraunce's voice is venomous and snarly, like a beast that's trapped in a corner.

"Fraunce—" whines Vincent, trying to snuff the confrontation before it gets violent. He knows it will. It always gets violent.

"We want no trouble."

"Neither do I, sir," says Kendrick in a gentle, submissive voice.

"Good. Then ye should know why to leave us be."

Kendrick nods in response. His older brother and the squire stare each other down for a few seconds. Vincent tries to open his mouth to apologize, but Fraunce drags him away.

"He was just bein' nice," mumbles Vincent under his breath.

"It matters not. It's dangerous to be around 'em. What if the others saw ye?" says Fraunce, his voice full of actual concern.

"What do you mean?" whispers Vincent as they cross into the common room. Fraunce places his hands on both of Vincent's shoulders. He leans down to get inches from Vincent's face.

"I love ye."

"Me knows," says Vincent. He searches his brother's expression, reading every minute feeling that crosses it. His brother is really scared of something. But of what? Vivian, Edmond, and Oswyn? *They wouldn't hurt us. They be our friends.*

"I will get you out of this," declares Fraunce. "I promise. But ye need to listen to me very carefully, ye hark?"

"What's wrong?"

"Nothin' ye can't fix." Fraunce smiles. Vincent frowns. His older brother puts too much of his happiness on Vincent. He knows he can never live up to it. "Just stay at the table for a while, ye hark?"

Fraunce rubs Vincent's head. Vincent nods. He starts to cross over to the table near the front door, but Vincent stops as he understands he needs to say one last thing.

"He really is nice," states Vincent.

Fraunce stares at him with an odd expression, one Vincent *can't* actually read, so Vincent looks away and meanders back to the table. Oswyn still sits at it, and he chows down on the pottage. He grimaces as Vincent sits down.

"Me could make this so much better," Oswyn whines. "How do they forget the salt? It's bloody pottage."

Vincent sighs and rests his chin on the table. How is he going to convince Fraunce? The only thing Vincent has convinced anyone of was for Fraunce to save his own life, but that was simple compared to this. It's a frightening world when it's easier to save someone's life than it is to change their mind.

Vincent watches his brother cross to the staircase where Edmond and Vivian stand.

The bard hurries back to his corner seat from the stables. Kendrick enters after him. Vincent waits for Warin to hobble through the door as well, but he never does. Strange. The squire sits back down at his barstool.

A sadness climbs over Vincent as he stares at Kendrick, who looks strikingly alone and forgotten. Vincent's leg drums against his seat as he tries to suppress a pressing need to be friendly to Kendrick. Something is bothering the squire, that much is clear, and he needs someone to help him through it. Why can't that person be Vincent?

Vincent stands up from the table. Oswyn gives him a funny expression but says nothing. Vincent takes a quick peek at his older brother. Fraunce seems to be in a heated discussion with Edmond. Unfortunately, there's nothing unusual about that. Fraunce and Edmond have been getting more and more agitated with one another over the last few months as the wedding has drawn nearer. *He won't notice,* decides Vincent.

Vincent scurries across the common room. The hay on the ground sticks to his bare legs as he kicks up the straw. Vincent didn't realize how much he was sweating. Every bit of grime and dirt clamps to his skin. Vincent taps the squire on the shoulder.

"Vincent?"

"Me wanted to apologize for me brother."

"He was trying to protect you, as a brother should."

"Ye be right," admits Vincent.

"About what?"

"I repeat what others say. Me needs to make my own decisions. Then maybe me can convince others to follow."

"And have you made your decision?"

"Yes." Vincent smiles. Kendrick grins back. He sticks out his arm. Vincent stares at it, bewildered.

"You're supposed to grab it," says Kendrick.

Vincent grasps Kendrick's forearm, and the squire does the same to him. Kendrick has a firm grip, so Vincent tries to squeeze tighter. It doesn't feel like he will ever match his strength.

"Hopefully we'll run into each other at the wedding tomorrow. I'd much rather spend the time with someone more normal. Sir Algor and I aren't admirers of the noble," confesses Kendrick.

Vincent's heart drops into his stomach. Kendrick's voice grew soft and purposeful when he mentioned the knight, and the reality that the squire's life will be irrevocably changed looms over Vincent. This is because of *him*. Vincent and his friends did this to Kendrick. Vincent represses the urge to vomit his pottage.

"You all right?" asks Kendrick with real concern. Vincent's face must be blanching. Vincent nods his head. He fights for control over his throat.

"Yes. Me should get back."

Vincent hurries to the table. He doesn't dare glance back at Kendrick. It will hurt him too much. Edmond and Vivian return to the table at the same time as Vincent. Edmond glares at him, and Vincent becomes self-conscious under the stare. Fraunce sits at the table across from him. The table goes quiet with the unspoken, as if a heavy weight has fallen on them all. The ceiling suddenly has an eerie shallowness to it, like it's slowly crushing down on them. Vincent imagines the dead knight upstairs, pushing down on the ceiling and putting a dent into it. The terrifying sight of an acidic body eating through the floor, gushing and spitting its foulness as it slops to the ground, overtakes Vincent's imagination. He stares out the window to banish that abhorrent thought from his mind.

Vincent stares off in space a lot, not really ever thinking about one specific thing, but usually mulling over many things or nothing at all. He is always at the two extremes. As Vincent stares out at the storm, he determines that this time he will think about nothing. His mind has been too busy the last few days. He'll simply watch.

The storm shrouds most of the view. Like they're behind a waterfall, a torrent of rainwater sprinkles down in fat drops from the roof. Occasionally, the sky flares to life, and the flat darkness bursts into a world full of depth and ghoulish shapes. In those brief moments when the heavens crack, between the skinny openings the torrent allows, Vincent espies the woodlands far in the distance and the rolling hills that go on and on forever. There is so much life hiding out there. It seems slightly less forlorn knowing there are people like Kendrick who, at the very least, are *trying* to do good deeds.

"Shit," hisses Edmond.

Vincent turns away from the window, from the fresh smell of the storm and the cool breath of its embrace, and glares into the stuffy heat of the inn, to the object of Edmond's vulgarism . . . to the pool of blood over Kendrick's head.

INNOCENT RETRIBUTION

<hr>

"**P**ERFECT. I WAS FAMISHED," says Kendrick.

He leans his scabbard against the bar. Edith watches him intently. He ignores the need to ask her why; perhaps, to her, this is a way of showing genuine hospitality. Still, it's a little weird for her to stare at him while he eats, especially right after she forced him to move over one barstool. Maybe she feels awkward for sleeping with Sir Algor? Kendrick strips a knife from his belt and uses it to take a bite.

It's terrible. The pottage burns his tongue, and his tastebuds instantly vanish into nothingness. Actually, that might be a good thing. Now he can swallow without tasting it. How do they forget the salt? Kendrick smiles anyway. He's unsure if Edith is the one who cooked it or not, and he's better off not vexing his mentor's muse. He slices another clump into his mouth.

"Mmm. This is a fine good meal, madam." Kendrick grins, hoping it is half-convincing. "Succulent as any food I've ever had."

"Glad ye like it, sir."

Edith quickly sweeps away something on the counter. Probably some dirt. Luckily, it isn't very hard for Kendrick to feign interest in the food; he *is* starving after all. He hasn't eaten since before Eliot showed up. Kendrick glances around the room for him. He isn't anywhere to be seen. Kendrick sighs with relief, which Edith seems to take as a sigh of enjoyment. Being able to talk with Sir Algor and that Vincent fellow had grounded Kendrick back to reality. The regret and self-hatred still brews inside of him, but the two of them have somehow made it a little easier. He's grateful for that.

"If ye need anythin' else, let me or Warin know," says Edith.

"Thank you, madam." Kendrick smiles at her warmly.

Splat.

Kendrick flinches. Something wet hits his face. His hand instinctively braces in front of him. The liquid rolls down his cheek. Kendrick furrows his brow, confused by the warmth of it. It's not cold enough to be rain, but what else could have hit him if not rainwater?

Thunder silences the room. The stool groans under Kendrick as he shifts his weight to wipe the liquid off his cheek. Kendrick lowers his hand. A dark maroon substance seeps into his hand. Kendrick tilts his head. His mind can't process what it is. Maybe blood? Did one of his head wounds reopen? He watches it soak into the back of his hand, transforming his skin to a darker hue.

Another drip hits him.

Kendrick jolts back, the barstool firing out from beneath him like some siege weapon. Kendrick loses his breath. The world constricts down upon him, and Eliot cackles at Kendrick like a loony. Kendrick glares up at the ceiling. His heart races faster than his mind can think. The lumber contorts under the force of crimson blood, and drips of it commingle with rain as it falls into this terrible plane.

Kendrick glares at Edith. Her lips quiver.

No, no, no, no . . .

Kendrick's mind never catches up with his body as he tears his sword from its scabbard. He pulls it out with so much force that it slices through the leather compartment. Eliot continues to cackle, rolling and writhing on the ground, his head separate from his body. Kendrick ignores him and sprints up the stairs.

He charges into a long hallway that stretches to the far side of the inn where a single window peeks out into the bleakness outside. There are four doors, and Kendrick takes a second to orient himself. It ends up being a foolish thing to do, though, since one of the doors is already ajar with its hinges kicked in. This is no time for thinking anyway. It's his duty to protect his knight. But more than that, it is his responsibility to help his friends.

Kendrick pushes open the door, ready to provide instant aid to Sir Algor. All he is greeted with is an empty, damp chamber. The window explodes with light, igniting a series of sparkles as the glare shimmers off dust particles which flitter from the ceiling beams. An intense rotten smell, like cheese left out in the heat for far too long, lingers in the air. Another scent similar to burning hair wafts toward Kendrick as well. He forces himself into the moist bedchamber.

He steps slowly. The floorboards creak under him, as if straining for him to not walk any closer, to not discover what is hidden past its boundaries. But he must. Sir Algor saved his life; he has to repay the favor. The bed at the far end of the space is in shambles, with its straw-filled mattress and animal-skin blankets discarded haphazardly over it. The light from the hallway casts a sharp beam into the pitch-black bedchamber, and a metallic object in the far corner redirects that light into Kendrick's eyes.

One of the door hinges.

Kendrick closes the door behind him. It doesn't make much logical sense to do so, but some animalistic part of him needs to be in the dark. Kendrick steps forward again, only this time, his foot slips momentarily on something. He holds the sword out in front of him, as if to slay whatever slimy monster made him stumble.

It isn't a monster, however, but a stagnant black pool on the floor. No light reflects off its opaque surface. It could be fathomless for all Kendrick knows. His mind finally finds some logic to grapple on to, and it tells him that can't be the case; but Kendrick ignores the soundness of logic and embraces the chaos of savagery. He gazes into the depths of the black pool and accepts the urge to touch it. He slides the tip of his sword through the darkness, and the thick, black liquid pulls at his blade as if it wants to drag it into its bowels. Kendrick proves stronger and lifts the sword before his eyes.

Lightning flashes and reveals it to be Kendrick's worse nightmare. Dark red blood.

Kendrick drops the sword. The serenity of his ignorance vanishes as he knows exactly what happened. Kendrick falls back against the door, almost pushing it into the hallway, and slinks to the ground. He grabs at his hair and hyperventilates. Tears build in his eyes as he accepts the truth.

That's so much blood.

Kendrick squeezes his eyelids closed, begging, hoping the world will magically revert back to how it was that morning. He prays for the sunlight of a new day, for the warmth and excitement dawn brings.

"He's riding next to me," Kendrick mumbles through streaking tears. "He's right next to me. We're in the fields. The sun is rising. Sheep are roaming. Hills are rolling. Sir Algor. He's next to me. He's next to me . . . "

But he's not, and the truth of reality buries into Kendrick like the fangs of a snake. It injects the venomous combination of pity, grief, and anger, which courses through his veins. His eyes scorch in his skull while fiery tears leave an ashy trail down his face.

Kendrick bursts up from the floor. Blinded by the fury of desperation, he overturns the bed in a vain hope of finding Sir Algor hiding beneath it. He hurls the nightstand against the wall where it explodes into a shower of splinters. It was the only thing left in the chamber, but the destructiveness of the bereaved has no remorse, and so the nightstand was doomed for demolition. Kendrick flies to the open window, eyes squinting, rain assaulting, as he searches hopelessly to find Sir Algor in that great beyond.

"Algor!" screams Kendrick into the thrust of wind.

Water soaks his face, and Kendrick has no inclination whether it is tears or rain. He stares out into the storm. Sir Algor is gone. He was destroyed here, in this very room. Whoever had committed the crime had even managed to hide the body. Kendrick's mind, desperate to stay active, scans through a list of suspects.

He knows Edith was with Algor, but something inexplicable tells him it wasn't her. He isn't particularly good at reading people, and he has no reason to believe he is an adequate judge of character, but Edith has a simplicity about her that tells Kendrick to not suspect her. She is probably a victim in all of this.

Who does that leave?

Kendrick doesn't have a clue. Sir Algor warned him about those peasants by the front door. *Vincent is a member of that group,* remembers Kendrick. He shakes his head. Vincent is too innocent to kill, and he definitely seems too timid to ride with murderers. *Besides,* reasons Kendrick, *he was with me in the stables.* There's also the bard, but Kendrick knows he was with Leif and Warin. That's everyone, as far as Kendrick knows.

Wait, wasn't there some man by the hearth when we came in?

Kendrick tries to think back, but the day has turned into a giant blur in his memory. It could have been his imagination. Hell, it could have been Eliot.

His mind exhausted, Kendrick gives up on the detective work. He kneels beside the dark pool. The blood spreads to his knees and soils his leather armor. A tear falls from his eye and splashes into the gore. The wind dies down outside the window, allowing for a brief respite from the noisy calamity. The soft, repetitive *thud* of rain hitting the roof is all he can hear.

This is a world of life or death. When we have an advantage over death, we must take it. Always.

Commander Rayner's words sound in the depths of Kendrick's soul. He is right. A shudder moves through Kendrick as he accepts the commander's words as truth.

The world isn't kind to us. People want us killed.

A second truth. Sir Algor had told Kendrick that. He didn't want to believe that one was true, but now it seems that he has been proven wrong yet again. It should have been Kendrick that died, not Sir Algor, the experienced knight. The world seems so drastically different from how it was this morning, when he was riding atop Fortune looking at the fresh dew. His reality has been mutilated since then, carved out and trampled on like some gladiatorial sport.

We must take it. Always.

Kendrick's nostrils flare. His neck pulses. His hands shake. He glares at his sword.

He is no longer a boy. He must become a knight.

Kendrick picks up his bloodied sword and stomps across the pool. He pulls open the door. He needs to suppress this upheaval. He needs to find who did this to Sir Algor. He has only one lead, and he will make her talk.

Kendrick descends the stairs, one step at a time. The common room has remained quiet. He stops on the final step, his body still drenched from his confrontation with the storm. He appraises the room. Everyone is silent and unmoved, as if the world had frozen over while Kendrick was away from it. Kendrick steps in front of the hearth and stares into its blazing fire. His knuckles scream at him to loosen his grip on the handle, but he finds that it is particularly hard to do that. His muscles w*ant* this fight. Kendrick takes a deep breath, watching the fire jump around in the stone encasing. He convinces himself that he must do this.

He trained to become a knight, and a knight dispenses justice. He isn't doing this out of revenge and anger. He's doing this because it's his destiny.

"You. You were with him last."

Kendrick turns to face Edith. She shakes her head. He has to be forceful, powerful, like Commander Rayner. Kendrick rushes up to her. She slinks against the wall. Only one person has ever looked at Kendrick with such fear, and that person is likely watching him this very moment, in this very room. Everything has come to a head on this day. He never thought he'd have to make two decisions that would decide his life on the same day. The glacier that encases his heart will be reinforced yet again.

Kendrick searches for any sign from the bar maiden. Edith holds strong. She's clearly in distress, but she doesn't back down from him. He quashes an uneasy feeling starting to build in his gut. He hates that he has to do this, but he must. He swore fealty. Someone killed Sir Algor, damnit! He has to stop them.

"He loved you." Kendrick's voice trembles.

"He thought he did." Edith's voice trembles back.

"He did."

"I'm so sorry."

Kendrick tries to keep back tears, but it only forces more to leak. He keeps his eyes pinned on Edith as he leans in to whisper to her.

"I know it wasn't you," says Kendrick softly, praying that she'll make this easy for him. "Edith, don't let me hurt the wrong person. Just look at who it was."

She doesn't answer. Her eyes stay defiantly on him. *Blasted woman! I may have already killed the wrong person today, don't make me do it again.*

"Please," he begs.

"You can let it go. You don't have to hurt anyone."

Why would you say that? This isn't about me.

"Edith, just look."

"Don't make me do this," she whispers. Kendrick ignores the part of him that cries out for him to stop. Everything is too far gone now.

"Look."

He stares intently into her eyes. They tremble together in mutual dismay. *Please, Edith, please.*

"Look."

She sticks out her chin at him. *Why are you making me do this?!*

"LOOK!"

Her eyes finally flicker to someone else in the room. Kendrick spins to face the perpetrator, his sword ready to strike down—

"V-Vincent?" stammers Kendrick, utterly baffled.

Vincent stands alone next to the stairs. Kendrick's mind fights with itself. It's not possible. Vincent was with him. Kendrick glances back at Edith, but she says nothing. Kendrick glares back at the peasant.

His name is Vincent. He's more than a peasant.

Exactly, he's a killer.

Kendrick raises his sword. His shoulders and arms burn from the weight of it. He's so tired. It'll all end soon.

"How could you?" questions Kendrick. "Did you do it before or after our talk?"

Kendrick steps toward Vincent, who doesn't move from his place. Kendrick waits for Edith to say something, to tell him that it wasn't Vincent, to say he doesn't have to kill two innocent-looking people in one day. She doesn't.

"You did this to me?" cries Kendrick. His blood boils as he thinks of Sir Algor. They were going to achieve so much together. They were going to make things right. They were going to follow the Codes of Chivalry and act the way knights should. And now he's dead. "Why?"

Vincent puts his hands up and shakes his head. Kendrick steps within sword reach of him.

Respond to me!

Kendrick huffs. He raises his sword, ready to put all his weight behind the slice and sever this murderer in half.

"Why did you kill him?!"

"Not him," says a voice from the peasant table. Vincent's brother steps forward. *This makes more sense,* decides Kendrick.

He moves his blade to face this new foe. "What do you know of this?"

"'Twas me who killed the knight."

Kendrick lowers his blade slightly. His words devour Kendrick's soul. So, Sir Algor *is* dead. No matter how stupid it was, some part of Kendrick still hoped he was alive. At least now he knows who it was. Now he can dispense justice.

The man looks at Vincent and smiles. He's smiling?! Why would he smile at something like this?!

"It was me," says the peasant boldly. "Don't hurt him. Vincent is pure. He's the kindest soul I've ever known. He would never—"

Kendrick doesn't think. He acts.

Kendrick thrusts his sword through the peasant's stomach.

It is too easy. The tip punctures skin, muscle, and bone alike with the ease of cutting through water. All of the man's body seems to sever before the blade. He hears bones crack and tendons rip. When the tip jettisons out Fraunce's back, bits of spine and offal spray out onto his fellow peasants behind him. The man slumps to the earth and convulses over himself. Kendrick snarls.

He shreds the sword from the twitching corpse. The sound of steel slicing skin rattles in the room. Justice has been done.

OBVIOUS REVELATIONS

VINCENT STANDS STILL, GRIPPED by the unexpected zap of shock. Fraunce falls to the ground. His body writhes as life spills out of him. Fraunce twists his head up, and the two brothers share one final moment.

Fraunce's body quits. His head slams into the dirt. He never moves again.

Shock holds Vincent in its clutches. Not even a single emotion of sorrow rises to the surface, only disbelief. His older brother is alive one moment and gone the next, slaughtered by that demon with the face of a savior.

"Ye killed our mate!" Edmond launches from his seat, flourishing his dagger.

Vivian jumps up from her seat and points her knife at the squire. Kendrick waves his sword back and forth between them. "You're all killers, ye lot," says Vivian.

"And now he aims to kill us!" Edmond moans theatrically.

"I don't," cries Kendrick. He steps back from them. "I brought justice to the man who killed my friend."

"Justice?" squeals Vivian. "Ye didn't even question him. Ye were out for blood, like all ye filthy knights."

She's right, thinks Vincent as he remains aloof from the conflict. His eyes keep lingering on Fraunce's discarded corpse. Life is so easily dispatched.

Vincent flashes back to the night they lost their parents, their town, and their innocence. Vincent has fought viciously over the years to reattain it. Now, all that work has vanished in an instant. He's never been so wrong in all his life. Only a fool could believe in preserving goodness through this.

Oswyn stands. He takes out his knife and joins the other two. They slowly circle around Kendrick, who pivots between the three of them.

The bard still sits in the corner, rocking back and forth on his chair like some lunatic. Edith stands behind the bar. She looks every bit as shocked as Vincent.

The first wave of reality blasts into Vincent like a flurry of wind. He has no family left. He is the only survivor of his line. All he has left of Fraunce is his dream of assassinating Duke Rowan, and whether they succeed or fail, that'll end tomorrow. All he'll have after that is his memories, and those have been particularly dark these last few years. The happiness they held in childhood is long gone, perverted by knights on that fateful night seven years ago. Now that happiness is finally brutalized to death by the next generation of the duke's knighthood.

For the first time in his life, Vincent understands the full extent of hatred.

PARIS WATCHES THE SQUIRE pierce the farmer from a peephole in Chamber 1. One of the planks on the floorboards has a circular hole that spies down onto the common room below them. The burning blood he felt before killing the knight shoots through his veins again.

Vivian and Edmond jump up from their table, and a primal need to join with the turning tide holds Paris hostage. He has never been one to be influenced by the whims of the mob. He isn't introverted necessarily . . . just private about his personal affairs. He has a simple life, or rather, he *wants* a simple life. A life away from conflict, where he can spend his days resting alongside Verona on those long summer nights.

But Paris can't deny it, it feels good to be connected with these other people, connected by their common enemy in life: the knights, the nobility, the royalty.

Paris is starting to understand what their coup is all about. Together they are strong, and together they have meaning. Yes, it feels *really good.*

Verona moans in the bed. Her symptoms, which were so deadly before, have slowly been decreasing. Even the strong, odorous scent is fading away. Paris can once again smell Verona's lovely fragrance, the one he wakes up to each morning that rejuvenates him for the day ahead. He didn't realize how enchanting her natural smell truly was, nor the power it held to make him believe in life again, not until it was stripped away. Edith's remedy worked. He will be indebted to her for the rest of his life. Edith is compassion personified. She's selfless, merciful, and, most of all, truly empathetic toward people. No matter if they were born between the legs of pristine royalty or a dirty street urchin, Edith would help them.

Now it's Paris's turn to help back.

Paris reaches into their last remaining burlap sack and pulls out Verona's knife. He cracks open the door, giving his wife a final glance, reminding himself, solidifying the integrity of his decision. These knights think they're above everyone else. They wanted to take his wife, to dehumanize her to nothing more than an item of pleasure for the "just" duke.

Paris can take his life into his own hands. He doesn't have to be impotent any longer. For this one night, Paris will take control of his own destiny. Tomorrow, if Verona fully recovers, they'll be with his parents and start life anew.

It's time to burn all allusions to the old one.

Paris moves into the hallway and closes the door behind him. A red handprint is left on the coarse wood. He looks down at his hands. Tiny slices are punctured into his palms, and blood slinks out between his fingers. The blood clotted beneath his nails reveals those to be the culprit. His nostrils flare. His body is ready for this. Holding on to Verona's dagger, Paris rushes down the stairs.

The last peasant at the table stands and takes out his knife. The squire now has three people surrounding him with weapons. The corpse of a peasant lies next to the hearth.

Paris halts at the bottom of the stairs. Vivian catches sight of him. Her eyes light up. "Join us," she says.

The squire swirls around to face him. Paris hesitates for a moment. Earlier in the night *he* was the one holding a sword. It isn't as comforting on the other side. No matter: he needs to commit.

Paris readies his knife and takes a step toward the squire. His limbs grow tense, and his fingers twitch to use the dagger. Vivian, Edmond, and the final peasant step forward. The squire swivels. He swings his sword to ward them off. The squire, now with his back to Paris, allows him the opportunity to step closer. The boy waves his sword around at Paris. They slowly surround him.

"Stay back," says the squire. "I want no harm."

"Hah. Too late for that, it is," sneers Vivian.

"He killed my friend!"

"Then ye killed ours," snarls Edmond. Vivian and Edmond glance at one another for a moment and make some unsaid decision. "Our most beloved friend," finishes Edmond sorrowfully.

The forlorn-looking boy who stares at the dead peasant glances up at those words. A tear falls off his chin, and Paris swears he spots the faintest hint of a smile. Paris steps closer to the squire.

"I just wanted to help," the squire says softly, his arms trembling.

"Help?" laughs Vivian. "Fine help ye've done."

The squire swings his sword, brushing back the onslaught. Sweat trickles down Paris's body. It feels like the hearth is evaporating the very air around them. The storm outside becomes a distant sensation, barely noticeable on the outskirts of their passion. The squire slices his blade through the air again.

"Take care where ye swing it, mate," says Edmond.

"Let me go. We'll forget all about this," begs the squire.

"Easy for you to say, after ye already killed one of us."

"My knight was murdered."

"So that be it then," Paris cuts in. The squire bends his head back to look at him. "A body for a body? Methought ye knights were supposed to be better than that."

"That be the hard truth," says the other peasant with a knife. "These knights are the worst sort. They pretend to be everythin' they are not. This boy is a murderer, a rapist, a thief."

"I'm not." The squire shakes his head.

Those words struck him, Paris realizes. He squashes the desire to smile. He shimmies his limbs loose as confidence rebuilds his strength. He smells the fear shedding off the squire. The other three conspirators must as well, as they circle in closer to the boy.

"I'll leave," says the squire. "I'll leave, and this can all be over."

"You think this stops?" questions Vivian harshly. "Oh no. 'Tis but the eve of a revolution. There be hundreds of us, in taverns across the land. T'morrow the duke will fall, and we will be free once more."

The four of them step closer, staying just out of the sword's reach. Paris is close enough to see the squire's turmoil. His bloodied armor and frantic movements reveal multiple openings for attack. The energy in the room changes. Paris feels connected, *truly connected*, with these people. They will make their own world, and it starts here with a dead knight Paris killed and his terrified squire. They hold unfathomable power.

He wrought his own destruction.

Paris's confidence crashes as the squire raises his sword, turns about, and lunges toward him. Paris trips over his heels and scurries backward. The squire's sword pierces down at him—

"AGH!"

The squire's sword rattles to the ground, unused and unthreatening. The squire falls to his knees right in front of Paris. Paris shoots up to his feet, his mind reeling from the squire's attack. He finally sees it.

The squire's hand lowers to the right side of his stomach, from which a knife handle protrudes. The squire's face blanches. He feels the gash in his side. It doesn't look terribly deep, but blood slinks down his side all the same. The boy tries to speak, but only a soft squeal leaves his mouth. He and Paris look up at the perpetrator.

Vincent stands there, hand bloodied, with a quivering chin and perplexed look. He glares at his dagger in the squire's side.

◦◦──◆──◦◦

"WOOHOO!" SHOUTS EDMOND IN jubilee. "That's how you do it, boy!"

"Vincent . . . ?" moans Kendrick, hands prying at the knife Vincent lodged into his side.

It was too easy to pierce through his armor. Vincent wasn't purposefully aiming for it at the time, but he must have sunk it right between the gap along the side of Kendrick's leather cuirass. Since the squire isn't wearing his chainmail, the weapon found its way into his body.

Edmond bounces up to Kendrick and shreds the knife from his side. Only about a quarter of the blade was bloodied, but Kendrick collapses onto his hands, nonetheless. Vincent observes the squire as he stares at his loss of blood. Vincent feels nothing. He didn't even grimace as the blade slid between skin and muscle under his command. Vincent shuns the shameful eyes of God. He shouldn't have any say in this matter. What would the priest think?

This is me retainin' my goodness. Now these brutes won't hurt anyone else.

Then it hits Vincent: the disbelief comes first, but that's quickly swept aside by the erosion of guilt.

Ye will rue this, Vincent's younger self says to him.

The remorse and shame stack on top of Vincent like bricks. These emotions grow heavier the longer he surveys the breadth of his destruction. And with his body failing to find an adequate way to release the tension of dismay, it resorts to buckling under the weight. His legs wobble, his gut vibrates, and his teeth chatter. His state of mind must have been obvious to everyone, as Vivian wraps her arms around Vincent and pulls his head into her bosom.

"'Tis fine, Vincent," she consoles. "Ye did it! Ye avenged your brother."

"Be proud, son," says Oswyn.

Vincent nods. Not to anyone in particular but to the cosmos so that they can disintegrate his penitence. To his surprise, they do. It comes in the form of indignation. Vincent glares down at the dying squire on the floor, and an umbrage coils inside Vincent's body like a nasty parasite.

"A real difference?" mocks Vincent, thinking back to their talk in the stables.

Kendrick looks away from him, too prideful to even accept his betrayal, no doubt. He's a liar and a wretch, the snake who convinced Vincent to bite into the fruit. Edmond, Vivian, Oswyn, Fraunce . . . they were all right about the knights, about the aristocrats, about the world. Now his older brother paid for Vincent's naivety with his life.

But why is there this naggin' part of me that still feels regretful?

Vincent buries that thought away. It's his youth trying to deceive him. He won't let it happen again. He can't. He needs to be a man now. Based off the examples Edmond and Oswyn set, that means being willing to do whatever it takes to secure your freedom from this oppression. Fraunce would want this from Vincent—to follow in his footsteps. Vincent will make sure he completes his brother's wish.

But he has to squash those pesky thoughts first, the ones attempting to bring him back to "goodness." They don't know what it means to be good in this world. They only know what it means to be stupid. Young and dumb.

Fraunce is dead, and while the grief hasn't struck him yet, Vincent knows he'll have to prepare for when it does. At least he has the other three, especially Edmond and Vivian.

Vincent didn't realize how much they cared about Fraunce until Kendrick slayed him. They were ready to give their lives to fight for Fraunce. They really loved his brother, and they really love him. It's an empowering feeling, one Vincent won't soon forget. There was a time when Vincent doubted the friendship Edmond and Vivian had shown to Fraunce. Something about it had appeared forced and manipulated, like the two of them were using Fraunce for some other purpose. But now he knows that was his misplaced morality once again, another "fact" that innocence had misinterpreted. Vincent should have never doubted them.

Vivian releases Vincent from her hug. Her warmth lingers with him for a benevolent moment, and the sweat from her skin glistens off his tunic. They are all connected in this inn, the one place that can bring all members of society together. It's the perfect place for Vincent to have learned the truth about humanity.

"Ye did good," Vivian says to him comfortingly.

Edmond nudges Kendrick with his foot. "Now what shall we do with ye?"

Kendrick doesn't respond. He's on all fours, but Vincent can't help but be impressed with how he keeps himself up. Vincent must have missed any lethal parts since Kendrick has yet to succumb to death.

He has to bleed out sooner or later.

"I say we stab him with his own sword," declares Edmond. "Give him the death he gave Fraunce."

"That'd be too quick for him," says Vivian. "Me suspects he won't be goin' anywhere. Let him think 'bout what he's done."

Vincent notices that Edith and the bard move uneasily after the comment. They aren't a part of the coup. Will they say anything, or report it to someone?

No, they can't.

They're stuck here in the storm with them. Besides, they are as culpable as them now. If anyone with higher power knows they stood around and watched someone within the knighthood get murdered, they would have them hanged or beheaded with the actual killers. Nothing that happened within this inn will escape.

"We should throw him out into the storm," says Edmond eagerly. "Let him think 'bout it out there."

"Me likes that plan," snickers Vivian.

Annoyance begins to sprout inside of Vincent. They are having a jolly time discussing ways to torture the squire, but there's something more important that needs to be taken care of.

"We need to clean Fraunce first," says Vincent bitterly. Oswyn nods his head in agreement. He was Fraunce's friend the longest. He understands.

Edmond and Vivian glance at one another, and, for a split second, Vincent swears he sees them debate it.

"'Course we do," smiles Vivian warmly. "Then we must bury him in consecrated ground."

"'Tis what our *leader* deserves," says Edmond, grimacing. Vincent doesn't pay it much mind. Everyone's emotions must be as jumbled as Vincent's. They cared about Fraunce as much as he did.

They stand in lamentable silence as Vincent approaches his brother's sprawled body, which extends across the floor. Strands of hay stick to Fraunce, and his blood congeals around him, giving him a ghastly red shadow. The fire from the hearth keeps his skin warm though, and from Vincent's angle, he almost looks alive. Almost.

Vincent bends down and flips his older brother over so his face isn't planted into the dirt. The wound through his stomach has stopped hemorrhaging, and now his body looks calm and serene. He could have been sleeping. Vincent waits for his grief to finally arise from deep within, for the lifetime of memories now locked in the past forever, to swirl through his mind like a fairy that he'll never be able to grasp. He waits for the pain . . . and waits . . . and waits. . . .

After a minute of staring at his brother, anticipating the despondency of sorrow, he realizes it won't come. Concern seizes hold of Vincent. Shouldn't he be crying by now? Doesn't he love his brother, for Christ's sake?! Where are his tears, his dirge, his wails?

Something isn't right. There's some part of him that's blocking this transition toward moving forward. It wants something from Vincent, but he's not sure what. He *wants* to grieve. Vincent knows how ridiculous that sounds, but he wants to feel the pain of losing a brother. That would be better than not feeling anything at all. Vincent forces himself to weep. He squeezes his eyes and thinks of his best memories with Fraunce. He thinks of when Fraunce and him teamed up to chase other kids through their wood. He remembers back to when Fraunce taught him to cut meat properly. He puts himself in the shoes of a forsaken Vincent, when Fraunce held him tight in that glade. Vincent rubs his chest subconsciously.

No tears form in his eyes.

Leif blasts through the door coming from the stables. Half the room jumps in surprise. The kid looks frantically at everyone, not even appearing to notice Fraunce's body on the ground.

"Knights!" yells Leif.

The bard springs up from his seat. He stumbles quickly over to the boy, swinging his arms wildly, trying to block the boy's view of Fraunce's butchered body. "Leif, stay back!"

He really does care about that boy, thinks Vincent bemused. Why is he bemused? He should be grief-struck. Why is he like this?!

"The knights are here," says Leif.

"'Course they are," laughs Oswyn.

"No. More knights," says Leif, pointing.

"What do you mean?" asks the bard.

"Outside."

Vivian runs to the window by their table. She squints through the storm. The room rests in limbo while she searches through the night.

"Fuck."

Her simple word echoes through the inn. She holds them all in her grasp—all waiting for her to explain her phrase of dismay. Horror seizes ahold of her. She doesn't explain further.

"What?" blurts Edmond finally, unable to contain the tension any longer.

"Get him by the fire!" orders Vivian, pointing to Kendrick. "Vincent, keep watch of him. Barmaid, tidy up the place quick."

"What is it?" questions Oswyn.

Vivian looks utterly terrified. Her foot taps nervously on the ground. She throws up her hands. "There be four knights outside, with weapons and horses and the lot. Looks like they're tidying up in the stables first. So now unless you all want to die, I suggest ye get to fuckin' work."

ANARCHY ERUPTS AROUND EDITH—AS if the previous set of circumstances weren't chaotic enough. How many things have gone wrong for her now? Way more than should be given to a hardworking woman, that's for sure. Edith shakes her head as she hastily sweeps up the blood-covered hay on the ground, more vexed than anything else. This whole night, with everything going from bad to worse to horrible to God-knows-what, is getting on her nerves. The storm refuses to let up too; in fact, it appears to be getting even worse. How much more tumultuous can a damn storm get?

She watches Vincent drag Kendrick to his feet. The squire doesn't put up any fight. That wound the peasant had given him didn't look immediately deadly; however, it certainly slowed him down. They fumble their way toward the hearth where the hot air shimmers off Kendrick's sweating body. He probably has a fever. Edith restrains her pity for him. She has been doing that a lot tonight. Everyone has. This is what happens when a lifetime of suppressed emotions boils over in a single night. It is a shame it had to happen here. Kendrick is such a sweet boy. From her brief meeting with him, he struck her as a kind soul. Generous people don't survive in this world, however, and Edith had to take that into account.

She needs to get back to Emma, and that involves *not* being slaughtered by a bunch of revenge-hungry knights.

Paris and Edmond carry Fraunce's body to the kitchen. Edith tries to object, but they ignore her in their rush to discard of any wrongdoings. She sighs as they dump the body —rather disrespectfully—onto the kitchen floor. Edith shakes her head.

It's time for her to switch up her demeanor once again. She has to play the part of an innocent bar maiden, particularly one who hasn't experienced death, death, and more death tonight. Edith humors that she could have been a thespian in another life. As a bar maiden, she always has to play different roles for different customers. This is doubly true in the bedchamber. She's gotten good at manipulating others and building up a specific allure around her. That being said, she hates doing it. She likes her authentic self the best, the one that comes out when she's around Emma. The quiet mother who wants to enjoy life one little moment at a time. But she can't be that person right now, and so she needs to become the best thespian she can.

Do what needs to be done. Do it smart, precisely, and fully. We'll get out of this yet. Us and the lovers. We still need to get Verona and Paris out of here. We should try to help Kendrick as well—his wound might be survivable yet.

Edith frowns. She shakes her head.

No. Me can't help them. I don't have the time. They can save themselves.

Can they?

Edith groans. She pushes back all other thoughts. First thing first, she needs to make the common room look normal. Oswyn and Godfrey are setting up the tables, chairs, and barstools. Leif scrubs at the drops of blood over the counter. Fortunately, the ceiling has dried up, and so it isn't leaking gore anymore. Edith glances up at it. The planks are stained a dark red, but luckily, it blends in with the grain quite a bit. It will be hard to spot unless specifically searched for, and even then, it can be confused for some other mess. No one will suspect it to be the internal remains of Sir Algor.

Vivian, Edmond, and Oswyn rush back to their original table. Godfrey sits at his corner while Leif sticks close to him.

Good, thinks Edith, *that bard will keep Leif safe.*

The stomping of multiple horses echoes from the stables. They managed to clear up the main room in under a minute. It's amazing how quickly people can move when their lives are at stake.

Edith grabs a torn piece of cloth and hands it to the peasants. At her issue, Oswyn wets it with rainwater outside the window. Edith runs over to the squire. Vincent forces Kendrick to sit before the hearth. The fire burns fiercely in front of them, and Kendrick's blood glistens as it slowly leaks from him. Edith approaches him with the wet cloth.

"Let me clean it," says Edith.

"Hey!" hisses Vincent, pushing her hand away. Edith does her best to imitate the glare of vexed mother, and Vincent immediately cowers down like a petulant child.

"They will see the blood if me doesn't clean it."

Vincent doesn't respond, so Edith bends down and wipes the blood off Kendrick's armor. After she finishes cleaning the immediate area around the wound, Vincent forces Kendrick's hand to cover it.

"Keep it over the wound," dictates Vincent.

Edith spots Vincent's knife for a split second as he presses the tip of the blade against Kendrick's other side. He positions it so it is impossible for anyone else in the room to see the dagger. The personal tension between them is overwhelming. Edith throws out her desire to figure out what is going on between the two of them, and she quickly wipes away the rest of the blood on his leather armor.

"Why?" Kendrick whispers.

"Don't move," responds Vincent. "Not a word."

Edith feels Kendrick's muscles tighten up as Vincent pinches the knife deeper into the squire's skin. Kendrick flinches.

"I got it," says Kendrick.

Edith shakes her head. She can't keep up with all the plots and relationships that are constantly forming and evolving and disintegrating. This night is really going to shit. She finishes up on Kendrick's armor and bounces away from that awkwardness. She hobbles back over to the bar, the only place she can think to be. At the corner of her vision, Paris hurries up the stairs.

The room goes silent. Everyone listens.

The horses' footsteps go quiet. Four loud *booms* rumble from the stables. The knights dismounted. Edith takes a deep breath, ready to face whatever comes through that door.

PARIS SLINKS BACK INTO Chamber 1. His breaths are heavy, and his heart thumps inside his chest. This is the worst thing that could have happened.

"Paris?" croaks Verona.

"Shh," says Paris. He lowers her head back onto the pillow. "Remain still."

"What's wrong? Paris?"

He kisses her on the forehead but doesn't answer the question. It's best she doesn't know what's happening, lest it worsens her condition. Her body needs to be focused on healing, nothing more. Paris scurries to his tiny peephole in the floorboard and peeks down it to the middle of the common room.

He waits.

EDITH TAKES ANOTHER DEEP breath. Footsteps thump chaotically from the stables. The clamor of metal rings out. *Great, one of these knights has a suit of metal armor.*

The air inside the inn goes dead. It's a startling contrast to the storm outside. The fury of the heavens ploughs their building, yet everything inside of it remains stagnant. Edith spots particles of dust floating in the air, perfectly still, while the candle lighting everywhere hardly flickers. The Earth knows this is a volatile situation in a room full of capricious individuals, where more oil will be tossed onto its skittish flames.

A belly laugh erupts from the stables. Deep, muffled voices spill out. Older men. The voices grow louder . . . louder . . . more clear . . . more boisterous . . .

A final laugh erupts as the stable door flings open.

Three knights in leather jerkins and a greenish-brown coat saunter into the room. Edith doesn't recognize any of them, yet they all bear the raven sigil of Duke Rowan.

But then a final man enters.

His armor reflects all the world around him, and his heavy footsteps send shivers through Edith's spine. The fire of the hearth makes the whole front side of his body glow with an unearthly hellfire. Edith's knees buckle under her. Her mouth goes dry.

Vivid green eyes shine out under a brown hood. Edith could recognize those eyes anywhere. They're the eyes of her daughter. Edith forgets to breathe as the father of Emma—that formless void that Edith has tried so desperately to put behind her—pushes back his hood.

Commander Rayner appraises the quiet room.

UNORTHODOX PROPRIETY

THE LAUGHTER OF THE knights falters as soon as they cross into the common room. Commander Rayner's eyes pass over Edith, not spending any more time to take her in than any chair in the space. A brief anger stabs into Edith over this fact. He didn't seem to recognize her . . . surely, she isn't that forgettable.

Edith pushes away the stupid emotion as soon as she can, letting cold reason take her over instead.

Why would he remember me? Edith scoffs. *Me was only some peasant he slept with five years ago. He probably sleeps with lots of women.*

There's a childish part of her that wants to stomp up to Commander Rayner and slap him across the face, to yell at him that he has a child, and *this* is why you don't finish inside a prostitute. She could have died in childbirth like so many other women. She lets that part of herself run rampant in her mind so it can get its kicks out. Like letting a child jump around to tire themselves out, Edith has found that releasing those ridiculous thoughts to play out scenarios in her head often leads to it fizzling away.

It's for the best that he doesn't recognize her anyway. That would be a whole other predicament stacked above a night full of them. To be fair, Commander Rayner did unintentionally give Edith the best thing in her life. He is just another man she has known, but now he'll forever hold a place in her mind.

He's a lucky man.

Commander Rayner finishes his appraisal of the inn. He smiles—*or is it a snarl?* The commander became a living legend amongst the peasantry, or more accurately, a living nightmare. Whether anyone would actually recognize him without an introduction is another question altogether. It's gotten to the point where people believe every knight they spot is Commander Rayner, and so every knight is met with common dread. Now, it appears, he'll add his new suit of armor to the mystique.

He doesn't want to be confused with other knights. He wants people to know it is him. Vanity is an addictive beast.

Commander Rayner points to an empty table at the center of the room. The other knights sit at it, throwing back their hoods and relaxing into their chairs. Commander Rayner and one other knight wear swords at their hips while the other two have axes. They keep them on their person as they make themselves at home.

"You, bar maiden," says Commander Rayner at Edith, pointing at her to make it obvious who he is speaking to. "A keg of your finest ale. Tell Warin it will be compensated by our liege lord."

Edith glances at Edmond, Vivian, and Oswyn. Not necessarily for permission, but to see how they are reacting. They've survived the first wave of the commander's great detective skills, but she can't help but shake a feeling that he always knows more than he lets on. Commander Rayner peeks over at the three farmers. He furrows his brow in suspicion. He snaps back to her.

"Make haste!"

"Yes, sir," says Edith, careful to keep her voice neutral.

Edith races past Commander Rayner. He's one of the tallest people Edith has ever met, and he towers above her as she maneuvers around him. Edith catches a bright glint in his eyes—Emma's eyes—as she goes by. A hint of recognition?

Edith scurries into the stables. There are now eight horses tied to the picket line, each one appearing to be bigger than the next. Horses have always frightened Edith. They are horrendously big beasts, and the look of cunning never leaves their faces. No animal like that is made for riding. She turns to the far northwest corner of the stables where there are five kegs of ale stacked up against the firewood.

When she crosses to it, her legs forget how to stand. Edith tumbles to her knees and gasps in surprise. She braces herself against the wooden kegs. Her long black hair catches in the coarse grain and pinches her scalp as she pulls her head away.

She rests there, surrounded by the pleasant fragrance of soggy wood, rain leaking on her from above, as the exhaustion of the day finally catches up to her. Her bones tremble for respite. Her legs beg to stay motionless. She has done nothing but move all day and all night, from one location to the next, ticking off the endless to-do list of her life. Edith has always been a structured person, preferring to have an ordered set of things to accomplish. Life is meaningless without a constant goal to move to next. But occasionally a person needs to rest, and Edith's body clamors for a chance to do so now. She leans her head against the kegs, stretching her legs out in front of her. She doesn't have time to nap or sleep, but a few seconds of quiet never hurt anyone. Edith closes her eyes, slows her heart rate, and subdues her muscles. She lets her mind wander away, opting rather to feel than think. She's done too much thinking tonight. And she'll have to do some more; this night isn't over yet. An ominous part of her knows that the worst is yet to come.

It speaks to her, warning her that this is her last chance. This is her final moment of rest, so she better get rejuvenated.

Edith cracks open her eyes. The horses at the picket line nudge gently against one another. She plays with the idea of stealing one and riding off into the storm. She could try to ride to Emma and get away from this whole mess. But she has no skill at riding, and her fear of horses will likely worsen if she's on top of one in a thunderstorm. That doesn't seem like the smartest place to learn. She best do what she's told. *Delay, delay, delay.*

Edith stands begrudgingly, ignoring the pleas of her thighs, and pulls at one of the kegs. The deft thing is quite heavy. She struggles to grapple with it, spinning it around in her hands to try and get a better grip. It almost falls, but she saves it with a well-timed knee thrust. Edith wobbles toward the door.

"My dear, *loyal* peasants," Commander Rayner's voice thunders through the wall. "No need to be frightened. We are friends who seek respite after a long journey."

Edith uses her shoulder to nudge open the door. Commander Rayner glances back at her as she walks in. He paces around the room, turning his eyes from one person to the next. He still hasn't noticed Kendrick, it seems, as Vincent has blocked off the squire from most of the room with his body.

"But," begins Commander Rayner, changing tone, "to admit the truth, we did not stop here coincidentally. We are searching for two fugitives. A man and woman who beget from the village of Salisbury. He goes by the name of Paris. She by Verona—"

Edith drops the keg. It slams onto the ground, the wooden barrel splintering. Ale spouts from it, soaking the floorboards in alcohol. Edith covers her gaping mouth.

Of course they're searching for Paris and Verona.

"Sorry, sir. 'Twas heavy," says Edith quickly, hoping to avoid any further suspicion. She tries to lift the keg, but ale squirts all over her. The sticky residue clamps her tunic to her body. She'll smell even worse now. She battles with the keg, trying to find her grip on the rapidly slippery barrel.

"Sir Tobias," directs the commander.

One of the other knights crosses to Edith. Sir Tobias takes the keg from her and carries it to the table with relative ease. The keg cracked on the upper side of the barrel, so it quits leaking by the time the knight gets it to the table.

"Bar maiden. Where is Warin?" asks Commander Rayner. "I must speak to him."

"Don't know, sir," says Edith truthfully. It has been a while since she's seen the foul man. Usually, his presence can always be felt thundering around the inn.

"Lovely," sighs the commander. "Go seek him."

"Yes, sir."

This is a chance for her to get away for a bit. Perfect. Edith uses the opportunity to confront Paris. Verona had told Edith about their past, how they had eloped from their previous town to escape the lust of Duke Rowan. What Edith didn't know is that they are actively being hunted down, and that they left a trail of clues leading to this inn. Now Edith is wrapped up with them. That's dangerous for her, but, more infuriatingly, that's deadly for Emma.

Edith darts up the stairs. It's not often that she loses control of her temper, but all the events of the night have filled her tolerance to the brim; now this final threat to her daughter has overflowed her cup of acceptance and spills out of her in the form of unadulterated wrath, all of it focused on one person.

She throws open the door to Chamber 1 and slams it shut behind her. Her eyes lock onto Paris. He stumbles back from the floor, putting his hands up in submission. Verona struggles to lift her head from the bed. Edith storms to Paris.

"Edith. Edi—"

She lifts him up by the tunic and pins him next to the window. He cowers before her. A sense of overriding power swells through Edith. Lightning and thunder crash right outside the window, flaring them into a brilliant white light.

"Who be ye?"

"She told you," says Paris, horrified.

"Knights don't travel across the kingdom chasing a single peasant woman. Now tell me. Who be ye? Who?!" Edith thrusts him against the wall.

"Me . . . me name is Paris."

"She said ye were elopin'. But he says you both are fugitives. So which be it?!"

"He's lyin'. Me promises."

"What's wrong?" asks Verona, coughing into the air.

"All me wants is to see my baby girl again," says Edith, frowning. All her emotions leak out of her at once, as her voice goes through a harmony of sadness, anger, and detachment. "But this night ain't gonna end in anythin' but more death. I helped ye. I helped ye both. But now me has a wounded knight downstairs, two fugitives up here, a coup, and a missin' innkeeper. So tell me. Who. Be. Ye."

"'Tis the truth," cries Paris. "Please, Edith. We need ye. Believe us. We just simple folk."

"Then why are they hunting ye down?"

"Me don't know, honest."

"This makes no sense."

"Please, Edith. Listen to your heart."

"My heart?" shrieks Edith incredulously. "You dare tell me to listen to my heart?"

Paris doesn't respond. She supposes there isn't a proper response to that. She stares into Paris's frightened eyes.

Pity, that pesky emotion, finds its way into Edith once again.

This isn't me.

Edith needs to be careful of straying too far from her true self, the woman and mother she wants to be for Emma. The one who helps people in need. She doesn't harbor the same hatred toward knights that others do, but that doesn't mean she trusts them. Paris shudders, shaking Edith's hands with it. She slows her heavy breathing, now aware of how rapidly her chest is beating. She loosens her grip on Paris, and he releases a sigh.

"We need to get ye both out of here," Edith finally says.

"How?"

"'Tis 'bout to be a bloodbath." Edith sighs introspectively. "When it starts, ye both need to be out the door. Me will be right behind you."

Paris crosses to the bed and feels Verona's forehead. Edith looks the woman over. Her hair has a sheen to it that wasn't perceptible before, and the perspiration on her skin now appears in healthy amounts rather than soaking her like before. The most striking difference is the smell. That foul stench of rotting meat that Edith smelled when she first entered the guest chamber is no longer perceptible. It's clean and fresh now. The storm must have helped it some, but it is certainly a good sign for the woman.

"She's getting' better," says Edith.

Paris and Verona smile. Seeing the two lovers together, made closer because of her, sends goosebumps up and down her body. It feels nice to have played a part in saving her. It almost makes this whole night worth it. She needs to get them all out alive, and then she might even be proud of this night.

"Now hark," says Edith sternly. "Me cottage is in Cudworth, a nearby village, a bit in that direction."

"Me knows it," says Paris.

"We meet there. My place is on top of the hill, faces the risin' sun." Edith wanders to the window again. She peers out into the chilly storm. She's been cold for so long. "I forgot what the sun feels like," she mutters quietly to herself.

"We will."

"Me daughter is there. She's but five. Tell her Mummy sent ye," says Edith softly. She crosses to the bed. Verona smiles up at her and grasps her arm.

"Tell me 'bout your daughter."

"Her name is Emma," begins Edith, hesitant at first but finding power in Emma's description. "She be like an angel, only, more divine. Mane as dark as mine, but her eyes are green as grass. She does this thing where she taps her cheek when she thinks. Like this."

Edith recreates the motion: puffing up her cheeks and tapping on them.

"She sounds lovely," Verona says sweetly.

"Ye have no idea."

Verona squeezes Edith's hand. Now that her fever is subsiding, Edith can see how beautiful Verona really is. It's a shame she has to go through this. *We could be friends outside of here. Me does really like her. Paris is very fortunate to have her.*

The three of them stand silently in Chamber 1, allowing themselves to forget the destructive combination of individuals downstairs.

*T*HIS IS POSITIVELY THE *worst time this could have happened. Thanks a lot, you useless, cretinous body. Thanks so much.*

Godfrey's body screams for a smoke. Sweat drips down his spine, soaking his doublet to the chair. His hands twirl the empty pipe. It turns and twists and flies, yet it never regrows the herbs needed for it. He notices the pipe shaking, so he looks down at his hands only to discover that they're trembling. His eyes twitch between all the knights. There's so many of them now. The need to smoke always invades his thoughts with more unrestrained zest when he is anxious. The past hour or so has taken care of that. Everyone here in this blasted inn wants him to have a panic attack apparently. Why is everyone being a psychotic murdering dolt tonight?

That Fraunce fellow killed the first knight. Idiot. The squire murdered him in front of all his friends. Idiot. Then the kid stabs Kendrick but doesn't manage to kill him. Idiots on top of idiots.

He shouldn't have ever left Regina. He should have taken her offer and spent the night there.

Then you wouldn't have met Leif.

Godfrey nods in agreement with himself. Leif is the one bright spot in this dark night.

Now, back to smoking.

The urge to smoke squeezes his lungs closer together. His body is moving on to phase two of the get-Godfrey-to-do-what-we-want spectrum. This is the part where his muscles start to strain and his bones begin to ache. His body has a civil war with itself. It'll keep the pain and discomfort up until he smokes, where it'll then magically disappear. Funny how it does that.

Idiot.

Godfrey knows the next phase is the dangerous one, where his body gives up completely and becomes a mind of its own. He can't let it come to that. He needs to stay in control. He's a man, and he's supposed to have sovereignty of his own body. He read a manuscript by Aurelius, or maybe it was Cicero, that forewarned of the battle of control that every man fights within himself. Scholars really love their Romans. He can't let that demon within him get out.

Leif watches him closely. *He knows something is wrong with me,* worries Godfrey. An itch tunnels into the lower-right side of his back.

The boy will find out. He'll leave you like they all do.

Godfrey's anxiety doubles. He shakes his head. That isn't true. *He* is always the one disappearing. He can't trust himself to stay in anyone's lives. He did it to himself earlier today. Regina and Juliana were so nice to him.

Too nice for me . . . Godfrey's fingers scratch at his arm.

Smoke, smoke, smoke. He must smoke. Smoking will make this all go away. All this pain, all this doubt, all this self-hate. Smoke it all away; let it vanish with the fumes.

Leif touches Godfrey's trembling hands.

His muscles steady. He looks at the little boy, who gives him a strange expression in response. Godfrey sighs, and the strong desire to do anything but be in this moment disappears at his touch. Godfrey takes his hand away and smiles. The boy smiles back.

"You better, Mr. Bard?"

"Thank you," says Godfrey warmly.

Leif turns his attention back to the knights. Godfrey can see the awe in the young boy's eyes. Commander Rayner does look magnificent in his metal armor; although, Godfrey has been alive long enough to recognize the peril it projects. The armor appears impregnable to any weapon of man and exemplifies the ingenuity of modern craftmanship. The commander finally sits at the table with the other knights. The four of them fill their tankards up from the keg and drink it down in long gulps. Their long cloaks that flow to the ground make them appear mythical and godly. They are truly intimidating.

He needs to get Leif out of here.

Godfrey has seen enough squabbling for one day, and Leif has seen one too many dead bodies, not to mention he is now an orphan . . . like Godfrey. This situation has to be handled with the utmost care. Prudence is key to surviving the volatile. He decides to start with getting Leif out of immediate danger.

"Leif," whispers Godfrey, sweat soaking his face, "I need you to hide in the stables."

"Why?" he whispers back, following Godfrey's lead.

"Do you trust me?"

Leif shrugs.

"Fair enough," says Godfrey. "Can you indulge my wish, for only a short while?"

"Me suppose. You will owe me another story, though." Leif smiles impishly.

"I can do that."

Leif sighs. He walks alongside the wall and goes into the stables. Commander Rayner watches the boy do so. Godfrey's muscles tense up, and his body forgets it is supposed to be aching. He readies to protect the boy. But

Commander Rayner doesn't do anything, and his eyes drift directly to Godfrey.

Smoke—

Not now.

But Godfrey's body ignores his command, and the lizard part of his mind begins to covet that delicious, smoldering exhaust.

Commander Rayner squints at Godfrey, as if he can glimpse the war happening within the bard. The commander eventually moves on and does the same stare and squint at every person in the room. Everyone sits impeccably still.

"Sir David," yawns Commander Rayner. One of the knights looks at him. Sir David is a tall man with a scruffy beard and broad shoulders that give him an imposing air. "I believe we need some company. Hark, peasants! Pull your table to ours. Don't be timid."

"Yes, it is rather drab in here," says Sir David, a suspicious grin on his face.

Vivian, Edmond, and Oswyn glance at one another. Godfrey stares at Vincent and Kendrick at the hearth. They keep their heads ducked down, pretending like they aren't in the room.

"You in the corner, join us too," says Commander Rayner.

It takes Godfrey a few seconds to realize he is speaking to him. The spike of desire hammers into him yet again, and his skin turns cold from the metal incision. Godfrey wraps his arms around his chest and shivers. Sir David leans closer to Commander Rayner. He whispers to him. The Commander gives a lengthy, shrouded response.

"Sir Ivan," shouts Commander Rayner. His voice booms out from him, and Godfrey gets the impression that he's purposefully this boisterous. "Check the kitchen for food. I believe the bar maiden is predisposed toward laziness."

"Certainly, Sir Commander," says Sir Ivan. He is the skinniest knight of the bunch, with narrow hips and small arms. His axe does most of the work for making him look intimidating.

Lightning flashes through the single window, and the rumble of thunder shakes the air above them.

Wait. Go to the kitchen? That means he'll see—

*T*HE BODY.

Edith halts on the stairs as a brief stint of dread slaps her across the face. Her head swivels from Sir Ivan to the kitchen door. She spots Fraunce's foot, which is visible through the cracked opening. Sir Ivan quickly crosses toward the bar. Edith's guts launch into her throat. She springs forward, almost running, to reach the door before the knight.

"Sir Knight!" blurts Edith. She doesn't know where to take the conversation from here, but she had to do something to slow him down. It works.

Sir Ivan hesitates for the briefest of moments, and it allows for Edith to block his path to the door. She stands between the wall and bar, instinctually spreading her arms out to take up even more space. It's not lost on her how Sir Algor used this same tactic on her earlier.

"I'm grabbing our food," says Sir Ivan bluntly.

"Me will get it right now, sir." Edith smiles as politely as she can. Now is probably a good time to play docile and innocent.

"You've done enough." Sir Ivan makes a move to squeeze past her, but Edith shimmies over to block him again.

"I insist. Ye be a knight and shouldn't have to get your own food."

"Do you doubt my ability to provide for myself?"

"What? No, sir. Me was—"

"Then I suggest you move out of my way," he warns with a low growl. Edith's eyes dart to the axe at his waist. She grimaces but holds strong, not wavering from her position. The farmers glare at her with trepidation.

Sir Ivan pushes past her. Edith shoves him. The backside of Sir Ivan's hand suddenly meets her face. Edith flings backward from the force of the slap, and her body crashes into the wall next to the kitchen door.

Edith can almost *feel* Fraunce's dead body right next to her. Blood slinks from her nose. The knight stomps over her.

"Don't push me, wench! Get out of—"

"Sir Ivan?"

Sir Ivan turns toward the center of the room. Commander Rayner stands at their table with an expression that is somewhere between disappointment and annoyance. Everyone stares at them.

"Sir Commander?" rebuts Sir Ivan defensively.

"Stop accosting the poor woman and sit down," says Commander Rayner calmly. "She said she'll get it."

"Sir—"

"Sit. Down."

Sir Ivan backs down under the commander's stern tone. He steps away from Edith.

"For the love of God," says Commander Rayner, exasperated. "Help her up first."

Sir Ivan whips his head from Commander Rayner to Edith. He mumbles to himself and growls.

There's some tension there. Maybe me can use that.

Sir Ivan lends his hand to her. She takes it. When she's up and standing, Edith rubs the line of blood beneath her nose. Sir Ivan keeps his eyes on her.

"Apologize," says Commander Rayner like a vexed parent.

"My apologies, madam." Sir Ivan scowls.

The knight stomps away without waiting for a reply, puffing a hot stream of air from his nostrils. Edith glances behind her at Fraunce's body. She sighs. Another disaster averted.

Commander Rayner stares Sir Ivan down as he sulks to the table and throws himself onto the chair. The commander turns his attention back to Edith. Her heart flutters as he honestly takes her in for the first time. There's certainly something behind his eyes, but his face is impossible to read accurately.

"Did you find Warin?" questions Commander Rayner.

"No, sir," says Edith.

"Where is he?"

"Me ain't sure. Me hasn't seen him in a while."

"The innkeeper has gone missing? During a storm?"

"'Tis the truth, sir."

Commander Rayner bites his lip and uses his teeth to pull it into a smile. He glances around the room again before glaring back at Edith. "I hope he's doing well."

"Me too, sir," responds Edith. She thinks she played it off rather well, as everyone seems to take their eyes off her— everyone but Commander Rayner, that is. She knows he saw right through it with those bastardly green eyes. How dare he pervert something so lovely to Edith.

"Very good. You best get that food now," says the commander.

Edith humbly accepts the expulsion of his glare. She spins into the kitchen, entrapping her with the dead body. The fury of Heaven shines the room into light, and Fraunce's intestines glow with white radiance. This is the second time Edith has been stuck in a room with a person who was stabbed through the stomach. Her luck is undeniably terrible tonight. Edith pauses for a moment, understanding of how selfish that sounds when next to someone who was killed. She shakes her head.

What has this night done to me?

She hurries and grabs a wooden pewter dish and scoops pottage from the heated cauldron. The fire below it died long ago, but Warin's concoction still feels warm enough. Edith stops herself before she exits with the pottage. She peeks back at Fraunce's discarded cadaver. She sets down the pottage and drags the corpse farther into the room. She turns him so he is facing up, and she closes both of his eyelids. He still doesn't look proper. She bends down and adjusts his tunic so it covers his whole body, terrible stomach wound included. Once Edith deems to herself that the body is well respected, she grabs the pottage and heads out to the common room.

Edith places the large pewter dish in the center of the knights' table. Sir Ivan doesn't dare glance at her. Edith can't help but feel a little powerful at her influence over the knight now. Commander Rayner dismisses her with a nod, and Edith happily obliges, crossing back to the bar. The knights reach for the food when Commander Rayner claps his hands together.

"Pull the tables," declares the commander. "Come on."

The knights wait to eat their meal. Commander Rayner points for the farmers to move their long table alongside theirs. Edmond and Vivian glance at one another, and it is Oswyn who decides to follow along with the commander first. Edmond goes along with him, and the two of them carry the barrel and wooden pallet table next to the knights. They line up the tables parallel to one another.

"Sir David, Sir Tobias. Fetch the peasants their seats."

"We can grab our own," asserts Edmond.

"Never deny help, my friend," says the commander amicably.

Edmond bites his cheek, probably suppressing some backhanded remark. Sir David and Sir Tobias—the other one with the axe—bring Vivian, Edmond, and Oswyn their seats. The farmers and knights sit. Commander Rayner turns his attention to the bard at the corner of the room. Edith furrows her brow. The bard is acting awfully peculiar. He rubs his head against the wall and scratches the side of his arm with his nails.

"Corner peasant, don't make me beg," says Commander Rayner flippantly; although, it truthfully sounds like a threat.

The bard's static-fused hair sticks up. He glances at his hand. It scratches his arm again. The bard bangs it against the wall. Strange fellow. The commander watches him closely.

Edith uses the bard crossing to the table as a chance to get out of the room, lest she be called upon to join them. She needs to get Leif. Edith saw him cross into the stables, so she sneaks out of the common room as the bard sits at the table.

Leif sits above one of the piles of stacked firewood. The eight horses tied to the picket line neigh and bump into one another as if spooked by some unseen spirit. The boy kicks his legs into the air and swings them about. He almost looks bored, a peaceful luxury only a child could have at this moment.

"Leif, remember what me said to you earlier?" asks Edith, referring to when she asked him to ride to her cottage. Edith can see from his face that he does. "Good. 'Tis time for ye to go."

"What 'bout my pa?"

Edith pauses for a moment, contemplating. "He'll meet ye there."

"Promise?"

Edith lifts Leif off the firewood and places him on the ground. He gives her a stubborn expression, forcing her to respond in some way. She sighs.

"I promise."

Edith unwraps the reins of Warin's horse from the picket line and adjusts the bridle to make sure it rests properly in the horse's mouth. She can't have anything happen to him out there. She would feel devastated. Warin's horse doesn't have a saddle. He is too cheap to pay for such a "useless thing," as he would put it.

"Bar maiden?!" yells a voice from the common room. Edith grunts. Why is she needed so often? *Eat your damn food.*

Edith carefully walks the horse over to Leif. She peeks back at the animal multiple times, making sure it doesn't try to eat her or anything crazy. It wouldn't surprise her based on how this night is going. Edith holds the reins with one hand and places another on Leif's cheek.

"Me needs you to protect Emma," says Edith. "Ye tell her Mummy is comin' soon. Can ye tell her that? Tell her not to be scared and that Mummy loves her. Me needs you to be a man now, ye hark?"

"Me will," says Leif proudly. Edith kisses his forehead, and he only slightly recoils from it.

"Me loves ye," says Edith. She means it. Leif has helped her survive more nights here than she can count. Whenever she had to deal with Warin, Leif was always there to cheer her up afterward. Maybe if Warin never shows up, she could take care of him.

"Bar maiden!"

Edith hands the reins to Leif. He glances up at her with his little, innocent eyes. Some part of Edith tells her to stay here a little longer, to try and run along with Leif as he rides for her cottage. She'd only slow him down. That would kill them both. She smiles down at the boy, the real heart and soul of Warin's Inn.

"Thank ye," says Edith softly, choking a bit as tears try to burst out of her.

Leif looks from the reins in his hand up to the horse. A feeling grabs hold of Edith and chills her to the bone. She tries to shake it away, but she can't. As Edith watches Leif's small frame beside that giant animal, she can't help but feel that it is the last time they'll ever meet. Her heart shudders at the implications of such a thought.

Stay strong, Edith. Ye got this. Ye will see Leif again. Breathe, move, and fight.

Breathe. Move. Fight.

ASTUTE NAIVETY

EDITH LEAVES LEIF ALL alone in the smelly stables. There are too many horses in here, and they are pooping and peeing all over the place. Leif hates the smell. Not really because of how gross it is that it came from inside the animals, but because it means he's going to have to spend all morning cleaning it. Yuck. He'd rather spend time with Mr. Bard or doing something fun like running around with the kids at the village. He always has to stay and work. It sucks.

Maybe he can get out of it this time, since Edith asked him to go to her house. Leif has only been to Edith's house a few times, on rare occasions when Pa is hosting special, noble people at the inn. Pa has always confused Leif. He is so mean to Edith, but she is his only friend. There are many days where him and Pa have nothing to do but repeat the same chores over and over again. At least on busy nights like tonight, there's lots of people to talk to, and lots of things to think about. His favorite nights are when the nobles come over and Pa doesn't make him leave. The nobles have really interesting stories of far-off places, and it gives Leif plenty of things to dream about for months at a time.

Leif leads the horse to the edge of the stables. He climbs the stack of firewood and uses it to help him mount the horse. He's going to get a little wet outside, but he doesn't mind it. He likes rain and water. They seem more magical to him than the sun. The sun just hurts to look at, and it burns him quite bad when he's out in it for too long. Besides, he gets to go see Emma. She's a little crazy sometimes and a few years younger than him, but she's fun to be around. He doesn't get to be around other kids that often.

Lightning flares at the back door, shining off something that catches his eye. He cocks his head. The stable goes dark again. He dismounts the horse. Thunder shakes the walls of the inn, and the horses kick off one another behind him. They are really scared right now.

Leif moves to the back door, leaving the horse behind. A rivulet floods under the wooden planks and flows into a little puddle. Leif examines it closer, curious to see why this little puddle caught his eye so much. It's because it isn't just water; there's mud and . . . something else. . . .

Lightning brightens the room again. The stream glows red.

Pa had gone out this door with Mr. Bard earlier. Something tells him this red stream might have something to do with them. *What is it?*

Leif pushes open the back door and steps into the onslaught of rain. He shields his face. The storm is a lot worse than he thought it was. His tunic flaps and flitters around him as the wind blasts his body against the inn. Leif is determined though. He can be a big man. He can fight a little weather. He isn't scared.

Leif follows the red rivulet of mud and rain. It leads uphill against the side of the inn.

This is like an adventure. Me can tell Mr. Bard all about this story. He will be proud of it. The story of how Leif found the source of the red river. Mr. Bard can then teach me all 'bout stories and how to tell 'em. It will be fun.

Thus, Leif continues his perilous trek through sludge and gale, all to find the origin of this mysterious red liquid.

THUNDEROUS SILENCE

AS KENDRICK SITS BEFORE the hearth, a disquieting and painful wound in his right abdomen while Vincent's dagger pinches into his left, he finds himself amazed at how quickly death can sober a person. A light fever starts to make its rounds through Kendrick's body, and the edges of his appendages tingle with a constant buzz. The acidic, coarse scent of smoke that rises from the hearth does little to calm his tumultuous health.

A war wages within him, fighting for life, but all Kendrick can think about is what he did to Vincent.

Kendrick can feel Vincent's rigidity next to him. He hides his pain well, but his anguish courses through the blade of his knife, all of it pressured onto the tip of the dagger. The fate of Kendrick's life balances upon the capricious whims of grief that he caused. It's a fitting climax for a murderer to experience during their final moments.

Kendrick's right hand remains warm as he covers his wound. Occasional squirts of blood still try to scour out beneath his fingers. He applies as much pressure as he can, thinking back to the basic healing fundamentals he was taught during his first few weeks in the knighthood.

Kendrick never imagined he would be using those techniques on himself, especially within his first year as a squire. He isn't even a knight yet.

As true as it was that Vincent joined the knighthood to win over Lucia, and as pridefully stupid as it was that he abandoned being his father's ward so he wouldn't have to live in the shadows of his forge, it was equally true that Kendrick joined because he really, honestly, wanted to become a knight. He used to fancy himself a kind person, a hero being held back by stagnation, by his obligation to his father. Then when Kendrick was accepted as Sir Algor's squire, and he was forced to accept the Codes, he thought he finally discovered the person he wanted to be. The type of man he could be for Lucia, for Duke Rowan, and for the world. It's easy for a person to lie to themselves, and it's even easier to ignore the truth. Bulwarked with the soberness of near-death, Kendrick decides it is time for him to finally accept reality.

He *was* a shadow, he *is* a killer, but he *will* become a knight.

Kendrick shall follow his own Codes, no matter what path it leads him down. He forfeited his life when he killed Eliot and Fraunce. All he can do now is give back, save lives, and protect the helpless. That includes Vincent. He wants to save them all. He can still redeem himself. He just needs to regain Vincent's trust. When they were alone in the stables, Kendrick saw the goodness in Vincent. It still lurks in his eyes now. Vincent is trying so hard to bury it down, but it's there.

Together they can both get out of this. Somehow.

Commander Rayner certainly threw a wrench into the plan, though. He's going to have to play this smart. He can't usurp the commander, not him. He is going to have to play along to some extent, but the longer he can delay that confrontation, the better.

"You two at the fire, join us," shouts Commander Rayner.

Shit.

Vincent and Kendrick glance at one another. Vincent twists the knife deeper into his side, and Kendrick's muscles tense up at its contact point. The hate pulses through it.

Save him. Be a knight.

"You'll regret it more if we don't," whispers Kendrick. That isn't a lie. Whatever Commander Rayner is planning, it's best to go along with it. Follow the plan until precisely the right moment to break from it.

"Don't ye do anything funny," says Vincent. Rather languidly, the two of them manage to help each other stand.

"Why do you veil your faces?" asks Sir David.

They're all here then. Lovely.

Vincent and Kendrick spin around. Vincent pivots awkwardly to keep his knife hidden in Kendrick's side. Yes, all the knights are here. Commander Rayner, Sir David, Sir Ivan, and Sir Tobias. The peasants are drastically outnumbered. They'll have to play along too. The four knights gape at Kendrick. Clearly, he is the last person they expected to see.

"Kendrick?" wonders Commander Rayner. "Why do you not greet us?"

"I was lost in thought," grimaces Kendrick, as Vincent pushes in the blade.

"Sir Algor?"

"He's sleeping upstairs," says Kendrick. Edith enters from the stables, and Kendrick looks at her. "He had some fun earlier."

Commander Rayner glances at Edith.

"I see. He had quite a load to take off," boasts the commander. All the knights laugh at his jest. No one else finds it funny. They sit quietly at the table.

"Sit next to us," says Sir Tobias, waving Kendrick over. "Your little buddy too."

They stumble forward like two conjoined twins, Vincent keeping next to Kendrick's left side. They sit at the table. Commander Rayner gestures for Edith to come to him. She does, and the commander scans her up and down.

"Get tankards for our friends," he says finally. "We're having a toast."

Edith bows and scampers to the kitchen. Commander Rayner turns back to his guests and smiles at them. Now sitting clockwise around the two tables are Commander Rayner, Sir David, Sir Ivan, Sir Tobias, Kendrick, Vincent, Oswyn, Edmond, Vivian, and Godfrey the bard. No one reaches for the pottage in the center of the table.

"Look at us," says Commander Rayner, grinning and spreading his arms wide to mock-encompass all of them. "All cordial, not fretting about the typical squabble of class and virtue and other . . . *shite*, as you peasants say."

No one responds. While most people would cower down from such a silence, Commander Rayner basks in it. These are the moments he lives for, his power and intimidation on display for all to see and hear. After letting the silence drag on for far too long, the commander leans forward and points to the food. "Well, let's eat," he says.

The knights scoop the pottage and ravenously devour it. Food debris flies everywhere as they fling chunks from the pewter dish into their mouths. Knights are supposed to have great table manners, as not doing so is a great sin against civilization and human hospitality. They know this.

Kendrick has eaten with them and seen them eat proper on many separate occasions.

This is purposeful. This is a statement.

Everyone watches while the knights dig in. After a few minutes pass, Sir Ivan spares a moment to peek up at Kendrick. "Why don't you eat?" he asks. "You're one of us."

"I'm stuffed," says Kendrick.

Commander Rayner glares at Kendrick. Kendrick returns the favor. He isn't going to back down from a false knight like Commander Rayner. Vincent will see what Kendrick is doing. He knows that Kendrick is a principled knight. Kendrick just needs to hold strong, and the peasants will come around.

The commander glances around the table. The three peasants avoid eye contact. Vincent keeps his gaze centered on Kendrick. Godfrey the bard is the strangest of the bunch, constantly rocking on his chair. He has been acting bizarre ever since their confrontation with Warin. Kendrick remembers he meant to follow up with him on what he did to the innkeeper. He had obviously gotten distracted with everyone else.

Content with his presence, Commander Rayner leans back. He yawns, stretches his arms, and rests his hand on the hilt of his majestic sword. He sits silently like that for a while, appraising everyone meticulously without betraying a single thought he is mulling over. Kendrick can see how people find him frightening.

Edith enters from the kitchen with multiple tankards. She hands one to everyone. Sir Tobias picks up the keg and rounds the table, pouring the alcohol into the cups. Edith moves some scattered candles from around the room and places them on their table. Commander Rayner's metal suit grows brighter as it reflects the newly added lights. The open-flamed beeswax candles barely move in the dead air. The commander assesses every action from every person.

"Why do we toast?" scowls Edmond.

"Did the sir commander beseech you to speak?" bites Sir David.

"Sir David, please, the peasant can speak," says Commander Rayner. "We toast to Duke Rowan, of course. There's nothing more sacred than a toast given to a loved one under the eyes of God. Would you not agree?"

"'For thou cannot lie under the gaze of our Father, for the lie will be belied, clear for all to see,'" quotes Godfrey. Commander Rayner stares at him with newfound interest. He clearly wasn't expecting such eloquence from the fidgety peasant.

"Would you look at that," says the commander, smiling. "We have an educated man within our midst. It's been so long since I had a conversation with someone learned in the arts of ancient literature. Humor me, where did you study?"

"I was taught under the council of a great scribe," says the bard. "His name was Master Divinicus Ode. He sent me to multiple monasteries and cathedrals to study under the guide of monks and bishops."

"I take it he passed away then?"

After a few seconds, Godfrey nods. "Yes. He has."

"A pity. This world is short on benevolent old men. I hope the three of us get a chance to meet and discuss literature in Heaven above," says Commander Rayner, neither with earnestness nor mockery. It is simply a statement. "What is your name?"

"Godfrey. Godfrey the Bard."

"No surname?"

"I never knew my family."

"It's a pleasure then, Godfrey the Bard," says Commander Rayner.

Godfrey's outfit dampens with sweat. Kendrick leans forward to get a better look at the bard. In fact, Godfrey is perspiring from every pore.

"No need to be so nervous," says the commander to him. "Everyone here has our protection. As long as we're trapped in here together, we're safe."

Commander Rayner makes eye contact with Kendrick, as if to assert the statement doubly true for him. He wants Kendrick to know he's one of them.

But I'm not, I'm better than them. I can be the first real knight under Duke Rowan. I can. I must.

G ODFREY FIDDLES WITH HIS knees. He tries desperately to stay focused.

The knights continue to devour the pottage. Godfrey's stomach involuntarily convulses at the sight. If he had any of that food, all of his meals over the last day would come out at once. His body is moving on to the next phase in its plan to force him to smoke. He feels it taking over him, one body part at a time, and he curses at his inability to do anything. The urge stretches for him like the long shades of dusk. It's a looming shadow that he can spot from leagues away but one he is unable to ever fend off or hide from. It will reach him all the same, one way or another, and all Godfrey can do is watch as it approaches.

What's wrong with me?

"A toast," declares Commander Rayner, lifting his tankard.

Sir David, Sir Ivan, and Sir Tobias—if Godfrey can remember their names correctly—raise their tankards with him. Kendrick lifts his next, followed by Vincent next to him. Oswyn, Edmond, and Vivian hesitantly raise theirs last. Godfrey glances at his tankard, deciding it is best to go along with everyone else.

How did it get all the way over there?!

The tankard appears to be a full three meters away. Actually, the whole table is elongated. Godfrey flicks his eyes up, his heart pounding and his mind in shambles. He glances around the room. *Everything* is elongated. The succinct square room has mutated into an enormous hallway. The hearth at the far end of the hall will take a few minutes to amble over to. Only the people around him have retained their proportions. The knights face him, clearly wondering why Godfrey is the only one not to raise his tankard in a toast. Godfrey takes a deep breath and focuses himself for this monumental task.

He reaches forward. His arm extends with the table. It stretches and stretches, his fingers becoming longer at the end of him, until it reaches the full three meters to the tankard. Godfrey gulps. He squeezes his fingers, praying that he aimed right.

He didn't.

His fingers twitch. His arm flings across the table as it spasms, and the tankard tumbles along with it. The ale spills everywhere. The knights quickly reach for the dozen burning candles. Edith reaches for a few as well, pulling them out of the way right before the spilled alcohol splashes on them. Godfrey whips his hand back in horror as he realizes how close he was to setting the whole place alight.

Godfrey, you imbecilic, son-of-a—

Godfrey shuts down his mind.

No cursing. We can still control that. We need power over something.

"What's wrong with you!" shouts Sir Ivan, sounding more like a statement than a question.

"Apologies, my lieges," stumbles Godfrey.

His hand already fumbles at his pipe. He has no authority over his actions.

Leif. Leif can help me.

Godfrey tries to twist his body to move toward the stables, but all his legs manage to do is entwine with the chair. They collapse to the ground together. Water boils in Godfrey's eyes.

Why?! Why can't you do what I say?! Why am I so useless?!

Godfrey only vaguely hears Commander Rayner's order to seize him. Before Godfrey knows it, Sir Tobias has him locked with his arms behind his back. Godfrey kicks out. He hits the table, and the pottage bumps out of its dish.

You're a failure, Godfrey. There is no life for you. There is no future with Leif. Everything you have ever loved and wanted is gone.

Godfrey's tears fall down his face like molten steel. They're right. No one cares for him. Any love any person has ever had for him is centered around the pity they feel for him. The peasants took care of him as a child out of pity. Master Ode taught him out of pity. Regina invited him to her house out of pity. Even Leif . . .

No. Not Leif. Leif wants to be around me.

Godfrey clamps down on his thoughts before they can retaliate. He won't let them pervert Leif too. It's not true. It's not! Godfrey strains against Sir Tobias's grip.

Smoke. You want to smoke.

I don't need to.

Yes, we do. Leif only likes you when you're high. So why not do it? It's for Leif after all. You're lonely while sober,

but the world likes you high. We can love each other again,
Godfrey.

I can love myself?

You can. Just listen to us. Listen to your soul speak to
you. God put you in our body for a reason. Why not hark?

Godfrey shakes his head. It's all a lie. Leif is waiting for
him. Their story doesn't have to start like this. Godfrey
grasps onto that faint hope, the reality that *can* be. He snuffs
that pesky urge by setting his mind on one thing and one
thing only: his future with Leif.

V IVIAN AND EDMOND STAND in protest of
Godfrey's detainment. Sir Ivan and Sir David rise at
the other side of the table. They flash steel. Kendrick's heart
races. He has to stop this. No more cruel death. He needs to
deescalate.

Kendrick feels the pressure of the dagger leave his side for
a split second as the hate transfers to the other knights.
Vincent tries to stand. Kendrick reaches out and tugs him
back into the seat, saving him from the immediate wrath of
Commander Rayner. Kendrick opens his mouth to tell
Vincent why—

A slob of spit blasts Kendrick in the eye.

He flinches back, while the spit strings across his face. The
mucus oozes into his pores. Vincent wipes the excess spit
from his mouth and glares at him with an intensity Kendrick
has never seen before. Kendrick rubs the drying spit off with
his shoulders.

I'm trying to help you.

Vincent can't possibly despise him that much. He isn't
like these other knights . . . he's not . . . he can't be . . .

Commander Rayner doesn't flinch at the rising threats. He remains calm and collected in his seat. He doesn't appear to have noticed when Vincent spit on Kendrick. That's good. Vincent is still safe then. Commander Rayner is too focused on Vivian and Edmond. The commander sighs and places his tankard down.

"Let the poor bastard go," says Vivian.

"Look at how he shakes," says the commander evenly.

"I don't . . . I'm not—" trembles Godfrey.

Commander Rayner leans closer to the bard. He glares through him. "I can see it in your eyes," growls the commander. "Hark peasants, this is what our laws protect you from. Our enforcement is reasonable. Tie him down."

Sir Tobias pulls a small, skinny thread of rope from his trousers. He binds Godfrey's hands together and slams him to the ground. Godfrey's head rebounds off the frozen floor.

Edmond stomps forward, as if to tackle the knight to the ground. Vivian grasps his arm and pulls him back. Kendrick breathes heavier. It's rapidly becoming harder to maintain control over his emotions. His animal instincts, the need to survive, fight back against his better judgments. A true knight never surrenders to primal passions.

Kendrick peeks at Vincent who seethes with unrelenting grief. He sticks his dagger into Kendrick's side again.

Commander Rayner glares steadily at Edmond and Vivian. "You will sit and share a toast," he says.

Sir David and Sir Ivan hold at the ready, their weapons hungry. Vivian and Edmond smartly decide to sit. The commander smiles at their obedience.

"A toast," restarts Commander Rayner, raising his tankard once again.

Everyone raises their drinks. Godfrey squirms on the ground. His legs aren't tied, but he appears to have no desire to stand. Edmond and Vivian glare at Commander Rayner, who simply smiles at them in return.

"With this drink," begins Commander Rayner, lifting his voice so it echoes throughout the inn, "we bless the marriage of Lord Merek to that beautiful and comely princess, Lady Lorena. May no evil afoul them. May no chasm cleave them apart nor any usurper complicate their claim." Commander Rayner glares at Oswyn, Edmond, and Vivian. "And may Thou bless us, Good Lord, to be the succor to our king and duke.

"Grant us the strength to disembowel those enemies of the crown, to catch them with their backs against the wall, so we may laugh as they fall. This mighty kingdom stays intact by the goodness of its citizens and because of the just leadership of our liege lords. To the health of Duke Rowan the Just! May his puissance be ever held!"

"Hear, hear!" shout all the knights in spectacular unison.

"Hear, hear," follows Kendrick.

Commander Rayner holds his gaze on Edmond and Vivian as he downs his beverage. The other knights drink. Kendrick places his cup down, unwilling to solemnize the toast on a night such as this. He peeks at Vincent.

"Hear, hear," toasts Oswyn reluctantly. He drinks. The commander grins. He focuses his attention on the last three peasants now. Kendrick nudges Vincent with his elbow, trying to pressure him to toast. Vincent doesn't respond, and all Kendrick gets in return is a sharper prick from the dagger.

Commander Rayner holds his tankard toward Edmond and Vivian and states proudly, "to the life of Duke Rowan."

All attention turns toward the three of them. Edmond and Vincent glance at Vivian, who has taken on the role as leader. No one moves. The drum of rain on the sides of the building thumps hollowly through the inn. Kendrick turns his head close to Vincent's ear.

"Do what he says, and you all will get out alive," whispers Kendrick. "I want to help—"

Vincent thrusts his shoulder upward and cracks Kendrick's jaw.

Kendrick's head whiplashes backward and bobbles to the side. His hair flops over his face. The movement was so swift and immediate that, by the time everyone glances over at them, it isn't obvious what happened. Kendrick's hair covers devastation underneath. He spits out blood and a tooth. Vincent acts as though nothing happened.

Kendrick keeps his head bowed. His hair hangs over his eyes in long, greasy locks. It covers the tears streaming down his cheeks. He weeps.

Vivian raises her tankard to Commander Rayner's, shifting attention away from Kendrick and Vincent. She stares the commander square in the eyes.

"To those who deal with injustice," toasts Vivian. Vivian, Edmond, and Vincent all gulp down their drinks to this.

"Injustice," repeats Commander Rayner softly.

Kendrick grinds his jaw. Pain shoots through his gums at the movement. His chest rattles from the force of his tears. He sucks the lingering blood inside his mouth down his throat, where the bitter liquid descends like oil, burning and sticking to everything along the way.

Kendrick's life swarms around the perimeter of the table, sparkling in and out of existence like the dense streak of stars on a clear sky. His father materializes at the far end of the table. He's reluctant to look at Kendrick, to see what he has become. He thought Kendrick was meant for the forge, to craft steel into items worthy of God, but instead Kendrick has become *this*. He has become a symbol for resentment and animosity. Lucia hides from Kendrick behind the onslaught of memories, her beautiful features perverted by her blatant disgust for him.

Then it all disappears.

The happy memories, the sad memories, all of them evaporate into the emptiness of the room. Eliot's headless body collapses into a pile of dust and scatters into the windless air.

The world manages to do something even more cruel than throw Kendrick's fears back at him; it abandons him entirely. Kendrick loses touch with the earth. His body barrels through space, spinning, tumbling out of control. The world separates from him, and the nightmarish vision of the Earth, breaking apart and floating up into the stars, haunts Kendrick to his bones.

Kendrick doesn't know what else to do, so he weeps.

He cries as silently as he can, but his back and chest bob as his body reacts to the deep sobs within him. Today Kendrick learned the truth about himself and the world they live in. He is alone in it, abandoned and banished from its occupants.

That is, until Commander Rayner looks at him.

Kendrick glances up through his dangling hair. Commander Rayner raises his eyebrow. Kendrick's lips quiver. There's something in the commander's eyes, a special gift that Kendrick has forgotten in the darkness of the night: sympathy.

A conversation Kendrick will never be able to discuss, and one he'll never truly understand, is sent silently between the two of them. For the briefest of moments, Kendrick no longer feels detached from the earth. Commander Rayner listens to him. Empathy. The Codes weren't entirely wrong.

All knights are in it together. They share a bond no one else can possibly understand.

Before Kendrick knows it, as tears continue to stain his cheeks, he slowly lifts his bloodied palms to the commander. Kendrick nods to his side, and watches as Commander Rayner glances down at the open wound there.

Commander Rayner's lips furl into a smile. He nods at Kendrick, as if praising him "well done."

The commander now knows about the death, the betrayal, the vileness.

Kendrick lowers his head. He bawls. Vincent nudges him to quit, but Kendrick shakes his head. He can't stop. His life crumbles apart around him, and all he can do is watch.

G ODFREY WORMS ON THE ground. He twists and pulls at the bonds holding his hands together. They loosen ever so slightly. Godfrey grasps at the thought of Leif with every stone of vigor he can muster. When a person only has one mission left in the world, they must imprison that destiny into their being. It's their last grasp on the importance of life.

Leif is Godfrey's final chance at making something of his existence.

Godfrey observes from his low vantage point as Commander Rayner drinks from his tankard. After a contemplative moment, the commander speaks. "I suppose you peasants are heading for the wedding? Why else would you occupy a whore-house during a storm?"

"To whore," quips Vivian.

"That suits your fancy?"

"Surprise you?"

"I'm never surprised," grins Commander Rayner.

"Ye lot are a bunch of dolts though," says Edmond.

"Insult the commander again," growls Sir David. He starts to take out his sword, but Commander Rayner waves him down.

"How so?" asks Commander Rayner, keeping his tone light.

"Ye hang up scrolls all around the kingdom, inviting peasants to ye fancy weddin'. Yet ye know damn well we can't read," says Edmond. "Seems like a waste to me. If it weren't for the heralds—"

"You can find something wrong with everything the nobles do, can't you?" sneers Sir Ivan. "Everything is a slight to you. What do you think? That Duke Rowan put up those scrolls as some symbol for your inadequacies?"

"Everythin' ye do is to put us down," spits Edmond. "The way ye talk, the rumors ye start, the money ye take. It's all a game."

"That reminds me," says Commander Rayner, relaxing back into his seat. "There's been rumors of an assassination attempt on our great duke, supposedly to happen tomorrow at his son's wedding."

"What a travesty," dismisses Vivian.

Godfrey fumbles with the rope. The knights at the table sit upright, ready for whatever their commander dictates.

This is the perfect opportunity to escape.

Godfrey carefully pulls his body away from the table using his shoulders. He swivels onto his side, so he can hide his fingers as he manipulates the rope. His body is drenched with sweat, and his hands are slick and clammy. They struggle to grip the bonds.

Commander Rayner taps his fingers on the table. He sighs forcefully, as if he's being coerced into doing something he'd rather not deal with.

"Knights," he commands.

Sir David, Sir Ivan, and Sir Tobias blast up from their seats. They surround the table in the blink of an eye. The peasants at the table flinch. Godfrey glances up at the bar maiden, who has managed to stay invisible at the back of the room. She holds four flaming candles in her hand.

"What the hell?!" yells Edmond.

"Stop," Commander Rayner says bluntly.

"This is bullshit!" roars Oswyn.

"Stop. I know."

"Know what?" asks Verona, exasperated.

"I *know*."

The room freezes over. Even Godfrey halts at trying to slip from his bonds. The knights take out their weapons behind the peasants. Commander Rayner remains in his chair, alone on his side of the table.

"I've always thought of peasants as animals," says the commander pensively. "Did you know all animals ultimately bring their own demise? It's in their nature. The fall of every great civilization has come from the bottom of society. Why is that, I wonder."

"Because ye rely on us," says Vivian. "Our food, our money, our labor."

"No," asserts Commander Rayner. He shakes his head. "'Tis more than that. You see, I have a theory of my own. Before I state it, I want you to know it's not your fault. You can't blame an animal for never understanding, of course. What could an animal know of the thoughts of God?"

Not even the knights seem privy to the answer. They all stand silent under the fury of the storm, waiting for Commander Rayner to bless them with his distorted wisdom.

"I believe you do it out of boredom. I can't imagine being so bored with life that I'd herald the end of civilization just to make it interesting. The harsh truth of your world, the one you're terrified to accept, is that you are the scourge of humanity. The noblemen, the academics. Those of royal blood and lineages? *They* are the ones who are forced to rebuild humanity time and time again. They fashion a world you useless vermin can live in. Using *their* money and *their* resources, their benevolence stows upon you all the great comforts you enjoy in life. You have paved roads because of them. You have safety because of them. You have commerce because of them.

"But what do you spoiled, pathetic souls do in return for their grace? You tear down the very foundations they built. You provoke violence. It is you lot who wants wars, and it's you alone who incite the sparks for these calamities. You are so forlorn, so desperate to have meaning in life, that you would embrace the apocalypse all to ensure that you will be remembered for something, even for death.

"The truth is you can't live without hatred. You can't live without pain. To your sick minds, that's what gives you life. And then it is left to us, your betters, the true children of God, to clean up your mess in the next generation. We will do it too. We will rebuild a better civilization and a better society. But it's only a matter of time until your lot destroys it again, once society becomes too perfect, once your boredom claws back out."

"Ye sure like to fuckin' talk," hisses Edmond.

"Ye better get to your point, lest ye bore us again," says Vivian.

"I'll be succinct," the commander responds flatly. He narrows his brows and glares at them. He drops any veneer of hospitality he may have once had. He lets the beast out. "I abhor it, the incivility."

Commander Rayner nods to the three knights. Sir Ivan and Sir Tobias ready their axes. Sir David unsheathes his sword. They stand directly behind the three farmers.

Godfrey wiggles at the ropes. The bond around his right wrist slips over his fingers. He glances back at the table. From his view on the ground, he can see that Vivian, Edmond, and Oswyn have pulled out their knives under the table.

"Before you die," says Commander Rayner, smiling, "I wish to know why. How can boredom drive you toward such destruction? What purpose could you possibly have besides that?"

"Our purpose is life," says Vincent.

It's the first time he's spoken since they joined the table, and it catches everyone off guard. Even Kendrick, in his weeping state, glances up at him.

"A pity," sighs Commander Rayner. "You indoctrinate them so young now."

"No," grins Vivian. "The peasantry learnin' the truth. This is only the start. Killin' us matters not. This century will bring a great change in the world. Me can feel it."

"Is your arrogance so blinding?" asks the befuddled commander. "Do you not recognize the path you descend? Don't you feel it in those knives you hold?"

The farmers turn silent, stricken by pure fear. Godfrey writhes on the ground, rubbing his hand along the dirt. The rope pulls farther down his hand. He almost has it off. Edith stirs behind him. Godfrey peeks at her curiously as she white knuckles the candles.

She's planning something . . .

Vivian clears her throat. "So what now?" she asks coarsely.

The knights raise their weapons. The peasants ready their knives. Godfrey closes his eyes and waits for the violence to start. It always ends this way.

Bang!

Godfrey jumps out of his skin. He twists on the floor and looks toward the noise. Leif bursts through the door to the stables. Tears stream down the little boy's face. It breaks Godfrey's heart. The urge to smoke transforms into the urge to hug him. Blood and mud cover Leif's body. His short hair is smudged to his head, and his clothes are ripped and tattered.

"Me pa!" wails Leif. "He's . . . he's out yonder. And he's . . . he's . . . and the knight . . ."

The commander closes his eyes as if praying. He takes a deep breath.

"Animals."

Commander Rayner pounces after the peasants like a metallic demon. He shreds his sword from the scabbard. The table cleaves apart under his force. Lightning and thunder rock the inn.

Then, Edith moves.

She throws the candles onto the hay-covered ground. The straw instantly catches fire. And before Godfrey has time to scream, the flames barrel toward him.

ETERNAL RUINS

T HE IMMEDIATE wave of heat blasts Edith into the bar. The wooden counter bursts asunder under her weight. Her spine bends inward, and a loud crack trumpets from her bones. She crumbles over, knocking her head on the corner of the bar, and collapses unconscious onto a barstool.

Her mind reawakens within a second, just in time for her to smack into the hard ground. Her breath leaves her body. She groans.

Edith's decision to catch the inn on fire had been her last course of action. She went through all the lists she could think of. She scanned all her options and imagined all the repercussions they could hold. At the end, it came down to Commander Rayner forcing her hand, as Edith knew she would be executed with the rest of them. She'd rather take her chances with a fire rather than Emma's father. It may even give Paris and Verona a chance to get out.

What Edith hadn't calculated, however, was that the inn would instantly combust, and that the inferno would consume the entire room within seconds. She thought the storm would have wet the building enough that only the hay would catch fire. She was wrong.

The inhabitants of the common room scatter before the roaring flames. A wall of flames separates Edith from the knights and the peasants, who were continuing to fight on the far side of the inn.

The fire has eaten much of the furniture. The tables are glowing embers, and the chairs are pathetic kindling. Edith pushes herself to her knees as the blaze licks at the surrounding walls. Black smoke covers the ceiling, reflecting the glow of the hellfire in sporadic orange tints. Edith feels her skin cooking alive, like she's roasting inside of a community oven. Sweat can't even be used to describe the amount of water leaking from her skin, as she feels her insides practically evaporating.

Edith uses the bar counter to pull herself up on her feet. She shrieks, quickly pulling her hands away from the counter. She gapes down at her hands, which now glisten red. The counter burned her hands, and they tingle with an almost unbearable scorching sensation. Edith ignores the waves of pain that zap up from her hands. She glances around the room. The common room has been separated into subsections by the flames, and she can barely discern the moving figures behind them.

She steps uneasily across the bar. She has two options of getting out of the inn: the front door or the stables. She attempts to orient herself within the inferno, but all directions look the same. Flames and debris and unimaginable brightness. She panics. Edith's heart drums in her chest, and the oppressive heat of fire presses her down into a miniscule child.

Emma. Remember Emma.

Edith whips her head around, checking for anything that may give her perspective of where she is.

The stairs. A little ways directly across from her, briefly visible through the three-meter-high flickering flames, Edith catches sight of the staircase. That means the stables are right behind her. Edith turns around.

She keeps the bar to her left, using it to maintain a straight path. The firestorm crawls after her. Edith's body freezes before her mind tells her to, and the ceiling above her cleaves. A heavy oak beam collapses to the floor, blasting the bar in half. Edith braces her face as sharp debris and smoke flutters around her. A good portion of those fumes inject straight into her lungs. Edith coughs them out. The blazing refuge blockades her path to the stables.

Right. The main door then.

Edith turns herself back around. The stairs flicker in and out of existence before her. She uses it as her guide. As long as she keeps sight of the stairs, she can find her way through this maze of death.

KENDRICK PUSHES HIMSELF TO his feet as Commander Rayner lunges after the peasants. The tables bounce aside as the commander thunders through them. His momentum is stopped, however, as soon as the heat makes itself known. Kendrick's hair scatters back as the momentous explosion hurls a gust of painfully hot air at them. Kendrick and Vincent duck for cover. The initial rage of fire rushes across the inn, appearing like a stampede of hellish steeds scorching everything in their path.

The knights leap from the flames as it severs the room. Commander Rayner bounces back, his unsheathed sword and metal armor making him flare like Hell itself.

Vincent's dagger presses into Kendrick's skin. He twirls, grasping for Vincent's arm. The boy fights back, trying to set his knife into Kendrick's gut. Kendrick shoves him back. The blade strips out blood as it leaves his side.

The force of the push bounces both of them to the ground, and a wall of fire divides between them. Kendrick uses the opportunity to crawl away. He hears the shouts and screams of multiple people. The roar of the inferno builds as it devours more of the inn. The wooden walls and foundations catch fire around him.

They're trapped in here.

A war cry erupts as Kendrick forces himself to his feet. He hobbles around just in time to see Oswyn emerge through dense smoke. He rushes after Sir Tobias, dagger in hand, and slits the knight's throat. Kendrick loses sight of them as they both collapse through flames into a pile of chairs. They disappear behind the brilliant glow of Hell and the deathly blackness of smoke.

Kendrick stumbles onward, unsure what direction that is exactly. He loses control of all his senses. Every part of his body is overloaded. The scorching smell of smoke blocks his nasal passages. The intense heat, which burns the edges of his hair, suppresses all sense of touch. His mouth is parched and dry, and his tongue shrivels into a dead twig. He can't even hear properly, as the hellfire screams around him. Even his eyes feel like drying out into husks.

Kendrick eventually stumbles into a block of wood. After a long moment of his brain trying to calculate what he could have possibly run into, it finally occurs to him that it must be the bar.

He hears a loud blast of crashing wood come from his right. An obscured figure drifts toward him. Kendrick steps away from the phantom, ready to be confronted with Eliot or Lucia again.

"Reveal yourself!" shouts Kendrick over the blaze. The figure doesn't respond, but it keeps walking toward him. Kendrick takes a grateful sigh of relief as the bar maiden stumbles through the remaining smoke. "Edith!"

Kendrick runs up to her. A good portion of her face is smothered with soot, and her eyebrows and eyelashes have scorched off completely. She must have gotten the blunt of the first explosion. He shakes her, and her eyes finally seem to crystalize onto him.

"Kendrick?"

"We have to move."

Kendrick grunts as he helps lead her. Fresh blood drips from the wound in his side. He has to brace her against the bar as she stuffs a ripped piece of fabric from his armor into the hole.

"Behind ye!" yells Edith.

Kendrick swirls. Vincent's knife misses his face by only a finger length, and the dagger penetrates the bar counter. Vincent tries to pry it loose, but the knife holds, sunk too deeply into the planks. Kendrick swings his fist at Vincent, but he ducks under it. They grapple.

Kendrick pulls after Vincent's wrists, letting his brief training take over. It's all about controlling your opponent, taking ownership over their vulnerable limbs. That mainly involves focusing on their wrists and their neck. The human body follows wherever those two limbs go. They wrestle after each other. The fire smothers the air around them, and so the fight for air becomes as important as the fight for strength.

Kendrick overpowers him. He shoves Vincent against the counter, and it allows him a precious second to raise his fist and throw it. It connects with Vincent's skull. The kid slumps to the ground, knocked out.

Kendrick's eyes linger on Vincent. Somewhere in that infinitesimal space between them lies the truth of the world, its plainness dormant until the breaking point of human sensibilities finally decays after a single event. That iceberg which has taken place in the stead of Kendrick's soul reemerges its ugly head, and Kendrick feels it frost over with another layer of impenetrable ice. There is no escaping this world in one piece.

"Me knows the way out!" yells Edith, tearing Kendrick out of his trance.

Edith slinks past him. Kendrick gives Vincent one last glance. He's leaving him to die. Vincent may avoid the smoke that's quickly filling the air since he's sprawled on the ground, but the fire is rapidly devouring every square meter of space. It will be a painful death.

Kendrick grimaces. He pulls Vincent's leg and drags him away from the nearest wall of flames. Edith peeks back at him but doesn't say anything. He lifts Vincent's chest up, so he rests against the bar. This'll give him a chance to regain consciousness before the fire gets him.

"We need to go," says Edith.

Kendrick turns away from Vincent. He rushes behind Edith as they dodge flames and collapsing architecture. He doesn't hear Vincent stirring behind him.

EDITH SCUTTLES PAST A pile of burning planks. She and the squire stay low to avoid the smoke. The black fumes slowly descend toward them, like an upside-down layer of mystical water that is trying to submerge them into its foul depths. The smoke curls and entwines into strings of darkness that almost resemble a net. They cross past the engulfed stairs, and they carefully navigate around what Edith believes to be the hearth.

Emma. Emma. Emma.

Edith's mind stays on track. She no longer hears the screams and grunts of the other patrons of the inn. The room has gone quiet with cacophonous chaos. She has to be almost there. The door or window can't be much farther. Edith accidentally touches her skin, and the spot leaves an ashy, almost charcoal residue on her hand.

"HELP!"

The feminine voice squeals through the furious inferno, piercing it like the dart of an arrow. Edith stops in her tracks. She can't be sure of the voice, but it sounds like—

"UP 'ERE!"

Edith bows her head. That one is a male voice, and she did recognize it. *Shit.*

"Who's that?" asks Kendrick. He spins around, trying to find the source of the pleas.

"A man and woman," groans Edith. "Newlyweds."

"Upstairs?"

Edith nods.

"We have to help them," states the squire like it's blatantly apparent that they should rush back into the thick of the hellish firestorm.

"Are ye mad?!" She glares at Kendrick. He wobbles slightly. His face is ashy white. "Look at ye! Ye won't make it."

"HELP!" pleas Verona's voice again.

"We don't have time," urges Kendrick.

He rushes after the inferno staircase. Edith doesn't. She hears wood crash behind her. She turns and glimpses as falling debris collapses a hole into the side of the inn. It's only a few yards away from her.

Emma.

Edith discerns rain and darkness through the opening, an escape from their present deathtrap, a way to her daughter. All she has to do is stride forward and she'll be out. One of the knights, it looks like Sir David, jumps through the hole and into the abyss beyond.

"Edith."

Edith spins on her heels and glances at the squire. The fire burns furiously around him, and the plump sea of black smoke nearly reaches his head. His eyes water from the ash and fumes. "I need you," he says simply.

Damn it! Why did he have to say that so plainly.

Her muscles pull for her to leave, to abandon the fallacy of human morality. Her natural instincts as a mother, to survive so she can care for her daughter, pulls every stone of her weight toward the hole in the wall. It is certainly moral for a person to leave others to die so they can care for their child. That is justified. *She* is justified.

"Please," begs Kendrick behind her. His voice is so soft, and so selflessly pure, that it manages to pull back Edith's motherly instincts for a moment.

Her gut twists into a knot, and her mind transports her back to the last time she saw Emma. Her daughter runs around before her, chasing the local kids and living a life of unashamed enjoyment. A good life. A happy life.

"ANYONE!" screams Paris.

"HELP US!"

Edith swivels her head to Kendrick. He waits for her, begging. Edith glares back, keeping her eyes trained on the breach. She feels tears run down her cheeks, probably from the smoke as much as the devastation of her heart. She feels like she's being shredded through a world of knives, tossed about by the forces of Heaven.

She doesn't need to help. Not this time.

Edith walks toward the hole, afraid to look back at Kendrick. A small explosion of sparks and fire blasts before her. She falls back onto her butt and pushes backward from the hole. Her hands curl into fists and her veins pop out of her neck. She yells into the air, a ferocious and dreadful sound.

"Why do you have to do this to me?!" shrieks Edith past the flames, past the storm, far into the firmament above.

"Edith," says that squire's stupid, innocent fucking voice. Why is he doing this to her? Let her go. Let her see her daughter, for pity's sake. "We have to save them."

"Why?!" cries Edith. She pushes herself up, her whole body a wanton mess. She glares at the young man. What makes him so worthy? What makes him so gallant and courageous to look down upon her, to strike judgment on her about what's right and wrong? "Why should we save them?"

"Because it's all meaningless if we don't," he answers gently.

Edith lowers her head. Her face scrunches. She imagines Emma's features. Her black hair, her green eyes, her clear skin, and her lovely smile. She is so beautiful. She's hers. Emma is Edith's daughter. She's the one thing that has made Edith feel alive.

Now why is this decision so hard?

A rivulet of tears bleeds from her eyes, reflecting the colors of Hell around her. Edith gazes at the hole to freedom . . . the path to her daughter.

It's all meaningless if you don't.

CRUEL LOVE

T HE INITIAL SPARK OF flames barrels after Godfrey.

He rolls to the side, the blaze grazing him as it roars by. He fumbles with his bonds, desperate now to get out, to get to Leif. The two tables that housed the hospitality of English society shudders across the room as Commander Rayner bulges through it. Godfrey hears the crackle of flames, and he peeks back in time to catch the fire twisting before it reaches the far wall. It slithers back toward him like a vicious snake, its fiery fangs lunging forward to seize Godfrey in petrified fear. Godfrey clumsily stumbles to his feet and tumbles to the side as the flames make a second attempt at consuming him.

He falls to the earth unharmed. He tries again to free his bonds. He pulls at the ropes, and his fingers crack under the constrictive pressure. He finally manages to slip his right hand free. He rubs his right thumb for a moment, checking to see if it broke while he slid the rope from its thickness. It didn't, and he chuckles in relief. Godfrey quickly slips his left hand out and stands up in the center of the inferno.

It's time, Godfrey. Do something right for once in your life. Save Leif. Get him out of here. You can do it. You can do it.

Godfrey spins around, examining the room. He searches for a recognizable object, something to let him know where he is. A giant flame wall jumps in front of him. He blocks his face as the heat boils his skin. The few facial hairs he had singe to nonexistence. A breeze of smoke circulates around the multiple stacks of fire like an underwater current flows around rocks and flora, billowing out as it surges in its own nascent air pressure. It smacks into Godfrey's face, and his lungs retaliate by harshly coughing out toxic phlegm and debris.

Godfrey turns away from the monstrous wall of fire, but its ever-present heat scorches the moisture from the air around him. His skin dries up into infinite wrinkles, and when he breathes in, it feels like he's sucking on charred flesh. The flames reach from floor to ceiling, obscuring all.

"Leif?!" shouts Godfrey. "Leif?!"

A light cough erupts from the other side of some flames. A small cough, a *little* cough. There's only one person so little to make such a noise. Godfrey charges toward the rasp, unconcerned with the damages his body may take. It already betrayed him long ago when it deigned him unworthy of anything other than smoking and drinking. There is more to his life than that. He may be a terrible poet, and perhaps he does push everyone away, but he's human, which means he has the ability to change—regardless of what other's think, of what *he* thinks.

Take responsibility, Godfrey. Take responsibility of your life for once.

Godfrey bursts through smoke and almost trips into the inferno. He backs up. The small cough echoes out again. He strains his ears to find the direction of the sound.

Oh, you have to be—

A narrow path between two unfaltering barriers of hellfire leads to the stables. The door is nudged open at the very end of this flaming hallway. The path is no wider than Godfrey's body when he turns his shoulders sideways; in fact, it appears to be even narrower than that toward the center. He will have to shimmy down the narrow corridor between the two fiery partitions. The flames crackle and sparkle as if to greet him to their extravagant misgivings. There's no way Godfrey can move through it without getting burned.

"Leif, I'm coming!"

Godfrey turns his body so he can fit through the opening of the flaming palisade. He sucks in his stomach and wedges himself down the passageway. The incandescent fury churns ahead and behind him. He has to squint his eyes to not be blinded by its brilliance, and Godfrey imagines that he is shimmying through the sun itself. His skin simmers, but he surprisingly feels little pain. He catches a glimpse of the back of his hand, and he has to stuff down the urge to vomit as his skin bubbles up from his muscles. The narrowest part of the passage flares before him. There's nothing he can do but continue toward it.

Godfrey sucks in as much as he can, and then he presses himself into the fire. He moves fast, practically running sideways. The fire licks over his face. It doesn't immediately burn him like he expected it would, instead it feels as if his head is in the center of a bubble of flames, cooking him from its heat rather than bluntly charring him.

He thought time would flow slowly when experiencing intense pain, but it reacts oppositely. The few seconds that he is incased in the inferno is over within an instant, and the only clue he has that it's finally past him is when his body crashes through the door to the stables.

Unfortunately, the pain hits him now.

Godfrey writhes on the floor, banging his fists on the ground for no good reason other than to try to distract the agony by adding more pain elsewhere. His face is seething from the inside out. He can *feel* the heat actively transferring from his face to the air around him. Little entrails of smoke wisp from his skin. Godfrey yells. His agony refuses to alleviate despite his pathetic fist punching and puny screams. This torture is here to last. Godfrey ignores it as best as he can, focusing his energy on the most important thing in the world. Not his affliction, but his redemption.

"Leif!"

Godfrey crawls deeper into the stables. The horses neigh incessantly at the picket line. They prance and kick backward at the licking flames. The inferno stretches to the countless piles of firewood strewn throughout the room. The rain drops that leak from the ceiling evaporate before they ever reach the ground.

"Mr. Bard!"

Godfrey's heart thumps in his throat. His eyes dart around the room, peering between the glittering fire and over the bleak smoke. He finds Leif trapped on one side of the room behind a piece of fallen debris. A section of the roof had collapsed. Leif ducks below the layer of smoke with watering eyes.

"Leif," smiles Godfrey, moving closer to the boy. "I'm going to get you out of here!"

Godfrey examines the collapsed roof. The debris simmers, and he doesn't need to get close to realize his hands will burn off before he ever moves the rubble. There's no way for him to get to Leif, but there is a crawlspace under the debris that the boy can fit through.

"I need you to crawl under that to me," says Godfrey. Leif glares at the flaming beam between them. "You can do it. I believe in you."

Godfrey can see the miniscule whirling of flames reflected off the boy's eyes, and the fright behind them is glaringly apparent. Godfrey nods at Leif, hoping it gives him the courage to do what he needs. But it is Godfrey who gains fortitude from their interaction, and his heart calms as resolution grabs ahold of him. They can do this.

Leif maneuvers onto his stomach. He crawls prone under the blazing debris. His body barely fits. The heat burns his sides. Godfrey gets as close as he can to the flames. He reaches his hand out to help pull Leif.

A strange scent hits Godfrey's nose. He glances up. The stacked firewood all around the room starts to smoke. That can't be good.

Godfrey falls onto his knees, trying to get lower so Leif can reach his hand faster. The boy crawls, inch by inch, cautiously and hesitantly, under the collapsed roof. His skin glistens with the sludge of soot and sweat. Leif looks up at Godfrey with his innocent, little eyes. Godfrey reaches for him, desperately searching for the salvation to his life.

The firewood is really steaming around them now.

"Take my hand!" cries Godfrey. His voice strains to make any noise. The air is so thick and dry.

Leif extends for Godfrey. His hand reaches, reaches—

He freezes. Godfrey stares at him, baffled. Leif tilts his head, and his eyes grow wide like Godfrey has transformed into some malevolent demon.

"Leif?"

Leif flinches his hand away from Godfrey. A dark glint passes over the boy's face, and he grits his teeth into a half-snarl. Godfrey reacts. He dives under the debris and grabs after the boy, trying to muscle Leif toward him. But Leif shuffles backward, keeping himself out of reach from Godfrey's prying arms.

"Son, take my hand!"

"No!" retaliates Leif.

The boy shies away from him. He pushes himself back to the other side of the burning beam. He shakes all over. Godfrey stands, unamused and thoroughly disconcerted.

No, no, no. What's happening?!

"You killed me pa!" Leif's voice croaks as emotion overfloods his little frame. The horses ricochet off each other behind him.

"What? Leif, I would never—"

"Ye did."

He is no longer saying *you*. Godfrey's body trembles. The voice that he buried down with the help of Leif reemerges into his soul.

We did it again. We destroyed our connection with another person. Leif doesn't love you. Look at him, he despises us.

Leif's eyes turn puffy. Godfrey shakes his head, in denial that Leif would ever think of him as a monster. Godfrey has been fine tonight. Leif has kept him in shape.

A pop bursts into the air as a bundle of firewood splinters and explodes.

I have to show him. I need to prove to Leif that I am a good person.

Godfrey tries to maneuver around the debris. The roof crumbles and blocks his path to the boy. Rain and fire intermingle around them. A gale of wind whines through the hole in the roof and tosses up fire flurries between them.

Make it right, Godfrey. Make it right.

"Leif, I was protecting you."

"Ye lie!"

"I know what he does, Leif," says Godfrey. Leif takes a step back away from him, and Godfrey's lips quiver as the furious agony his body fights through subsides. Only pure emotion remains. He has to put everything on the line. "Those bruises on your arm, that scar. They didn't manifest from thin air. I warned him that if he touched you again, I would take you from him."

Godfrey wipes away tears. He doesn't know the last time he cried for anyone. Leif stares at him, trying to distinguish reality from fiction. The picket line whips as the horses use their collective strength to pull away at it. The fire roars around them.

This is your last chance, Godfrey realizes. You need to give him your all. Stop hiding how you feel. Stop suppressing all your self-hatred. Let him know. Open up.

"Come live with me," croaks Godfrey. He speaks slowly, deliberately, sure to make every word hang in the air. "I'm sick. I never thought I'd be a father, but I've always wanted to be a brother. You make me want to stay clean. We can travel, tell stories. I can teach you to read and write. Remember our story? The rock monster who wants to be friends with humans? Only you can bring out that friendliness in him. We can be a family."

There it is. It's all out there.

Godfrey reaches out his hand, a symbol of his openness and his trust. Leif glances down at Godfrey's warmth, and Godfrey can spot the million thoughts going through the kid's mind all at once. Slowly, agonizingly, the little hope for

Godfrey's future looks up at him. The expression on Leif is unreadable, and Godfrey's heart crawls to a halt. The world goes silent around him.

The storm disappears. The fire subsides. All the silly, unimportant turmoil of his past evaporates. All the aimless wandering and searching of Godfrey's life has led him here. None of it matters but this moment, the final destination of his soul.

"I hate ye," hisses Leif.

Godfrey's body somehow manages to blush through the searing pain. His world collapses into a thunderous menagerie of ruin. He begs, "Leif—"

"I HATE YE!"

The firewood surrounding the room explodes. A hole blasts into the side of the stables. Splinters, log chunks, and fire bursts into a ball of molten mayhem.

Godfrey and Leif launch across the room, their bodies thrusted about and shredded like nothing. Godfrey braces his hands uselessly in front of him, and his head hits the floor hard. His vision blurs, and all sounds mingle into a single unrelenting high-pitch tone, like a town bell who's ring never dissipates.

Godfrey's smarting body finally scuttles to a screeching stop. He lifts his head up, and an aching sting shoots down his neck to his tailbone. He watches the horses finally break the picket line, their manes sizzling, and their tails burnt to a crisp. All the horses race off through the open hole, hauling lengths of the burning rope with them.

The last thing Godfrey sees before he passes out is those majestic beasts vanishing into the spring storm.

BENEVOLENT WRATH

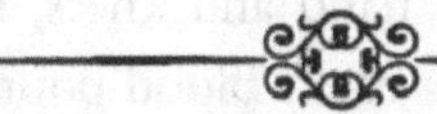

VINCENT REAWAKENS TO A discomforting throb in his head. He rubs his temples as he catches up to the present. He's propped against the bar, but he doesn't remember bracing himself against it. The last thing he remembers was when he was stopping Kendrick from getting away. Then they got into a scuffle . . . but the rest is a blur.

He groans laboriously as he strains to get on his feet. The whole place burned down so quickly. One moment he was at the table, the next he was in the middle of a firestorm.

Vivian, Edmond, Oswyn. I have to find them.

Vincent stumbles onward, wary of the falling debris and flickering flames. The inside of the inn has almost generated a windstorm of its own, with hot gusts blowing embers and ash through the air. Some walls of fire coalesce together into magnificent, swirling columns of flames that shine with the grace of damnation. Vincent swats away the deadly exhaust as it flurries around him. Something about it all seems right. The world has taken on the very form of Vincent's animosity, and now it's showering him in it with rancorous glee.

He's maintaining his goodness.

Vincent spots Oswyn, who pushes the corpse of Sir Tobias off him. Oswyn's right arm is sliced, and he braces it gingerly as he rolls off his back. Orange-red blood drizzles down his arm. His fingers hang uselessly from his hand.

He's going to have trouble cooking now, thinks Vincent. He shakes out the silly thought. There are more important things to worry about.

Oswyn climbs onto his hand and knees, but then an axe and a sword pierce into his back. Blood pours from Oswyn's mouth as the weapons skewer him to the ground. His body slowly descends down the blade of the sword and the head of the axe until his cadaver finally plops to the earth with an unadorned thump.

Commander Rayner and Sir Ivan wrench their weapons from his lifeless body. Vincent scuttles back until he is hidden behind the fiery rubble.

The knights share a contagious bout of coughing. Smoke and debris fly everywhere. The flame wall towers toward them. Commander Rayner swats away a black veil of smoke to reveal Sir David stumbling from it. Peasant or knight or noble alike, they are all equally affected by the forces of nature.

"Run to the keep!" Commander Rayner orders Sir David. "Warn Duke Rowan!"

"You think this is them?" asks Sir David.

"I have no doubt. The air was amiss the moment we stepped in. It's our lucky day, we stumbled right into the coup. We have to tell the duke!"

"What about you?!"

"We'll handle it."

"Rayner—"

"Go!" shouts Commander Rayner. He shoves Sir David away. "There's no time to waste!"

Sir David nods to his commander. He worms around some flames and searches for an escape. Commander Rayner and Sir Ivan remain, exposed and deadly. Vincent feels around his belt, but he left his dagger in the bar. He's weaponless.

The commander and the knight move. Vincent follows them, deciding that it's safer to keep them in view than risking accidentally stumbling into them while traversing through a cloud of smoke.

Commander Rayner and Sir Ivan hold their weapons up at the ready. The knights maneuver around flames, falling wood, flying debris, and opaque smoke. Vincent moves carefully behind them, mindful of the sudden bursts and flares of the columns of smoke. They reach out at random intervals, branching and attempting to scorch whatever dares curl around them.

Vincent's mind starts to go fuzzy. A serene calmness slowly overtakes the turmoil of the inferno, and he even begins to feel cozy in the heat rather than deleterious.

Vincent involuntarily hacks out smoke. The harsh, dry cough surprises the knights. They spin around, but Vincent dives prone onto the ground in time. The knights glance around the burning inn. Sir Ivan bumps into Commander Rayner, who shoves him off him.

"Sir Commander, I'm feeling light-headed," moans Sir Ivan.

"Belt it," silences the commander. "Do you hear that?"

Vincent watches the knights while prone. The earth burns his arms and legs, carrying the heat from the surrounding fire into their roots. Commander Rayner jerks around right as Edmond vaults over the wall of fire.

Edmond impales his knife into Sir Ivan's armpit, tearing into the only vulnerable skin that his leather armor doesn't protect. Edmond slices the dagger out and brings a healthy number of tendons with him. Sir Ivan swings his axe, but Edmond ducks under it. Vivian ambushes from the surrounding smoke. She tries to stab her knife into the back of Sir Ivan's neck. The knight pivots, however, and swings his axe at her. Vivian jumps to the side, avoiding the attack by a few hair lengths. She disappears back into the black air.

Sir Ivan uses his momentum to continue his strike. He swings around at Edmond during the same moment Edmond stabs down at him.

Edmond lodges his dagger into the knight's ear. Sir Ivan separates Ed's arm from the shoulder. They collapse together into the wall of flames, combusting the fire into a miniature explosion around them.

Vincent covers his mouth, suppressing a gasp that wants desperately to leave his throat. Commander Rayner spins in a circle, bracing his sword up in a guard position. Wood collapses to the floor somewhere in the room. The commander flinches. Vincent watches him scan his surroundings, which alternate between being insanely bright and incredibly dark.

"I know you're still here, wench!" Commander Rayner coughs. "You can't resist killing me, just like all you murdering peasants!"

A cough erupts from somewhere nearby. Commander Rayner and Vincent glare toward the sound. A giant wall of ash flies toward them like the front of some massive storm. It bears down on them. Within an instant, both Vincent and Commander Rayner are blasted in the face by thick fumes and smoldering embers. It burns Vincent's eyes, and his ears and nose become clogged by the substances. He sneezes it out. Vincent hesitates, wondering when Commander Rayner will slice him down for making that noise, but the commander never does.

The wall of ash surrounds them now. It's a magnificent sight. Darkness shrouds them, but it is alive and feisty. The smoke swirls about, and sections of the fumes burn red-orange for a brief moment, giving a glimpse at the surrounding hell. But inside their isolated cylindrical ash pile, the smoldering debris floats gently around them like black stars. The inn might not even exist for all they know. It becomes eerily silent, a hellish bliss.

"Come on, you whore," growls Commander Rayner.

Wood cracks. Commander Rayner spins. Nothing.

The commander relaxes his shoulders and lowers his blade from the guard position. Vincent sees the smoke behind him glow red. It silhouettes a woman with a knife.

"There."

Commander Rayner swings his sword. Vivian stabs.

The commander's arm blocks her knife. Vivian bounces back, stunned by the force of his defense. Commander Rayner grips the blade of his sword with his hand and yanks it toward him while he simultaneously punches the hilt. His metal armor clinks together as the pommel cracks into Vivian's skull.

She tumbles to the ground. Commander Rayner stands over her. The barrel of smoke around them blows away with another gust of hot air. Vincent crawls forward, trying to get a better look at their fight.

The fumes obscure Commander Rayner's face as he mounts Vivian. His green eyes sparkle through the darkness and mutate into a devilish red gleam. He grabs the blade with both hands, half-swording the weapon, and lifts it above his head. Vivian's frightened face reflects off his armor as she realizes what he's doing. He aims to use the hilt as a hammer.

Vivian slices Commander Rayner's shins.

The commander drops his sword and collapses to the earth. He writhes back and forth, slapping at his severed tendons.

Vivian, while trapped on the ground like a cornered hog, managed to find the only vulnerable spot on Commander Rayner's entire body. A mistake had been made while lacing up Commander Rayner's greaves, the long piece of leg armor that rises from the base of his foot to below his knees. The greave is connected to a small piece of metal, which protects his calf by three treads along their side. A foot protection piece called the sabaton is supposed to shield any exposed skin under the outer ridges of the greave; however, because of some miraculous moment of stupidity, or incompetence, or both, the lower thread that ties the frontal greave to the back one was loose . . . just loose enough for Vivian to slide the blade of her dagger above the sabaton and slice his shins apart.

"You fucking cunt! Whoreson!" weeps Commander Rayner. He tries to stand, but his ankle snaps in half under his weight. The commander slumps onto his head. "You bitch! I can't walk!"

Commander Rayner crawls forward. The blaze bursts through the smoke. He's surrounded and useless like the rest of them now. Serves him right. Vincent smiles. This is divine judgment at its very best.

"Me told ye . . . this century will change the world." Vivian coughs. "Ye kind will be gone by the end of it."

"I'm going to kill all of you!" Commander Rayner remains motionless on the ground while crying out into the inferno.

Vivian feels for her head, but Vincent sees her fingers pass right through her skull. The Commander's pommel bash did its job; however, it's only Commander Rayner who shrieks in pain now. His howls turn into gurgles, which turn into weeps of pain. Vivian beams the entire time, filled with satisfaction as she listens to his melodic agony.

Vincent stumbles over to her, the final remaining friend of his older brother. She gazes at the engulfed ceiling above them. Vincent cranks his neck to see what is so fascinating about it. Fire streaks around the outer walls and blows inward toward the spot Vivian looks at. The smoke disperses around these intense flames, and Vincent catches the magnificence of that ceiling. The planks grow a mixture of ruby red, emerald green, azure blue, lilac purple, and pure white within the hidden fissures and gaps of the grain. The colors whisk around, transforming and melting into different shades of various beauties, all instigated by the destruction of fire.

On that night seven years ago, as Vincent stood upon that knoll and watched the town of his childhood burn to nothingness, he believed it was the only time he would ever see something that spectacularly abhorrent in all his life. He was wrong.

"Vivian," says Vincent, his voice sounding hazy and distant. He shakes her. "Vivian."

She turns her head toward him, exposing her head gash to Vincent in all its horrible glory. Vincent applies pressure to it, unsure of what else to do with his hands. All he really does is get them bloody. Vivian smiles up at him.

"Kill the squire," she says. "Your brother would want it. Me knows it. He would want ye to avenge him. 'Tis what your parents would want. Kill him. Ye are the last one we have. Kill him."

Vincent nods at her, knowing it is true.

Vivian dies there under his arms, beneath the hypnotic wood above them. He rests her head down gently. She's right. This is what his whole life has built up to. All his doubts and theories about the goodness in the world, all those years he spent dissenting against Fraunce and his friends about the anger they hold toward knights, it has all led to this very moment of becoming a man. He had to go through all that inner turmoil so that tonight he could learn the full truth about humanity. He needed to feel the betrayal. He needed to understand the depth of its roots. He needed all of it, even though it hurts. It hurts like Hell. His quiet prayer with the priest was in a past life now. This is a new world; this is a life of fire that Vincent has been newly baptized in.

Now he knows what Fraunce really meant. This is why he was best friends with Vivian and Edmond. Now he knows what he needs to accomplish to become the man his older brother always wanted him to be.

To not be naive. To not be a coward. To not be a simpleton who ambles through life and experiences the basicness of marriage and child rearing.

Fraunce wanted me to be more than that.

A glint of firelight catches Vincent's eye. It's a reflection off a sharp, iron object: Commander Rayner's sword.

Vincent smiles.

It all starts with killing Kendrick the squire.

PREMEDITATED IMPULSE

P ARIS HELPS VERONA UP from the bed. Smoke seeps into Chamber 1 from the peephole in the floor. Paris can feel the fire smoldering beneath them as the warmth spreads through the wooden floorboards. He can't tell if it's his imagination or not, but the planks seem to be rising upward, bursting the floor into various tilted angles. It's disorientating, and it makes him dizzy.

He peels the animal-skin blankets off his wife and positions her feet on the floor. She has largely recovered from the sickness and only has minor symptoms, like a petulant cough and chapped lips.

"What are we doin'?" asks Verona.

"'Tis time to go," hurries Paris. "Ye heard Edith. We need to be out the door."

Verona simply nods. She grunts as Paris puts her weight onto him. He braces her while she stands. They remain motionless for a while, letting Verona's legs get used to their own weight again. Paris saw the initial blast of flames, but otherwise doesn't know the full extent of what is happening downstairs. The storm is still louder than the fire. And the air is mostly clear, other than the continuing rise of smoke from the peephole and through tiny cracks in the floorboards. Paris shuffles Verona forward. They make slow progress, and Verona has to stop for a break when they're halfway to the door.

"You have to keep goin'," says Paris.

"I know." Verona sighs, her breath coming out harsh and blunt.

One of her biggest fears is to be a burden on those around her. She had told Paris that on one of their first courting encounters. Verona curses to herself as she stumbles over her own feet and collapses to the floor. Paris is careful not to make her feel too bad about these circumstances. It isn't her fault. He knows that, but the longer he stays in this inn, the more the dread builds and builds inside of him like a never-ceasing wave; its colossal angst slamming on him again and again, raising his anxiety. The only escape is to get out of this hellhole. The only way to do that is to somehow move Verona downstairs and out the door without any of the knights noticing. So Paris isn't particularly hard on himself either, as his masquerade slips for a brief moment, and a glimpse of annoyance passes over his face. Verona doesn't say anything though. She'll keep that self-conscious burden locked away somewhere deep within her. It'll come out against Paris someday, but as long as that means they'll get out of here alive, Paris will take it.

With depleting vigor and strenuous fatigue, they manage to reach the door out of Chamber 1. *This is going to be a long way down,* humors Paris, trying to keep the mood light in his own mind.

"Got it," says Paris, reaching for the door handle and throwing it open.

They stumble forward, Verona dragging Paris with her, as the door swings around its hinges. Verona leans against the door frame and tries to catch her breath. Her eyes flicker back to the guest chamber as she suddenly remembers something.

"The sack," huffs Verona.

"We'll have to leave it."

"But my weddin' dress—my mum's weddin' dress, is in there. And some of our clothes, and other stuff we can sell to —"

"We don't have time," says Paris. "Trust me. We don't need it. We'll start our own life together, and we will find better stuff to replace it. Our stuff."

Verona gives in. She kisses her fingers and places them on Paris's cheek. She smiles at him. Paris leans in and they hug for a good, long second . . . until the smoke hits them.

Paris and Verona recoil from the blast of fumes, which curls into their nasal passages and stuffs burning embers into the crevasses of their nose. Paris jumps to the far side of the hall. The black smoke swirls up from the staircase. Paris sprints into the smoke, swatting it away as he tries to see what their descent will look like. Verona follows close behind. As Paris peeks over the edge to glance down the stairs, a fireball bursts up at him.

He flinches back. The flames devour the stairs under them. Heat swirls upward, while black smoke and fire flurries rush after them. The hair on their arms singe. Verona gapes at the hellish landscape below them. The entire main room is in flames, popping and bursting and scorching everything in its path. The stairs are completely consumed. There's no chance for them to get down it.

"What's happenin'?!" Verona gasps.

Paris pulls her away from the staircase. He thinks fast, calculating the rapidly evaporating options they have. He and Verona run back to Chamber 1.

Paris kicks open the door, only to be greeted by a blaze that shoots from the bowels of their guest chamber. It burns his face. Paris trips backward and crashes to the ground with a heavy *thump*. The floor cracks under his weight. Somehow the inferno has completely destroyed the bedchamber during the few seconds they were out of it. They are lucky to be alive.

Verona helps Paris stand up. "Ye all right?!" she asks.

Paris ignores her. Now is no time for talking. He spins to the window at the end of the hallway. The hellfire illuminates the hall from outside the window. Paris hesitates, the horror striking him all at once. They entire inn is encased in flames. Paris turns back to the stairs, but the inferno has already climbed up its steps. There's no escape, except—

"HELP! HELP!" Paris screams into the abyssal flames.

"HELP! UP 'ERE! HELP!" shouts Verona. They stand together, using the collective power of their voice to echo their pleas louder into the night.

"UP 'ERE!"

"HELP!"

"ANYONE!"

"HELP US!"

They wait for a response, but none comes. They've been abandoned. Paris pushes down the fright. There's no time to be scared. He must act. He pulls Verona and they duck into Chamber 2. The hallway fills with flames behind them, glimmering off a wet substance all over the floor. It takes Paris a moment to remember what it is, but by then Verona is already stepping onto it.

"Watch out!" warns Paris.

He pulls Verona back right as she trips over Sir Algor's pool of blood. She steadies herself against his chest. Verona wipes at the blood, confused.

"What's that?" she asks. Paris ignores the question. She must never find out what he did in this chamber. Never. "Paris?!"

"The window."

He tugs his wife with him across the space. Rain batters them as Paris appraises the drop out the precipice. The fall from the second story window isn't terrible. The rain has created a continuous mudslide below them, and the blaze has yet to harass the north side of the inn. It will be a dangerous fall, of course, but it gives them a chance.

"We need to jump," says Paris.

"What about the fall?" contests Verona.

"The smoke will kill us."

The fumes start to build inside Chamber 2. It skims along the ceiling, bubbling and foaming downward after them, until it passes out the window they stand by. Verona hesitates. She glances out the window to scan their fall. Her skin glistens with rain and sweat.

Hopefully, we won't land on the knight, prays Paris.

Verona eventually steps back from the ledge. She peeks behind her at the eerie orange glow that haloes the hallway entrance. She closes her eyes. Paris waits, more-or-less patiently, for a response. It finally comes in the form of a small head nod.

They move quickly, as much to escape the pace of the inferno as to avoid the little voice inside of their head that screams at them to not do it. This is their only option. They can't afford to be tentative. Resolution is the only cure to desperation.

Paris and Verona fling their legs over the ledge. They glare down at the muddy ground far below. Paris searches for Sir Algor's cadaver, but the clouds have still taken hostage of the moon, and so it is impossible to see much of anything, even with the inn's incandescent glow.

Paris and Verona look into each other's eyes. They say it all in an instant. An "I love you." An "I'm sorry." "Thank you." "See you on the other side, whatever that will be." They grasp each other's hands, holding their lover's grip tightly.

Verona smiles. Paris smiles back. They ready their final leg to wrap over the window. Paris takes one last look below them, and then they turn and—

"Wait!"

Paris and Verona stop themselves right before their bodies topple out the window. They glance behind them. A glossy figure, sheened over with a black shadow, steps away from the glow silhouetting him from behind. Paris's fingers curl around the edge of the window frame as he recognizes Kendrick the squire. Paris's blood drains out of his hands as his knuckles turn white. His veins protrude from his arms, and his breath turns into the exhaust of coals, a smoldering heat that could melt winter's fiercest snow. He turns to leap out the window again, opting rather to take his chances with the fall than battle another knight.

"Edith?" Verona exclaims.

Paris flinches back around. Disguised behind the frame of the young squire, and partially hidden by the glare of the inferno, Edith paces into Chamber 2. This is where it started all those hours ago. The chamber that instigated this night of terrors has turned into the place of their final decision.

"We're out of time," hurries Kendrick. "Come with us."

Paris glares at the squire. This is all because of *them*. The knights are who wanted to take Verona away. They're the ones who were going to tear their family apart before it even began. This squire is one of them. Paris won't let himself forget that. Kendrick is merely taking advantage of a situational opportunity. He'll turn on them, sure enough.

"Paris, we are *both* helpin'," says Edith. She can see straight through to Paris's hate. She has seen him like this before. But he was right then, and he is right now.

"So he can strangle us later?" argues Paris.

"I'm risking my life—" begins the squire.

"That redeems you, does it? Ye rapin', murderous pig!"

Paris is surprised by his own vehemence. He usually stays quiet and lets the thoughts fester in his own conscious like a plague. Not tonight. Tonight, everything gets out.

"Paris!" Verona gasps. "What are ye sayin'?"

"He's one of them. They are still tryin' to take ye from us."

"I *was* one of them," states Kendrick forcefully. "But from here on I'm going to be something more."

"Hah. It has always been the same," says Paris, sneering.

"What can I do to prove it?"

"Ye can finally die."

Verona's mouth drops. Her eyes drift over Paris, and a hint of shame climbs over him. She steps away from him, slowly backtracking until she's out of arm's reach from Paris. A chunk of the ceiling breaks off and crashes onto the bed. They all jump as the floor beneath the bed snaps. The bed, ceiling, and floorboards spiral down the hole and into the hellfire below. Flames jump up through the nascent opening, blazing them all with light as harsh as the sun.

"Either ye come with us now, or ye jump to your death!" declares Edith. She seems different now, more assertive and aggressive.

She's over this night, muses Paris. He pays no heed to any of the hard decisions she must have made to help them here.

All he can think about is this rotten squire, the scourge of the fiefdom.

Verona stumbles behind the squire, her eyes wide in something between terror and bewilderment. Paris remains alone in front of the window. Rain and lightning flash behind him; fire and smoke glow before him.

"I want to help," says the squire, his voice soft and tender.

He's tryin' to manipulate me.

An explosion shakes the floor. Debris launches through the hole next to Paris like a volcanic eruption. Verona's face scrunches into an undefinable emotion. She reaches her hand out for him.

"We will be fine, Paris," promises his wife.

How can we ever be fine with this bastard around us? We will never be safe with them around.

Paris bows his head and closes his eyes. They need to get out of here. They're trapped. They won't survive the fall. Maybe if they just use the squire for a little while, then they can abandon him when they're out in the open road. He looks devastated. He won't survive long.

"Fine," says Paris.

Only for a little while.

He grips the knife under his trousers.

*U*NGRATEFUL WHORESON, fumes Edith as she storms out of Chamber 1.

She has no patience for any of this. Her path to freedom had been right there; she could taste the damp air and smell the fresh wind. Emma was right on the other side.

I always have to fucking help.

Edith shakes her head aggressively, and her knotted hair flitters across her vision. She shoves it away. The inn bellows around her. She can sense its very foundation shattering apart, constricting into crisp embers that'll house the forgotten memories of this night for all of eternity. No one cares about the peasantry. It's up to them to live on and remember it for themselves.

Emma, I'm comin'. Mummy is on her way.

Edith, Kendrick, Verona, and Paris scurry past flames to a hole, about a meter in diameter, in the floor of the hallway. She glances down the opening, hoping and praying that the path is still clear. It is.

"This is where we climbed up," says Kendrick.

Edith couldn't care less whether Verona and Paris understood what was happening. This is her final good deed of the day. Her mind is finally set on her only remaining course of action, to get home.

Not wasting any time, Edith kneels next to the hole and grabs Kendrick's hand. She throws her legs over the opening. Kendrick helps lower her back into the common room. Edith drops to the ground with a solid rattle. She shakes it off. Edith peers back up through the hole where Kendrick, Verona, and Paris all crowd around.

"It still safe?!" asks Kendrick.

Edith glances around. The fire is nearby, but it seems to be focused on the walls at the moment. There is still a passageway, lined by flames, that leads back into the center of the inn. From there they should be able to navigate to the severed opening in the front of the building.

"Yeah! Hurry down!" Edith shouts back.

Kendrick leans over the hole above her. He reaches his hand out toward Verona. "Come on," he says to her. "Don't worry. I'll let you down slowly."

Edith hears a faint crackling noise above her. She tries to peek around the squire's body, but he blocks most of the hole. She can only see Paris's face. Paris glances up above them and then back down at the squire. His lips flash into a brief smirk, as he heaves Verona away from the hole.

The quiet crackle transforms into a loud snap. Kendrick's body jolts forward as he plummets headfirst through the hole. A large, fiery beam crashes down above him. The timber pummels him on the brief fall, cleaving in half over his body as they meteor into the earth. An explosion of ash and dust combusts into the air when they slam into the dirt. Edith has to swat it away.

Kendrick writhes in pain. He rubs at his shoulders, and even more blood spills from the knife wound in his side. Edith pulls him out from under the hole, lest more debris collapses on top of him. An almost parental need crawls over Edith as she quickly tends to the squire. *No time. No time.*

"He alive?!" Verona screams down the hole.

"Yes!" Edith rushes back under them. She waves for them to come down. "Now jump! Me will catch ye!"

"Shit," says Paris.

He stares up again at the ceiling to the second floor. Edith follows his gaze. The flames engulf the roof above them. Small fragments drop from the structural supports holding the roof up. It showers around Edith in little sparks of splinters.

"Hurry!" rushes Edith.

We need to go. We need to go!

Verona hangs her legs over the precipice. Edith reaches up and tries to stabilize her dangling feet, but she is too short to reach. All Edith can manage to do is slightly move the bottom of Verona's feet with the tips of her fingers. A sizeable chunk of wood breaks from the large beam. It shatters next to Verona's head.

She drops. Edith catches Verona right before she hits the ground. They stumble briefly before they both catch their balance again.

"God bless ye," says Verona.

"He better after this," Edith retorts. She and Verona gape back up the hole at Paris. "C'mon!" screams Edith.

Kendrick stirs on the ground beside them. He rubs his head and groans. If he gets out of this, his back will hurt like Hell in the morning. He crawls to his knees. Edith turns her attention back to Paris who timidly glances at the fiery ceiling above him. Splinters of timber fall all around him. He trips backward as the ceiling growls at him like some monstrous beast that readies to leap after its prey. His fingers twitch.

They don't have time for this. The whole inn can collapse at any moment.

"Jump!" yells his wife, clearly feeling the same anxiety as Edith.

Paris kneels next to the hole. He takes a deep breath but doesn't throw his legs around. This is taking too damn long.

"Jump down the fuckin' hole!" orders Edith. He doesn't listen. He keeps his stupid eyes on the deteriorating hallway around him.

Come on! We need to go. I need to get to Emma by morning.

"Paris!" Verona screams, desperate to get his attention.

Paris finally slings one leg over the hole. The ceiling creaks and roars. He raises the leg back up, right as Edith reaches for him.

"Fall!"

Paris jumps. The roof implodes over him.

Everything tumbles through the hole at once. Verona and Edith brace themselves. The second floor explodes. Flames splatter. Paris, part of the roof, and half the second floor crashes down onto them. Emma's bright little face flares before Edith in a flash of tranquil stillness.

Ash and smoke combust into the air.

Utter darkness remains.

THE FIRST SIGN OF life for Paris is when his lungs force out a terribly strained cough. He begins with the small movements. He tries to wiggle his fingers, one-by-one, starting with the thumb and moving toward the pinky. He does his dominant hand first. When those fingers all report back successfully, he moves to the left hand. All those fingers seem to be working, too. He focuses his power on his toes next, using the same method since it worked so well the first time. He starts with the big toe, curling it into his feet, and slowly moves down the line. He sighs in relief as all ten toes furl like he commanded them to.

Paris hacks out dust and smoke again. The room is thick with a haze of particles so dense that it blocks out the firelight around them. The only hint of the inferno's existence is the insufferable heat that permeates all around them. He tries to move his bigger limbs now. He shuffles his arms out ahead of him, propping his upper body off the ground. His legs decide to work as well, and they scrunch up under him.

Multiple other coughs erupt from elsewhere in the cloud of debris. Paris gingerly rises to his feet, swaying slightly from the laborious movement. His head throbs something fierce, and when Paris lifts his hand up to the source, it comes away bloody. Luckily, it only feels like a minor gash. Unluckily, however, the first person Paris spots in the debris field is the damn squire. Kendrick shuffles toward him. The squire appears deathly ill, but that's from his incident earlier. He looks largely unscathed from the imploded roof. *Damn.*

"You hurt?" asks Kendrick.

Paris ignores him. The squire doesn't actually care about his health, it's all a façade. Besides, he has to find Verona. That's more important than talking to him.

Paris stumbles through the haze, hands out ahead of him. The ash and smoke slowly fade away, and Paris quickly spots Verona before long. She vomits out a sludge that resembles a combination of water and charcoal. Paris rubs her back.

"I'm fine," she moans.

"Sure you are," Paris smiles.

Verona raises her arm, a subtle way of asking for assistance. Paris obliges and helps lift his wife to her feet. When Verona is confidently standing, she snaps her head around and peers through the dispersing cloud.

"Edith?" she calls out.

No answer. Paris and Kendrick glance around as well. Then, like a trickle of water after a terse rainstorm, a small cry splatters into the still air.

"Oh no," says Verona.

They rush after the faint cry, and it leads them to a pile of burnt rubble. There, under a rigid beam, twitches Edith on the ground. The heavy support brace crushes her chest. Verona gasps as they spot a piece of lumber impaled through her thigh. Edith's skin blanches, and her jet-black hair has mutated into a coarse gray from the ash pile that surrounds her.

Verona kneels next to Edith. She lays her hand on Edith's forehead, as Edith once did for her. Tears drip down his wife's eyes and land on Edith's skin, splashing it with a wet sheen that almost makes it look alive again. Edith's hand trembles as she grips Verona's arm.

"Emma . . . me daughter . . ."

"Shush, we're going to get ye out of here," says Verona softly.

"We will," assures Paris, focusing on this poor, pitiful woman; this woman who gave life back to his wife, who sacrificed so much for them.

"Do ye remember . . . remember what she looks like?" asks Edith.

Verona nods. "Black hair. Green eyes. Puffs up her cheeks. Me could never forget."

Edith smiles a wonderous, joyful smile. The type of smile that can only be expressed once in a lifetime. One that can't be defined but only felt.

"That be her . . ." sniffles Edith. "Me Emma . . . Me angel."

Kendrick pushes past Paris and kneels next to Edith. He reaches down and grips the impaled lumber with his hand.

"This is going to hurt," he warns. He pulls the lumber through her thigh. Edith squeals in pain but surprisingly little blood comes out of the wound. "God is watching over you, Edith," says Kendrick. "This wound isn't deadly. Come on. Get up. I'll be damned if you aren't seeing Emma today."

Kendrick motions to Verona, who helps him brace Edith up. She can barely put any weight on her leg, and she is forced to leave it lame and limp. They carry Edith over to Paris, where the squire leans her against him. Now it is Paris and Verona who must carry Edith, the savior of their lives and the burden of their escape.

Kendrick grimaces. "Now, let's get out of this hellhole."

INFERNAL RAPTRUE

❧

AT SOME POINT, DEATH loses all meaning.

If Edith would have died, the immense sadness of her passage wouldn't have stirred Kendrick any more than a general addition to the misery and gloom of the night. He's seen the demise of too many, and thus the shock of Edith's passing wouldn't have festered into an immediate contusion of grief and sorrow. There is only despondency and wretchedness left in his life. The world would have taken another, and Kendrick would have failed another. What's new?

Kendrick wobbles on his feet. His head is light as a feather on his neck. It's a strange feeling, like his head floats ahead of his body, which can only manage to follow behind him at a sluggish rate. Kendrick slowly realizes that a thick pocket of smoke hovers around his head. He ducks under the black layer, but his lungs are already sizzling from the embers of destruction. He coughs. It does little to alleviate the floaty sensations of his head. A part of him, Kendrick acknowledges with some panic, is serene and tranquil. That section of his being wants him to sit down on the heated floor and sleep gently into the night. It will be pleasant. He'll fall asleep almost instantly, and he knows he'll dream of Lucia, wearing that stunning, billowing emerald dress while backlit by the splendors of Duke Rowan's party. She'll smile at him, and he at her, and he can pretend that her tenderness pacifies the frozen tundra within him.

Maybe she can.

Kendrick hits himself in the head and shakes it belligerently to banish the temptation of the devil from him. It's all a mirage. The Lucia in his dreams will only be a hollow shell of her real self. He can never replicate her majesty, her command, her beauty. He lets himself remember her allure at that party so many months before. Then he forces himself back to the present predicament. Kendrick knows this is the smoke, or the wound, or the tingling in his spine seducing him to sleep. It is death waiting impatiently for him, but he'll allow the angel of demise to dangle the image of Lucia a brief second longer.

God, she makes that dress look good.

Then she's gone.

Kendrick uses the last of his remaining self-control to hold firm to wakefulness. He'll never know if Lucia will wear another dress at the wedding tomorrow. Never again will he be blessed with the softness of her touch or the sweetness of her fragrance. All he'll have for the remainder of his time on this earthly plane is the sacredness of their memories.

Kendrick sighs. His thoughts are getting increasingly morbid. He needs to remember he's still alive, and so he must fight. He needs to get Paris, Verona, and Edith out of here. Edith, at Kendrick's beckoning, almost gave her life to save them. He must survive for them. They must survive to reach Edith's daughter. This is Kendrick's final mission.

"We have to go before this whole place collapses," says Kendrick, watching the roof continue to crumble into the inferno. It only feeds the fire and causes it to grow stronger.

Verona glances over Edith at Paris. He avoids her eye contact. There's a growing tension between the two of them, but that's none of Kendrick's business. His duty is to escort them to safety. He won't quit trying to become a knight until every last bit of blood has dripped from his mortal body. This is the life he signed up for, and he will embrace it to the fullest. Perhaps his father can even be proud of him, after it's all over.

Paris and Verona balance Edith between them as they follow Kendrick around a flame. Kendrick's mind continues to remain fuzzy, and he has lost most of his sense of touch. After squeezing between two narrow piles of fiery refuse, they find the straight path to their escape. They rush toward the gap in the side of the inn. Kendrick sighs in relief. He's finally done something right.

Vincent leaps before the hole and blocks their path to freedom.

Kendrick buries his heels into the hard dirt, and the trio crash into his backside. Kendrick's eyes widen as he notices Commander Rayner's sword. Vincent lifts the weapon at them. Kendrick feels around his armor, but he has lost every weapon he had.

"Vince—"

"No." Vincent's voice is stable; however, his body is anything but. The sword shakes in his hand.

Kendrick shovels Paris, Verona, and Edith behind him. This is between Vincent and him. Even if he dies here, slaughtered by Vincent's vengeance, he can still give them a chance to escape.

"So much hate," says Kendrick softly, cautious of every word, "yet I never did anything to you."

"Knights," speaks Vincent, "ye rape, slaughter."

"I don't."

"'Cause one of ye do somethin' nice, we supposed to forgive? Are we supposed to forget everythin' ye lot have ever done?"

"Hark!" fires Kendrick angrily. "We're going to burn to death, for Christ's sake! Vincent, let's get out. We don't have to do this."

"I do," scowls Vincent.

He slices the sword at Kendrick. Kendrick flinches back at the last second, just getting out of range of the fatal blow. Vincent pulls the sword back up and points the tip at Kendrick again. Vincent's form is sloppy and easily readable, but Kendrick assumes that, given his current state, he will be unable to avoid even obvious attacks. Kendrick's body is slowly giving up on him. He has to get out of this fast, but he'll have to do it with the power of his voice and his mind, not with the fear that surrounds a sword.

Like a real knight should.

"If you're going to punish me for a crime I didn't commit, at least tell me what it was," reasons Kendrick.

Vincent lowers the sword slightly. His eyes drop for a moment. There's a world of hurt swirling in Vincent's mind. The lad peeks up. His pupils reflect fire.

WHO DOES THIS BASTARD *think he is? Why should he make* me *remember that night?*

Vincent tries to remember nonetheless, sparked by the damnable desire to shove Kendrick's benignity back at him.

The hot summer air presses at his skin. The distant screams of men, women, and children soar around him. He hears the crackle of fire . . .

"Do you even remember anymore?" Kendrick's voice reverberates through his darkest dreams.

Fraunce grasps Vincent's hand. He pulls him. They run. A crowd swarms around them. The crackle of fire . . .

What happened that night? There were knights, and they were killing. Fraunce was there.

Vincent grits his teeth, teetering the sword between his two hands. He stares into the squire's eyes. He will be a man when he kills Kendrick; he will see into the squire's soul and know what he is doing. *That* is justice. Fraunce wants him to kill Kendrick. Vivian wants him to kill Kendrick. His parents even want him to kill Kendrick.

They never did find their pa afterward. Vincent always wondered what happened to him. Did he get away? Is he living a life out there right now?

"Does it matter?" says Vincent softly, responding to both himself and Kendrick.

The hellfire blazes around them. Sweat slides down the side of Vincent's face. That night was only one experience, one circumstance dealing with the wreckage these knights cause. This is bigger than Vincent. He must stay strong.

The crackle of fire . . .

Something else happened that night, a dark secret Vincent chooses to forget. There was a knight chasing him through the wood, after Fraunce had left him.

Fraunce abandoned me.

"Let us go," begs Kendrick. "Look at me. I'm going to die anyway. Don't let them die, too."

Vincent appraises the squire. The puncture wound he pierced into Kendrick's right abdomen is festering. Kendrick's skin is white as a pearl, and his hair dryly sticks to his head. Vincent turns his attention to the bar maiden and the two peasants behind Kendrick. The woman is terrified, and the man appears to be close to a mental breakdown. The bar maiden is close to death herself.

They look like our neighbors from the village.

"Vincent. You're good," reasons Kendrick. His voice sounds so honest, so vulnerable. "I know you. Please, let them go. This isn't you."

"Maybe it is," says Vincent, forcing hostility into his voice.

It's a trap. Don't listen to him. Don't.

What happened that night in the forest? There was a clearing. The knight followed Vincent into the glade and stabbed him. That's what happened. That's what Fraunce had told everyone. That was the truth. He has the scar to prove it. *The fire crackles . . .*

"I'm sorry."

Vincent snaps his head up at the squire. Does he really have the fucking audacity to apologize to him?! Vincent tightens his grip around the handle. Kendrick dares to take a step closer. Vincent holds the sword toward the squire's neck.

Kill him. Do it now. Remember Fraunce. Remember your parents. Be strong.

Kendrick and Vincent stare at one another. There's something real in the squire's eyes. It is potent, and powerful, and manipulative. Damnit, there's compassion in them!

"Stop," warns Vincent.

"I'm sorry," says Kendrick again, his voice breaking.

Kendrick takes another step closer to him. Vincent slashes the sword, brushing back the squire's benevolence.

Remember. Remember that night.

A blade cut through his chest, but it wasn't the knight. No. Someone else was with him. Fraunce had abandoned him, and Vincent wasn't strong enough to care for his own wound. So who had stabbed him? It had to be the knight. It's always the knights.

Kill Kendrick. Kill the squire.

Kendrick takes yet another step. Every muscle in Vincent's body tenses at once, like a conglomerate reaction to some invasive poison—pure, unadulterated emotion.

"Stop!" cries Vincent, frowning at his own weakness. Unfaithful tears stroll down his cheek. Kendrick shakes his head.

"I'm sorry, Vincent," whispers Kendrick. He takes one last step.

"STOP!"

Vincent pinches the point of the blade against Kendrick's neck. Skin breaks. Blood trickles down Kendrick's collarbone. The pressure against the squire's windpipe makes his voice strain as he glimpses into Vincent's soul. The two of them remain motionless in the furnace.

"What we did was wrong," croaks Kendrick. "And I'm so sorry. Truly."

Vincent doesn't move. The blade's edge remains pressed against Kendrick's neck. All it will take is one easy movement. A simple flick of the arms, and Fraunce's killer will be dead.

But the fire crackles . . .

"It can't be forgiven," says Vincent.

"I know," acknowledges Kendrick, his voice sheared.

That summer night from seven years ago collapses onto Vincent like a tree falling under the force of immense winds. The truth reveals itself: Lucella's betrayal, Vincent's half-death, and his salvation by the hands of a knight.

I know.

Kendrick's words of understanding, his vow of responsibility, rings inside Vincent's conscious. The sword weighs heavy in his hands. A simple twist. A simple fate. A simple life.

I know.

Vincent removes the blade from Kendrick's neck. He steps aside, lowering the sword to an unthreatening position. The peasants and bar maiden behind Kendrick rush past them.

"Thank ye," says the peasant woman to Vincent as she runs by. They carry the bar maiden out the gap in the side of the inn, disappearing into the storm beyond.

Kendrick feels his neck. The two of them stand in the middle of pure hell. Vincent avoids any further eye contact with Kendrick. The decision bites at him like a tick. It gnaws and chews at his conscious. He feels the squire's stare. Vincent can't stand any more of his virtuous benevolence. No one deserves it.

"We could have been friends," says the squire.

"No," answers Vincent honestly. "Never."

Kendrick leaves without another word. Vincent understands. What can be said for so much destruction? All Vincent has is himself and the large world around him. The Church . . . the nobility . . . the peasantry . . . human society . . . it's all kindling for the crackle of fire.

KENDRICK STOMPS OUT INTO the humid air and breathes the freshness of the night. Never before has he been so grateful for the coolness of the spring storms. The inn burns behind him, illuminating the rain like the long streaks of flaming arrows. Kendrick spots Paris, Verona, and Edith waiting for him. He holds his side. The pain hits him harder now. Kendrick catches up to them.

"What happened to him?" asks Verona, genuinely concerned.

"He's lost," says Kendrick sorrowfully. "As am I."

No more is said. They turn and head for the direction of Edith's village. They truck through the diminishing rain.

VINCENT HANGS THE SWORD to his side. Tears evaporate off his cheek. He doesn't care about the fire any longer. It can devour him and burn him to his bones. Vincent's body tenses. He hits himself in the head and bends over as a monstrous yell escapes from deep within.

He let Kendrick go. How could he? He's failed again.

"Too weak, all of you," chuckles a wet voice.

Vincent glares over. Commander Rayner lies on the ground, his body half burnt, and his ankles bleeding out. Vincent hobbles over to the commander, sword in hand, and drinks in every expression that passes across his face. This is Commander Rayner, the great boogeyman, the living demon of the peasantry.

What a pathetic spirit. Vincent straddles him.

"Let me die," spits Commander Rayner.

Vincent puffs out steam. He grabs the hilt of Commander Rayner's sword with his right hand and its blade with his left. He holds the sword horizontally over Commander Rayner's face. Vincent lets his anger boil through him.

"Animal," says the commander, smiling.

Vincent chops down.

He slices through Commander Rayner's face. He pries the sword out. Then, Vincent chops down again, and again, and again, and again, and again. Blood. Bone. Spit. Mucus. Brain. A demon takes control. Vincent drools as he minces the face into mush.

He finally subsides.

Vincent wipes guts out of his eyes. His whole body is covered in gore, and he's sure he would be unrecognizable to anyone. Vincent drops the sword next to the faceless cadaver. The inferno glistens off his body. He hears a large section of the building collapse behind him.

There's only one thing left for him to do.

Vincent pushes open the door to the kitchen. Fraunce's body lies motionless on the ground, untouched by the fires of Hell. The kitchen's walls burn around them, and the once-fresh herbs float across the air like golden sparks.

Vincent knows no one will ever find Fraunce. The inn is going to implode at any moment, and Fraunce will be buried here for all of time. He'll never be buried in holy ground, and thus he'll spend eternity in Hell. Vincent sends a small prayer to the Good Lord, that when He shepherds Vincent into the next life, He'll send Vincent past the golden plains of Heaven and toward eternal fire, so that Vincent may be with Fraunce again.

Vincent ignores the chaos around him. He ignores it all. He's only here for his older brother. Vincent lies next to Fraunce's dead body.

"I failed," he whispers to Fraunce. "I could have stopped him, but me didn't."

Vincent convulses over himself, his body overtaken by raw emotion. He refuses to remove his gaze from his brother as he bawls. Fraunce was everything to him. He *is* everything to him.

And he let Fraunce down again.

Vincent couldn't even achieve his brother's last wish, as Vivian had said.

"I should have killed him," cries Vincent, busting down all the bulwarks he had set up over the last seven years. With Fraunce, he can be his true self, and that true self hurts. "'Tis what ye would have wanted. I'm too weak. I failed our parents. I failed you."

Vincent reaches out his hand and places it on Fraunce's cheek. He was reaching for warmth, for comfort, but all he finds is cold nothingness. Even in the midst of an inferno, his older brother still lacks the solace of human skin. Vincent sets his eyes on his brother's face while the inn implodes around them.

All he ever wanted, all Vincent ever dreamed of, was to be like Fraunce. To be strong, and confident, and loyal. But instead, all he ever turned out being was one thing.

"I'm a coward," sobs Vincent.

He removes his hand from Fraunce's face. He doesn't deserve to touch his brother, not even dead. A bloodied handprint remains on Fraunce's white cheek.

"Forgive me."

The inn collapses on top of the two brothers.

REALISTIC FABLES

GODFREY'S EYES SNAP OPEN between crusted mucus and smoldered ash. He grunts as he stands, wiping away blood that covers his face. He inspects the stables, or, more accurately, the ruins of the stables. Rain drenches the remaining fire, which lies scattered throughout the ruins of the space. A pile of ash builds up into a growing mound. The wind howls across the stable's remains, sweeping the cinders of the deteriorated inn off into the dark of night.

"Leif?" groans Godfrey.

He limps to where the boy stood before everything exploded to smithereens. Godfrey's outfit flutters helplessly in the wind, revealing ripped and mangled holes that expose Godfrey's bare skin to the elements. He breathes in. The air is brisk and scented with the syrupy fragrance of exposed amber. The discarded beam, which had entrapped Leif not long ago, now rests in three separate pieces. Lightning flashes a good distance away, but it allows Godfrey the chance to see the environment in more detail.

Buried beneath a small pile of waste, Leif's scorched tunic lies tattered and in ruin. Godfrey pulls it free from the refuse and holds it reverently between his hands. It's such a little tunic for such a little boy.

"Leif?!" Godfrey calls out again.

No human answers the bard's pleas, but the firmament above shakes the earth in a bout of thunderous claps. The world goes silent for a time afterward, and Godfrey impatiently listens for the sound of any movement. All he can hear is the natural drips of rain showering down walls and over ledges, intermixed with the occasional gust of sharp wind. Not even the inn groans behind him any longer, as it seems to have collapsed a while ago. The near countryside is still dimly lit from the lingering flames of that fateful inferno, but other than that and the remaining rubble, there is little evidence for the extent of human fallibility that developed within its walls.

That's like all ancient ruins, Godfrey supposes. *The world forgets the memories of those who lived within it. And if they do remember, it's only by its thinnest denomination.*

"Leif?!"

His voice echoes into the darkness around him. The rainstorm is finally slowing down. The precipitation is turning fatter and is becoming less frequent, descending to the earth in consistent and deliberate paths. The wind can't grab ahold of these showers as efficiently, and so the rainfall drops down in a straight line rather than sideways.

"Leif?!"

Godfrey searches through the ruins. He won't give up hope, not until he spots the boy's body. Not until then.

Godfrey delicately picks apart the waste of Warin's Inn. He lifts lumber, kicks over ash piles, and stomps out fires. The night trudges on. The cool wind that has previously dominated the storm subsides, revealing the multitude of sparkling stars across the sky as the clouds finally begin to depart. Exhaustion shoots through Godfrey's veins as he approaches a full hour of searching for Leif. Every time he interacts with an object, a new pierce of pain, like being stabbed with a hot iron, ricochets through his muscles.

With the additional light of the stars and the occasional glimmer of moonlight through the thinning clouds, Godfrey can see the havoc the fire wrecked on him. Blisters, which form a multitude of bubbles across his forearm, crawl up his skin and disappear behind his doublet. Every section of his body is tender, and the simmering heat of the fire has yet to leave his system. He can still feel it, the inferno, the hallway of fire, even after an hour of stomping through the chilly breeze. Godfrey ignores the pain as best as he can.

I deserve this pain. If I failed Leif, I deserve it.

As the night draws on, however, his self-imposed punishment does little to tame the increasing pain his failure presses upon him. By his second hour of searching, the sky showers on him in bursts of scattered gloom. To Godfrey, this new rain invokes the impression of a weeping human rather than the insouciant whims of nature, like Heaven itself is now sharing grief with the victims of Warin's Inn. Godfrey has to pause occasionally when the pain of his body grows too great. He stops and listens, hoping he can hear the shuffle of little feet.

He never does.

When he pauses during the sorrow-filled showers of the sky, he can't hear anything over the noise of its plump raindrops. But even when he stops during one of the brief, dry halts in the rainstorm, he can only hear the remaining fire flap in the faltering winds.

By Godfrey's third hour of crawling through the rubble, his desperation climbs to a climax. The first set of stars, which revealed themselves behind the thick clouds, have made their way toward the western horizon. The storm has mostly ceased, as it has ventured farther to the south. The wind has forgotten all cause of building to a gale and instead has left the remains of this area of their kingdom to their little brother, the breeze. There are no longer any direct, visual remains of the inferno. Every fire has been successfully snuffed by the rain or by Godfrey himself.

"Leif . . ." croaks Godfrey for the hundred-plus time. The words barely leave his mouth, as his throat loses all inclination toward speech.

Godfrey's heart stops for a beat as he stubs his toe into something both solid and flimsy. He bends down and pushes over a pile of planks. His fingers burn at its touch, but he bites through the affliction anyway. He brushes off a small layer of ash, only to find himself hunched over the nude body of Sir Algor. Sure enough, just next to him is Warin's corpse.

Godfrey squints his eyes closed. He squeezes back tears but is unable to keep back a whimper that slinks out between his lips. His hands clinch into fists, and his legs give way from under him. He falls to his knees within the dilapidated ruins as another round of scattered showers falls upon him. His wails become swallowed by the suppressing force of God. Godfrey is alone in his grief, alone in his agony, and alone in his journey.

He knows the truth. The world has already moved on from the devastation of this night. It is only another brief distraction in the longer story of human civilization, like all the lives of the Romans and Egyptians and Hebrews that he was taught about in his academic upbringing. What difference does the death of a little boy make when there are the stakes of a king's succession at play? What does it matter of the misery of a forgotten bard when factions of religion are at war with one another?

What does it matter?

It matters to me.

Godfrey bows his head and lets the heartbreak tear away at him. He'll remember this night. He'll remember the tragedy within Warin's Inn, and he'll never forget the image of the little boy who was full of exuberance and dedication toward self-improvement, and how his life was taken too early. He'll remember.

There is a single bright spot in the remains of this devastation; this is the longest he has ever gone without thinking about the need to smoke.

Godfrey climbs to the top of a hill. The first light of dawn fights back against the oppressing blackness of night, and he can see the last remnants of the storm disperse in the far south. It is a wonderous sight.

Godfrey still carries Leif's scorched tunic with him. His body screams at him to lie down and rest, to dwindle the immense pain of his burns and to recalculate all that has happened in the last day, but Godfrey wants to get far away from Warin's Inn before he does so. He wants to be nowhere near that graveyard when he awakens again. He pauses on top of the hill, scanning the horizon of Duke Rowan's fiefdom.

Where do I go from here?

Godfrey decided he's better off not going to the wedding as he originally planned. He has had enough of knights and nobles and scheming peasants. There may very well be another bloodbath there, and Godfrey believes it is best to not be caught up in such death two nights in a row.

Yeah, that would certainly be bad for my morale. Godfrey's own joke doesn't make him laugh. Laughter seems hard to come by nowadays. A pity.

He looks to the east, not only to the rising sun, but toward the town of Sherborne. He thinks of Regina and the distress she must have about her husband. Then his mind wanders to Juliana. He imagines her tossing and turning in bed, unable to sleep, her mind a scattered mess of worry after her father left. They seemed so well put together when Godfrey was invited into their abode, but he should have known better. Everyone who has ever lived can seem simple and normal. It takes some strength, and a little courage, to explore deeper than that. Godfrey considers traveling back to Sherborne. Maybe Regina will be willing to house him for a little while longer.

What would I do there? Sit around all day and leech off their kindness?

No. Godfrey shakes his head. He can't do that. *So where then?*

Godfrey turns his eyes to the northeast. He has never been to London. He's heard of all sorts of strange and wild stories coming out of that city. He has spent the majority of his life avoiding people and watching them from the outside. Perhaps it's time for Godfrey to blend in with them. He can struggle with them, work with them, and live with them. He can even give his poetry a try at one of London's various taverns or present them at one of the city's many public celebrations and merchant extravaganzas.

Godfrey takes a deep breath. He is tired of the countryside. He nods to himself. The city it is then.

The bard stretches. He needs to find a place to rest. The sky shifts into a dull lavender color, and the stars near the eastern horizon bask in the generous glow of day. Godfrey grasps Leif's tunic, feeling the rough fabric between his fingers.

He has a story to tell. It will probably flop like all his other poems, but this one actually has importance to him. It won't be about fame or proving his talent. This one is different.

Godfrey smiles. A part of him scolds himself for releasing such an emotion. Godfrey buries that thought. His whole life, Godfrey has had that pesky voice putting him down. Another part of him really believes he deserves it, too. Perhaps he does. He gets defensive when someone calls him a vagrant. Godfrey likes to believe that he travels with purpose, that he isn't baselessly wandering and munching off the miniature economies of each village he passes. A greater part of him knows that's false.

Why does there have to be so many different parts of me?

Godfrey sighs. He sits down on the crest of the hill to watch the sunrise. He supposes it doesn't matter if he was truly a vagrant or not. That was in the past, and it'll be vanished from time as quickly as the circumstances within Warin's Inn. The future is ahead of him, and he has purpose in that now. He needs to go to London and tell this story, not because anyone may actually want to hear it, nor because it may have any actual importance in their life, but simply because it is something he needs to say. It's necessary for the happiness of his own life, and that makes it worth something.

Godfrey relaxes. He leans back and lets the grass brush at his burnt arms. He must look like a beast in some regards. Maybe that'll get him more attention. Either way, he needs to start developing how he'll orate his story.

The story of a lonely rock monster, and how his appearance betrays the kind nature of his heart. It'll be about the plight of this rock monster—how he stomps around his forest in hope of befriending all the various critters within, and how he also seeks to make connections with the humans who wander through it. The story will climax with the rock monster saving the life of a human during a raging forest fire, finally gaining a human friend for life. The twist is the rock monster did more than save the human from burning in the flames. He saved the human from taking his own life as well.

The rock monster will never know that he saved that human's life twice that day.

Perhaps the metaphor is a little obvious, muses Godfrey, *but* fuck *them all. I have always liked the obvious.*

CHIVALROUS KNIGHT

❧

KENDRICK, PARIS, VERONA, AND Edith continue to head south through the open English countryside. Unfortunately, the storm has decided to follow them, and thus, they continue to be bombarded with rain well into the early morning. The four of them push through it, their determination and dogmatic drive overpowering all sense of self-preservation. They need to get Edith back to Emma. They made a promise to her, and that promise is the only thing keeping them sane. Kendrick's body begins to give up on him before his mind does, so he slowly starts to fall back behind them.

He watches Paris, Verona, and Edith trek next to each other before him. The massive grass field they are passing across brushes at their knees. It's a tranquil sight, all things considered. The sky is still slightly overcast above them, and a few odd drops of rain fall here and there. But the black sky breathes its first color of day, and that gives Kendrick the vigor to keep going. He wants to feel the warmth of the sun one last time.

His mind bounces from one thing to the other as he tries to distract himself from the bleakness that forms at the edges of his vision. He thinks of Sir Algor. Only a day ago they were traveling together across the openness of Duke Rowan's land. He had so much hope then. They were jesting, enjoying each other's company, experiencing life best they could. It was a good morning. His mind uses that juncture to think of Fortune. Kendrick wonders what happened to his horse, his friend, his companion. The stables were completely destroyed when they sprinted from the inn. He scanned the area for her, hoping Fortune would spot him. She would ride up to him with her mane blowing in the wind, and the four of them could have used her assistance to get to Edith's house faster. Kendrick shakes his head. That was the practical reason he had hoped to find Fortune. The actual reason is he needs someone to comfort him. Fortune knows him better than most humans. He would have liked to feel the barrel of her body pressing against his legs, and he would have loved to rest his head against hers. She is truly a spectacular animal. He hopes she got out in time.

His mind, of course, thinks about Lucia. He plays through a whole imaginary scenario of how their night would have gone during Lord Merek's wedding. He imagines how awkward their initial conversation would be, and how they'd navigate all the little complexities of being both young and enamored. He thinks of as much detail as he can, even accidentally saying one of his lines out loud and getting a peculiar glare from Paris.

There is something about that man that Kendrick doesn't trust. But what use does that lack of faith do for him now? He's dying. Whether he trusts Paris or not is of little importance.

Kendrick thinks of his father. He reckons his father is getting out of bed right about now. He'd be warming up the forge and getting ready for yet another day of following the commands of the nobility. Kendrick should be next to him, supervising the less intricate matters of blacksmithing. Pa would have wanted him there. Kendrick knows his father loves him dearly. He was so proud the first time Kendrick tempered metal, and the first time he helped him craft a sword. Pa sauntered around for the rest of the day, glowing with the pride only a father can have over something so insignificant their kid has done. Kendrick should be next to him now, making his father's day by following in his footsteps.

Now Kendrick will die in the middle of a field, and his father will have to receive the message of his death while under the furnace of the forge. What will he think then?

Will he weep for me? Will he be disappointed? Will he remain indignant and use it as an opportunity to prove he was right all along?

Kendrick doesn't know, and perhaps that's for the best.

They keep roaming across the pasture. The sky brightens with every step, glistening off the fresh dew upon the blades of grass. The brisk morning air gives way as the warmth of all things edges toward the eastern sky. It'll be another beautiful day, which will be sadly scorned by the viciousness of the world. It's an endless cycle, one day after another, only to be broken briefly when someone finally stands up and does the right thing. Sir Algor had called the plight of human ignorance, hostility, and hypocrisy "virtuous sins." Kendrick finds that label to be aptly correct, but that's not the end-all-be-all of the world. Civilization can be so much more, and the individual can be so much greater than that. Everything in the modern world is about the collective: the Church, the royals, the patricians, the peasantry. It's all about the collective souls of God's creation, not the individual spirit of each. Something about that leads to the creation of virtuous sins, but that's a thought for another time . . . for a man who isn't on death's doorstep.

After deciding that they won't find cover any time soon, the four of them relieve themselves before trudging onward. Kendrick sneers at the ridiculousness of such a circumstance. The body keeps on operating until its final beat, it seems.

They eventually reach what must be the center of the humongous grassland. Verona and Paris continue to take turns helping Edith forward. Kendrick glares at her wound as he stumbles along after them. She'll need to find help in her village, and if she survives, she'll certainly never be able to use that leg again. Kendrick turns his attention to his own stab wound. It has completely dried up, and the skin around it has turned purple.

Kendrick glances up across the plains and finds that they are coming upon a singular European ash that stands alone in the countless miles of empty grassland. The tree is stunning. The trunk is solid, and the brown bark commands attention, as it contrasts brilliantly against the whitening sky. It would take a few men to wrap their arms around the entirety of the tree's torso. The wonderful width of its branches spread around the trunk in a perfect half-sphere. Spring has already taken over this European ash, and the leaves look as vibrant and fresh as if they sprouted yesterday. Maybe they did. The world is always moving forward.

Things die, and things birth anew.

Kendrick's legs finally give out on him as he crosses the lone tree. He collapses to the dirt in a terrible crack that sounds worse than it feels. In fact, he doesn't feel much of anything anymore, except the soft breeze caressing his skin.

"Paris!" yelps Verona, slapping Paris's arm and spinning around after Kendrick.

She rushes over to him and helps lay Kendrick against the tree trunk. The bark presses firmly against Kendrick's back, and a sense of awe spreads over him. This European ash must have existed here for hundreds of years, facing the elements alone in the middle of the pasture. It has seen things Kendrick can't even imagine. He can almost feel the roots set deeply into the solid earth.

"Can me get ye anythin'?" Verona asks him. There's a comforting, almost motherly, tone to her voice, which puts Kendrick at ease. He never had a chance to meet his real mother. She died during childbirth. He supposes he will soon, if the Good Lord forgives as much as the good book promises . . . as Sir Algor promised.

"Thank you," says Kendrick, smiling, trying to make this easy for her.

Verona's face betrays her true sorrow. He doesn't want his death on her conscious. Paris and Edith amble their way over to them. Paris's face is a bulwark of impenetrable evaluation; if anything, Kendrick fancies he spots annoyance and indignation.

"Paris?" Verona asks her husband wistfully.

"Nothin' we can do," says Paris.

"I'll be fine," says Kendrick. That's a lie, of course. Everyone knows it, but sometimes the world is a little easier when a lie is allowed to bloom.

Paris helps Verona stand up from Kendrick's side. He places his arms around her and gives her a tight squeeze. This could have been Kendrick and Lucia . . . perhaps in another time. Whoever the lucky bastard is that wins her heart, he hopes their love is true.

"Go on," Paris tells Verona.

"Why?" she retorts.

"'Cause I told ye," he says with a stern kiss to her temple. She gapes at her husband. "Go," nudges Paris.

Verona rolls her eyes at him and turns to Kendrick. "Thank ye," she says softly. "Thank ye for everythin'. We will never forget you."

That's nice, to be remembered.

Kendrick smiles at her. He knows it is a kindness to Verona's gentle soul to not respond back verbally. He has found out that many things are better said in silence. He learned that lesson from Lucia. Silence is the language of love.

Verona turns and leads Edith west, away from the rising sun. Paris and Kendrick watch them as they leave. Kendrick isn't sure if Paris's command was one of authority or of pity. Did he send her away so that she wouldn't have to watch Kendrick's final moments, or did he do it so he can have Kendrick all to himself?

It doesn't matter, Kendrick supposes. *I'm about to find out either way.*

"Do ye know who we are?" questions Paris at last.

"You both wed a few nights back, but the duke wanted her." Kendrick nods, remembering the discussion after the beheading.

"Will they come after us?"

"No. They'll forget."

Paris sighs. His shoulders drop to a relaxed position. Kendrick knows he took a large weight off the man's shoulders. There's another graceful interaction he can add to the right things he's done.

At least I'm ending on a high note.

A warm gust of air flounders across the plains. It hits Kendrick with a rejuvenating breath. Paris stands motionless over him. He has splotches of burn marks all over his skin, and a decent chunk of his forehead is scarred pink. Kendrick checks himself. The scars of the inferno have wrecked his body as well. These are visual memories they'll hold for the rest of their lives. It'll be the last remnants of that night.

At long last, Paris turns and heads after his wife. Kendrick cranks his neck to look after him.

"Wait," strains Kendrick. He meant to shout, but his mouth and throat have completely dried up. "If anyone asks, tell them I was a vassal of the people, not the court."

Paris halts, his back turned to Kendrick. The man lets the words disperse into the fathomless sky. Kendrick waits for a response. It finally comes.

"You saved no one."

Kendrick frowns as Paris waits another second before leaving him alone with the lonely European ash.

So be it. It isn't Kendrick's place to dictate his own legacy any longer.

Kendrick turns his vision to the east. The grassland stretches out before him like an endless ocean, its mounds and knolls rolling over the flatness like incoming waves of earth. The sun will soon peek over that wide green expanse, and Kendrick will be hit with the rays of life for the final time. Kendrick awaits that feeling.

His mind goes completely blank. There are no thoughts of Sir Algor, or Eliot, or Vincent, or Lucia, or his father. There is only Kendrick, this sturdy tree, and the nascent morning. A bliss grabs hold of Kendrick, and it keeps him locked in its grasp. In some nearby wood, a bird finally stretches its voice and screeches its first song of the day. Kendrick knows somewhere out there, beyond the endless pasture of the countryside, some shepherd herds his sheep across the plains; and somewhere else, in some quaint cottage under some magnificent snowy mountain, a family awakens and prays their thanks for another day of life; then even beyond that, on the edge of some terrible battlefield, two commanders, under differing banners of spirituality, line up their troops for another battle; and even elsewhere, across a great, desolate land, merchants travel over the long winding roads toward civilization, appreciative that their wares haven't yet spoiled and money is still to be made. Everywhere else, all around the world, life moves on as it always has, and Kendrick can't be more grateful for that realization.

He now understands how this European ash has survived so long on its own. Here, in the center of the grassy plains of southern England, they can see the entirety of the earth. Right here in this spot, they are the least lonely organisms in the world.

The sun peeks over the horizon, shining its dazzling light onto all of the great and terrible people of the Earth alike, and Kendrick glimpses those Heavenly rays that will live on to greet every generation of mankind. In some nearby farmstead, a cock crows its shrill beckoning of that magnificent radiance, only doing what it has done since the beginning of time, unknowing of its importance in the final moments of Kendrick's mortal existence.

Kendrick smiles as he beholds the spectacular beauty of the world before him, the sun banishing the shadows of twilight, while the veil of gloom—which has enraptured Kendrick for too long—finally ceases coverage over his soul. The final warmth he'll ever feel touches his face, and the torrent of ice, which has solidified the glacier within him, shatters into a million speckles of white stars under the immense heat of that warmth.

Kendrick relaxes as the Holy Paradise lies open for him. His methodic breaths crawl to a halt. The birds continue to sing, the rooster continues to crow, and the sun continues to shine. Kendrick accepts his lot in life.

In that moment of truth, during the final beat of his heart, Kendrick becomes one with himself, with nature, and with God.

GUILTY ABSOLUTION

THE VILLAGE OF CUDWORTH, Edith's village, looms ahead of Paris and Verona. Edith had sent them ahead so they could get to Emma faster. She promised she would be right behind them.

The village is fashioned at the base of a large hill, which spans the better part of two furlongs. In the early morning sun, Paris spots a number of buildings and houses climbing up the eastern side of the hill. A dry moat and palisade surrounds Cudworth, its pointed stakes at various heights and effectiveness to protect the village from the dangers of banditry and other unknown perils. His eyes linger on the highest point of the hill, and therefore, the highest point of the village where a few cottages remain aloof from the others. If Paris remembers Edith's directions correctly, one of those should be her home.

"Me hopes the guards let us in," says Verona.

"'Tis late enough, they should," says Paris.

They stumble around the northern side of the hill, following alongside the moat. Paris's legs feel ready to break off his body at any second. His bones ache with fatigue, and the nascent blisters on his skin are developing an increasing itchiness. Verona, somehow, survived the fire mostly intact. Her skin is a few shades darker, and her lush eyelashes and eyebrows are burnt into nonexistence, but she doesn't appear to have sustained the same level of deeper burns that Paris has. He's grateful for that. She had to survive too much over the course of the night, and she certainly doesn't need lifelong scars to remind her of it.

The sun quickly rises in the east, burning the distant clouds into wisps of gray. The sky takes on a yellow-blue discoloration, which contrasts nicely with the emerging haze. The evening storm has completely disappeared into nothing more than a forgotten memory. The leftover moisture from the night fills the morning breeze, and a great dampness clamps down onto them. The earth smells of fresh life, and Paris can hear the movement of villagers on the other side of the wooden stakes. It is time to embrace a new day.

"Halt," announces a guard as they approach the main gate.

Paris and Verona cross a drawbridge that spans the moat and do so. The village is so small that there is no walkway for town guards to patrol at the top of the palisade. Rather, it is simply two guards with long pikes who stand before an open partition between the wall of stakes. They look no older than teenagers.

"Who be ye? What do ye seek in our village?"

Paris steps in front of Verona. "My name is Paris. This is me wife, Verona. We are here to take care of Edith's daughter," answers Paris.

He has found that it's best to always answer guards truthfully. Guards aren't usually trained and tainted by the crudity of the noble class like knights are. In most cities, towns, and villages, the guards are local, honest folk who are simply trying to make a living. They are almost always younger, like these teenage boys, and hired by the reigning lord or lady. Guards understand the fundamental flow of their domain because they actually live amongst their fellow peers that they protect. They don't deserve the hostility that knights do.

"We heard about Warin's Inn," the second guard jumps in. "Is Edith all right?"

"Wait, how have ye heard?" asks Verona, her ears perked up.

"A boy rode in early this morn. He told us it burned down."

Paris and Verona glance at one another. He turns back to them. "Edith was injured in the fire. We promised her we would watch over her daughter," says Paris hesitantly.

The guards' shoulders slump a little at the truth. The first guard licks his lips and sighs while the second guard covers his gaped mouth. There is earnest devastation on their faces. Edith was well liked, it appears.

"Will she live?" questions the second guard incredulously.

Paris nods. The second guard leans back against the palisade, the relief taking away his core strength. The first guard takes a deep breath. "Good," he says. "Emma loves her mum."

"Her mum loves her," says Verona.

"No one doubts that," smiles the first guard. "Ye won't find a single soul who doesn't like Edith. If there's ever a problem in town, she's there to help fix it."

"Sounds like her," says Paris.

The first guard clicks his tongue and forces himself to stand straight again. "Ye will find Edith's cottage at the top of the village. Follow the main path, it will lead you there."

"Thanks," says Paris. He and Verona walk by them, but the second guard stops them short.

"Tell Emma," he begins, "that if she ever needs protection, her favorite guards will help her. We be here for her. Always."

"'Course." Verona grins, placing her hand gently on the guard's arm. The guard smiles back at her and straightens up again. Paris pulls Verona to follow him.

It takes longer for them to hike through the village than Paris expected, merely because of its vertical height rather than the actual land mass of the place. Paris and Verona are already exhausted from being up for a full day, and the extra effort to climb a steep hill is doing little to help their cause. If Paris didn't know better about Edith's resilience, he'd wonder how she would get up this hill.

Cudworth awakens around them. Women are out and about, carrying empty buckets to the nearby stream or hanging up their soaked clothes on the line racks between their houses. Men are moaning as they head to their stores or to their laborious jobs once again. A few drunkards here and there groan as they recover from their hangovers. From some house deeper within the village, a newborn wails to be fed. Paris feels like a ghost moving through all these blissfully ignorant souls. They don't know what it's like to have to take a life, what it's like to fight tooth-and-nail for their survival. They're the lucky ones. Eventually, after too much strenuous effort, Paris and Verona make it to the top of the hill.

"Do ye remember which one it is?" asks Paris.

"She said it faces the risin' sun," says Verona.

Sure enough, at the eastern-most edge of the hill, a single cottage peeks out at the new day. A medium-sized horse is tied up next to it. Paris and Verona nod at one another. They cross to the dingy cottage. Its walls are thin, and the exterior surface has been crudely whitewashed. The roof is a mess of cluttered thatch, with leaves and debris clotted all around it, presumably from the storm last night. The two of them stand before the closed door to Edith's home.

"Ye ready?" asks Verona anxiously.

"Ready?"

"To finally have kids," she grins. There is some fear in her eyes, but she's also excited. That fear jumps to Paris. Edith will be lame for life now, and she had asked Paris and Verona —well, mostly Verona—to stay with her and Emma for a time. They really are going to have a kid now. He thought it would never be possible, but here they are.

Paris nods timidly. Verona takes a deep breath and knocks on the door. They hear the shuffle of feet inside, and a few brief, hushed whispers. Paris glances at his wife, who keeps taking big breaths. *She's really nervous about this*, appraises Paris. The door opens, and it takes his eyes a second to adjust to the darkness within.

"Hi." Verona smiles, her eyes adapting first.

"Who ye?" asks a charming, high-pitch voice.

"Ye must be Emma."

His wife bends down to the girl's level. Paris finally sees Edith's daughter. She is precisely as Edith described, with her jet-black hair and vivid green eyes forcing all attention to turn toward her face. Emma wears a white gown that stretches all the way to the floor. Her tiny toes poke out of the bottom trim.

"Yes," Emma answers.

"Ye mummy sent us," says Verona.

"Me mum?" Emma rubs her eyes. They probably woke her from her sleep. Her eyes are red, like she hadn't slept for most of the night. He wonders if she's scared of storms. Emma tilts her head at them. "Who are ye?"

"Me am Verona. This is Paris, me husband."

"Hi," says Paris in a terse voice. For some reason, the word caught in his throat, and it came out as a gnarled cough.

Emma glances behind her into the bleakness of the cottage. "Look," she exclaims. "They says me Mummy sent 'em."

Emma steps to the side to let someone squeeze next to her in the doorframe. Paris peeks his head around his wife to see who it is. The patter of more feet rings out from the darkness, and a little boy crosses into the sunlight.

"Me knows 'em," he says.

"Ye Warin's boy?" asks Paris, making sure he isn't imagining things.

"Me was," hisses Leif. The sourness in his voice stops everyone cold. Leif dons a female tunic over his body. That's strange. Did his actual tunic get too wet when he rode here?

Leif didn't escape from the hellfire as gracefully as Verona did. He has a line of scars and blisters along the left side of his face. It almost creates a perfect line down the center of his body.

"We're so happy ye made it," says Verona, smiling.

Leif doesn't respond. An awkward few seconds pass between the four of them.

"Why don't ye grab your things," suggests his wife.

"Why?" wonders Emma.

"Your mummy wanted us to take ye somewhere."

"Like a trip?" asks Leif. His question is steeped in a sort of weariness, almost in an accusing manner. Paris, Verona, and Edith had decided that their best course of action was to leave the south of England. One of the knights had escaped the inn, and there's a chance they'd be hunted for their crimes. They can start life anew someplace else.

"Exactly."

Leif's eyes flicker between Paris and Verona. He doesn't trust them. *Why should he?* These two kids are alone in the world, and all they have are each other. Paris knows that feeling.

"Come on, Emma," says Leif, nudging her to come with him back into the cottage. Emma doesn't move. She keeps her eyes up on Verona. She puffs out one cheek and begins to tap on it.

"Ye do look like an angel," says Verona, scanning Emma's body. "With eyes green as grass."

Emma blushes. She turns and disappears into the cottage. Verona rises from her kneeling position. The sun gleams behind them, warming their backs and loosening their joints. From their vantage point on top of the hill, Duke Rowan's fiefdom can be seen for leagues and leagues in all directions. Someday, the top of this hill will be used to build a castle or a cathedral, but now it harbors only beautiful views. Verona keeps her eyes locked on Paris, though. She studies his face, and her slender lips dive into a frown.

"What?" questions Paris.

Verona turns away from him. Paris furrows his brows, confused by the newfound hostility. He reaches out for her. "Verona, what is it?"

He turns her toward him and tries to pull his wife into an embrace, but she twists away from his hug.

"Verona—"

"Me just . . ." begins Verona, jumbling her words as she tries to search for the right way to express herself. "Me can't wrap me head—"

Paris takes a step toward her. Verona takes a step back. She's never acted this way before. It sears a hole through Paris's heart.

"What?" says Paris in a harsh tone.

Verona looks him dead in the eyes. "Did ye hurt anyone?" she asks. "Did ye have any part of that . . . death?"

Paris freezes. He wasn't expecting a confrontation like this.

She must never know what I did, Paris reiterates. *She must never know I killed a knight.* A section of Paris's mind screams at him that he did more than that, but surely the murder is the worst atrocity he committed last night.

"Who do ye think I am?"

"Answer me," says Verona sternly.

Paris takes a step toward her, considering all the repercussions that any answer could cause. He will put the whole world on his shoulders for her. She stuck with him when no one else would. She married him. Paris will carry this guilt all his life to be with her, to not *lose* her.

"My actions are pure," says Paris. "Always. Now come here."

Paris pulls Verona into a hug. Her body leans lifelessly against his for a few moments, but then her arms clutch around his back, and he feels her chest press against his. They connect in their embrace, which forms an unspoken, sacred bond between the two of them.

Paris promises the virtue of his decisions, and Verona accepts the lies he tells her.

He stares into the distant landscape beyond them, toward the rushing rivers and rising fog.

"I would never hurt anyone," reassures Paris, not leaving a hint of doubt in his voice. *Unless they threaten you.*

A noise seeps out from the cottage, and they turn to find Leif and Emma standing before the front door. Emma drops her burlap sack full of supplies as she stares at something past them. Her eyes sparkle with the light of the sun.

"Mummy!"

EDITH FALLS TO THE dirt, uncaring of the pain shooting up her body. Emma sprints across the small space that separates the two of them. Her little feet almost stumble over themselves in their frantic rush for her. Edith reaches her arms out, desperate to touch her daughter as soon as she can. The jubilee that flickers across Emma's face as she barrels toward her is something Edith will remember for the rest of her life.

Emma runs into Edith at full speed.

Their arms wrap around each other. Emma's tiny hands grip and pull at the back of Edith's torn tunic, grasping for the security of her mother. Edith buries her face into her daughter's black hair and sobs into their thick strands. She feels Emma giggle before the cute sound even leaves her mouth.

"Why you cryin', Mummy?" she asks.

"Because Mummy loves ye," says Edith.

She pulls Emma tighter into her. Emma snuggles her cheek against Edith's, and with it, the horrors of the previous night vanish in an instant. She got back to her daughter. She did all she needed to do.

Now she can be at peace. Now, she can rest.

VERONA SMILES AT THE loving form of Edith and Emma. They let them have their moment, the mother and daughter laughing together in joyous contentment. The connection of their love even speaks to Leif, who stands back at the door without uttering a word. Verona glances sideways at Paris.

"Ye sure you're ready?" asks Verona again.

Paris turns his gaze to Verona. In this moment, they are the only two souls in the world.

"I love ye," says Paris.

"I love ye."

Verona steps forward and taps Edith on the shoulder. Edith, with great labor, stands with Emma in hand. The little girl only reaches the height of her knees. Emma follows next to his wife and Edith as they walk the long path leading down the hill. Leif grabs the reins of the horse. He clicks his tongue, which causes the animal to follow after him. Leif gives Paris a suspicious glare before he vanishes behind the body of the beast.

Paris halts on the crest of the Cudworth hill. He watches Edith and his wife venture downward with the two kids following after them. He has two children now . . . that'll be difficult. They're an odd family of five.

Paris peeks behind him at the vast English countryside once more. Way in the far west, he can see the towering keep of Duke Rowan, the "just" bastard. Paris pulls his dagger out of his belt. He stares at it.

He flicks the blade around in his hand, and it grazes lightly against the tips of his fingers. The serrated edge pricks against him.

Me would never hurt anyone.

He sounds like a knight. Paris spits in disgust. *Everyone got what they deserved,* Paris supposes. He puts the dagger back into his belt. He glances down the hill and finds that Verona, Edith, and Emma are waiting on him. Leif keeps leading the horse with his head bowed.

Of course, this couldn't be easy.

Paris takes a deep breath, sucking in the energy of a new life before he rushes down the hill after them. There's a pile of guilt stacked on top of him, a weight he'll never be able to shrug off. It'll take a lifetime of work to keep Verona from spying it.

But that's fine. He was always in the right.

CIVIL INSURRECTIONS

EPILOGUE

SIR DAVID SAGS TO the ground under the weight of his drenched armor. The fucking leather was already burdensome enough, but the damn rain made it five times as heavy. He drags his feet behind him, still spitting out the smoke and debris that lingers within his lungs.

"Stupid, fucking peasants," Sir David mutters to himself. "Damn cowards, the lot of them."

He's still a half league or so from Duke Rowan's keep. He can see the castle over the canopy of trees stretched out before him. The sun is close to the zenith. He's been traveling for half a day straight, and every muscle inside of him wants to roll over and die. He won't let it. He's in control of his body. *He's* in fucking charge.

That being said, Sir David isn't particularly thrilled to have to admit to Duke Rowan that there's going to be an assassination on him tonight. There's sure to be quite a bit of screaming and berating and whatever else angry lords do. On the bright side though, he'll likely be promoted to commander. He's been in Rayner's shadow for far too long. Duke Rowan will need someone to protect him and his son at the wedding tonight.

A trail of dirt lifts into the sky from Sir David's right. He stares toward the dust. It grows larger and denser as it makes its way toward him like a dark, flying snake. Sir David moves his hand to his sheath, only to find out that he left his sword at the inn.

"Damn dolt," Sir David curses at himself.

The perpetrators of the trail of dust soon make themselves known. They ride upon horseback, and one of them holds a banner attached to the top of a long pole. A grizzly red splotch scattered across an azure sky: the banner of Duke Richard.

"Fuck me."

The knights of Duke Richard surround Sir David. There's seven of them in total, and two of them wear pristine metal armor similar to what Commander Rayner had. Their steeds neigh and prance back upon their hind legs. The men hoot and holler at Sir David like he's some exotic animal stuck in a cage. Sir David has only had the displeasure of meeting these assholes twice.

"You look like an utter embarrassment, Sir David." Commander Braxton, one of the two knights in full metal, sneers. "Did you get doused and tumble into the peasant's latrine? Should I search for your comrades in such a manner?"

"Belt it," bites Sir David. "I need to be transported to my liege lord."

"I'd say so," says Sir Rithe.

"I realize entry into your knighthood is rather pathetic," says Commander Braxton, "but don't you lot realize you have a wedding to attend? Your baron won't be happy if he has to be protected by the knights of Duke Richard."

Sir David ignores the stab at Duke Rowan's honor. There are more important things to do than pick a fight with them.

"Take me to the keep," commands Sir David.

The knights laugh at him. Sir David remains calm and cautious. The second knight in full armor, Commander Hurst, steers his steed toward him. Duke Richard's fiefdom is large enough that he needs two commanders to control it all. Sir David has heard rumors that the two commanders often squabble over Duke Richard's favoritism.

"Where is Commander Rayner? We'd like to have a discussion with a real knight," says Commander Hurst. Sir David feels his face flush red. His mustache twitches under his nose.

"I don't have time for this petty bout of insults," declares Sir David. He pushes past them, but the knights quickly surround him again.

"What's the hurry? You're already tardy for preparations," jabs Commander Braxton.

"Rowan's knights are always slacking off." Commander Hurst sneers.

"They died trying to protect his land!" shouts Sir David defensively. He bites back his tongue, but it's already too late.

"They died?" asks one of the lesser knights in stunned awe.

"Butchered by peasants," Sir David clarifies. "And the rest of you will be, too, if you don't get me to the Goddamn keep."

"What is this all about?" questions Commander Braxton. "Be frank with us, Sir David. My patience is running thin."

"*Your* patience?" Sir David laughs mockingly. "We discovered a plot, a coup attempt by the local peasantry, to assassinate Duke Rowan and possibly Lord Merek and Lady Lorena. We've done more work than you cowards have in the past decade."

"And you say your fellow knights have all died?" asks Commander Hurst.

Sir David nods solemnly. The commanders face one another, and then they turn their expressions to the other knights. Some unspoken declaration makes their way between them. Sir David feels the hairs on his neck stand up tall. A shiver passes through him. Commander Hurst cranks his neck back down at him with an intimidating smile.

"Sir David, we're placing you under arrest," he announces.

"Like balls you are!" Sir David shouts back.

Too late. The next thing Sir David feels is the force of a mace slamming against his backside. His armor protects some of the blow, but his spine crumbles in as he falls to the hard dirt. The knights laugh around him in viscous mockery. Sir David groans. He tries to pull himself to his feet, but he finds his limbs won't work like they're supposed to.

"I knew you knights were useless," says Sir Rithe in his vexing, nasally voice. "Died by the hands of peasants?! Useless."

"What about Lady Lorena," Sir David pleas to their sense of honor. "She's in danger as well."

"Yes," says Commander Hurst indifferently. "As it turns out, Duke Richard doesn't care very much for his younger daughter. It was an asinine betrothment by King Henry in the first place, further proof of his inadequacies and overreliance on the importance of women."

"Yeah," spits some knight behind Sir David. "This whole fiefdom will be Duke Richard's once Stephen finally takes the throne."

"I thought you bastards weren't even coming out this way," coughs Sir David. Blood spills from his mouth.

"Duke Richard believed your paltry defenses needed some bolstering." Commander Braxton smiles.

"No," Sir David says in disbelief, the clues coming together in perfect harmony. There is only one conclusion. "You knew about the coup all along."

Commander Braxton jumps off his horse. His feet land right next to Sir David's head. He squirms. The knights laugh at his flinch. Commander Braxton kneels down close to Sir David.

"It's not our duty to inquire on the intelligence of our liege lords." He gleams maniacally. "It's our duty to follow his command, and if we get a little something out of it, I see no problem with it. Do you?"

Sir David growls at him. Commander Braxton reaches over Sir David and grabs something. He hears the clanking of metal and iron as the commander pulls a mace into Sir David's view.

"I think our duke will be rather pleased to hear about the destruction of Rowan. What do you all think?"

The other knights cheer and jostle. Sir David yells and tries to worm forward, but his body betrays him for the final time. He was never in charge.

"Do you feel it in the air, Sir David?" Commander Braxton whispers to him. "The world is changing. This is only the beginning of a wonderful generation. But, unfortunately, it'll have to come at the cost of a few others."

Sir David doesn't get a chance to retort. The mace thunders down onto his head, and the world vanishes in an instant.

THE END

The Anarchy Saga will continue in Part 2

THE ANARCHY SAGA

WHAT IS *THE ANARCHY SAGA?*

The Anarchy Saga will be a five-part story that follows the plight of numerous eclectic individuals (and their ancestors) throughout the 12th century—specifically through the turmoil of the Anarchy. Each novel will work as its own standalone story; however, the collective whole of the saga will have a complete narrative that gives a fully realized depiction of life during the High Middle Ages. You can expect the same level of humor, violence, religion, drugs, sex, heightened realism, twists, and betrayals to be present throughout the subsequent novels. You can also expect a broader mix of individuals in the following stories—more female characters, characters of different racial and religious backgrounds, etc..

While Part 1 of *The Anarchy Saga* was focused exclusively around southwestern England, future installments will be set in other parts of the world as well. And while the majority of characters in each novel will be new, they'll all be connected to the characters of the previous installments in some way.

And, of course, you can expect your favorite characters from this book (and perhaps, even their ancestors) to make appearances throughout the saga.

WHAT'S NEXT IN *THE ANARCHY SAGA?*

Part 2, the follow up novel to *Virtuous Sins*, will begin with Lucia as she attends Lord Merek and Lady Lorena's wedding—hoping to find the blacksmith boy she fell for the following year. . . .

Part 2 will be a story about a woman trying to find her place in a patriarchal society, a father going down a warpath to get revenge for the death of his daughter, and two brothers fighting on separate sides of the Anarchy.

WANT TO STAY UPDATED ON *THE ANARCHY SAGA?*

If you enjoyed *Virtuous Sins: A 12th Century Thriller* and want to stay up to date for the next installment of *The Anarchy Saga*, then consider joining Derek Roy's mailing list (you'll also get early access to the prologue of Part 2):

https://www.derekroystories.com/anarchy-mailing-list

You can also join the official *Anarchy Saga* discord if you wish to interact with other fans (and get updates from Derek Roy):

https://discord.gg/kdKqyjEMKu

ACKNOWLEDGMENTS

WRITING A DEBUT NOVEL is no small feat, and thus there are a series of individuals I would like to express my gratitude for.

I would like to thank my family for never doubting my dreams. Whether I was staying up until 4:00 a.m. to film in the freezing cold or staying locked in my room for eight hours writing, they never pressured me to opt for a "comfortable life"—especially my sisters, who are always keen on keeping me humble. I am truly blessed.

I'd like to give a special thanks to Cindy and George Feeser whose generous donation allowed for the editorial process of this novel to be possible. I would further like to thank Carly Catt, the wonderful editor of this novel, who did a fantastic job fixing my prose. This novel wouldn't be as streamlined without you. I would also like to thank my close relatives for their beta readings. Your advice was invaluable.

I would further like to express my thanks for my friends, many of whom had to endure countless hours of my complaints about the complexities of twelfth-century politics. A special thanks to my roommates, who took on the blunt of these protests. I'd also like to shoutout my D&D

players; being a DM for you all while writing this novel helped refine my storytelling to a degree you all can't imagine. If I could keep a campaign of you murderhobos on track in our sessions, then I could certainly wrangle in the plot of *Virtuous Sins*. Praise the Stormdaddy! #NeverForgetDroop

Finally, I would like to thank my friends, film peers, and followers on social media for your feedback on the design of the cover as well as your continual support. It's truly beautiful when artists can brace each other up.

ABOUT THE AUTHOR

 Derek Roy is a film graduate from the University of Nevada, Las Vegas. He is an international award-winning filmmaker and has been a finalist in international screenwriting competitions. He has written three feature film spec scripts, as well as multiple short film screenplays, and is hoping to find representation for his writing/directing in the film industry.

Derek Roy loves to tell stories in any medium he can. Along with writing *Virtuous Sins*, he plans on writing a whole saga of novels depicting life in the 12th century. He also has ambitions to write stories for video games and television/streaming as well. He dreams of one day becoming a showrunner, while having the luxury to pursue any medium that one of his stories might fancy.

You can find a link to his other writings and directorial work at:
https://www.derekroystories.com/